The Café on
Dream Street

The Café on Dream Street

ADRIANE BROWN

STOREHOUSE
MEDIA GROUP

This is a work of fiction. Names, characters, places, and incidents are the product of the author's imagination or are used fictitiously, and any resemblance to actual persons, living or dead, businesses, companies, events, or locales is entirely coincidental. Oakmont, New York, is a fictional suburb, not meant to represent any actual locale or its inhabitants.

LCCN: 2019910381

Paperback ISBN: 978-1-63337-301-3
E-book ISBN: 978-1-63337-302-0

Printed in the United States of America

1 3 5 7 9 10 8 6 4 2

Acknowledgments

I would like to give special thanks to Ivan Graciano and CISPES (The Committee in Solidarity with the People of El Salvador), whose advice and support made this book possible. Ivan Graciano, a veteran civil war fighter in El Salvador, spent his youth fighting to achieve better living conditions for his people. He lived in the United States and then returned to his country. Today he continues to work for his people.

Special thanks also to the following people for their support in researching information for this book:

- Anne Taylor Carsel, friend and lawyer- Much gratitude and appreciation for providing invaluable assistance in writing the courtroom scenes.

- Cindy Hallberlin, friend and lawyer, for her enthusiasm and support for this book from the very beginning, her legal advice, and her dedication to the struggle for immigrant rights.

- Florence, Arizona Immigration and Refugee Rights Project— Many thanks for phone consultations regarding the Arizona landscape and immigration issues in Arizona.

- Leonard Gianessi, for his ongoing friendship, encouragement, and support during the writing of this book.

- Linette Tobin, immigration attorney, for sharing her extensive knowledge of immigration law and history.

- Mariana Boneo, former Executive Director, Hispanic Resource Center, for sharing her story.

- Nadia Litwack, for her invaluable friendship and her support for the writing of this book.

- The New York Immigration Coalition, for their advice on New York immigration law and history.
- Ronald B. McGuire, lifetime friend and lawyer, for his advice and information on the New York legal system and his lifelong dedication to the cause of human rights.

The following individuals and organizations provided incredible support and advice in the writing and editing of this book:

- Allyson Machate, publishing consultant and CEO of The Writer's Ally, for going above and beyond the editorial process to be helpful and supportive.
- The Writer's Ally Creative Services team for their expertise and skill in the editing process.
- Jaimee Garbacik, Footnote Editorial, for her creative and insightful editorial support.
- Emily Hitchcock, project manager, Storehouse Publishing, for her support in putting this book together and her willingness to field all my questions constantly and cheerfully.
- The Bethesda Writer's Center, where this story began.

And of course, infinite gratitude to my family for their unwavering support throughout the writing of this book. Immeasurable thanks to my husband, Syd Brown, who was willing to give his opinion on infinite versions of the same line and whose love and devotion make everything possible, to my sister, Liz Price and my brother-in-law, Tom Shcherbenko, the best family anyone could have.

Dedicated with love to Syd, Joe, Ariella, Liz and Tom,
the best family anyone could have.

Oakmont, New York
Fall, 2005

One

Twenty years had passed since Felipe found his front door cracked and broken, nothing left but jagged pieces of brown wood hanging off the frame. Unfamiliar voices, shouting, threatening voices, spilled through the doorway, mixed with sobbing and loud wails.

He had a new life now, but the memories remained, intruding at the most inconvenient times, squeezing the breath out of him, leaving him lightheaded and dizzy as his heart hammered in his chest and the room filled with the odor of death.

Felipe shook himself, wiping the sweat from his forehead with the edge of his sleeve. El Salvador faded and he was in Oakmont again, fifteen miles from New York City, in the little storefront restaurant owned by his uncle, Miguel. Customers were sparse this time of day, the usual mid-morning slump, so he wiped down all of the tables, then stepped into the storage room to replenish the kitchen supplies. He was reaching for a bottle of cooking oil, when the sound of loud voices stopped him in his tracks. The storage area had no door, only a curtain that served as a barrier between the two rooms, but there was a small space near the shelves where he could flatten himself against the wall and peer through a tiny opening in the curtain. A hand was waving at Tio Miguel—a hand extending from the dark blue sleeve of a uniform.

"Officer Bradley, Oakmont PD, and this here's Officer Dawson." Bradley, the bald one with the big belly, stepped behind the counter, his eyes wandering over the stove, the sink, the grill.

"How many people you got workin' here?"

"Three. Five on the weekends."

Officer Bradley brushed against the storeroom curtain as he bent down to inspect the cabinet under the sink, then yanked open the oven door and peered in. "Names?"

Tio Miguel squeezed the water out of the sponge, watched it trickle down the drain. "My nephew and his wife. They have teenagers who do a few shifts after school, and we have extra people working weekends."

El Patio Café was not much more than a kitchen with a front counter and a few tables and chairs, but it was Felipe's refuge, his sanctuary, his hope for his children's future. He especially loved making pupusas; he made them from scratch, and his rough hands delighted in the softness of the flour as he kneaded the dough, a softness that reminded him of the dirt under his bare feet back in his village. He would roll the dough into a ball in the palm of his hand and press a filling of cheese, pork, or refried beans into the center, then gently slap it from palm to palm to flatten it before he browned it on the griddle. His creation, his work of art—an art he hoped would send his children to college.

Officer Bradley slapped his hand loudly on the counter. "What is your nephew's *name?*" Tio Miguel squared his shoulders, glaring icily at Officer Bradley as he began wiping down the stove, moving the sponge slowly around the burners.

"Your nephew's name!"

Tio Miguel's black hair was thinning and peppered with gray, his face lined and leathery, but his body was lean and his arms thick and muscular from his early years of farm work and migrant labor. When Felipe had arrived in New York at the age of fourteen, frightened and alone, it was Tio Miguel who welcomed him, opened his home and helped him begin his life again, a life filled with the sweet aroma of frying onions, garlic, and cilantro, the sizzling of grilling chicken and beef.

Officer Bradley grabbed the back of Tio Miguel's neck and slammed his head into the counter. "Give me your nephew's name, now! You don't cooperate with us, we can close you down, buddy. We have a problem with people who break our laws, sell drugs to our kids, and don't pay taxes. Your nephew pay taxes on the drugs he sells?"

"No, no, we're not like that. We always pay the taxes, and we just sell food here. We don't sell no drugs!" Tio Miguel muttered.

"You got a lot to say, Gonzales, except when I ask you a question," Bradley snapped, slamming Tio Miguel's head into the counter again. A trickle of blood ran from his nose and dripped onto his shirt, leaving a dark red stain. "Now tell me your nephew's name, unless you want to come down to the station with us. Got a nice little cell that would fit you just fine!"

"Sanchez. Felipe Sanchez," Tio Miguel whispered through clenched teeth. He grabbed a cloth from under the counter and held it up to his bloody nose.

Officer Dawson leaned against the counter, his fingers curled around the handcuffs that hung from his belt. He had the round, ruddy cheeks of a rookie and the powerful arms of an athlete, his burly frame pumped up from hours of lifting weights. He slowly unhooked the handcuffs and twirled them in the air, inches from Tio Miguel's face, then picked up a salt shaker and rapped it on the counter three times as though he was summoning a servant. "Been here ten minutes and you haven't offered us anything to drink. That's not a very good way to do business."

A glass of water appeared on the counter, next to the salt shaker.

"Water? That's what you're offering me? Water?" Dawson barked, shoving the glass back at Tio Miguel. The glass slid across the counter, toppling over with a thud. A pool of water trickled from the glass and dripped over the edge, forming a puddle on the floor. "Get me a Coke or a root beer!"

Dawson glanced over at Bradley, who was fiddling with the knobs on the stove, turning the burners on and off. "Soda for you?" he asked.

"Nah, I don't drink that sugar water. I prefer the real stuff, but you wouldn't be serving beer, would you, Gonzales? I don't recall seeing a liquor license."

The water disappeared and another glass appeared where the water had been. Officer Dawson took a sip, cradling the glass between his hands, his eyes fixed on Tio Miguel. "Your nephew come through customs at JFK airport?"

"Bet he swam across the bay from Jersey," Bradley snickered. "You take the Staten Island Ferry, you can see them saluting the Statue of Liberty as they swim by." Their laughter, sharp as a knife blade, was tempered only by the thin cloth that hung between the two rooms.

Officer Bradley picked up a can of scouring cleanser, poured some out on the counter, pinching it with his fingers, smelling it. "Tell Sanchez we got our eye on his kids, too. If they're dealin' outta here, we'll get 'em."

El Patio was the social center of the neighborhood, and people often stayed long after they had finished eating. It was not unusual to see small children playing while their parents caught up on the news of the community, and frequently a group of men sat around one of the tables outside, socializing or flirting with the women who walked by. An

15

American flag and a flag of El Salvador hung side by side in the front window, along with a menu and a set of Christmas lights that were still up, even though the holiday was long past.

Bradley studied the kitchen area for a moment, then stared at the curtain. "Whoa—think we missed something here. What's in there? You store a lot of—" The jingling chimes of a cell phone intervened and he talked briefly, motioning Dawson toward the door.

Felipe's white cotton shirt clung to his body, damp and clammy from sweat, and he was seized by an overwhelming desire to get away, to run and hide somewhere. He plunked down shakily onto a box, clutching the edge of a nearby shelf to steady himself until the moment passed. The police wanted to arrest him, take him from his beloved family, his children. Julia had been upstairs with Marisol and Camilo, for which he was intensely grateful. She would have defended him, stood up to the police, demanded her own answers, and Marisol, her mother's daughter all the way, would have joined in. It was better that they hadn't been there. His family didn't need to hear the police insulting him, making jokes about their Papi.

He pushed the curtain aside and stepped warily out of the storeroom. The customers had scrambled out the door, leaving the restaurant silent and empty, and a bloody cloth lay idly on the counter, along with the glass of Coke. Tio Miguel was drifting around the room aimlessly, pushing in chairs, straightening salt shakers and napkin holders. He had a gash on his forehead and a purple bruise under his eye.

"You okay?" Felipe asked. "Looks like your nose stopped bleeding. I'm going to toss this," he said gently, picking up the bloody cloth with two fingers and dropping it into the trash can. He dumped the remains of the soda in the sink and placed the glass in the dishwasher.

"*Cabrones!*" Tio Miguel muttered angrily. "Don't they have anything better to do than to hassle us?"

Felipe sponged down the counter, then grabbed a mop from the storeroom and began hurriedly soaking up the water on the floor. He and Tio Miguel had big plans for El Patio, to expand it, make it a full-service restaurant, maybe a nightclub, too. They had been working seven days a week, filled with excitement, energy, and hope, but now Felipe felt rattled, uncertain about what the future might hold. A shadow passed over the window, and he peered out nervously as a police car cruised slowly up the street.

Two

Colin Sullivan could see six of them congregated by the fence across from the Quik Shop grocery. Brown-skinned men in work boots and jeans and T-shirts, leaning against the fence waiting patiently for someone to drive up and give them a job to do. One wore a baseball cap with a New York Yankees emblem and shuffled restlessly from one foot to the other, looking uncomfortable, as though he knew he wasn't wanted there. Colin's father said they were criminals just by being in the United States, sneaking into the country and expecting to be welcomed with open arms and given a bunch of handouts.

His father, Frank, rested his left hand casually on the steering wheel of the white Ford van, his gray and white warm-up suit covering the worn places on the seat. The old girl had been taking the Sullivan family and Colin's football team for burgers for as long as he could remember and still ran like a charm, even after a hundred thousand miles and years of scrapes and dents that had never been fixed. Frank circled the van around the mall parking lot, looking for a space. It was really more of a small shopping plaza than a mall, but everyone in Oakmont called it "the mall." Still, you didn't have to go anywhere else in Oakmont—you could get about anything you needed there. The Quik Shop grocery, Hamburger Heaven, a hair salon, a hardware store, the bank, a pharmacy. Across the parking lot, there was a big box discount department store, where you could get clothes, toys, furniture, and whatever else you might want.

The van rumbled down the fire lane between the parking lot and the sidewalk, then spun around in an abrupt U-turn, tires screeching as Frank slammed on the brakes, throwing everyone in the vehicle forward. Wouldn't want to drive with Dad without a seat belt, Colin thought. Frank pressed the power button on the window, gave two short blasts on the horn, and waved at the men standing by the fence across from the Quik Shop.

"Want a job?" he yelled, beckoning to the men.

Two men sprang toward the car and hovered there expectantly. "Sorry, no jobbo," Frank said, pressing the window button again, leaving the men standing there staring at him as the window closed.

"C'mon, Dad. Forget those guys. Don't know about you, but I'm ready for some grub."

"Forget them? Like hell I will. You let 'em hang out in the mall today, they'll be movin' into the neighborhood tomorrow, takin' your job the next day. Already have a lot of people without jobs, sure don't need 'em moving in on us. Property values'll go down, house won't be worth fifty cents. You think they want to live in Grover Hill, stand out here in the sun waiting for some little painting job? They want what we have, and they'll take it if you let 'em, any way they can. Laws don't mean nothin' to them. Hell, they got here by breakin' the law."

Colin studied his father's face, the tightening of the muscles in his jaw, the wrinkle in his brow, the downturn of his mouth as he sucked on a cigarette. A stream of smoke flowed out of the side of his mouth, drifting off into the van, mixing with the smell of sweat and funky old car seats.

Frank turned the van back into the parking lot and spotted a vehicle pulling out at the end of the row. A car waited nearby with its blinkers on, indicating that its driver had already claimed the space. The engine roared as Frank zoomed in front of the waiting car, the van swaying wildly as it lurched into the empty space.

"Guy was waitin' for the space, Dad."

"What is your damn problem? You can't see the lot is full? We'd be waiting here another hour. Gotta go for what you want in life or you'll be left behind like the trash in that garbage can over there."

"Way to go, Mr. Sullivan," Luke said.

Frank turned to Luke and winked. "Think they made a mistake at the hospital. Maybe Luke's really my boy."

A piece of ash fell from his cigarette and landed on Colin's pants, leaving a dark gray stain. Colin stared out the window at a little red sports car zipping around the parking lot. Looked like a Porsche, or maybe an Audi. Wouldn't mind having one of those.

As his teammates piled into the red plastic booths at Hamburger Heaven, Colin ambled nonchalantly in the direction of the restroom, stopping to glance at the TV screen above the counter, making small talk with a guy in a gas and electric company uniform about the golf game playing on the screen, hoping enough of the guys would fill his father's booth so he could ditch him today, eat with his friends without his dad hanging over him like he was a little kid. He watched the golf game from the counter for a few minutes, keeping an eye on the booths, but the spot next to Frank remained available.

Colin gazed wistfully at the second booth as Frank patted the empty space, then slid in next to him. A cute young server sauntered over and dropped a pile of menus on the table. Hot body, too, with long dark hair and a stretchy yellow top that was super-tight under her Hamburger Heaven apron. Couldn't have been much older than him.

Frank waved his hand at the menus. "Don't need those. Two orders of the number three burger, fries, and Cokes for my son and myself." Colin had been thinking about trying something different today, maybe the fishcakes, but didn't want to look like a jerk in front of everyone. Not worth it to challenge Dad on something like that. Nothing wrong with burgers and fries. Frank stared at the server as she took orders from the other guys, his eyes following her rear end as she walked away. "Nice, huh?" he snickered.

"Yeah, must be new. Never seen her here before," Colin responded.

Sam Evans laughed. "Too hot for you, guy."

"Don't need her, dude. The whole cheerleading team lines up for me after games. She's all yours," Colin shot back.

The arrival of the burgers and fries killed the conversation for a while; not much to say when you were stuffing your face with food at Hamburger Heaven. Colin grabbed a French fry from the plate, dipped it in ketchup, stuck it in his mouth. Hamburger Heaven had the best fries, a little crunchy, a little salty, just the right amount. He took a bite of the burger and savored the charcoal flavor. It was a pretty good burger, cooked on the grill—probably better than fishcakes, anyway. The table quickly became a trash heap of empty plates splotched with red ketch-up, half-eaten pickles and crumpled up napkins. The server grabbed the dirty dishes and slipped off to tend to other customers as the team shuffled outside, well-fed and sluggish from their meal.

The morning had been sunny and crisp, but the late afternoon sky had turned ominously dark and leaves swirled through the air as the wind picked up speed. The same guys were hanging out by the fence across from the Quik Shop, or maybe they were different ones. It was pretty late in the day to be getting work, but Colin guessed they could do inside painting or put up drywall any time. He and his dad had done some work on the family room in the basement last year, not an easy job.

Colin wondered if the guys who were there earlier had gotten any jobs. There were only two of them now, sitting on some old boxes, probably cartons that had been tossed from one of the stores, chatting with each other, laughing and joking, maybe telling stories to pass the time. Made sense for them to sit down while they were waiting. Someone should stick a few chairs out there so they didn't have to sit on boxes. Mom probably would have helped them if she had been here, maybe run into a store to borrow some. She might even have gone home and brought some of the old folding chairs in the basement. He hesitated for a moment, glancing at the stores, wondering if he should see if anyone had some extras. Dad would have a fit, though, and with rain threatening, it was time for everyone to pack up and go home.

Colin climbed into the van and occupied his usual place, the passenger seat next to his father. The seat of honor, Frank called it.

"How's about we give 'em hell for hangin' out where they don't belong?" Frank said, turning around to address the team.

Luke shook the plastic cup with the remains of his Coke, rattling the ice. "Got it right here, Mr. Sullivan!"

"You gonna waste a perfectly good Coke on them? Give it to me, dude—I'll drink it." Colin stuck out his arm and grabbed the Coke from Luke.

"Wasted? Hey, I can't think of anything better to do with a leftover Coke," Frank said.

"Got another one right here, Mr. Sullivan. Nice and sticky. Bring all the flies in Oakmont to that fence," Sam chuckled.

The branches of the trees were jagged and black against the ashen sky, the colorful fall foliage turned sallow and brown. Colin watched as a lone yellow leaf swirled through the air and landed on the windshield, a bright patch of color on a bleak afternoon. The van crept down the fire lane and rolled slowly past the two men sitting on boxes in front of the fence. The first drops of rain had begun to fall, large drops that sent people scurrying to their cars or ducking for cover under the awnings.

Colin rolled the plastic soda cup around in his hand, swishing the remaining ice back and forth, feeling its coldness. The windows in the back rattled and groaned as they rolled down and the remains of the Cokes flew through the air, splattering on the men's clothes. The two men bolted from their seats on the boxes, shouting angrily as they moved toward the van.

Frank poked Colin's cup with his finger. "What the hell's the matter with you? Go on, help out your team. Go. Throw a long bomb."

Colin had been promoted to first-string wide receiver on the Oakmont High football team this year, his junior year, a position that brought all kinds of perks. In fact, sometimes he loved the admiration and the privileges more than the game itself. Otherwise, most days were pretty much the same, not much unusual ever happened. A few bad grades, losing a game sometimes, but nothing worse than that. "You do what you're told, follow the rules whether you like them or not, and things will work out for you," his father always said. It seemed like everyone believed that, at least adults did. Teachers, cops, parents—they all said that.

"They're right there—get 'em, quick!" Frank yelled.

Colin flipped the cup out the window and watched it bounce on the cement, a ribbon of brown liquid dribbling down the sidewalk as the van picked up speed and roared away.

Three

Felipe leaned against the railing as the boat drifted out into the choppy, green waters of New York Bay. The hubbub and the commotion of the city faded away, the only sounds the squawk of seagulls, the slapping of water against the boat, the excited chatter of the passengers. A medley of languages floated across the deck, an intermingling of nations, united in their quest to see the statue that had welcomed so many into American life.

Ricky stood next to Felipe at the railing, skinny and gangly at fourteen, but already as tall as his father. A few weeks had passed since they had gone to the Yankees game together to celebrate Ricky's birthday, but Felipe still delighted in reminiscing about the great time they had, rehashing the details over and over again in his mind. Despite Ricky's initial protests about going, he stopped complaining about wanting to be with his friends and enjoyed every minute. They had strolled around

Monument Park looking at the statues of famous Yankees, chomped down several hot dogs and a bag of peanuts, and Felipe bought a beer and let Ricky have a taste. When the Yankees won the game, they let it all out, high-fiving each other and cheering and screaming raucously along with the crowd. On the way home, Felipe surprised Ricky with a stop at the game store, where they picked out the new video game he wanted.

Felipe's own fourteenth birthday, spent fighting for survival as he stumbled across the Arizona desert, seemed so long ago, another lifetime. Someday he might try to find the little church that gave him a safe haven. He had always wanted to thank them, but he had never known the name of the church or even the last names of the people who had rescued him.

He watched the rise and fall of the breakers, remembering a river, clear as glass, that provided all the drinking and cooking water for a small village in El Salvador, where his mother washed clothes with the women of the village, the sunlight dancing on the water like a thousand *luminaria* candles. The Rio Escondido, where he floated on his back, filled with wonder at the clouds drifting across the brilliant blue sky, as white and soft as the flowers that bloomed on the coffee plants. A beautiful green parrot named Verdito, winking at him from his perch on the branch of a laurel tree.

A light wind was blowing, ruffling Julia's dark curls as she sat on a bench nearby with Marisol and Camilo, breathing in the sea air and doing a pencil sketch in the little notebook she carried everywhere. Marisol, his little girl, was turning into a woman, looking more like Julia every day. Men were already checking her out—maybe they thought he didn't notice, but he saw the glances, the double-takes as they looked her up and down. If any guy ever tried to hurt her, an army wouldn't be able to hold him back. She would be okay, though. She had the grades to apply to fancy colleges—Ivy League, she called them—and to get scholarships to pay for them, too. His wife and his daughter, the most beautiful women in the world, and the smartest, he thought, as he turned away from the railing to check in with them, see how they were doing.

"Papi, the Statue of Liberty," eight-year-old Camilo said excitedly, shaking his arm. On their right, a towering statue of a woman stood astride an island, verdant with green lawns and the foliage of maple, horse chestnut, and linden trees, all dwarfed by her spellbinding physical presence. A woman with a crown and a gold torch, embracing everyone who traversed these waters on their way to a new life in the United States. Camilo had a report to write about the statue for school, and Felipe had insisted he would learn more if he could actually see it.

The ferry pulled into the dock, rocking from side to side, kicking up white foam onto the wooden pier. Felipe clutched the metal guardrail, watching the tourists stroll up and down on shore with their cameras, suddenly not sure he belonged here. When he had first suggested this outing to Julia, she had objected, and maybe she had been right.

"The Statue of Liberty and Ellis Island?" she had responded, rolling her eyes and shaking her head disapprovingly. "They don't tell our story. I'll take Camilo to the library and help him with his report, and then maybe we can go to the Bronx Museum of the Arts or to the Museo del Barrio to see some Hispanic art. The kids need to learn about their own culture, too."

"I don't see a problem," Felipe said cheerfully, trying to be reassuring. "They're American citizens, and this is the history of their country. And mine, too, because I live here. There's nothing wrong with learning about history, even if it's not yours," he had countered.

"I just don't want you to be disappointed," she had said softly, putting her arms around him and kissing him gently on the lips, but in the end, she gave in.

Now memories were creeping up on him, shadowy at first, as they always were. He tried to shake them off, to think about the good things he had, his family, the good time they were having today. He wheeled around abruptly, staring helplessly at the New York skyline and the bottomless green water in between. Julia would understand and have no problem with taking the next boat back to Manhattan, enjoying the rest of the day at a park or one of the museums she had suggested. Maybe these symbols were not about him or how he had arrived, just as Julia had said. Central Park might be nice, a better idea than this.

He turned to her, but she had started down the gangway holding

Camilo's hand tightly, with Ricky and Marisol following closely behind, and a crowd of people had filled in the space between them. He shouted their names until he was hoarse, but found himself voiceless in the din of the departing passengers, their feet thundering toward the gangway. The boat rocked and swayed in the shallow waters of the pier, and Felipe's gait became unsteady as the ground shifted under him and the back of Julia's head disappeared.

Remembrances of things lost, people left behind, were flooding through him now, tormenting him. Soldiers with bayonets, a *guardia* with steely black eyes and a jagged red scar on his face patrolling the coffee plantation, the whine of bullets, flesh rotting in the heat. Empty places where loved ones had once been. He took deep sucking breaths through his mouth as the crowd closed in around him, but couldn't seem to take in any air, and felt himself gasping, choking. Dizzy and disoriented, he sat down on a bench as the crew barked at people to move along, watch their step.

Someone shook him, and he found himself staring at the dark green uniforms of two National Park Service security officers. "You need to be movin' along," one of the officers snapped irritably. "Looks like he might'a had one too many," the other one added, narrowing his eyes disdainfully at Felipe.

Muffled voices, then Julia's concerned face appeared. "He'll be fine," Julia said quickly, handing Felipe a water bottle. "He just gets a little dizzy in the heat. We're just going to sit right here for a few minutes, but we'll be getting right off at the next stop, at Ellis Island. There's no problem, sir. Thank you so much for your help." Felipe took a few sips of water, feeling air seeping into his lungs and four sets of arms around his back, at his waist, around his shoulders, holding him up.

He leaned back on the bench as the boat began to move again. The last few passengers had already disembarked for the Statue of Liberty and new passengers had boarded for the trip to Ellis Island, one half-mile away. The boat wouldn't be returning to Manhattan for a while, and he had promised Camilo this trip, so there was no turning back now. He had no choice but to go through with it, to forge on.

As the boat pulled away from the dock once again, an announcer's voice boomed from a loudspeaker above his head. *"America is a nation of immigrants and New York City is a gateway for them,"* the announcement declared. *"Ellis Island was the principal gateway for immigrants from 1892-1954. What do these monuments symbolize to us, to the immigrants who came through here?"*

A castle rose up in front of them, a three-story red brick castle with arched entranceways, crowned with four copper domes and ascending spires that disappeared into the clouds. "That is a very old building, *niños,*" Felipe said excitedly, feeling more grounded now, ready to get on with the day. "You are going to learn something about the history of your country, and I am going to learn about the country of my new life."

31

"Isn't America your country too, Papi?" Camilo asked.

"I wasn't born here, but you were, so you are a real American citizen, and no one can take that away from you," he said in a low voice, as though this was a special secret just between them.

They followed the crowd down the walkway that led to the main entrance of the Ellis Island Museum, where a woman dressed in a blouse with billowing sleeves and a long, full skirt held up a sign. A printed scarf framed her face and a brown, woolen shawl was draped over her shoulders.

"What does the sign say, Marisol?" Felipe asked.

"It's about a play you can watch when you go in there called *Through the Gates.* The next show is in ten minutes. There's a movie, too, called *Land of Hope, Land of Tears.* About the immigrants who came through here, I guess."

They stepped through the arched entranceway into the Baggage Room, a vast hall decorated with immense photographs of wide-eyed immigrants carrying all their worldly belongings in their arms, their faces clouded with fear and confusion as they were hustled into the very room in which the Sanchez family now stood. Behind a glass enclosure lay dusty wooden trunks and wicker baskets of all sizes, the wooden boxes, leather cases and embroidered pillows the immigrants had clung to as they descended the gangway after months at sea, the only remnants of their previous life that they could touch. They cherished those belongings, placing them in honored spaces in the corners of tenement rooms, passing them on to their children and grandchildren, who returned them to Ellis Island to live on in history.

The Sanchez family meandered through the building, perusing documents and photographs, maps describing the changes in migration over the centuries, actual artifacts the immigrants had brought from their native countries. A tin plate, a fork, and a cup that had traveled from Russia, a teapot, a tablecloth. A bent, rusty donkey shoe, a good luck piece a father had given his son as a gift before he left Ireland. Handmade wedding dresses, beaded wedding shoes. A red velvet jacket with floral embroidery and a lace collar over a lace trimmed floral skirt from Moravia. A small girl's dress, a boy's suit. Bibles from Poland, Russia, Italy, Ireland, Lithuania; a shofar from Russia; rosary beads from Italy.

"Over twelve million immigrants entered the U.S. through Ellis Island," Marisol read from a sign. *"Only two percent were turned away, mostly for contagious diseases or if they were not physically or mentally able to work."*

"They had to pass a two- to three-minute legal exam," Marisol explained as she read further, "and had to state whether they were married or single, what their occupation was, how much money they had, and whether they were ever convicted of a crime. Polygamists, prisoners, and anarchists were not allowed to enter. They never would have let you in, Ricky," she teased.

"What's a polygamist?" Ricky asked. "Am I a polygamist?"

33

"A man with more than one wife," Marisol explained, which brought titters from all except Camilo.

"Sweet," Ricky said. "I should have been born back then."

Felipe smiled. "Hard enough to handle one wife," he said and jumped out of the way as Julia tried to slap him on the arm.

They wandered back down to the first floor, past the gift shop and the cafeteria, through the glass doors to the American Immigrant Wall of Honor—a long, circular stone wall overlooking the bay, inscribed with thousands of names. Stone picnic tables nearby were occupied by people in saris, kaftans and sarongs, shorts and T-shirts, quietly savoring grilled chicken sandwiches, hot dogs, and French fries. Gulls and pigeons bobbed their heads in the grass, hoping a tasty morsel might be dropped their way. The Statue of Liberty and the New York skyline reigned majestically on the horizon, and a yellow tugboat floated across the water.

"Six hundred thousand names are inscribed on this wall," Marisol read. "It says that the wall celebrates immigration from its earliest beginnings right up to the present day."

"Did you come here when you came from El Salvador, Papi?" Camilo asked. "Is your name on the wall? Let's find Papi's name."

For a moment Felipe was quiet, the words stuck in his throat. His little boy, with the long lashes and eyes of liquid chocolate, waiting expectantly for an answer. When he was born, Camilo's eyes seemed to take up his whole face, the most beautiful eyes Felipe had ever seen.

"Beautiful eyes, just like yours, *mi corazon*," Julia had said. He took a deep breath, swallowing hard as he took Camilo's hand, holding it tightly, little fingers warm against his.

"You're hurting my hand, Papi," Camilo said, trying to pull it away. Felipe lightened his grip but held onto his hand and squatted down next to him.

"I came here a different way," he said softly, "from another place far away from here, across a big desert, where the sun was very hot and the sand burned your feet if you stepped in it without shoes."

"Like the sand at Orchard Beach when it's a very hot day?"

"Even hotter than that, and much bigger."

"Did you see the Statue of Liberty when you came across the desert?"

"No, *mijo*. There was no Statue of Liberty at the border I crossed."

"Then how did they welcome you when you came here, Papi?"

Four

Frank Sullivan watched the front door at Tony's Steak 'n Brew swing shut behind the last customer, then peered into the kitchen to make sure the final cleanup was done. The bartender was wiping down the bar one final time, pausing briefly to grab empty beer mugs and the remaining bowls of pretzels.

Frank's eyes followed the sweep of the bartender's arm, inspecting the counter for any remnants not picked up by the rag. A low hum of voices came from the back room, where an active poker game was in progress. "Join us in the back, Rob?" Frank asked.

The bartender tossed the rag into the sink, shaking his head as he moved out from behind the counter. "Thanks, but not tonight, Frank."

The back door slammed as the kitchen staff threw their aprons into the laundry bin, punched their time cards, and filed out. Frank loosened his tie, slid it off his neck and folded it, then stuffed it in the pocket of his jacket that was hanging on a hook behind the cash register.

The restaurant had a policy that the male employees wear red ties with little steaks on them, a stupid policy, Frank thought. It wasn't that kind of clientele; in fact, he wondered if he had ever seen a customer wearing a tie in here. The little steaks covered up any food stains, though, so maybe that was the reason. It was important in a restaurant to look fresh, even when you weren't. He stepped outside the back door, slid a cigarette from the soft pack in his breast pocket, placed it between his lips, and pulled out a matchbook. The match made a slightly sulfurous smell as he inhaled deeply and blew a long stream of white smoke into the dark, then tossed the burnt matchstick on the ground. In the old days, bars and smoke went together, but that had changed, like so many other things. You couldn't smoke in restaurants anymore on account of some law pushed through by government bureaucrats. No one ever asked his opinion, things were just here today, gone tomorrow, decided by somebody he never saw.

The face of a full moon stared down at him, a fall harvest moon, illuminating the ebony sky with radiant yellow light. He stood there transfixed, taking in the panorama of Oakmont at night, the shimmering lights from houses and office buildings, the blinking of a neon sign, the glowing red taillights of passing trucks. Oakmont, his town. His lips tightened around the cigarette as he took a final puff, then tossed the butt on the ground and stepped on it, grinding it back and forth with his shoe until it was nothing but a pile of dust. Ten years in this restaurant, and they give Jim Kelly's job to someone else.

A check of his watch showed ten-thirty, time to get started. He pushed the door open with his palm, leaving behind the solitude and the peaceful silence of a town at rest. Chitchat and laughter emanated from the backroom—the guys were back there, waiting for him. He made a quick stop by the kitchen, where he grabbed some bowls of salsa from the refrigerator and picked up several baskets of chips and bottles of beer, which he placed on a tray and carried into the back.

"Beer's on the house, guys. Tap? Bottled? Long neck? What's your pleasure?" he announced loudly over the din.

"One of them bottles right there would be good, and how about a couple'a steaks, Frank?"

"Yeah, you invite cops to a party, you're gonna have to feed us. Thought the place was called Steak 'n Brew. Can't have steak and brew without the steak. I might lose weight and become thin and puny."

"No danger of that, Bill."

Tony's Steak 'n Brew was your standard American chain restaurant, rows of booths with scuffed plastic seats and a six-page menu that served everything from scrambled eggs, hash browns, and bacon strips to hamburgers, fries, and triple-decker ice cream sundaes. It was best known for its eight-ounce steaks at reasonable prices—sirloin, T-bone, rib-eye, prime rib, and New York strip, rumored to be the best in Westchester County, as well as a wide array of beer.

The back room was a smaller version of the main dining room, but with long tables to accommodate party groups and a smaller bar, not as grand as the long bar in the main dining room, but well stocked for any group. The same giant TV screen above the bar, a favorite gathering place for local sports fans.

"Sorry, dining room's closed, but we have plenty of snacks." Frank placed his hands on the table and leaned into the group. "Finish up the game, guys. We have some business to take care of."

Ten years he had managed this place and never asked for a raise beyond the measly one they gave him five years ago, so when Jim Kelly, the regional manager, announced his retirement, Frank was sure this one was for him, his chance to move up, make more money, secure a place for himself. He was perfectly situated, inside the one-yard line, poised to fly like a gazelle across the goal line. Regional manager now, then into the higher levels—east coast first, then national.

He stood over the table and waved his arms in the air. "Guys, guys. Got some pictures to show you. You're gonna be interested in this." The cards were sitting on the table now, and several cops were staring at him, probably wanting him to get the talk over quickly so they could get back to their poker game. There were a few familiar faces, regular customers of the restaurant, and several he had never seen before. He had asked

Mike Torelli to bring some of his buddies and a whole roomful of cops had shown up.

"Apply for the regional manager position online," the secretary in the office had said. Bonnie worked on the application with him, checking his spelling, making sure he hadn't missed anything. No room for errors, it had to be perfect. He waited, one month, then two, with no response. Jim Kelly's family threw a big retirement party for him in the ballroom of one of the fancy hotels, with a live band and dinner buffet—still no response.

Frank pushed the button on the remote and some fuzzy pictures appeared on his laptop computer. Damn cell phone didn't take very good videos, but you could make out a group of men gathered in a park, food wrappers scattered on the ground around them. The next scene showed a truck pulling up to the curb, picking up two of them and driving away, while a group of children played on a brightly colored climbing structure, flying down the slide.

Mike Torelli turned to him and grinned. "What are these? Home movies of your family's afternoon in the park?"

"You should see the ones of his trip to the mall. Best photographs of the men's shirt department I've ever seen," Greg Bradley chimed in.

"Thought you were bringing in strippers, Frank."

"No strippers, Mike. Strippers are on a bring your own basis. BYOS. Bring your own stripper." Uproarious laughter and whoops and hollers filled the room, accompanied by the resounding thud of fists pounded on the table.

The new regional manager had come in the next day, a young guy in a suit and tie, looked like he never worked at a restaurant in his life. Probably studied business somewhere, at some fancy college. Frank had never liked school much, so after graduating from high school, he had enlisted in the military instead of going to college. Thought he would go a different way, serve his country instead of sitting on his ass in a classroom.

"So what do we get tonight besides the Sullivan family home movies? Torelli said you were showin' porn films."

"Frank is going to pass out Victoria's Secret catalogs so you can look at women's underwear." More laughter.

"Thanks a lot, Frank. Could'a stayed home and watched my own porn movies," John Loman said.

"Next meeting is at John's!" someone yelled.

Kevin something, the new regional manager's name was. When the east coast manager first brought him around to introduce him to everyone, the guy had given some dumb little motivational speech, made Frank's stomach churn just having to listen to it. Uppity fella, acting all snooty because he was in charge of everything. Kevin had reached out to shake his hand, but Frank didn't move, just stood there rooted to the floor, not believing what he was seeing. He went home sick that day, barely ate anything for three days, just lay on the couch watching TV and sleeping. He had to go back to work eventually, though, had a family to feed, had to have the paycheck.

Frank held up his palms to quiet the chitchat, begin the serious stuff. "Thought you guys might like to know about a new organization in Westchester County," he declared.

"What kinda organization, Frank? You a peacenik now?"

"It's about these guys, these damn immigrants sellin' drugs to our kids. We're startin' a new group to run 'em out of Oakmont."

He'd had to walk back through the door like a dog with his tail between his legs, face everyone who had said that he had it in the bag and joked with him about being the new regional manager, calling him "boss man" and "Mr. President." It was the hardest thing he ever had to do, hold his head up like nothing had happened, smile at the customers, kiss the boss's ass when he wanted to beat him silly. Couldn't believe he'd have to take orders from some kid who had stolen his job and was pocketing the money that should have gone to his family. His job, his money.

Ken Dawson took off his Mets cap, slapped it down on the table in front of him and hunched forward, as though moving closer to the table would make him more effective.

"Stop illegal immigration!" he said pounding his fist on the table to emphasize each word. "SIM for short!"

Frank had their attention now, so he kept going. "They're passing laws against illegal immigration all over the country, so the immigrants are all coming to New York because we let 'em run wild. They're all over Oakmont. I don't want 'em in my backyard and I'm sure you don't, either. Brothers, I'm asking for your help on this."

Bradley nodded. "I'm itchin' to get these guys off the street. They're bringin' drugs into the county from the Bronx and their kids are all in gangs. Me and Dawson got a place we're watchin' right now. The son is a known associate of the Miller Avenue Kings, the dad is illegal, and they're dealin' drugs from the back room of their ratty little restaurant. Let's go after them first—it'll scare the hell out of the rest of 'em." He paused, scanning the faces in the room, appraising what kind of support he might have. "Problem is, they've tied my hands with this due process stuff."

"A situation like that, Bradley, just shut 'em down for health violations and get 'em out of the neighborhood. You don't need any laws to get rid of scum like that. It's just like bowling. Set 'em up, knock 'em down."

"Then what? They come up to our neighborhood? Need somethin' stronger than that," Mike Torelli said.

"Got family out in Jersey where they've tried to pass laws deputizing cops as federal immigration agents. That way you wouldn't have to call immigration to bust 'em," Bradley added.

Dawson raised his fists in the air. "You got my vote!"

Frank grabbed some more beer bottles from the bar and set them down on the table. He picked a chip, scooped up some salsa, and shoved it in his mouth. "The laws'll make it easier. Right now, you gotta bust 'em on a criminal charge."

"Where my sister lives, the cops can make immigration checks even if they're caught jaywalking or living too many people to a house."

"Make it illegal to rent to 'em."

"Yeah, the rent thing. That's the bottom line. Make it illegal for them to live anywhere. Bust any landlord who rents 'em an apartment. They'll have to leave then."

Things were turning out a thousand times better than Frank had expected. They were definitely on board, ready to make things move, bring in new people. Jobs would be given back to Americans, playing fields left for American kids. Thoughts were racing through his mind so fast he could hardly keep up with them.

"You guys are right on the money. Thirty towns have already passed ordinances making it against the law to rent to illegals."

"Then we can bust 'em for vagrancy for sleepin' under the bridges. That's an easy one."

"You can get 'em on traffic violations, too. You see one of 'em driving, pull 'em over. Chances are you'll find a violation somewhere."

"Yeah, a crooked license plate."

"Hey, I'll bust 'em for too many dents."

"That would land you in jail, too, Bradley."

Frank bounced up and down on his heels, his face flushed, his eyes wide open. They were looking to him as someone important, a leader. It was a small group, but he would move on to larger ones, speak in front of larger crowds, thousands of people cheering and screaming when he finished his speech. Oakmont would be clean again, its old comfortable self, but he would continue on to other locations, other states, and clean them up, too. They would see him as a man with a place in history, a hero, the one who had started it all. The hell with Steak 'n Brew. He wouldn't need their crappy job anymore.

"Yeah, this is all good, but we need somethin' bigger, guys. Get 'em out for good," Frank declared.

"What, Frankie boy? Tell it, boss man."

"NAPO, baby," Greg Bradley interrupted.

That wasn't one Frank had heard of. "What's a napo baby?" he asked.

"National Association of Police Organizations. Very strong group with a lot of pull. Represents cops all over the country. Best lobby for laws that affect law enforcement in the country. They have a big convention coming up next month—we all gotta go, guys."

Frank wouldn't be able to go to that one, but he was elated that the cops were going.

They would be talking to other cops, finding ways to expand anti-immigration laws across the country, maybe come up with some new ones that really did the job.

"Forget the laws. They don't work anyway. You need to check out my boys in the First Militia," a young cop with a blond brush cut said. "We been working for a lot of years on this down in Arizona and Texas where they come over the border. We don't have meetings like this—we just hide in the bushes and shoot. Watch 'em run like rabbits and then *boom!* Right between the eyes."

Five

J ulia Sanchez had worked the breakfast and lunch shifts at El Patio, then spent the afternoon with a group of teenagers at the West Oakmont Community Center, assisting them with a large triptych that integrated graffiti art with a New York street scene.

She lay back on the couch, gazing out the living room window as the late afternoon sun cast an orange glow over Grover Hill, glad to finally be off her feet. For a few minutes, the aging brick, the pockmarked streets, and the dull brown of old wood were transformed into a work of art, a painter's canvas. Art was a comfort to her, a respite from the pressures of daily life, and she was always trying to find ways to beautify her surroundings. She had discovered art in middle school, where a teacher noted her talent and gave her a small sketchpad that fit into her purse.

When she graduated from Morris High School and took a job in the shipping department in a run-down warehouse in the East Bronx, it was her creativity that sustained her, allowed her to create bright color where there was darkness, spring where there was winter.

Julia glanced at her watch, then grabbed her drawing pad. Ricky and Marisol were downstairs at the restaurant helping Felipe and Tio Miguel with the busy dinner hour, and Camilo had finished his homework and was watching TV in the bedroom, so she had a few minutes to sketch before she had to start dinner. Ricky and Marisol would grab something to eat during a break, but she needed to feed Camilo soon, maybe something quick she could just stick in the microwave. A hot dog and some fries—that would work, give her a little more time to rest and do some drawing. Hot dogs were his favorite lunch at school, and he was always bugging her to make them.

Felipe wouldn't be home until much later in the evening, after the dinner shift was long over and he and Tio Miguel had cleaned up, locked away the cash, and tallied up the receipts for the day. El Patio was doing well, they had said, but sixteen years of marriage taught her to observe subtler things, rely on reading his body language. Felipe's usually bright smile seemed thin and strained lately, and he seemed out of sorts, as though he was upset about something, hiding some problem that he wasn't sharing with her. That was Felipe, trying to protect everyone, even if it was at his own expense, putting his best face forward no matter how he really felt. Maybe she just worried too much, and he was just coming down with a cold or something, feeling a little under the weather.

She outlined an image of the sun setting over the buildings, then flipped slowly through her sketchpad perusing old drawings, testimonials to the special moments in her life, chronicled in pastels or colored pencils or just pen and ink. The sweetest drawing was a rendition of the first time she met Felipe, a drop of honey that forever remained on her tongue.

She had come to Oakmont from the Bronx with Willie, her boyfriend at the time, to attend the communion of one of his nieces. On the way home they had stopped at El Patio for some food to take out, and she had noticed immediately that there was something different about the guy behind the counter, definitely not a New York look. *Campesino*, maybe, from the countryside somewhere. His eyes were the color of deep, rich coffee, and his thin white T-shirt clung to his chest, accentuating the muscles underneath it. He caught her eye and smiled as he handed her the bag of pupusas and she felt fluttery, like a flower shaken by a sudden gust of wind.

She and Willie returned to his Bronx apartment to eat and watch a movie, but she was distant, preoccupied. Her heart had already broken up with him and when she left that night, she knew she wouldn't be back. The following Saturday she took the forty-minute ride from the Bronx to Oakmont on the Metro-North train, returned to El Patio and ordered another pupusa just to see him again.

He picked up a cheese pupusa, placed it in a bag along with a can of Coke. "Hey, how are you today?" he said. "You were here last week, weren't you? New in the neighborhood? I'm Felipe. I didn't catch your name."

Her heart was beating way too fast and she hoped he couldn't hear it, or maybe she hoped he would. "Julia," she responded. "I don't live here, but I come to visit sometimes, and your pupusas are so delicious, I just had to come back for another one!" she said, trying to make her voice come out low and breathy, a sexy voice that might attract him.

"I put a special ingredient in them," he said, grinning.

"Well, whatever you put in there was so good—really, the best I've ever had!"

Disgraceful, her mother would have said. Not any way for a lady to act, showing up uninvited and flirting shamelessly, but then he was smiling at her again, his fingers brushing hers as he gave her the bag, and she felt weak and desirous, not at all in control of herself. She checked to see if he was wearing a wedding ring and didn't see one, but she did notice that his hands were rough, and when she examined his face she thought there was something in those coffee colored eyes she couldn't quite identify, maybe a sadness. His hands were scarred and weathered like an old person's, and she wondered what would have given a young man an old man's hands.

Despite the muscles and his rough hands, his voice was gentle and there was a kindness in it that she rarely heard from New York guys, who tended to be pushy about everything. "I was thinking, maybe you would like to go out next weekend. Then I can tell you all about how I make them, and I can find out all about you!" he said.

The following week, she met him at the Melrose station, on the Metro North line that ran from the Bronx to Westchester County, and they took the bus from there to Orchard Beach, a mile long strip of sand and shimmering blue water at the end of Pelham Bay Park in the East Bronx.

The beach was packed with people that day, but Felipe took Julia's hand and they walked past the people playing music and barbecuing in the grassy area, past the sunbathers lying in the sand and the children digging with paper cups. At the end of the beach, they found a quiet spot away from the crowd, behind some rocks. It was there he first kissed her, a memory that would forever be infused with the smell of the sea and the feel of warm sand. They were both eighteen, passionate and idealistic, brimming with enthusiasm.

They watched the seagulls swooping down over the water looking for fish, and he shared his dream of owning a classy restaurant where people sat down for dinner and were served by waiters in white shirts and black pants. "White tablecloths," she added, "a vase with a rose, a candle on every table, and a pianist, playing soft jazz while people sip their wine."

Julia had never liked riding the bus, they were usually too hot and too crowded, full of irritable, grouchy passengers looking for any excuse to get into a fight, but the bus ride home from Orchard Beach that day was unlike anything she had experienced before. It was as though she was floating inside a magic cloud, a special place where she could not be touched by meanness or cruelty, a place of beauty where only good things happened to people. She could vaguely hear an argument at the back of the bus, something about somebody having a grocery bag on an empty seat and not allowing the other person to sit there, but the angry words drifted over her head, which now rested on Felipe's shoulder.

Her bus stop was a block from the Metro North train station, so she walked Felipe to the station, marveling at how charming the neighborhood had become and how sweet the air smelled, as though rose petals had saturated the air, enveloping her in a rainbow of colors and scents.

The next week Felipe invited her to go dancing at a club in Oakmont, and as they drifted down the street with their fingers entwined, she could feel his body heat, smell his aftershave lotion and the cream he had put in his thick, black hair. The beat of the music was loud enough to be heard out in the street, and her fingers began snapping and her hips moving, right there in the middle of Oakmont.

The velvet tones of Ricky Bonaro floated over the dance floor as their bodies moved in perfect harmony, like the instruments in a finely tuned orchestra. The last call was sounded at 2 a.m., and although Julia would have been content to dance the rest of the night, they headed back to Fourth Street, where Felipe shared one of the apartments above El Patio with his uncle and aunt, Miguel and Rosa, and their two children.

"I have a key," he whispered, motioning her toward El Patio. The storage room in El Patio was a small space off the kitchen that was cordoned off with a curtain, but plenty big enough for her to find his lips and to pull off his shirt and feel the strength of his chest against hers. They lay in each other's arms and she told him about growing up Puerto Rican in the Bronx, while he told her a little about his life in El Salvador. She had been right about the sadness in his eyes, but that only made her love him more. It took many months of loving him, though, before he was able to share the whole story.

El Salvador
1985

Six

Green with tropical forests and crimson with blood, hot with the fire of volcanoes and the relentless sun that beats down on coffee pickers, cold with death. When the rains come down, it is not really rain at all but the tears of a grieving people that soak the land and make the coffee grow.

Felipe rose with a sense of foreboding, just couldn't shake the feeling that something bad was going to happen. Mama roused him at dawn most days, but today she didn't have to coax him at all because he had been awake most of the night.

The morning sunlight filtered through the leafy green branches of the laurel trees as he carried the pear-shaped dried gourd, the *tecomate*, to the river, where he would fill it with water for Mama, who was preparing their breakfast of tortillas, beans, and salt. He was already too warm in his thin white shirt, so he threw it off and tossed it by the bank of the Rio Escondido, next to the *tecomate*. The river was still chilly from the night air, but his body warmed to it quickly as he plunged in and floated on his back for a few precious minutes. The river water lapped gently against his skin, soothing him as he floated, gazing up at the glorious blue sky of early morning, listening to the birds warbling to each other as they scouted for breakfast while the sun came up.

High above him, a green parrot squatted on a branch blinking one black eye, maybe the same parrot he had seen a few days ago in a tree by the *choza*, the one-room hut he shared with his parents and his sister and brother. Such a beautiful parrot deserved a name, so he made one up on the spot. *Verdito*, little green one, he would call him. "*Hola*, Verdito," he called to the parrot. There were no clouds in the sky today, and he wondered where the clouds went when they weren't in the sky.

Papa had been coughing all night, a rumbling, hacking cough that awakened Juanito, the baby, who was frightened by the noise. Mama sat on a straw mat, rocking him, singing a lullaby. *"Vaya cierre sus ojitos,* close your little eyes, *canasunganana, canasunganana,"* she had cooed, but Juanito continued crying and Papa continued coughing, so no one got much sleep.

The sun was higher now, its bright yellow face reminding Felipe that it was time to go to the *finca*, the coffee plantation, to begin the day's work. He slid the *tecomate* into the river, holding it steady, the water gurgling softly as it rose to the top. His shorts were cool against his skin from the river water, taking the edge off the heat that was already baking the dirt under his feet and drying the dampness in his hair.

The scent of smoke wafted through the air and Mama appeared in front of the *choza*, her black hair tied into a bun, her slender body bent over the *hornilla* cooking tortillas. The *choza*, a one-room hut built of wood, had a thatched roof covered with dried grass and only a tiny window to allow in natural light, but this morning a streak of sun streamed across the dirt floor, dancing on the straw sleeping mats and Papa's sombrero that sat in the corner.

The mats were usually rolled up and hung from the wall during the day, but today Papa was still lying there long after the sun rose. Felipe placed the *tecomate* in the corner next to a small bag of cornmeal, two machetes, and Papa's sombrero, then sat down on the floor next to Papa. Papa clutched the sides of the mat and attempted to push himself to a sitting position.

"Papa," Felipe said quietly. "Papa, maybe you shouldn't go to the *finca* today."

"I don't get paid if I don't work, *mijo*, and they were not happy about the sick days I took last week. If I don't go in today, they'll fire me for sure—then what will I do?"

"I'll work extra hours until you feel better, Papa. I can do any job there, even loading trucks," Felipe answered, pleading with him now.

Juanito had finally fallen asleep, wrapped in a blanket, breathing rhythmically on the straw mat. Mama put her arm around Felipe, squeezing his shoulder. "I'm very proud of you for wanting to help, Felipito, but nine hours a day is plenty for a thirteen-year-old. Papa will manage."

Felipe and Papa trudged down the long stretch of road that led to the *finca*, a trip that usually took them an hour if they moved along at a brisk pace. Today they had gotten a late start and needed to hurry, but Papa kept stopping every few minutes to catch his breath, and they couldn't seem to propel themselves faster than the armadillo that poked sluggishly across the road in front of them.

More than an hour had passed before the multi-hued shirts of the coffee pickers appeared in the distance, splotches of color peeking through the green leaves of the coffee bushes. Gauzy white tropical shirts, plaid sport shirts with buttons opened to the waist, some white T-shirts, some brightly colored ones.

Felipe's friend Ernesto and his father, Oscar, were pulling coffee beans from the plants and putting them into baskets strapped around their waist, while other families washed them and spread them out to dry on stone terraces called drying platforms. Men with muscled brown arms and faces damp with sweat peered out from under their straw hats, as they loaded the jute sacks filled with coffee beans onto trucks. The beans were transported to a *beneficio*, where they were processed—small separated from large, red from yellow from green—then washed to take off all the debris and loaded into a machine to remove the pulp.

As they entered the *finca*, the freshness of the earth in the early morning and the sweet smell of coffee beans mingled with another odor—the acrid smell of gunpowder from the rifles of the Salvadoran National Guard as they shot into the air for sport, letting the pickers know that their life could be extinguished with the squeeze of a trigger for any reason at all. They swaggered up and down the rows of coffee pickers in knee-high black boots, bandolier bullet belts slung across their dark green military uniforms, the bayonets on their rifles sharpened to a razor point, keeping a close eye on how much each person was picking. They made detailed reports to the owners, and when payday came, they exacted vengeance upon those whose counts were not sufficient.

"You're late!" The bayonet with the razor sharp tip waved angrily in the air, piercing Papa's threadbare white shirt, a red stain now inching its way slowly down his back. Papa stood stiffly in front of the *guardia*, not moving, his spindly arms dangling helplessly from his frayed sleeves like bent branches after a storm. His eyes followed the bayonet as it moved toward his right ear.

"Yes, sir. I wasn't feeling so well this morning, but I'm here to do my job."

"You're late!"

"I'm sorry, I-I—"

"You'll be sorrier on payday."

"Please, *señor*. We'll stay later to make up the time. We need the money."

"Are you talking back to me, old man?" The rifle twirled and the butt of the gun jabbed Papa in the chest, pushing him into a coffee bush. Felipe could not see any life in the *guardia's* face, and where there might have been a spark in his eyes, there was only stone. A jagged red scar ran down the side of his face, and there was nothing but an angry line where his mouth belonged.

Felipe strapped a basket around his waist and began pulling the red, ripe coffee beans from the bush. Pull the beans, toss them in the basket; pull the beans, toss them in the basket; pull toss, pull toss, pull toss.

His thoughts drifted to another time, when he and Ernesto and Rafael made a soccer ball out of a nylon stocking filled with rags, imagining themselves to be great soccer players who would bring glory to their country. He would kick the ball, higher, higher, until it sailed over the heads of everybody, flying with the speed of lightning, landing between the goal posts. The goalie from the other team would scramble to get it, but it would be too late. Another goal by the great soccer player, Felipe! A stadium filled with adoring fans would chant his name, *Fe-li-pe, Fe-li-pe,* cheering until they had no voices left, and money would flow like a river into his hands. He could feel the weight of the money in his pocket, money to buy a house for his family, beautiful clothes for his mother, land for his father. He would go to San Salvador to find a doctor for Papa and bring back treats for Ana and Juanito.

The *guardia* with the scar was paying close attention to Papa, whose frail body was hunched over the coffee bush, pulling the beans with awkward, weary strokes, his breathing labored, his face contorted from the effort. A ledger waved in the air, a black boot swung out, leaving a dusty footprint on Papa's leg.

"Go on, faster! You are worthless to me today. Another piece of trash for me to clean up!" he thundered.

Felipe wanted to scream at the *guardia,* to tear him apart, scatter his limbs in the bushes the way so many villagers had been scattered, but his mouth didn't move and his fingers kept picking. Pull, toss, pull, toss, pull, toss. He felt like a coward, letting Papa be pushed around by these devils. To be a man would be to defend him, to stand up to the *guardia,* but they needed the money and a wrong move could bring even more trouble. They would fire him on the spot, maybe him and Papa both, and they wouldn't hesitate to kill Papa, right there in front of everyone.

A horn blared loudly, interrupting his thoughts. The *carreta*, the lunch truck, had arrived, calling the coffee pickers to lunch, bringing tortillas, one or two for each picker, sometimes with beans.

Felipe joined Papa and a group of men sitting in the grass eating tortillas. Their voices were low, whispering, glancing around cautiously for any sign that the *guardias* might be within earshot.

"That one with the scar is bad today," Manuel said in a barely audible voice.

Oscar nodded at Papa. "Go over on the other side where he can't see you."

"There's no place where they can't see you," Rolando muttered under his breath. "We found Diego's body yesterday in the bushes by the latrine."

Felipe surveyed the men sitting in the grass, men he had known all his life, the fathers of his friends, chewing their tortillas without even any beans today. Manuel and Rolando had been schooling him in the ways of picking coffee since he was seven years old, sharing the secrets of survival they had acquired over the years. Oscar taught Ernesto and Felipe how to play soccer, and showed them how to make a soccer ball that was strong and would last for a while.

"We have no land, no food, and still the *hacendados* want more." Oscar was looking at Felipe, directing his words to him. A teacher talking to his student, a father to a son. Felipe had left school after third grade, but the *finca* became his classroom, these men his teachers, his protectors.

"We're standing up now, fighting for land reform, which makes the rich landowners very angry," Oscar said.

"And when they have all the land and all the food, who will be left to—"

Felipe stopped short as the whistle blew, calling the coffee pickers back to work, and his eye caught one of the *guardias* moving toward them. The *guardia* smacked Oscar with his rifle, then fired a shot into the air as everyone scrambled through the grass toward the coffee plants.

The coffee sacks weighed two hundred pounds, pulling at the muscles in Felipe's arms until they ached and burned, straining his back until he could barely stand. Felipe and Ernesto would each lift one end of the coffee sack, then swing it in the air so that it landed on the back of Rafael, who carried it over to the truck to be loaded.

The *guardia* with the scar kept his eyes on Papa, glaring at him as he pulled the beans from the plants and threw them into the basket. "I told you—faster!" The butt end of the rifle crashed into the back of Papa's head. Papa collapsed into the dirt and the rifle came down again and smacked him squarely across the mouth, a trickle of blood running down his chin. As the rifle rose a third time, a voice rang out across the field, loud and strong, causing everyone's head to turn.

"*Basta*, enough!" The thundering roar of Oscar's deep voice reverberated across a silent field, as rows of coffee pickers stared mutely into the bushes, beans flying through the air into the baskets at lightning speed. "Enough, *señor*. He's not harming anyone. He's not feeling well today, but he's still been working very hard."

Another sound rang out, louder, more powerful. Oscar fell to the ground, motionless.

Where his words had been a few minutes before, there was blood, and then silence. Oscar, who had been eating tortillas without beans, the father of Ernesto, Celia, Roberto, and Carlos. Oscar, who helped them make a soccer ball and taught them how to play. Oscar, the one who defended Papa. Felipe didn't look, but he knew the smell, and the scrape, scrape of a body being dragged off into the woods.

Oakmont, New York
Fall, 2005

Seven

Frank was kicking back in his old easy chair with his feet up on the coffee table when the brassy honk of the doorbell jolted him out of his catnap. He had been alternately dozing off and watching the game on TV, nursing a beer and dipping into a bag of barbecue-flavored chips. He shook himself out of his drowsy state and peered out the window to see who might be banging at the door.

A blue and white police car was sitting at the curb and two cops in uniform were standing on the front steps, ringing the bell and knocking impatiently. Probably had to do with the Stop Immigration meetings, some news about getting the illegals out of the mall. Ever since the SIM meeting, cops all over town knew he was in their corner on this, more than willing to help out any way he could.

Frank recognized one of them right away—Tony Scoletti, worked the east side of town, came to the Steak 'n Brew with Greg Bradley and the others. He had showed up at the SIM meeting last week and brought two new guys with him. Frank didn't know the other cop, looked young, maybe new to the force.

"Officer Ringold, Oakmont PD. Colin Sullivan your son?"

There was a bite in the air, a late November chill, a reminder that winter was around the corner. Frank shivered as a nippy breeze pierced his shirt. Monday was his day off, and nothing beat kicking back in an old shirt and a pair of shorts, not doing much of anything. He sure as heck hadn't expected anything big to happen today.

Frank stared at Tony, puzzled. "What's this about?"

"Frank—"

Scoletti dropped his eyes, as though he was conversing with an invisible person sitting on the front steps. "Frank, uh, we have Colin down at the station, and uh, you might wanna come down there."

"What? What happened?" Frank said, completely alarmed now. His mouth was so dry he could barely get the words out, and he could feel sweat collecting on the back of his neck and under his armpits, despite the cold air. Should'a grabbed his beer before he answered the door, because he sure could use a swig of something right now.

He fiddled with some loose coins in his pocket, a dime and a few pennies he had forgotten to put in the spare change jar. He took them out of his pocket and jiggled them in his hand, leaned against the door frame, trying to appear casual.

Officer Ringold unfolded a piece of paper, stared at it, folded it again slowly as he watched Frank's face. "Colin Sullivan. Arrested for drug possession down at the East Oakmont mall."

"Whoa, whoa–hold on a minute. This has gotta be some kind of mistake. My son is a good kid, plays wide receiver on the football team at Oakmont High. He's college bound—never been in trouble in his life. You sure you got the name right?"

Frank dropped the coins back in his pocket, ran his hand through his hair and shook his head. "No, no way, not possible. You got the wrong kid on this one."

The East Oakmont police station was situated next to Oakmont High School in a nondescript, square brick building sandwiched between the high school football field and a small park. Frank had been through those white double doors before, when he was taken into custody for punching a referee at one of Colin's Pop Warner football games. It had turned into a brawl, with several fathers flailing at each other—one guy actually got knocked out. The worst thing was that they ended up arresting the wrong guys, should have been the lard-ass referee who couldn't tell a foul when it was in front of his face. Instead, Frank had to go to a hearing and sit for hours until charges were finally dropped. That was small change, though, compared to having everyone know your kid was busted for drugs.

Johnny Loman was sitting behind the counter, typing something into a computer. "Hey, Frank." He turned to the other cop behind the desk. "Frank manages Tony's Steak 'n Brew. You oughta check it out. They got the best steaks in the area and free beer for cops," he said, winking at Frank. "So, uh—you're here for—" he said, pointing his thumb at the staircase. "Yeah, he's up there."

Frank surveyed the lobby, the hard plastic benches, the large counter that separated the public from the police. He was mortified at having his family business on display, at Colin being on the other side of the counter, the criminal side. They always blamed the parents, like it must have been something about the way you raised him that made him do something bad.

He leaned on the counter and nodded at them. He did have a few things going that could work for him. He was known around here and had friends in the police department. All those free beers he gave away had to be worth something. A few conversations in the right places could make this all go away.

"How's it goin', bud?" he said, his eyes riveted on Johnny's face. "Hey, I saw your boy the other day. I hadn't seen him for a while, actually not since our kids played Pop Warner football together. He's turned into a big handsome guy. I bet the girls like him." A laugh from behind the counter. "Is he playin' any sports these days?"

Johnny shuffled through some papers, tossed a few in the trash, put the rest in a manila folder, and walked to the file cabinet. "Tell you the truth, Frank, he sits around playing guitar all day—you know, that loud screechy music the kids like. He thinks being a rock star is his destiny. He's gonna be a little surprised when he finds out he has to work for a living."

Frank lowered his voice and leaned a little further over the counter. "Listen, Johnny, Colin's a good kid, just got himself into a little trouble. You got kids—you know they don't always think. And, uh, Johnny, I'd appreciate it if you could keep this from gettin' around town, know what I mean?"

"You can count on it, Frank. C'mon, let's go see him. Scoletti's already up there."

The interrogation room was stuffy and warm, and Frank found himself peeling off his jacket, laying it on the back of the chair, unbuttoning his shirt collar. Despite his confidence that he could manage this, he was speechless as he sat down at the gray plastic table across from Colin, the boy he raised, and wondered what he had missed.

Tony Scoletti rolled up his sleeves, leaned forward with his elbows on the table. "We've been investigating drug activity in the area for a while, Frank. Your boy here was arrested with eight ounces of marijuana and an ounce of cocaine."

Colin, his boy. His eyes were the deep blue he had inherited from his mother and his dark blond hair had grown quite a bit. Past the middle of his neck, definitely needed a haircut. At sixteen, his hands were large, a good size for a wide receiver, but not quite the hands of a man yet. Frank could remember those hands when they were smaller than his finger, and then later when they became big enough to catch a ball. A five-year-old boy who could already hold onto the ball and couldn't wait to play catch with Daddy.

Frank folded his arms and glared at Colin. "Well, son? You got somethin' to say for yourself?"

Colin was slumped in the chair, staring at a spot on the table. "I was hangin' out in the back lot behind Hamburger Heaven while one of my friends went inside to get a soda," he mumbled stiffly, folding his arms tightly across his chest. "Next thing I knew the police were there holding up a backpack they found behind the dumpster and searching me. It wasn't my backpack and I don't know whose it was."

"One of your friends, Colin? Someone toss it there when they saw the police?" Scoletti asked.

"My son says it wasn't his backpack, Tony. Did you find it on him? His fingerprints on it?"

"I'm sorry, Frank, but we showed up because we had word from an informant that a deal was about to go down there. We pulled up in the squad car and saw a bag go flying, land behind the dumpster. Colin is facing possible felony charges, Frank. Possession with intent to distribute—a Class E felony. We need the truth about what was going down there."

Frank stood up, towering over the occupants of the table. "You're damn right we need the truth!" he said vehemently, stabbing the table with his finger. "Look, Tony—you and I both know where those drugs are coming from, where the real crime is coming from. It's those damn illegals standin' around the mall every day. They're the ones with the Mexican connections—Mexico, cartels, they all speak Spanish and play soccer together—you know what I'm sayin', bud."

His voice rose, a deep bass that he had cultivated in the Marines, a voice that commanded respect, the voice of a righteously indignant tax-paying American citizen.

"I know you guys are just doin' your job, but we're done here. Time for us to lawyer up so we can straighten out this crap."

Officer Scoletti leaned back in his chair, clasping his hands behind his head. "Whoa, wait just a minute, Frank. If our boy Colin works with us to help collar some of those guys you're talking about, the bigger fish, we may be able to find some ways to cut him a break. We can probably get it cut down to a misdemeanor and he'll just have to do some community service. You go to trial, you could win or lose, but if you lose, bye-bye football scholarship."

Frank leaned over the table and narrowed his eyes at Colin. The look, Bonnie used to call it. It had always worked in the past; he had kept Colin in line with that look since he was a little tot.

"What about it, son? You with us on this?"

"Dad—"

"You are if you want to walk out of here, do you un-der-stand?" Frank said sharply, emphasizing each syllable.

Colin cradled his head between his hands, his body motionless as though he was frozen in place. A minute of excruciating silence filled the room while Frank waited for a response.

"Do you un-der-stand?" Frank repeated angrily, raising his voice.

"Okay, okay! Fine—I'm cool with whatever," Colin finally muttered, staring down at the table.

Eight

Felipe rose at 6 a.m. and moved silently around the tiny apartment, pulling on a pair of faded jeans and a blue work shirt. He tried to step lightly so as not to wake anyone, but the old wood floor creaked and groaned under his feet, causing him to take one step at a time, pausing frequently. He headed toward the refrigerator where he found two pieces of cold pizza Ricky must have left, wrapped them in a napkin, and slid them into a brown paper bag. No telling how long they had been there, but they would do for now. One for breakfast, one for lunch.

The world was dark, the streets empty and silent, the only light coming from the glow of streetlamps or the headlights of an occasional car that meandered down the street, the only sound the yip of a dog being taken out for a walk in the early dawn hour. It felt strange to be doing this, like something out of a bad dream. Maybe he would wake up and find himself in El Patio getting ready for the breakfast crowd—setting up the coffee pot, putting out a supply of napkins and white paper bags. All they usually wanted was coffee and a roll, a pupusa or a burrito to take for lunch.

El Patio looked as it always had, except for the padlock and the sign on the door. *Closed, Order of the Westchester County Department of Health for multiple health code violations.* The envelope was still taped to the door, courtesy of the New York State Liquor Authority, indicating a one hundred dollar fine for selling alcohol without a license and a summons to appear before a judge. A second envelope fluttered next to it, from the town of Oakmont, for operating a club without a cabaret license. Julia had read him the fine print, which said that continued operation of a club without a cabaret license would result in a fine of one hundred dollars a day for each day the club operated.

The same two cops that had been harassing them, Bradley and Dawson, had appeared at El Patio a week ago during the dinner hour, found the radio playing and two beer bottles in the trash that he and Julia had shared after closing the night before. A quick scan of the kitchen turned up a burner on the stove that wasn't working, and a few specks on the floor that Bradley insisted were rodent droppings. Bradley had rummaged around, opening cabinets and drawers, checking the storage space behind the curtain, searching for drugs, demanding Felipe's citizenship papers. The next day an inspector from the health department arrived and cited them for multiple health violations: stove inoperable due to leaking gas, rodent infestation.

El Patio had been his haven, his anchor in a stormy world since he arrived in New York at the age of fourteen, and its closure made him feel disconnected and lost, as though his body no longer had any ground to stand on and was floating aimlessly in space. El Patio was where everything good in his life had happened, where he and Julia made love in the back room behind the curtain, where his children played while he rolled out the dough for pupusas and filled burritos with chicken and rice. He wondered if he could get in there to get his family pictures off the wall, and Julia's drawings. Marisol had been drawing lately, too, and she and Julia actually had a little business going, selling their artwork to the restaurant customers coming up from New York City.

Ramón Sosa, a long-time customer and patron of the social scene around El Patio, went to the mall quite often to pick up work and had offered to go with Felipe, show him the ropes.

"Painting, construction, cleaning, moving things. Whatever they need, you do," he told Felipe.

"I've never done any of those jobs," Felipe said. "Do they need anyone to make pupusas?"

Ramón laughed. "You just work hard, that's all. Just stick the paint in the bucket and slap it on. Stick the shovel in the ground and dig. The pupusas, bring for your lunch. You're going to need them."

Streaks of dawn were appearing in the sky as Felipe, Tio Miguel, Ramón, and three other guys leaned against the fence in the parking lot across from the Quik Shop grocery. A white pickup truck with several dents and duct tape around the back window swerved out of the parking lot and slammed into the space in front of the Quik Shop, rock music blaring from the radio. A twenty-something white guy with a baseball cap on backward and a black T-shirt speckled with paint stains rolled down his window, stuck two fingers in his mouth and delivered a piercing whistle. "Need two guys to put up drywall," he called. "Hurry up. You two, get in." Felipe scrambled toward the truck, but two guys who looked too young to shave moved faster and jumped into the back of the truck, which zoomed away as quickly as it had come.

Ten o'clock arrived; store managers fished for their keys, inverting sleepy *Closed* signs to a more zippy *Come in, Open for Business.*

Eleven o'clock. Felipe meandered around the lot, perusing store windows to pass the time as he listened for the sound of a truck engine, but the street was empty except for a lone police car. From the corner of his eye, he saw the door of the car opening, the cop loping toward him waving his club.

"Felipe!" Ramón called in a low voice, motioning to him to come back to the fence.

Ramón had warned him about standing in front of the stores while they were waiting for contractors to show up with work. "The store owners don't like us hanging out near their doorways. Bad for business, they think."

Felipe felt a sting on the back of his leg as he stumbled backward, away from the swinging club. "Against the fence! Move across the parking lot, against the fence!" the cop barked at him.

Twelve o'clock. Felipe grabbed a box that had been tossed into the trash behind one of the stores, took off his backpack, and sat down on the box to eat his pizza. A mottled gray pigeon flew down from its perch on the roof of the Quik Shop, then another. Somewhere in El Salvador a green parrot named Verdito sat on a branch, waiting for the return of the dark-haired boy who floated in the river, contemplating the cloudless blue sky and the green leaves of the laurel trees. Felipe broke off a piece of pizza crust, tore it into tiny pieces and tossed them at the pigeons, who dove for the bread, bobbing their heads as if to thank him.

A chorus of voices intruded on his thoughts, a rhythmic chant. A clump of people was advancing through the parking lot like a swarm of angry bees looking to see who had disturbed their hive. They were carrying signs and yelling, something about illegals, parading in a circle around the spot where the trucks were supposed to stop.

Another pickup truck rolled through the lot, splashes of mud on its dingy gray fenders, its bellowing muffler and racing engine temporarily drowning out the shouts of the picketers. The truck made a wide circle around them and screeched to a halt in front of the fence. Ramón grabbed Felipe by the arm. "In the truck. Fast!"

"Can you paint?" the driver shouted.

"Yes!" Felipe shouted back and hoisted himself up into the truck bed.

"Go back where you came from!" a shrill voice screamed. Several people in the crowd were shaking the back gate, kicking at the door and the fender. A rock sailed from somewhere and hit the passenger side window, chipping the glass.

"Come on, get in!" Felipe yelled to Tio Miguel, but the driver gunned the accelerator and the truck hurtled down the fire lane. As the truck sped away, Felipe caught a glimpse of Tio Miguel, clutching his brown paper lunch bag, staring as they drove away without him.

The parking lot and the day laborers, the picketers and the police all melted into the horizon, into another realm where they couldn't touch him. He had a job, even if it was a small one. He hadn't wasted the whole day and would have some money for Julia tonight. The side of his face felt moist and sticky, and he pulled an old tissue out of his pants pocket to wipe it.

"What's on your face?" Ramón asked.

"Spit," Felipe answered. "They were spitting at me."

El Salvador
1985

Nine

A landless and hungry population demands land reform and is met by violent opposition from wealthy landowners. Death squads begin executing peasants and the United States dispatches Green Beret trainers to teach the Salvadoran Army techniques for defeating insurgents. It is not tears but rivers of blood that irrigate the soil, the dust of bones that fertilize the coffee plants and make them grow.

Felipe had made the trip home from the *finca* so many times he could do it with his eyes closed, but tonight a gray mist blanketed everything, turning the trees into hazy shadows, the path ahead a blind alley. Papa stumbled over a rock in the grass, the wheezing from his chest making a whistling sound as he leaned on Felipe to keep from slipping. Heavy rain had begun to fall, the dusty road fast becoming muddy, pools of water appearing where the road had been. The rain slapped against Felipe's face and soaked his sandals, which made sucking sounds as he slid in the mud, trying to keep them both from falling.

"You can make it, Papa. Mama is going to fix you up, and then you can go to sleep. You can make it. Mama is there waiting for you, and Ana and Juanito."

Papa pressed his back against a tree and closed his eyes, his body sagging, as though the tree was all that prevented him from toppling over completely. "Can't go on right now. Need to sit—"

"Hang on to me, Papa. We can't stay here. If the *guardias* find you they will shoot you, the way they shot Diego and Oscar. You can lie down when we get home."

Papa took a few steps forward, then stopped and sat down again, breathing hard.

"Papa—"

"I'll be okay, I just need to rest for a minute," he said. "Just a minute—"

"The *guardias*, Papa," Felipe said desperately, but Papa didn't move.

"Those thieves—they've taken everything from us. Chickens, pigs—we can't even have fiestas anymore," Papa said wistfully, staring off into the distance. "Someday we'll go to the *posadas* again and give presents to the children," he continued. "Do you remember the *nacimiento* in the square?"

"Not too much. Mostly I remember the food and the dancing. Let's talk at home, Papa. We can't stay here. We need to go now!"

"The priests built a manger in the marketplace and they even put in animals and made it look like a farm. I guess you were too small to care about that. I think you were more interested in the gifts," Papa said, a faint smile crossing his face.

Felipe placed his hands under his father's armpits and dragged him to a standing position.

Papa gripped Felipe's arm as they stumbled along the muddy road, pausing every few minutes so that Papa could catch his breath. The dried grass covering the top of the *choza* emerged abruptly through the mist, like a gift that had fallen from the heavens.

"See, you made it! There we are, there's the *choza*. Just a little bit more. You did it."

"We did it, *mijo*. We did it together, you and me."

A small figure appeared at the entrance, silhouetted against the wooden door frame.

"What happened to you? Why are you so late? I've been so worried!" Mama said anxiously, peering at them from the doorway. "Look at you—you're soaking wet," she said, scurrying into the *choza* to find them some dry clothes.

"Papa's hurt, Mama. We got to the *finca* late and the *guardia* said Papa worked too slowly, so he stuck him with the bayonet and hit him with a rifle. Oscar tried to stop them, and they shot him. Oscar is dead, Mama."

"*Ay, dios mio*," Mama said, her lips quivering, as though she was trying to hold back tears. "What is wrong with those people, that they have to do this to us? We never hurt anybody," she mumbled bitterly. "Get a mat, Felipe, quickly."

Felipe helped Papa lower himself onto the mat, and together he and Mama pulled off his torn, bloody shirt and tossed it in the corner. "*Te amo*, Fernando," Mama whispered, leaning down and kissing Papa on the forehead. "You're going to be okay, *querido*. We're going to help you."

Oscar, lying on the ground, being dragged away. Sorrow was ripping at Felipe's heart, threatening to drown him, but there was no time for sadness—they needed to help Papa.

"I can go visit the *curandera*, Mama, to get some medicine for Papa."

When Juanito had gotten a fever a few months ago, Felipe ran to see Father Rodriguez to ask him how to get a doctor, but the priest had explained that there were three doctors for every ten thousand people now and they were mostly in the cities, not in the countryside. Father Rodriguez told him where to find Esperanza, the healer, who said prayers as she rubbed garlic paste on Juanito's body and hung a ring of garlic around the baby's neck.

A cup of water and a rag would be Papa's medicine now. Mama dipped the rag into the water and began to clean Papa's wounds.

"You can go to the *curandera* tomorrow, *mijo*," Mama said. "Papa will rest tonight, and you can go early in the morning, before you go to the *finca*. It's late and you've had a very hard day. Tomorrow morning is soon enough."

"But Papa—"

"Felipe!" Mama said sternly. "You are not going to see Esperanza tonight! I know you want to help, but the soldiers are out there patrolling. If they see you out there at night, they'll think you are going to meet up with the FMLN and they'll arrest you. Besides, Esperanza sleeps, too. Papa will be okay until morning." She pushed a straw mat toward Felipe and blew out the candles.

"Mama," he whispered, and found himself telling her about Oscar and the *guardias* and trying to get Papa home in the rain.

When the growling in his stomach woke him a few hours later, he lay in the darkness for a while, listening to the ragged breathing of his father and the quiet breaths of Ana and Juanito.

Mama's breath made no sound at all, so he rose silently and crawled over the dirt floor toward her, just to make sure she was alright. She had told him to wait until morning, but that might be too late for Papa, and the *curandera* might not mind being visited during the night in an emergency. Felipe stepped softly past his sleeping family, past a half-empty sack of cornmeal and a small bag of beans leaning against the wall, past the machete and the *tecomate* he had filled with river water that morning, and gently pulled open the door of the *choza*, slipping into the cool night air.

The *Guardia Nacional* was not in sight, but he knew they could be hidden anywhere, their dark green uniforms camouflaged in the darkness, their fingers curled around the trigger of their rifles. The rain had stopped and the air was smoky and acrid, as though a fire was burning. He made his way down the main road of the village, the *chozas* dormant except for one, the yellow light of a *candile* flickering in its window.

On Sundays, the marketplace was held here. People came to spend the meager pay they earned picking coffee on the *finca*; they bought food for the week or brought things to sell, met their friends to socialize, share food and catch up on the news. The marketplace opened early, at 6 a.m., with oranges, bananas, and avocados arranged neatly on small tables, women bustling about in long skirts with red, green, purple embroidery, carrying baskets on their heads, children by their side. Fish caught in the river sizzled over fireplaces in the ground, and guitarists played music while people put money in their hats. Mama had once bought him a special treat, candy made with tamarindo and sugar, but thinking about it now reminded him too much of his empty stomach, so he turned his thoughts back to finding Esperanza.

Felipe had crossed the river before, but it had been daytime then, and now it was pitch black, without even a sliver of moonlight to help guide his way. The sky was full of stars, though, and for a moment he wished he could lay down by the river and watch them for a while.

There was one that was larger than the rest and less shiny, and he wondered what it was. Papa had once shown him how some groups of stars were arranged to look like pictures of animals and people, and if you sat very quietly and observed carefully, you could make them out. He could not make out any animals now, but he saw one that maybe had the shape of a man, or maybe a woman.

The Rio Escondido was dark, asleep with the rest of the village. The fish that drifted through the glassy water in the morning light had disappeared into the murky blackness, but Felipe could make out the larger rocks, glistening with slippery moss, their jagged edges gleaming like silvery knives.

His footsteps crunched in the grass, loud as thunder in the stillness of the night, and he crouched behind a tree, his eyes peeled for a hunting animal or the appearance of human clothing through the bushes. Somewhere above him, a night bird fluttered its wings as it took flight, startled by his presence. A twig snapped, and the branches of the trees were sharp, angry bayonets silhouetted against the leaden sky. He tiptoed, one step at a time, toward the bank of the river, stepping carefully onto the boulders that were visible, stretching out his arms to balance himself.

The first two were flat, but the third was uneven and slanted, slippery and treacherous as the river sloshed across it. He raised his right leg to position it on the flattest part of the rock, the chilly water drenching his sandals, but his foot slipped as it touched the slimy surface and he was catapulted into the river, the edge of the rock piercing his bare leg.

He paddled furiously toward the other side as a dark stain formed and was sucked down the river. Soaked and shivering, he dug his fingers into the muddy river bank and heaved himself onto the grass, desperately scanning the area for the dwelling place of the *curandera*. He spotted a *choza* that looked much like his own, peeking out from behind the trees. He inched through the grass toward the front door.

"Esperanza," he called, knocking lightly. "Esperanza, I need your help."

There was no answer, so he knocked a little harder, then sat down on a fallen log to wait.

Grabbing a pile of leaves, he fashioned a makeshift bandage and held it against the gash in his leg, trying to stop the flow of blood. He wondered where the *guardia* hid at this time of night and whether they could see him through the trees. Mama had told him to wait until morning, but he hadn't listened, and there was no one to defend him if they found him alone out here in the dark.

"Esperanza," he called, louder this time, hitting the door with his fist.

There was a faint rustling—a shuffling of feet, the rattle of a rickety wooden door, and a tousled gray head appeared in the doorway. Creases and lines covered every inch of her face, as though she had been in the sun for centuries, and the gray head presided over the thinnest body he had ever seen, nothing but skin and bones. Her eyes were the most remarkable—deep green and as bright and clear as the Rio Escondido in the morning sun.

"You are here in the middle of the night, *niño*. Something is very important to you. I remember the last time you came, there was a sick baby. I remember your name, too. You take good care of your family, Felipe. How is the baby?"

"The baby is fine, but Papa is the one who's sick now. He's coughing all the time and he can't breathe. Then, at the *finca* yesterday, the *guardia* stabbed him with a bayonet and beat him with a rifle. I'm sorry to wake you up at night, but we don't have anybody to help us."

"Of course—come in, come in—you came to the right place. I'm going to prepare some medicine for your Papa, and for you, too," she said, bending down and examining the cut on his leg. "That doesn't look too bad, but I'll put something on it."

"Esperanza, I have nothing to pay you with right now, but I can come back and help you later," Felipe said.

"I don't expect pay from a boy trying to help his family. If I need help from you, God will bring us together again. Please come in and let me put some *chichipince* on that wound on your leg and bandage it for you."

Esperanza lit some candles and Felipe could make out an altar with pictures of saints and various kinds of plants. Little bottles of liquids and packets of powders filled a small table, and the room had a spicy, perfumed scent. A brightly colored piece of cloth hung toward the back of the hut, creating a small private space.

"That is the place where I call the spirits, *niño*," Esperanza said when she saw him looking at the curtain. "If you have a problem of the heart or a family problem, I call on the spirits to help you. But you are too young to need that. For now, I am going to give you some things to help your papa, and if he does not improve, I will come to see him myself. Bring this bottle to your mama and have her give him a spoonful of this syrup for his cough three times every day. Tell her it has things in it that will help him a lot— eucalyptus, mango leaves, ginger and anise, boiled into a syrup," she said, gazing proudly at her creation. "Those are the best things for his cough, Felipe. The little bag has more *chichipince* to put on his wounds and yours, and this one has a special powder to put on his skin to protect against the *mal de ojo*, the evil eye. Your mama will know what to do with it."

Something shiny caught Felipe's eye and before he could ask what it was, Esperanza pressed it into his hand. "An amulet, to protect you. Keep it close to your body, around your neck or in your pocket to keep you safe and bring you luck. I'll pray for you tonight."

"Thank you so much, Esperanza. I promise, I'll return and pay you back."

"Someday you will, Felipe. Someday you will," she said, draping her arm across his shoulder for a moment. "Come back anytime if you need more help."

The impenetrable darkness was softened by the approaching of dawn, but Felipe slipped and slid over the soppy grass, holding the bag with the medicine tightly in his hand. Crossing the river further down this time, he avoided the wet rocks, balancing precariously on a fallen log as he headed to the *choza* where his family was sleeping. The amulet hung on a string around his neck, and he felt protected, the spirits on his side now.

The acrid, smoky smell had grown stronger and the clamor of shouting voices wafted through the trees, muted by the deafening rumble of planes circling overhead. Felipe crept along the ground, ducking behind the bushes, hoping the dim light and the foliage would provide cover. Just beyond the grove of trees, he could see an open field, thick with the green military uniforms and black boots of the Salvadoran army, the *rat-a-tat* of guns blasting through the smoky dawn. Hatless men in threadbare shirts and ragged pants were running toward the woods, as camouflaged figures snaked through the high grass on their bellies, shooting at them as they ran. The field was littered with bodies and pools of blood already turning brown; the air was thick with the suffocating smell of smoke and the foul odor of putrefying human flesh.

Several men in military uniforms stood on the sidelines. One was a giant of a man, towering, husky, with a shiny bald head, shouting orders in barely understandable Spanish, then speaking to the others in a language Felipe didn't understand at all. Tourists had once come to the marketplace speaking a language that sounded like that, and a vendor had told him that they were Americans, speaking English. These must be the American soldiers one of the coffee pickers had mentioned, helping the *guardias* and the army, and he wondered how they could be so powerful that even the *guardias* listened to them.

Felipe clutched his bag of remedies and crept gingerly through the woods until he was sure he was far enough away that he was out of earshot of the soldiers. Stumbling and tripping over rocks and fallen branches on the ground, he dashed toward the main street of the village and the *choza* that was his home. As he approached the front door, something seemed amiss. The door appeared to be cracked and broken in several places, and he could hear the buzzing of voices, booming, angry voices, mixed with softer ones.

"Please, *señor*, he is sick and needs to rest," he could make out Mama's voice saying. "Please, please don't hurt him."

"We know who you are, Señor Sanchez. We saw you making contact with the guerillas yesterday."

"Guerillas? No, no, I was at work yesterday, picking coffee. My son was there—"

Felipe heard Papa's voice stop short. "Where is he? What did you do to my son?"

He could hear crying now, softly at first, then loud sobbing pierced the thin walls and the broken door. It was Mama sobbing, followed by a man's voice. "Maybe he ran away to join the guerillas, which makes things even worse for you. There is a battle going on about a half mile from here between the FMLN and the army. We know many FMLN come from this village and are hiding somewhere in this area. Maybe your son is out there with them. Tell us where we can find him, now!" the strange voice bellowed.

"I don't know where he is. He was here last night, sleeping on that mat."

"Whose shirt is that on the floor?"

"Mine," Papa mumbled.

Felipe heard the stomping of feet, and then a thump.

"A torn shirt, with blood on it? So you were out there fighting, too."

"No, no, that happened at the *finca*. I got hurt at the *finca*. I-I fell—and the machete—"

"Your son is gone, your shirt is bloody, and you think I believe that? You were seen talking to Oscar Valenzuela yesterday at the *finca*. We know Valenzuela has been meeting with the FMLN guerillas in this area. This is your last chance! Where is your son?"

"I don't know—I don't know where he is."

There were several more thumps and a crash forcible enough to make the wall shake, followed by the sound of Mama screaming and loud wails from the baby. Someone inside the house kicked a piece of the broken door and it fell off completely, landing with a thud in front of the *choza*. Two *guardias* appeared, dragging Papa with his arms twisted behind his back and his face in the dirt. Mama followed close behind, throwing herself on top of Papa as they dragged him away. Ana stood in the doorway holding the screaming baby, tears running down her eleven-year-old face.

Felipe's body shook the way it had when he ran a fever, an uncontrollable trembling from the top of his head down to his feet. He felt dizzy and violently sick to his stomach, but worst of all were his legs, which threatened to collapse under him any minute. No, not Papa. Please not Papa. *Papa,* he screamed, but only in his head. Felipe could see them from his hiding place behind the *choza*, one short, stocky man and one tall, thinner one in the dark green uniform of the *Guardia Nacional.* He had to tell the *guardias* where he had been, that he hadn't been fighting with the FMLN, so they would let go of Papa, but he was frozen, rooted to the ground.

They shot Oscar when he spoke up for Papa, and they probably wouldn't believe him—it might even make them angry enough to shoot him right in front of Mama and Papa and his sister and brother and then shoot Papa, too. If he was quiet, didn't upset them more, maybe they would leave Papa lying on the ground and go away.

The shaking had turned to numbness, as though he had no body at all, and he couldn't tell if his heart was still beating or if it was completely broken, a dead weight taking up space in his chest. He tried to draw a breath, clear the dizziness in his head, but his chest was tight and wheezing, the trees swaying, shimmering like the road in the burning heat of the midday sun.

"*Dios mio*, no. No, please, he was here with me last night," Mama screamed. "Please don't take him, please!"

The *guardias* kicked at Mama furiously with their boots, but she continued to hold onto Papa, her hands wrapped around his arm as she was yanked along with him, then his arm was slipping away, slipping out of her hand, so she grabbed his leg and held onto the cuff of his pants until the pants leg ripped and she was lying in the mud holding a piece of torn cloth that was all she had left of her beloved Fernando Sanchez.

If he had listened to Mama, stayed in the *choza* until morning, the *guardias* would have seen him there, might have let Papa go. Felipe stumbled on wobbly legs toward the trampled earth imprinted with the outline of Papa's body, toward the front of the *choza* with the gaping hole, breathing raggedly as Papa's body disappeared behind the trees, followed by the muffled *boom* of rifle shots. Mama lay on the ground sobbing, her arms stretched out in front of her as though she was still trying to reach for Papa.

Felipe and Ana helped Mama into the *choza,* laying her down gently onto the straw mat.

Mama gaped at him, her mouth half open in disbelief. "You're here, Felipe, alive. Is it true what they said? Were you fighting with the guerrillas?"

"No, Mama. I went in the middle of the night to get the *curandera* to help Papa. Look, she gave me some medicine."

Mama closed her eyes, took a deep breath and let it out slowly. "I told you not to go out there at night. You could have been killed. Papa would have been—"

Felipe bent over and placed the amulet around her neck, gently wiped her mud-spattered face with a wet piece of cloth. "Mama, you need to rest. Ana will take care of Juanito."

"No, no, we need to leave here right away. Now the *guardias* think you were fighting with the guerrillas last night, and they'll come back for you the way they came for Papa. The truth is not important to them. They are *cabrones* who only care about themselves."

"Where can we go, Mama? How will we live?"

"We'll go to Father Rodriguez, to the church. He'll find a place for us."

Felipe took out the packet of powder and rubbed some on her skin, and then on his. "This will help protect us from evil, Mama. Ana, hold out your hand and put some of this on yourself and some on Juanito. Esperanza said it will give us strength."

Mama was already picking up the tortillas she made that day and putting them in a small woven bag. Ana helped her with the *covita*, the blanket she wore around her shoulders to carry the baby. Felipe took a last glance around the hut that had been his home since he was born, and followed Mama through the space where the door used to be, where Papa had been.

Oakmont, New York
Fall, 2005

Ten

Colin assessed the football spiraling toward him, felt the smack of the leather as he pulled the ball out of the air, curved his hands around it and held it tight. His legs were moving, dodging, racing toward the goal line. They couldn't touch him—he was invincible, Superman flying across the sky. The goal line was in front of him now, and he raised his arm in triumph as he flew across it. A roar went up from the stands, and he quickly glanced over to where his father had been sitting, spotted his faded red and gold Oakmont High sweatshirt bobbing up and down amidst the cheers and the stomping feet of the crowd.

The team swarmed around him, hugging him, pouring water over his head as the coach waved his fists in a victory salute. Cheerleaders were gathered around the locker room door, casually twirling pom-poms, conversing with each other, tossing flirtatious smiles at the players.

Frank raced down to the field, grinning from ear to ear. "You did great, son. Pick your college, buddy—they're all gonna want you," he said proudly. At least Colin could safely bet that today wouldn't be one of Dad's grumpy days.

"Yeah, thanks, Dad. Big celebration at Sam's later, so don't wait up for me!" Colin chuckled.

"Big day tomorrow, too, son. Don't stay up too late!" Frank shot back, grinning again.

"What's tomorrow, Dad?" Colin asked quizzically. "I didn't know—"

"See you later, guys," Frank announced, loud enough for everyone in the crowd to hear. "Congratulations and all that, but we gotta run. I'm taking the best wide receiver in the county out for dinner! C'mon, son—it's family time right now. You can see your friends tonight."

"I'm not ready to leave yet, Dad," Colin said quietly, desperate to avoid an argument with his father in front of everyone.

"It's okay, bro," Luke interjected, coming to his rescue. "Have dinner with your family. We'll see you at Sam's."

"What's it gonna be, Dad?" Colin asked, leaning back against the seat, his legs sprawled casually out in front of him as the van pulled out of the Oakmont High parking lot. "The Super Combo Special at Hamburger Heaven?"

This had to be the best day of his life. He had done it— made the final touchdown that won the game, sending the team to the regional playoffs. No reason why he couldn't go along with the family thing for an hour or two. Even Dad would be tolerable today, and a whole evening without having to listen to him complain wasn't half bad.

He smiled to himself thinking about tonight. That was going to be one great party, with everyone treating him like a hero. His teammates would be bringing lots of booze, and he was definitely going to get bombed. Guys would be bringing stuff to smoke, too, but since he had been picked up at the mall Dad had threatened regular drug testing, so he better lay off that one. At celebrations like this, the parents would often look the other way, might even leave and let the kids have the run of the house, figuring they had earned the privilege to blow it all out for one night. Either way, he would be cruising, totally mellow, laying back and enjoying life.

"Better than that," Frank was saying. "We'll go to that nice Italian place. You can order whatever you want; you've earned it."

"Where's Mom?" Colin asked. "I thought she was coming today. Are we picking her up?"

Frank rested his left hand on the wheel and reached for the radio dial with his right as the van swerved at the exit to the highway. "Yeah, she had planned on being here, but couldn't get off work today. They're short-staffed because one of the nurses fell and broke her arm this morning. You know, an emergency in the emergency room, ha, ha!"

Mom had missed his big day—not her fault, though, and he could fill her in later. She wasn't much of a football fan, anyway, didn't really understand the game, but she would have been happy that it went well for him.

"So, Dad—what were you talking about? What's happening tomorrow?"

Frank pressed the power button on the radio, but there was no music on his favorite station right now, just a commercial that went on and on. Colin didn't mind Dad's music that much—some of the oldies were pretty good—but he really didn't feel like listening to that old stuff today, and he was grateful when Dad punched the button again and the radio went silent.

"Well, got some good news for you, real good news," Frank said. "I pulled a few strings in the right places, said some nice words to the right people, along with a few free beers, and you're going to watch those drug charges get flushed," he continued, looking totally pleased with himself. "Especially after today—your future is hot, boy. We can't afford to let all that talent go down the drain."

Colin straightened up in the seat and stared out the window, the excitement of the day quickly vanishing. He should've known this wasn't just a dinner celebration, that something else was going on. He gazed back at his father, appraising his mood. "Is it gonna be that easy, Dad?"

"If you cooperate, it will be. We'll go over to the police station tomorrow, and the cops will put you in front of a one-way glass so you can pick out the person who is selling drugs to the kids at school. You win, they lose."

No way he could explain the drug scene at school to Dad—that he had no idea where anything came from—it just seemed to show up, and everybody did it, even the football players.

The only people he could rat on were his friends, and that would be the end of his life if he ever did that. He could never show his face in school again, that's for sure, which would be worse than losing the scholarship. Better to keep your friends and find some other way to pay for college.

"But, Dad, I—"

"We know the drugs are there, but we're not blamin' the kids. We're going after the people who are bringing it into the country. Maybe you think it's all no big deal, but you're wrong. It's a big fucking deal, and if you're involved in any of it, you need to get uninvolved, like now," Frank said, glaring at Colin. "If you're as innocent as you claim, I'll be the happiest guy around. But right now it don't matter one bit if you're innocent, because the cops think you're guilty, and you've got charges hanging over you. Those charges are gonna haunt you if you don't get rid of 'em, and it's not worth throwin' it all away for somethin' like this."

"It's just that I'm not sure I can do that. I don't really know any big suppliers, and I wouldn't want to pick out the wrong person, ruin somebody's life for nothing," Colin said.

"You won't be ruining anyone's life. The guys in the lineup are known criminals, and you're doing a community service, putting them away. Think of it this way. You could probably pick any one of 'em and be right."

"That's—that's my only choice?" Colin pleaded, his voice cracking the way it sometimes used to when he was in middle school. "Maybe if I go to trial I'll get off. What does Mom think about this?"

Frank pulled a cigarette out of his shirt pocket and stuck it between his lips, then took it out again and waved it at Colin. "There's a lighter in the glove compartment. Grab it and light this for me," he said, frowning. "Look, there's no need to bother your mother with this. She doesn't know a damn thing about police business," he grumbled, as Colin searched the glove box for the lighter. "I deal with these guys all the time, know how the system works. You might not get off, and you'd be a damn fool to sacrifice your life for some guy who's probably guilty anyway—if not for this one, then for some other crime he didn't get caught for."

Colin clicked the lighter several times but nothing happened, then a flame shot up and Frank sucked in a long drag, blowing a column of smoke into the van. Colin racked his brain desperately for some tidbit of information that might sway his father, convince him that there was a better way to go. "Dad, I'll just do the court thing. It's the first time, and they'll probably cut me a break. Shit, I'm on the football team, got pretty good grades, and I've heard from my friends that if you're under eighteen, they seal the records."

"Goddamn it—*I* got you a break—*this* is your break, and if you don't get that, then I'll help you get it," Frank said irritably. "It's not just about you, okay? It's also about criminals who break our immigration laws, sneak over the border without papers, bring in their drug culture and disrupt our communities, turning kids on to harder drugs, like crack or heroin—that's the real goddamn issue here. Something about that you don't get, son?"

The victory party was awesome. Colin got really blasted, danced and made out with a cute girl until about 3 a.m., then dragged himself out of bed at noon because his father insisted that they go to the police station to look at those guys in the lineup. His head was pounding and his stomach felt wretched, but Dad had promised that this was the best way to dump the drug charge, keep his life on track. It probably wouldn't take too long. There's no way he would recognize anyone in the lineup unless it was a kid from school, and there was no way he would rat on any of them. He definitely didn't know any illegals, the ones his father was always blaming for everything.

Seven men dressed in work clothes stood motionless behind the one-way glass, their arms dangling awkwardly at their sides. Seven men in faded jeans, khaki work pants, and T-shirts, like the men in the parking lot next to the Quik Shop. They seemed to have lost their hats—maybe the cops made them take their hats off to make it easier to identify them. Colin looked away, but the glass took up the entire wall of the room, nothing else there to look at, to divert his attention while he decided what to do. He felt like he was in prison himself, stuck in this dingy room with the faded green walls and cracks where the white plaster showed through. Breathe in and out slowly when you're nervous, Coach had taught him. Breathe in, breathe out.

His father had hired a lawyer, Charles Reiter, from some fancy law firm—Bainbridge, Reiter and Mangum. He must be maxing out his credit cards to pay for that one. Detective Scoletti was standing to his left, keeping his eye on the men behind the glass.

"Scholarship," Frank whispered in his ear.

The lawyer slipped in between them, scowling at Frank. "Don't coach him, Mr. Sullivan, or you'll have to leave."

"Colin," Detective Scoletti began. "Did any of these men sell drugs to you at school, at the mall, or any other time?"

Charles Reiter loosened his red tie, took off his gray pinstripe suit jacket and laid it across a chair. "You need to be sure, Colin, absolutely sure." Colin could see wet circles of sweat under the armpits of his starched white shirt. He must be suffocating in this stuffy room in that fancy suit. Colin hated wearing suits and ties, tried to avoid them whenever he could. He was thankful Dad hadn't made him wear a suit today. Dad could be cool sometimes; he just wanted him to have a good life, didn't want him to ruin it before he even got to college. Colin still had about a year and a half to go, but he couldn't wait to get there, move out of the house and live in a dorm, play on a Division I team. Penn State or the University of Miami, stepping stones to the big leagues. He wouldn't want to miss that action.

Eeny, meeny, miney, mo, didn't really matter which one, they were all criminals, his dad had said, but his body seemed to have ceased to function. His arms and legs were concrete slabs, his feet frozen in cement. Must be what it's like to be dead. Wouldn't be such a bad idea right now.

"Recognize any of these guys, Colin?" Scoletti repeated.

Silence descended over the room while they waited for him to answer. His father, who had taken the day off from work; Charles Reiter, the expensive lawyer he couldn't afford; Detective Scoletti, who had offered him a deal; the seven men behind the glass. Ten people waiting for him to decide so life could move on and they could go home.

He had everything to lose, and maybe just this once, Dad was right. It wouldn't make much of a difference to the guys behind the glass. He didn't think they had much of a life anyway, always in and out of jail, nothing to do when they came out except stand in that parking lot every day trying to make a few bucks. Seven faces, expectant, hopeful. Six would get to leave, one would get busted. Even that one probably wouldn't get much time, maybe a few months, a fine for being a public nuisance, and a warning to stay the hell away from the mall. This whole lineup thing would be a warning to all seven of them. Hang out by that fence again and you might end up in a jail cell.

Dad was depending on him to do this right, to help him clean up the problems in Oakmont. Hell, the whole town was depending on him, at least the eastern side. When you won a football game, you didn't cry for the other side. The whole idea was to win for your team, and the people in this room were his team. If he didn't do it, Dad and the cops would be all kinds of pissed off at him. They were going out of their way to help him, to straighten this out for him. There was no telling what they would do if he didn't go along.

Colin breathed in, breathed out, the way Coach had said, did eeny, meeny, miney, mo in his head, and pointed to the one that was holding card #2, second from the end on the left. He didn't even look at the guy, didn't really want to see the expression on his face or think about him at all. Mom wouldn't like him picking out a random guy, but she had made a big deal about the football scholarship, too, and she would be happy for him, that he fixed a mistake and could get on with his life.

A cop was behind the glass now, escorting the other guys off, leaving the one he had picked. One man, standing there alone, under the glare of the lights, wondering what the hell just happened. He didn't think the guy could see him—they said it was one-way, but the way the man was staring it felt like his eyes were burning right into him. He sure hoped the guy couldn't see him, because his life wouldn't be worth two cents if all of Grover Hill knew he was the one who had fingered him. His ass would really be in the toilet, then. He would probably have to leave town and go live in some other state permanently.

The cop was back, slapping handcuffs on the man, shoving him out of the room. Colin felt some relief, the tension in his stomach easing up some. The cops were taking care of things, locking him up. By the time he got out of jail, Colin would be safe in college, far away. The guy would never remember him, even if he had seen him. This was over, this whole screwed-up mess was over—that's what really counted.

Frank clapped him on the back. "That's my boy! I knew you could do it! Let's go pick up Mom and then grab a bite. We can scarf down some burgers and fries, then we'll go to see Nana. She's seventy-nine years young today, and I bought her favorite chocolate cake with butter-cream frosting and some flowers."

Hamburger Heaven was mostly empty, not unusual for an unseasonably cold afternoon in November. It had snowed this morning, and there were only a few customers scattered across the restaurant, mostly students sitting alone, sipping coffee and staring into their laptops. Colin was grateful to his dad for handling the drug case for him, glad it was over so he could move on.

His mind drifted back to the party last night. Music was one of his favorite things, and the music last night had been totally hot. The girls were hot, too, but he hadn't met anyone he was really into.

He had made a dumb mistake, dealing in a public place like that, but he had learned his lesson, wouldn't do that again. Fortunately, a few months of community service would wipe it all away, and he could start over with a clean slate. The court had given him a list of approved places to check out—hospitals, homeless shelters, places like that. Helping people who were down on their luck might even turn out to be a cool thing to do for a few months.

The ketchup was dripping down the side of the burger, so he licked it off with his tongue and took a large bite, chewing it slowly, savoring the charcoal flavor, the sweetness of the ketchup, the tartness of the pickle.

His mother had ordered a chicken salad but hadn't taken one bite, was just pushing it around with her fork. Bonnie Sullivan worked the night shift as an emergency room nurse, which allowed her to have more time to spend with her family during the day. She arrived home at seven-thirty in the morning, when everyone else was just getting ready to start the day, and slept until three or four, doing errands and household stuff until she left again around 10 p.m.

"How did it go today, Colin?" she asked.

"What?"

She stabbed a piece of chicken, which sat patiently on the end of her fork waiting to be eaten while she studied Colin's face, searching for an answer. "Whatever you did at the police station."

"I, we—" Colin began, but Frank intervened.

"He fingered one of the guys in the lineup who's been supplying the drugs to the kids, that's what he did," Frank said. "Very brave of him, if you ask me. I'm very proud of how he cooperated with the police and helped us get rid of one of those parasites."

She lay down the fork, the piece of chicken still sitting on the end. "You know who the big drug dealers in the area are? How do you know that?"

Colin sucked on the straw, observing the brown liquid as it flowed upward, the fizz zapping his tongue, the icy cold jolting his brain. "I've seen some older Hispanic guys hanging around outside school at the end of the day—"

"He looked like someone you saw outside school one day? How do you know he wasn't a parent picking up his kid, or a coach waiting for team members?"

"Dad said that all those illegal immigrants sell drugs, so one is as good as the other. I've seen that guy around—I think I saw him at the mall that day they arrested us, too."

Bonnie turned to Frank. "What if he really is a drug dealer? What if someone figures out who picked him out? What kind of danger are you putting him in?" she said testily.

"I thought about that, Mom," Colin said. "I was behind a one-way glass, and the guy was handcuffed and taken to jail."

"And what if someone saw you go into the police station, just around the time his buddy was brought in? You think he didn't have any friends backing him? Maybe they were in a car across the street, watching everything that was going on," Bonnie retorted. "So either way— either you stuck your head into one hell of a dangerous situation, or you sent an innocent guy to jail. Terrific."

"Would you rather that Colin go to jail? Give up any chance he has of a future because of some little problem that can be easily solved? Is that what kind of mother you are? You'd rather see your son behind bars than some drug dealer?" Frank said angrily.

Bonnie was the one raising her voice now. "I didn't raise my son to tell lies that put innocent people in jail, and I sure don't want him killed over this. You don't know anything about the guy—you seem to have no idea who he is."

"Actually, the cops know all these guys," Frank declared. "They're all a bunch of troublemakers who they've been watching for a while. There wasn't an innocent one up there. It's too bad Colin could only pick one. It would've been better if he could've put them all away."

Bonnie stared at Colin quizzically. "I don't understand how you got mixed up in all this, honey. I hope it was a mistake, or just about being with the wrong kids at the wrong time, and that you're not involved in some kind of a drug scene. But if you are, you need to take the consequences for your own actions. That's the kind of mother I am," she said, sending Frank a withering glance. "We'll get you some help if you need it. I can talk to one of the doctors at work—"

"I got him some help—help to get rid of the damn charges completely. It's over, it's been fixed. Can we talk about something else now?"

"Well, I didn't raise my son to have other people take the rap for him or risk his life because he doesn't have the courage to take the consequences for what he's done," Bonnie continued. "You have a lot of things going for you, Colin, Ivy League or not. A lot more than the poor guy you picked out of the lineup."

"Poor guy?" Frank snapped. "Do you know what those people are doing to our community?"

Bonnie rolled her eyes and shook her head impatiently. "Not that again!" she said wearily, rubbing her temples with her fingers. "Exactly what are 'those people' doing besides trying to get some work and feed their families, just like you? You'd be better off hassling the management at Steak 'n Brew to give a you raise."

"Don't roll your eyes at me!" Frank retorted. "You know what they're doing, Miss goody two-shoes!"

Colin gazed out the window at a motorcycle roaring up the fire lane, a 750 cc Harley, two-tone metallic blue, shiny silver chrome. Definitely cool to have one of those. Guy had on a leather jacket, black with metal studs—wouldn't mind one of those either. Two day laborers in jeans leaned against the fence, lucky guys that didn't get picked up in the police sweep. One had a baseball cap sitting backward on his head, the other was bareheaded with longish brown hair pulled back into a ponytail. Dad would be furious that new guys had shown up after they swept the mall, meaning there would probably be more police sweeps and more lineups, but he didn't have to be involved in those.

One of the men raised his hand slightly as a mud-splattered black pickup truck with a bad muffler lumbered down the fire lane belching smoke. There was something familiar about the truck, so he squinted, trying to read the writing on the dirty red and white sign on the door. Jim Gardner, Painting and Contracting—he knew that sign. Yup, that was him—the truck with the smudge covering part of the sign, causing it to read Jim Gardner, Panting and Contracting, something Colin always found funny as hell. Jim Gardner, their next door neighbor, was hiring illegals from the parking lot at the mall.

Eleven

The sky was pearl gray, almost white, as Felipe, Tío Miguel, and Ramón leaned against the fence across from the Quik Shop, keeping an eye on the police car that was parked at the curb while they watched the parking lot for trucks, hoping that if they stared hard enough, a contractor might magically appear. An icy blast of wind tore through Felipe's light fall jacket, warning of an approaching storm, one of those late November snowstorms that instantly turns autumn into winter.

They made sure they were following all of the police guidelines: stay off the sidewalk, away from the customers, against the fence. Put all trash in the trash can, don't leave litter on the ground. That was a big one—made the store owners very upset. Felipe had even called a little meeting early one morning as the sun was coming up to talk to the other day laborers about following the rules so that they could continue using the lot to get jobs.

Large snowflakes were beginning to fall now, swirling through the air, landing in his hair, on his neck, sliding past the collar of his jacket, dripping down his back. Maybe someone would have an indoor job today. Julia had been asking him for food money, the rent was due, and he had promised the kids he would take them to the movies this weekend, but there was no possibility he could come up with the price of admission tickets for five people right now. Julia had picked up some work cleaning houses, but it wasn't enough to support the whole family. In El Salvador he had survived on tortillas and salt; he could live on that until things got better and save the food money for the children. Tortillas and salt, with a few beans.

He knew now why his mother had put him on that truck, had sent him away. Now that he had children, he understood her pain—the anguish of a mother who can't provide for her children, keep them safe. Nothing was more painful than watching your children suffer. Mama wanted him to have more than tortillas and salt with a few beans. He had hoped to bring her to New York soon, to show her his restaurant and how successful he was, to have her meet Julia and his wonderful children, but that plan would have to wait.

Felipe's hair was damp and his jacket was speckled with wet spots, a brown jacket with dark polka dots. Icy flakes burned into his face; his fingers were stiff and frozen. No trucks had shown up yet this morning; maybe he needed to stop dreaming and stare some more. The eye that was watching the police car noted movement—the door was open-ing, probably to tell them to go home, that there wouldn't be any work during a blizzard.

A blue uniform strutted toward them, his head tilted to the left, one thumb tucked into his belt. A slow swagger across the pavement, his eyes fixed on Felipe. Leave, walk fast in the other direction, he thought, but hesitated because he needed the work, and the cops might think he had done something wrong and come after him for sure, maybe even shoot him.

The blue uniform was closer, coming toward him. The squeezing in his chest was choking off his breath, the dizziness playing games with his eyes, blurring his vision. The snow hitting his face was now mixed with sweat, the back of his knees and his armpits damp, his pants pasted to the back of his legs. The policeman's eyes weren't black like the *guardia* with the scar; they were gray, a cold blue-gray, like ice on a frozen lake, a treacherous lake where the ice was thin in some places and thick in others so you didn't know where it was safe to walk. Felipe didn't know what lay behind those eyes or what was safe to do at this moment. A hand was on his chest now, pushing him, and a voice was speaking, distant, muffled, like the voices of the *guardia* who had murdered Papa. Perhaps it was too late—he had already hit the thin ice and was slipping through the cracks into the deadly water, already drowning without so much as a rope or a branch to grab.

"Hands against the fence." Cold metal pressed against his fingers, hands ran up and down his back, his sides, in his pockets, his New York Yankees cap jerked from his head, thrown on the ground. "Who's your boss?" Gray Eyes barked.

"No boss. I work for myself," Felipe mumbled. Gray Eyes grabbed his collar, rammed his face against the fence. The metal cut into his lip, a trickle of blood dripped into his mouth.

"Don't play games with me, buddy. I'm not takin' crap from you. You know what I mean. Cocaine, heroin. Your connection in the city. You ain't standin' here all day in the cold for no painting job."

Felipe tried to sound as polite and cooperative as he could, but the words came out hoarse and flat, as though all the energy had been sucked out of him. He wasn't sure what the policeman wanted to hear, and it was hard to find the right words in English when you could feel everything slipping away.

"Lost my job, just trying to get some work."

"And what kind of work do you do?" The policeman stuck his finger into Felipe's chest, gave him another push.

"Drywall, painting–"

"Drywall, painting." The cop imitated him, ridiculing him in a high voice with an accent. "And selling a little on the side to make extra money? You live here in Oakmont? Haven't seen you around here. Did you go to Oakmont High?"

"Oakmont, I live here in Oakmont."

"Name?"

"Felipe Sanchez."

"What part of Oakmont do you live in, Sanchez?"

"Grover Hill."

"Need to improve your English, Felipe. You don't sound like someone who was raised in Oakmont. Where are you from? Colombia? You come here to make a lot of money?"

The snow in the parking lot was seeping into Felipe's shoes as the policeman jerked and twisted his arms, yanking them behind his back. A set of metal handcuffs clicked, digging into his wrists. Another police car had arrived, a van this time, and two more blue uniforms were rushing toward the fence. Tio Miguel, his beloved Tio Miguel, Mama's older brother, was being handcuffed and dragged toward the van, struggling to keep his balance on the slick, icy pavement. His blue watchcap fell off, and a white carpet of snow blanketed the thin strands of gray hair plastered to his head. They had celebrated his sixty-fifth birthday just last week.

The dank odor of mold and dead leaves tracked in on wet shoes permeated the van, and Felipe, Tio Miguel, Ramón, and four others who had been standing at the fence were pressed together in a sodden clump, chilly and miserable, as the van rattled and bumped over the potholes in the street. He wouldn't be able to give the landlord the rent money today or anything extra to Julia for food. Julia, expecting him home, would be cooking something warm for him to eat, and he hoped he would be out quickly, before she had time to worry.

The van growled and lurched until a click of a key quieted it and the back door opened with a screech, revealing the red brick of the windowless West Oakmont police station, a block from where El Patio sat shuttered and silent.

Still handcuffed, they were pushed and prodded into a closet-like room, lined up in a row facing a long mirror. A short, stubby cop with flabby jowls and a large double chin slipped behind the line, jingling a set of keys, removing the handcuffs. "In America, you're innocent until proven guilty, so we're going to put you in a lineup. If you're identified, you'll be arrested. If not, you're free to go."

A lineup, he said, and the mirror in front them was a one-way glass, with people on the other side who would pick out the guilty one. Felipe wondered who they were, and whether someone he had never met could accuse him of a crime. He looked out over the lineup, at Tío Miguel, who had opened up his home and helped him start a new life, then at Ramón, who had brought him to the day laborer site even though it could mean less work for him. No criminals there. He didn't really know the other guys; maybe it was one of them they were looking for. They stood for a few minutes—seven men in a line, trying to appear at ease and nonchalant, their eyes glued to the one-way mirror. Felipe attempted to rotate his neck without moving his body as the door opened with a bang and Officer Bradley, one of the cops who had threatened Tio Miguel at El Patio, sauntered into the room and stopped in front of the lineup.

One by one, he pointed each person toward the door, until Felipe was standing there alone. "Guess I wasn't too far off. Trust your instincts, I always say. I knew it was you all along, runnin' drugs outta that hole in the wall restaurant up the street." Felipe gasped, gaping at him in shock. "No, I have never—we followed all the—"

Officer Bradley jabbed his finger into Felipe's chest, then gave him a shove, causing him to lose his balance. Felipe stumbled, as he tried to catch his balance to keep from falling. "Oh, yeah? Well, I have a surprise for you, asshole. You're not going to be such a big man anymore, because you're the one he identified."

El Salvador
1985

Twelve

Catholic priests open their hearts to their dispossessed and bereaved parishioners, calling for land reform and an end to the death squads. The Archbishop of San Salvador, Oscar Romero, is assassinated after saying mass in the chapel of a church-run cancer hospital. Four American church women are raped and killed by the Salvadoran National Guard. Flag-draped coffins fill the vestibules of village churches; the wails of mourners deluge their sanctums.

The small stone church with the red wooden door was silent, the windows dark, the voices of the priests quiet as the village slept. "Father Rodriguez! *Por favor, por favor, ayudanos,* please, please help us!" Mama called, pounding on the door, but seemed unable to raise her voice loud enough to be heard. Felipe banged until his knuckles were bruised, but no response came.

"Maybe around the back."

Another wooden door appeared as they approached the back of the church, but the only greeting was the distant crowing of a rooster somewhere in the misty dawn. Later in the morning, when Father Rodriguez opened the door, he found them huddled together, sleeping on the ground behind the church. "You need to come in quickly," he said, hustling everyone inside.

Felipe kept a close watch on Mama as she struggled to hold back the tears that slipped silently down her face, leaving streaks on her dusty cheeks, still spotted with mud from the day before. Her hair, usually pulled back neatly into a tight bun, was a tumble of black standing out in all directions on her head, her thin, white cotton shift torn and caked with soil. Felipe was the man of the family now, the one who had to be Mama's strength, the Papa for Ana and Juanito. Ana, pressed against Mama's skirt, clutched her hand tightly, and the baby stared wide-eyed from the *covita*.

"Father, the *guardias*—they took, they took my Fernando—" she sobbed, pressing her face against the baby's soft fuzzy head. "They'll come back, Father, and take my son, too. We have to leave, go somewhere where I can protect my children."

The priest nodded sympathetically. "I understand. I'll do everything I can to help you. For now, we have a small room in the basement where you can rest, and I'll try my best to arrange something. We have a network; we can get you out of the country," he said gently. He had the round, smooth cheeks of a young person and a full head of thick black hair, but Felipe could see deep wrinkles around his eyes and across his forehead, along with a drooping at the sides of his mouth that gave him a permanently worried expression.

"Follow me," he said, guiding them down a narrow hallway into a tiny back room, then down a rickety staircase to a storage cellar. The cellar felt damp and had a moldy smell, as though the rain seeped in and never entirely dried out. Felipe could see some big plastic bags that looked like they were filled with clothes, several sacks of rice stacked up in a corner, and some straw mats near the back wall. "You can stay here until we can arrange a safe way for you to leave," Father Rodriguez said. He turned away abruptly and stomped back up the stairs. A few moments later, Felipe heard the old wooden door at the back of the church creak and slam shut.

When he returned, he was carrying a basket of tortillas and beans, which he placed on a small table in the room. "You must be hungry," he said. "I brought you some food because you have a long trip ahead of you. Tomorrow at dawn, you can go to the marketplace and look for an old blue truck with a driver with a white cap. Wave him down and say the words 'what's for breakfast?' and he will say, 'mangoes,' and you both will know you have the right person. I will wake you to make sure you get there at the right time. You can stay here until then."

They arrived at the marketplace early Sunday morning, before the sun had even begun to rise, but it was already bustling and crowded, a place to blend in, to be invisible. The air was fragrant with the smoky, nose-tickling aroma of beans and tortillas cooking over fireplaces built into the ground, the tantalizing fragrance of grilled meat, humming with the patter of women chatting as they put out their baskets of food.

"Avocados, mangoes, and *platanos*, fried bananas. Wouldn't you like some sweet *platanos* for breakfast? Mine are the best; they melt in your mouth."

Mama pressed something into Felipe's hand, a few coins to buy a bag of tortillas for the journey. Four tortillas in a small bag—one for now, three for later. A weathered blue truck appeared in the distance, rolling slowly down the road, its once shiny paint faded and dotted with rust. It meandered past the vendors, the driver surveying the crowd, stopping briefly as though he was perusing the stalls to purchase something. Felipe could make out the driver's white hat, so he gave him a small wave and the truck ground to a stop near a grove of orange trees. A green parrot perched on a branch, peering down at him. It's Verdito, coming to say goodbye to me, Felipe thought. *Adios*, Verdito. Maybe I'll come back to visit you sometime.

Felipe had to take a great deep breath to keep the sadness away; no time for sadness now, only time to be strong for Mama and Ana and Juanito. Strong for Papa, who couldn't take care of them anymore but would have wanted him to take over as the man of the family. That was the most important thing, to make Papa proud of him, and he thought about Papa smiling down at them from heaven, where there were no *guardias* or soldiers, and he could finally rest. The man in the white cap was sizing him up, eyeing him cautiously.

"What's for breakfast?" Felipe asked quickly.

"Mangoes," the driver responded. "I'm Hugo. You—get in the back, quick," he said to Felipe, motioning toward the rear of the truck. "*Señora*, you and the children are going to ride in the front with me. If the *guardias* stop us, you are my family going to Don Cristobal's *finca* to work."

Felipe climbed into a tiny crawl space in the bed of the truck, where he could scrunch down behind the bags of cornmeal, hidden from the prying eyes of anyone who stopped the truck to peer in.

"Cover yourself! Hurry!" Hugo said, tossing Felipe a blanket. "Be very still until we leave this area. I'm going to throw some sacks of cornmeal on top of you."

The heat was suffocating and the truck rocked and bumped over the holes in the dirt road, smacking Felipe's head against the floor, but at least they were moving now, away from the *guardias* and their dead eyes and their guns. The bouncing and rocking continued for a few minutes and then the truck was still.

"Where are you headed?" a deep voice said.

"Bringing supplies to Don Cristobal's *finca*."

The bags pressed against his chest were making it hard to breathe, his right arm was completely numb, his legs cramped and aching, but he was as motionless as the corpses that littered the roads, silent as the dark earth on which they lay.

"Who are these people?" the voice demanded sharply.

"My wife, Maria Elena, and my children, Ana and Juanito."

"Where are they going?"

"My wife and my daughter cook for Don Cristobal at the *finca*."

"Open the back!"

The squeaky, grating sound of rusty metal sent a chill through Felipe's teeth as the back gate was pulled down, dropping with a thud. "What's in here?" the voice rumbled, just a few feet away now.

"*Harina*, cornmeal, for Don Cristobal," Hugo called from the front seat. The squeaky gate slammed with a furious screech, and the truck lumbered forward, bouncing and rattling as it crept along the dusty road. Felipe sucked in some air, flooded with relief that the *guardia* had moved on, and that Mama, Ana, and Juanito were still sitting in the front seat next to Hugo, alive and safe.

After what seemed to Felipe like days, the truck screeched to a halt again. He heard the gate clang open, then the blanket and the bags were being pulled off him by two shirtless young boys about ten years old. Sunlight filled the truck, and he saw that Mama was already outside, conversing quietly with Hugo, their bodies nearly touching as they spoke.

His head was pounding and his back ached from the bouncy ride, but he stumbled over the remaining bags and crawled out of the truck.

"Where are we?" he said groggily, blinking in the bright sunlight.

"Honduras! We're in Honduras, *mijo*. The *guardias* can't find us here."

Outside the truck were rows and rows of tents, lined up as far as the eye could see, children playing in the dirt and women sitting listlessly watching them.

"Felipe—" Mama began, then stopped and turned to Hugo. "Explain it to him, Hugo."

"Well, you are going to come with me," Hugo said solemnly, letting the words out slowly, as though he was about to share a secret of great importance.

"You need me to work for you?" Felipe felt a little excitement, that he might be able to save some other people's lives the way Hugo saved theirs, maybe earn some money, too.

Mama was twisting her fingers and looking away from him. "There's nothing for you here, Felipe, and you can't go back to El Salvador. They'll take you, the way they took Papa."

Hugo clapped Felipe on the shoulder reassuringly. "The United States, Felipe. There are opportunities there for a young person like you, a new life, jobs. I can take you to meet a coyote who is leaving today, taking people across the border to the United States."

Mama's body was rigid, as though she had tied herself in a knot to keep from breaking apart, but her hands kept moving, tapping her leg, stroking her hair. Her fingers shook as she pushed a strand of hair away from her face, a trembling Felipe hadn't seen before.

"My oldest brother and his wife, Tio Miguel and Tia Rosa, have a restaurant in New York," Mama said quietly. She came from a family of twelve children—she had seven brothers, five still lived in El Espino, picked coffee on the *finca*.

"That would be nice for you to see Tio Miguel, Mama. We could find someplace to live near them and I could work in the restaurant."

Mama placed her hand on the truck as if to balance herself, but she seemed shaky and frail, as though she might fall over with the slightest touch.

"Felipito," she murmured so softly it came out as a whisper, her body so still it appeared as though she wasn't breathing at all. "Felipito, I'm not going with you. I have a baby and couldn't make the trip right now. Maybe someday we will be able to join you, but not now."

His stomach was churning, making him feel as though he was going to be sick. Things had been bad, but he still had Mama and Ana and Juanito. He put his hand in his pocket and tightened his fingers around a smooth stone he had picked up by the river.

"You can work in Miguel's restaurant, maybe send us a little money to help us when we leave here. Tio Miguel and his family will look after you."

"Mama, I can help you here. I can work here and help you take care of Ana and Juanito."

Mama's lips trembled, her voice wavering as she struggled to get the words out. "There is no work here, and back in El Espino, the *guardias* are looking for you. You know how they are—they will kill you, *mijo*. They think you were fighting with the FMLN, and they will hunt for you and kill you, like they did to Papa."

Hugo glanced at his watch. "The truck is leaving this afternoon. If you are going, you need to get ready now."

Mama picked up a backpack that had been sitting on the ground next to the truck and handed it to him. "There's a bag of tortillas and some water in here, and a little money to buy more when you need to."

Felipe's eyes widened, as he gaped at Mama in disbelief. "Mama, no! Please let me stay! I want to stay here!" he pleaded. He clenched his jaw tightly, desperately trying to hold back the tears. When he was a little boy, Mama would hold him, soothe him when he was upset, but he was a man now and it was his job to soothe Mama, be brave for Ana and Juanito.

"This is what Papa would have wanted." She removed Esperanza's amulet from around her neck, placed it back around his. "You are the man of the family now, so go, *mijo*, and make a life for yourself." She embraced him tightly and kissed him on the cheek, then turned and walked away, her head bent so he could no longer see her face.

Arizona
Winter/Spring, 2006

Thirteen

The streetlamp outside the window cast an amber light on the empty space beside Julia, illuminating the white pillowcase that lay smooth and uncreased, as ghostly and silent as a deserted road in the darkest hour of the night. When Felipe hadn't shown up by six, she thought it was a good sign, that he had gotten a big job and was just too busy to call. She waited for him until the sun disappeared behind the buildings, but Camilo needed to eat so they went ahead and ate without him—rice with the last of the meat she had left and some salad.

The ring tone on Julia's cell phone sliced through the darkened room like the blade of a knife, threatening and ominous. Her white cotton blanket and light blue top sheet slid onto the floor in a rumpled heap as she rushed to grab the phone from her purse, tipping over a glass on the table, sending a stream of water trickling over Camilo's homework and a math book Marisol had left there. The glowing red numbers on the digital clock read 1 a.m.

The voice on the phone sounded like Tio Miguel. It definitely wasn't Felipe. "Julia—"

"Miguel? What is it? Where's Felipe?" she stammered, cradling the phone against her ear while she grabbed some paper towels from the kitchen. Her hand moved feverishly across the table as she wiped up the water and threw the wet paper towels at the kitchen sink, then flung herself into a chair with a thump.

"…arrested this morning, well, we all were," a muffled voice muttered through the static on the cell phone. The person was stumbling over his words, with pauses that were too long. Maybe it was a wrong number—someone that sounded like Tio Miguel but was calling for someone else, someone who had been arrested.

"Miguel? Miguel? Are you there?"

"I'm here, Julia—it's me, Miguel. Can you hear me? The cops busted us at the mall this morning and put us in a lineup, Julia. Felipe was the one they picked."

"Picked? Picked for what?" she said hoarsely.

"Something about selling drugs to kids at Oakmont High. Sorry for calling so late, but I stayed with him at the station while they booked him, and it took hours."

"Booked him?" She pressed the phone against her ear, but Tio Miguel's voice was stifled by the poor connection, his words punctuated with buzzing and hissing.

"Miguel?"

"The police… ICE, Immigration and Customs Enforcement…" the phone crackled, and then went dead.

Winter had come and gone and spring returned again while Felipe spent his days on trial for the felony drug charge, his nights at the Westchester County jail at Valhalla. An aggravated felony, due to his undocumented status, the public defender informed her when Felipe was convicted. Five months passed as Julia visited him twice a week, the maximum allowed, talking to him through a glass window, assuring him she would always be there, sharing how much the children missed him, encouraging him to stay strong, he would be home soon. Then last week she had gone for her regular visit and he had vanished.

"Sanchez? No longer here," the clerk reported. "Been transferred to the detention center in Eloy, Arizona, to await deportation."

Julia had not gone a day without Felipe since she was eighteen and didn't know what else to do except to try to contact him, remind him of how much he was loved and missed, and do everything she could to help get him released from the detention center so he could come home. She immediately phoned Steven Rosenbaum, the public defender who had represented Felipe on the drug charge. He agreed to contact the detention center for her and to represent himself as Felipe's lawyer, but when he called, he was informed that attorneys were not allowed to do any consultation over the phone and the detainees were not allowed phone calls out.

"The best I can do," he said, "is to give you the name and phone number of an organization in the Eloy area that specializes in helping undocumented immigrants. I'm sure you're not the only one dealing with a situation like this."

The Southern Arizona Immigrant Rights Project was not located in the town of Eloy, but was in the area, about thirty miles away. "There's nothing you can do over the phone," the woman who answered said, "but we can give you the info we have about how to get in to see him. The detention center doesn't allow phone calls, but they do have visiting hours, like any prison. But, uh, you'll have to come down here to do that. Getting him out, well, that's another story. It's a complicated, difficult process, especially if you don't live in the area. You know—lawyer meetings, court dates—all that stuff. Be better if you could stay awhile. If you do decide to come down here, give us a call and we'll try to support you."

Marisol had agreed that Mama should go to Arizona to help Papi and promised that she could manage things, feed Camilo and get him to school, put him to bed at night, but Ricky was sullen and withdrawn, next to impossible to communicate with. Julia had tried to talk to him about Felipe's arrest, but it was as though he had retreated into a secret life where no one could touch him. The past week he had stayed out late every night, not even coming home for dinner. "Ricky, why don't you stay with Tio Miguel and Tia Rosa while I'm gone? You love Tia Rosa's cooking, and she said you could eat with them anytime you wanted. You can sleep there—"

"I'm not a baby, Mama," he snapped. "I can take care of myself."

"I know you're not a baby, *mijo*. I just thought you might like some company at night—"

"Aren't Marisol and Camilo going to be here? Why would I need to sleep there?"

"Marisol will be here, so yes, you can sleep here, but she will have her hands full, and I don't feel comfortable asking her to take care of Camilo and cook for you, too. I'll make a big pot of *carne guisada* and leave it in the refrigerator for you all to eat this week, but if it runs out, the offer stands—you are welcome next door. If any other problems come up, things we haven't thought of, go to them, they will be more than glad to help you—"

"I'm fourteen, Mama. I can take care of myself. You don't need to treat me like I'm some kind of little kid. Go to Arizona to help Papi. I'll be fine," Ricky had shouted, storming out of the room, but Julia wasn't at all sure about that. Fourteen years of being his mother meant she could not help but catch the tremor in his voice, a tell-tale sign that he was holding back tears.

"Keep an eye on him," she whispered to Marisol. "You don't have to take care of him, but please, call Tia Rosa if anything comes up. I'll leave you each some spending money."

Julia withdrew most of the money she and Felipe had saved to expand El Patio—cash for Marisol so she could buy food for the house, along with a pre-paid cell phone card to use in case of an emergency, a bank check so she could pay the rent if Julia wasn't back in time, and pocket money for Ricky. Cash and another pre-paid cell phone card for her to take to Arizona didn't leave much in the account. She would need to be very frugal about how she spent money on the trip because the next month's rent would need to be paid, too. Hopefully, things in Arizona would work out and she could come back quickly, look for a job that would pay the bills.

Julia slouched in one of the gray plastic chairs at the Greyhound bus station and stared distractedly at a women's magazine someone left on a chair. *Two Hundred Forty-Five Ways to Celebrate Summer,* the bold print on the cover read. *Seven Secrets to Being Happier Right Now—how to feel in control of absolutely everything,* in smaller print. She flipped idly through the magazine, gazed at a recipe for tuna casserole, read some of the ideas for summer fun. Her favorite purse, an oversized red and black woven bag, straddled her lap and bulged with sandwiches, bottles of water, a small blanket, and a change of clothes for the trip to Arizona.

Felipe, alone in a jail cell in Eloy, Arizona. She hoped they weren't hurting him—the thought of that was more than she could bear, so she thumbed through the magazine again to distract herself from thinking about it. Two days and ten hours on the bus would bring her to him. She might not be able to get him out of the detention center right away, but they could talk and come up with a plan, and it would boost his morale to see her, to know that the family was behind him, doing everything they could to bring him home.

"Casa Grande, Arizona," the bus driver's voice boomed. Closest stop to Eloy, the Greyhound office in New York had informed her. A sleepy desert town, flat and dusty, one hundred miles from the Mexican border. The nearest big city was Tucson, fifty miles south. The bus station in Casa Grande looked the same as any other: scratched up plastic chairs, weary people in dingy white undershirts and faded cotton house-dresses carrying their belongings in shopping bags, munching on potato chips or sipping cans of soda, chatting to each other while they waited. Julia had finished her sandwiches on the bus ride, so she hiked her bag over her shoulder and moseyed around Casa Grande, found an inexpensive diner where she ordered two burritos and bought two more bottles of water. One burrito to eat now and one to carry with her for later.

The waitress shoved the burritos across the counter and shuffled toward the cash register. A blonde wig framed wrinkled brown cheeks, as furrowed as the dollar bills Julia pulled out of her change purse.

"How far are we from Eloy?" Julia asked.

"'Bout sixteen miles," the waitress answered indifferently, not even looking up at Julia when she spoke.

Being this close to the immigration detention center, she must get asked that constantly, Julia thought. She's probably totally bored, answering the same question over and over again. At least food appeared to be cheaper in Arizona than in New York—that was good news.

"Where would I catch the bus to get there?"

The waitress pushed a cup of coffee toward a young man in a cowboy hat sitting at the counter, scooped up the bills and dropped them in the cash register. "No buses here that go to Eloy," she said, grabbing a piece of chocolate cake from a glass case, placing it on a small beige plate and slapping it down next to the coffee.

"She knows me, all right," the man said, turning toward Julia. "Never has to ask what I want. Get the same thing every time I come in, chocolate cake and coffee." He eyed Julia as he took a bite of the cake and washed it down with a gulp of coffee. "Headed to Eloy?"

"Trying to," Julia answered. "Is there a train that goes there?"

"No trains, either. Take you there myself, but I'm working, on a coffee break. Work down the road on a construction project, be there until after dark. You wanna wait, I can take you then, 'bout nine tonight."

This was a strange place that had no public transportation. Maybe they were afraid that the inmates would escape and run away on the bus.

"Thanks, I appreciate the offer, but I need to get there soon as possible. I'm picking up my husband, and he wouldn't like it much if I showed up late."

Adriane Brown

"Well, I was gonna ask if you wanted to go dancing tonight after I get off work, take you to Eloy in the morning, but sounds like you're taken. Not surprisin' a pretty woman like you already be spoken for," he said grinning, his eyes surveying her body. "I come here every morning at this time, if you change your mind."

He was cute in an impish kind of way, and seemed nice enough, but who could tell—for all she knew she might accept a ride from him and end up dead in a ditch.

"How do I get to Eloy without a car?" she asked, ignoring the flirtation.

"Shuttle van'll take you there."

"Where do I get that?"

"Greyhound station, up the street."

Julia packed up her burritos and her water and raced down the narrow sidewalk back to the Greyhound station, feeling more energetic now that she was getting closer to Felipe. Sixteen miles and she would see him, let him know the family was there for him.

"The shuttle to Eloy—how much?"

"Thirty-five dollars," the agent replied, not even looking up from his computer screen.

"Thirty-five dollars for one bus ride? Is there another way?"

"Sure, you can walk. Take you a while, but you'll get there."

The broiling midday sun burned Julia's face and the top of her head, and

144

she could feel sweat collecting on her neck. It had to be over one hundred degrees. Open, flat fields bronzed by the sun stretched for miles, fuzzy white cotton plants on thin brown stalks and fields of wheat and hay, the remainder nothing but prickly cactus, rolling tumbleweed, and a few scruffy trees and shrubs to shade the scorched earth from the blistering heat. She should have thought to bring a hat, but that was the last thing on her mind when she left New York. More scrub brush, RVs moving slowly down the hot tar of the highway, teenagers in old cars spotted with primer where they had patched up dents. The cars whizzed past her, people going to work or home to their families. Nobody would care about a stranger, especially one going to see her husband in jail. Her illegal, jailed husband with the warm, coffee-colored eyes and the beautiful smile. Felipe, who never harmed a fly.

A strange feeling came over her as she trudged along in the desert heat. It was as though she had entered an alien world where she was completely invisible, unable to be seen or heard by anyone. She was nothing to anybody here, and nobody would care if she fell down dead right in the middle of the highway. Felipe would care, though, and she would keep tramping down this road if it took another three weeks. They beat people in jail, kept them in solitary confinement until the demons took them over and their laughing, loving spirits were ground into dust. A blister was developing on her heel, and her pink tank top was thoroughly soaked with sweat, but she pushed on. There wasn't much to look at on the road, so she tried little tricks to help her pass the time—she thought about good times they had, the little trips around New York they had taken with the kids.

The air was dusty and her throat was parched so she stopped for a few minutes by the side of the road to rest and drink some of her water. She needed to call the kids, to let them know she was okay. Marisol had been instructed to only use the pre-paid phone card in an emergency, because there wasn't much time on there, and she should probably follow her own advice and use it sparingly, too. She had discontinued their landline service and their main cell phone accounts because she wanted to leave Marisol with enough cash to take care of things while she was away, and there just wasn't enough money left over to pay phone bills.

The police hadn't stopped her, but she thought if they did she needed to have an explanation as to why she was wandering along the highway. The Sanchez family didn't need two people in jail. She would say her car ran out of gas and she was headed to a nearby gas station. No, she didn't have a gas can. It might be better to say her car broke down and she needed to get home; her husband would give her a ride back to the car and they would have it towed. A more convincing story, maybe.

The heat was diminishing, which was good news for walking but not such good news if it meant that it would be getting dark soon. The cement girders of a highway overpass were in front of her, a large shady area where she could rest and cool off. The place was full of rocks, but she found a patch of smooth dirt near the back wall, as far away from the road as she could.

She was so hungry—if she could just eat and rest for a few minutes, she would have more energy to continue on her way. The sun was fading and darkness would soon cover this road, her only guide to the immigration detention center in Eloy where Felipe was being held. Waves of drowsiness washed over her as she battled to stay awake. This was definitely not a safe place for a woman alone to fall asleep. Marisol had found a Super 8 motel in Eloy on the internet and had written the address on a piece of paper for her, and if she could keep walking, maybe she could get there tonight, get some sleep there and take a shower so she would be freshened up and ready to see Felipe first thing in the morning. She put the remainder of the burrito in her purse and took out the paper with the name of the motel and stuck it in her pocket. Hoisting her purse over her shoulder, she forced herself to stand, but after two and a half days on the bus and several hours walking in the grueling afternoon heat, her feet felt like lead weights and the blister on her heel rubbed against her shoe every time she took a step. Five more minutes rest wouldn't hurt, so she sat down again. Five more minutes, and then she would continue on to Eloy. The last thing she heard before she passed out was the sound of traffic whizzing by her on the road and the rumble of trucks overhead.

Arizona
1985

Fourteen

They flee to the desert by the thousands, craving safety from the death and destruction of the war, searching for a safe haven to protect their children, but death pursues them, threatening them at every turn. They battle to survive another day, another hour, another moment, as they trudge over endless miles of parched earth and rocky hills, nothing but cactus to quench their thirst.

The silence of the Arizona desert at high noon was broken by the whine of a helicopter circling overhead and the sound of a car engine growling somewhere nearby, like wild animals tracking him, looking for fresh meat. Felipe would have preferred a wild animal to the Border Patrol, the immigration agents who could find you more easily than a wild animal and send you back to wherever you came from, even if it meant certain death.

The blazing sun burned through his threadbare white T-shirt, drenched and sticky from the rivulets of sweat trickling down the back of his neck. The thin soles of his sandals did nothing to protect his blistered feet from sharp rocks or the gritty dust cutting into his toes, and when the wind blew, dust filled his eyes, his mouth, his throat. He licked his lips, but his tongue was dry, like sandpaper rubbed on an open wound. He could see mountains rising up far away in the distance and imagined the coolness of the trees and water, maybe a lake he could jump into when they arrived. If they arrived.

Twenty of them had begun this journey together, led by a coyote, a smuggler hired to guide migrants over the border and across the treacherous desert terrain. The coyote, furtive and tight-lipped, was known to the migrants only as El Pitón, the python. El Pitón had met them at the Mexican border, told them the trip would take four to five days and that the temperature could go as high as one hundred and thirty degrees.

"Not everyone makes it," he said. "I can show you the way, but staying alive is up to you."

Felipe tried to keep track of the days since he left his village and thought today might be the day, his fourteenth birthday. It was sometime around now—he was sure about that. Before the war, the whole village used to come to sing *Las Mañanitas*, to wish him happy birthday, and Mama always made something special, tamales or pupusas. A soccer ball sailed back and forth through the air and he and Ernesto and Rafael were stars, adored by everyone. Oscar, Ernesto's papa, strummed cumbia and merengue music on the guitar, and they danced into the night and drank *chicha*, an alcoholic drink made of fermented fruit and black corn. He thought maybe now that he was fourteen, they would have let him have some, just a little, this time.

He knew Mama loved him, had wanted the best for him when she sent him here, but he wondered if she had also been a little bit angry with him for disobeying her, sneaking out at night to see Esperanza when she had told him not to. If he had listened to Mama, stayed in the *choza*, the *guardias* wouldn't have thought he was out fighting against the army, and Papa might still be alive. Everything had happened so fast, he never had a chance to explain it to her so she would understand and forgive him. Maybe she would have let him stay, and he could have worked on a *finca* in Honduras or in a factory in one of the big cities, brought in money for his family.

He desperately missed her and Papa, his dear Papa, whom he would never see again, ever, and Oscar, who died defending Papa. Papa's friends, the coffee pickers, who had always loved and protected him as though he was their own son, his sister and brother, and his friends, Ernesto and Rafael. He tried not to think about them, because when he did, sadness would creep up on him, a sick feeling that would overwhelm his body, causing him to feel shaky and weak when he needed to be strong, to keep going.

He wondered whether he would ever see Mama again, and if she had any idea that to get to New York you had to cross this land of death first. If he died here, he would die a stranger, another body in the desert, never having a chance to say goodbye, with no one around who cared enough to find his mother and let her know he was gone, that she should pray for his soul.

The other migrants were grabbing handfuls of dirt, rubbing them over their bodies in an attempt to camouflage themselves, as El Pitón pointed furiously toward the bushes. No words were exchanged, no shouts, no orders, but they heard the car engine and understood the gestures, knowing that any sound could alert the border patrol to their location. They scattered in all directions, taking refuge behind whatever vegetation they could find, squatting behind a creosote bush or a mesquite tree. A family with a young child ran toward a dry river bed, laying themselves flat beneath a rocky overhang, the mother covering the boy with her body as she tried to shield him from the prying eyes of whoever was approaching in the car. Jimenez, they said their name was. Rogelio and Esmeralda Jimenez and their son, Cheyo.

Felipe rubbed dirt over his arms and legs and crouched behind a mesquite tree, sitting as still as the tree itself. He pulled his knees up to his chest and wrapped his arms around his legs as tightly as he could, his backpack with the empty water bottle and the few tortillas he had left providing a thin cushion for his back as he pressed his body against the bark of the tree. He was small for his age and his legs were as thin and brown as the branches, his body barely wider than the trunk of the tree.

Folding himself into a small bundle, he might have been just another piece of vegetation in the desert.

A rapid, clicking sound distracted him, the ominous rattle of a snake with a flat, triangular head and diamond-shaped markings, inches away from the exposed skin on his feet.

The snake paused, sensing the heat of his body, its black tongue slithering in and out, as though it was mocking him, laughing at the trap he was in. Felipe's heart was pounding so loudly he was sure the border patrol agents could hear it, and he quickly touched the amulet around his neck and whispered a prayer Father Rodriguez taught him. Rattlesnakes could pick up fear, smell it. Above him, a vulture circled hungrily and the snake turned away from Felipe, its long body jerking and twisting in the dry grass as it slithered to the safety of a nearby hollow in a rock formation.

The vulture swooped low, aiming at something in the grass. A woman's body, bloated and sun-blackened. He knew the smell, the urine and the blood, the oozing fluid and the maggots. In El Salvador, lifeless bodies were sprawled out under trees, on the sides of roads, in the bushes. Mama had sent him here to save him, but death had followed him to this desert, to this tree, where he had to hide from *la migra* the way he hid from the *guardias* in El Salvador.

The bloated body in the sand was not alone. There were two others, as well as a backpack, an empty water container, a yellow shirt abandoned in the heat, a shoe. Two feet sticking up, wearing rubber soled shoes. Felipe crawled on his belly through the grass toward the body and sucked in his breath and held it, swatting away the flies. He untied the shoes, pulled them off the body and darted back to the mesquite tree, breathing hard. They were a little big, but they would protect his feet from biting desert creatures, searing heat, and knife-edged rocks. New shoes, white with a blue stripe, that felt soft under his feet.

A blast of rifle fire shattered the sultry desert stillness, followed by loud, angry voices. He understood the shouting, the bellowing voices, the crack of rifle fire, and tried to make himself even smaller. He turned his head slightly and from the corner of his eye he could see Rogelio Jimenez handcuffed, being led into the vehicle, to be sent back to Mexico. Someone he couldn't see was screaming, panicky wails that echoed over the dry river beds and the *bajadas,* the shallow slopes at the base of the rocky hills.

"*Parense!* Stop!" shouted one of the border patrol agents as he chased sixteen-year-old Horacio through the high desert grass. Horacio sprinted across the dry river bed, his arms and legs powerful from a childhood spent cutting sugar cane in El Salvador, putting distance between himself and the agent, who was slowing down, panting hard. Felipe could just make out the agent's face; a red face covered in sweat, wearing a straw Stetson hat that flew off as he ran. The agent's dark hair was cut close to his scalp, like the soldiers in his country.

"*Detenganlo!* Stop him!" the agent yelled again.

155

A rifle barrel protruded through the window of the jeep, pointed in Horacio's direction. Shots rang out and Horacio dropped to the ground, making moaning sounds, and then no sound at all, just a red river soaking into the red earth.

An engine started up and the jeep began to move, creeping slowly over the rocky ground, circling around the prickly cactuses, the creosote bushes and the mesquite trees, flattening the grass under its wheels, prowling for migrants hidden in the bushes. It was close enough for Felipe to smell the exhaust, to see the tread marks in the sand. The jeep continued to make figure eights between the bushes, then whirled around and went in the other direction toward the red-faced border patrol agent, who was standing under an overhanging rock formation waiting for the jeep to pick him up. They edged along, watching for signs of human presence, then meandered away.

A tumbleweed bush rolled by, turning over and over again, closely followed by a plastic bag. A page from a newspaper dangled from a cactus, impaled on its thorny spines, letting him know that somewhere nearby there were people, houses, a town, close by but far enough away that they wouldn't be able to hear his cries for help, his last screams as he perished in this endless, burning graveyard.

A murmuring of voices drifted through the shimmering heat, followed by a faint whimpering. He was not alone! His eyes caught the flash of a blue bandanna beyond the bushes, the outline of bodies by the dry river bed. It was El Pitón, addressing the group of migrants!

Felipe lingered behind the bushes for a moment, watching for any sign of the border patrol, then inched cautiously through the grass to join them.

Five men huddled tenaciously around El Pitón, clinging to his every word, his knowledge of the terrain their only hope for survival. Twenty migrants had crossed the border, but these five and Felipe were the only ones left. The others had been caught by the border patrol and deported or chased far enough to become separated from the group, lost in the vast open space, disoriented from the heat. Horacio, dead, staring into the sun, sightless, hearing nothing.

The whimpering was coming from a small boy, maybe six or seven years old, seated on the ground next to the group of migrants. It was Cheyo, the boy whose mother had been trying to shield him from the border patrol, the son of Rogelio and Esmeralda. Felipe looked at the others quizzically, but he already knew the answer, so he stood there not speaking, just nodding his head, letting them know that he understood. The wailing coming from the border patrol jeep had been Esmeralda, Cheyo's mother.

Felipe squatted down on the ground next to Cheyo. "We're going to take care of you, *niño*. We're going to find your parents," he said quietly, trying to be soothing, but Cheyo continued to whimper, shuddering with each breath as he sat crumpled up in the dirt, the red and white stripes of his little shirt muted under a layer of brown dust.

Gilberto pushed a rock around with his foot and kicked it hard, sending it bouncing into the grass. "How do you expect to do that? We don't know where they are from, or where they took them. You see a telephone out here? You going to call somebody?"

"If you yell loud enough, *la migra* will come," one of the others said. "They'll be glad to help you."

"Try praying to God, maybe God will call the border patrol," Gilberto said, bringing a few half-hearted chuckles from the group.

El Pitón squinted, gazing into the distance as though he was talking to someone far away. "We can't take him. You'll be lucky if you get your-selves out of here."

Felipe took off his shirt and wiped the boy's face. "I have a little brother at home. I'll take him with me."

El Pitón laughed, not a real laugh but a kind of snorting noise. "You're crazy, boy. He'll never make it, and he'll hold the rest of us back. Better that some of us survive than have all of us die trying to save a seven-year-old." He stomped away, shaking his head, grumbling to himself.

Felipe slipped his shirt back on, damp with Cheyo's tears, and took him by the hand. "Where are you from, Cheyo?" he asked, trying to sound as gentle as he could.

"El Salvador," Cheyo whimpered.

"Don't worry, we're going to find your parents," he said, although in his heart he knew it was impossible, they never would. If a miracle happened, maybe they would reach a city and an American would adopt him.

"Where is my mama and my papa? I'm thirsty."

"We will find them, *hermanito*," Felipe repeated. "We will find them." He took his last two tortillas out of his backpack and gave one to Cheyo.

"I'm thirsty," Cheyo said again, and sat down on the ground, tears rolling down his chubby round cheeks. "I'm tired. I can't walk."

El Pitón glared at Felipe. "Leave him here or we're going on without you."

"You can't—"

"You think I can't? I can and I will. Leave him here, or you're on your own."

The tortilla stuck in Felipe's throat, a lump of dust, a fish trying to float down a bone-dry river, lodged in the unrelenting cracked mud. He coughed it up, chewed it more so it would go down, sit like a rock in his empty stomach.

Felipe trailed behind El Pitón and the five migrants struggling to keep up with him, clutching Cheyo's hand as they trudged toward the base of a rocky incline. Cheyo's short legs were no match for El Pitón's urgent pace and he stumbled, pitching forward into a mound of gritty earth, coughing and choking from the rust-colored soot that filled his eyes and covered his nose and mouth, his ear-splitting shrieks reverberating across the desert. Felipe lifted Cheyo from the ground, brushed off the dust, and

held him for a moment. "You have to walk, *hermanito*," he pleaded frantically, as the blue bandanna disappeared over the top of the hill.

"I can't walk!" Cheyo howled. "I want to go home. I hate it here!"

The beads of sweat on Felipe's neck turned cold, dread running
through his body as Gilberto, the slowest of the group, vanished over
the ridge. If he left Cheyo behind he could run, catch up with the others, save himself. That's what Mama wanted, for him to survive, to not
become another bloated body staring vacantly at the brutal, pitiless sun.
Without El Pitón to guide him, he had no chance.

"Pitón!" Felipe screamed again and again, but his words just floated
away, lost in the desolate expanse of desert before him. He turned away
from Cheyo, stumbling toward the base of the incline, grabbing at the
rocky, crumbling earth as he lurched forward, slipping and sliding in his
haste. His hand landed on a sharp rock, blood oozing into the dirt, dust
filling the ragged gash across his palm.

The highest point on the slope was within his reach; a few more
steps brought him to the summit, where he stood gazing out at five
T-shirts and a blue bandanna plodding across the unbroken expanse of
rocky soil, tumbleweed, and cactus. Felipe stood frozen, Cheyo's screams
clawing at him from below, the T-shirts shrinking in the distance. He
edged slowly down the hill, one step at a time.

"Okay, you don't have to walk," he said desperately, kneeling down
on all fours in front of him. "Climb on my back and I'll carry you. We

can't stay here. We have to catch up to El Pitón, find your mama and papa." Cheyo climbed on Felipe's back, his arms wound tightly around Felipe's neck, his legs wrapped around his waist. "Not so tight. If you choke me to death, we'll never get there."

Cheyo was a dead weight on his back, but at least they were moving. If they traveled quickly enough, he might still catch a glimpse of the migrants in the distance or spot their footprints and follow the trail they made. He crawled along with Cheyo on his back, slow as a snake edging through the grass in his village, inching up the slope, down the *bajada*, until he was upright again, feeling the earth flat under his feet. The T-shirts had vanished, so the craggy mountain peaks silhouetted against the cloudless blue sky were his only guide, his guardian angel. His village in El Salvador was in the mountains, too; he would know better how to survive there. It would be cooler, and there would be trees with fruit they could eat.

Just before the next rocky incline, his eyes caught a spot of blue, maybe a lake. "See, there's a lake," he said to Cheyo, pointing to the isolated patch of color shimmering between two parched sunburned hills. "When we get there, you can have a drink." God had answered his prayers, sent him a lake to drink from and a mountain range to guide him.

"I don't see it," Cheyo said. "I don't see any lake."

Felipe wasn't sweating anymore, and his skin was hot and itchy. El Pitón had warned them about *El Diablo*, the devil, the heatstroke that came knocking at your door, calling you home. His head was filled with cotton, and somewhere far away he could hear the sound of Cheyo crying, feel his arms loosening around his neck as he drifted to the ground. A wave of calm washed over him, a feeling of peace.

In his dream, his body was floating in the air, moving of its own volition, out of his control. Strange noises: rumbling, roaring, screaming. Someone was yelling. His eyes were stuck shut, but he fought to get them open, to view the strange world he had entered. A truck was there, not green and shiny with a border patrol emblem, but old and rusty—a black, rusty old truck with a dent in the door. Two faces were peering down at him, lifting him, hoisting him into the back of the truck; a man with long, black hair tied behind his head and deep brown skin, a woman with a huge straw hat. Felipe told himself to run, but he couldn't move a limb. He drifted back to the dream for a moment and then woke up. Something warm was next to him, moving. Cheyo, staring at him with his big brown eyes, watching over him. Felipe's chest was bare and a pretty woman with green eyes and long, curly red hair flowing from the big straw hat was sponging him with a wet cloth, giving him small sips of salty water.

"*Hermanito*, are you okay? Cheyo?" he mumbled, still fading in and out of his dream.

"I have Coca-Cola," Cheyo answered, holding up a bottle, his voice steadier and calmer than it had been.

The pretty woman spoke a little Spanish, funny-sounding Spanish. "I'm Sarah, and this is Danny," she said softly. "The boy is fine, and you're going to be okay, too." Her Spanish was just perfect for him. She was not *la migra* or a bandito. Just a pretty American woman with a pink face, wearing a big straw hat and a thin white shirt with long sleeves covering her arms, speaking perfectly decent Spanish.

"*La migra* took Cheyo's parents," Felipe whispered through cracked lips that split more when he tried to talk. He could taste blood, salty in his mouth. "You have to—"

The woman touched his arm gently, as if to tell him he didn't need words, that she understood the situation, had seen it before. "This is not the first time a child has come through here alone. We have contacts in many places and we don't give up. We'll do everything we can to find them."

The truck was slowing, rolling to a stop in front of a church, its white steeple radiant against the unbroken blue sky, reminding him of Father Rodriguez, and Mama. Two pairs of arms held him steady as he crawled out of the truck and stumbled along on wobbly legs toward the front door of the church. He could smell food cooking and hear the chatter of voices. People speaking Spanish, people like him. "Where are we?" he whispered. His throat was still scratchy and there was a throbbing pain in his head.

"*Un santuario.* A sanctuary," Sara answered. "*Casa de seguridad.* A safe place. You can rest here, then we'll help you find a bus or a train that will take you wherever you want to go."

"New York," he said. "Oakmont, New York. I have an uncle who lives there."

There were butterflies in his stomach, a feeling of excitement, thrilling, hopeful. He had done it—he had survived the brutal trip across the desert, and these people would help him get to New York, where he would work in Tio Miguel's restaurant, maybe even earn enough to send for Mama and Ana and Juanito.

"*Gracias,*" he said, glancing shyly at Sara. "*Muchas, muchas gracias.* A safe place!" He repeated her words excitedly, continuing to stare at her in amazement. "A safe place!" He had spoken his first English words.

Spring, 2006

Fifteen

Colin stared up at the ornate stone walls of the church, the stained glass windows, the curve of the gold door handle, and forced his foot up to the next step. He gripped the banister, dragged his other foot up and stood there, not moving. Funny that he would end up in Grover Hill to do community service, of all places. Dad never stopped railing about Grover Hill—said the guys that hung out by the fence at the mall lived there—violent criminals from violent countries, bringing drugs into Oakmont. Colin had barely slept a wink last night, worrying about gangbangers who didn't like white boys from the east side, wouldn't miss a chance to beat the crap out of him. Dad had driven him, wouldn't let him walk around Grover Hill alone, promised to pick him up at the end of the shift.

He pulled open the massive wooden door at the top of the stairs and peered cautiously into the church lobby. A bulletin board with notices about church things and community events stared down at him, as well as several signs with arrows pointing out the direction of different rooms. *Dining Room*, the sign said, pointing toward the first room on the left.

Colin had expected strange smells, the odor of food cooking amidst the urine-soaked clothing of chronically homeless people, but instead found himself in a pleasant room with hardwood floors and long white plastic tables with matching chairs. Everything seemed to be made of white plastic, simple but clean. Napkin holders and forks and spoons on white paper tablecloths, paper placemats and paper plates at each setting, a vase of yellow, red, and white cut flowers on a small table in the corner.

A wrinkled old man with an elfin appearance and a gray ponytail greeted him, stuck out his hand. "I'm Wesley, and you are—"

"Colin Sullivan, here to do some community service."

"School or court?"

"Court, I guess."

"Ah, got yerself in a little trouble, did ya? This is as good a place as any to work it out, make good on what ya did. No one'll judge you here. This is the best place you could be, son. Teach you more than you'll learn going to school for a lifetime."

Wesley seemed nice enough, but Colin hoped he wasn't going to be lectured with religious morality stuff while he was here, given little cards with Bible sayings on them. A guy at the mall used to hand those out to the shoppers, but everyone just tossed them. Going to church wasn't something his family did—the last time he could remember being in one was when his father's younger sister got married, and he had just been a little kid then. The only thing he could recall about it was that he had to wear a suit and that it was boring, except for the part where he got to chomp down a lot of cake.

"Come on, let's walk around. I'll explain what you'll be doing," Wesley said, pointing out a small alcove across from the dining area. "You'll be over there, serving food to the people who come in."

A long table stretched across the front of the alcove, covered with aluminum pans labeled with black marker: *beef stew, ham, coleslaw*, bowls of apples and bananas, plates of chocolate chip cookies, a wicker basket full of bread, a pitcher of apple juice, and a silver coffee urn.

"The rest of the food is kept in here," Wesley said, as they stepped into a large kitchen directly behind the alcove. A walk-in closet was filled with bags of canned food and cereal, groceries people picked up and took home to feed their kids, and the shelves were lined with institutional-sized cans of vegetables, soup, and beans. A massive aluminum pot sat on the stove, simmering with vegetable soup.

"At noon, folks start drifting in, coming to you for their soup. They pick up their own bowls over there," Wesley continued, pointing to a table that contained a pile of lunch trays and a stack of plastic bowls, along with an assortment of plastic forks, spoons, and knives, paper cups and napkins, all neatly arranged. "You stick the ladle in the pot and fill their bowl—that's it— that's all you have to do."

It was a diverse group that shuffled in at noon, another surprise, and not at all what he had imagined. Some old people, some his age, mothers with children, an array of colors and races, sizes and shapes, some chattering in English, some in Spanish, a family speaking a language that was unfamiliar, maybe Russian, a few silent, searching out a spot at the end of the table where they could be alone. Colin felt the tension that had been gnawing at him since last night easing up. Doing his community service here would be manageable, and Wesley seemed like a nice guy. The place was definitely not the freak show he had expected. No sign of violent criminals or any of the people Dad was always complaining about.

Mom would be pleased to hear how friendly the place was, and he might even try to convince her to come and help out sometime. He wasn't sure what to tell Dad, maybe he wouldn't use the word "cool," just mention that it was going okay, that he would be able to deal with it, do his time and get on with his life, which was what Dad wanted.

The alcove faced the dining room, where a long row of people bent over their soup bowls, their chairs scraping faintly on the wood floor as they rose to toss the bowl in the trash and return to the alcove for the rest of their meal. A young woman who appeared to be about his age sat across from him, next to a boy of about seven or eight. She had to be older than she looked, couldn't have had a child that young. Beautiful, though. He was struck by her eyes, almond-shaped, the color of molasses, with long black lashes. She wore a lacy white tank top that didn't quite reach the waistband of her pants, leaving a swatch of brown belly showing above her jeans. Colin tried not to stare but found himself watching her movements out of the corner of his eye as he filled the bowls with soup.

A line was beginning to form in front of the alcove, so maybe he needed to observe less and ladle faster. Some of the people were standing patiently, holding their bowls quietly between their fingers, but others were shifting impatiently, their eyes fixed on him. An elderly woman with white hair that stood out in all directions held out her bowl, but her hands shook and the soup threatened to drip all over the tray as she carried it. Her thin flowered dress didn't quite fit right, seemed way too big for her small body, and she wore what looked like a pair of pink bedroom slippers on her feet, the kind his mom wore around the house, making the same shuffling sound when she walked.

"I'm sorry, sonny—I'm a bit shaky here," she said, a little sadly. "You're a nice boy, to come here and help people. My Ralphie—"

"I've got it, ma'am," Colin said, gently taking the tray from her hands. "Where are you sitting?" he asked, carrying the tray to the long table and setting it down for her. His grandmother, Nana, had white hair like that, and he had always thought it looked pretty cool, but then he had always thought Nana was just about the greatest person he'd ever known. She still lived alone in an apartment in the old Bronx neighborhood Dad grew up in, something his parents were always fussing about. They thought she should live in Oakmont with them or in some kind of a nursing home or something, but Nana didn't think so and refused to move.

Despite what his parents thought, Nana bought her own groceries, carried them home in a shopping cart, cooked her own meals. She had turned seventy-nine this past fall, and they had held a small birthday party in her apartment, although she had really organized most of it herself, invited the people she wanted. Feisty as hell, made sure everyone knew what she thought about things.

Colin pretended not to notice as the girl with the kid tossed two soup bowls in the trash and sashayed in slow motion toward the alcove, a sensual dance in jeans that accentuated the curve of her hips, the movement of her legs. She glanced back at the child, who sat at the table zooming a toy truck up and down, and held out two plates to the other servers. "A little ham for him, and some bread—he likes that," she said. "I'll have a little of everything."

Curious that she would be in a soup kitchen, Colin thought. She didn't look homeless or down and out, and the kid looked well cared for. "How was the soup? Okay today? We aim to please," he said flashing a big grin. She looked at him quizzically, as though she was wondering what was wrong with him.

"It's food." He wasn't sure if he was being way too pushy, or if she was just not in the mood to talk.

"Your son's a ham guy, it looks like." He wondered again about the kid, and how old she was.

Another puzzled look. She looked him over this time, as if she needed to decide whether it was safe to answer. "He's my brother. He's a little picky, but he likes meat." Her brother, not her kid. She turned away, sashaying back toward the child sitting at the table. There was a seriousness about her, a maturity, definitely different from the girls he knew at school. Colin never had to make much effort there, always had someone to take to a dance, to the after game parties, so he had never ventured much beyond the line of cheerleaders. He couldn't imagine any of the girls he knew spending their Saturday afternoon in a soup kitchen in a church, babysitting their kid brother. Most likely they would be hanging out at one of the bigger malls in the area with their friends, browsing the stores looking for bargains or going to the movies.

Colin knew he could never ask her for a date—Dad would have a heart attack—but he could still be friendly, talk to her a little if she came back to the soup kitchen. Mom wouldn't mind, said the Hispanics she encountered at the hospital were nice people. Anyway, it didn't really matter what his parents thought—the girl didn't seem too interested in him, and it was probably better that way. He had just gotten out of one mess and certainly didn't need another.

Sixteen

The early morning light was dim beneath the overpass, and it took a few minutes for the grogginess of sleep to clear before Julia realized what had happened—that she had fallen asleep under a highway in Arizona and had slept there all night. She peered around anxiously for her woven bag. There it was, right next to her leg, where she must have dropped it last night when she passed out, totally drained from walking all that way in the sun. Today would be another exhausting day, but if she kept going, she would get to Eloy and see Felipe! The morning was still cool, at least as cool as it got in Arizona, and if she started walking now, she could probably cover a lot of ground before the heat became ferocious and slowed her down.

Julia quickly gobbled half of her remaining burrito and stuffed the rest back in her purse. For some reason, burritos were always huge, no matter where you were, so you could eat half and save the other half for another meal, if you wanted. The remains of this one might have to be breakfast, lunch, and dinner today.

A strange noise interrupted her thoughts, startling her, a noise coming from a pile of raggedy old clothes near the far wall of the overpass. Julia grabbed her bag and leaped to her feet, flooded with fear, appalled at what she had done. She had spent the whole night here, and anything could have happened. The noise was probably rats foraging around for food, and she shuddered, totally disgusted by the thought that a bunch of rats could have been running over her while she slept. A rat could have bitten her, and people died from rat bites. Panicky now, she checked her clothing, her arms and legs, but didn't see any obvious bites, and they hadn't gone after her burrito, which had been sitting in her purse.

The pile of clothes moved again, but it wasn't a rat—it was a body moving—another person sleeping here; in fact, she could now make out two other bodies stretched out on the gravel near the wall. She wasn't the only one who had slept under the highway last night. The body under the pile of clothes had raised himself up on his elbow, gawking at her. It was a man, an old man with wild gray hair and a grizzled beard.

"I must be dreamin'!" he said with a grin, creeping toward her, scrutinizing her with red, watery eyes. An empty whiskey bottle lay on its side next to him, and the place was littered with trash. Crumpled brown bags, wadded up tissue paper, empty food containers. She had slept on gravel, surrounded by garbage.

She held her bag tightly against her chest and backed away from him, smacking into the cement wall of the overpass. Her legs were shaking as she moved quickly toward the highway, but one of the other men had crawled in front of her, blocking her path. A homeless encampment, full of scraggly looking men. Not a place she wanted to find herself alone.

"What brings you here, beautiful?" the gray-haired man asked, eyeing her curiously.

"She's better lookin' than most of the folks we see around here," one of the others mumbled. "Better dressed, too," which brought snickers from the other two.

"My car broke down and I couldn't get home last night, so I sat down to rest and fell asleep," she said quickly. Maybe if she showed she was friendly, wasn't afraid of them, they would leave her alone. "Thanks for letting me sleep here, but I'm heading out right now."

"Good place as any to sleep. Where ya headed?"

"Eloy," she said and moved toward the road.

"You're not too far, 'bout eight miles. Live in Eloy?"

All that walking yesterday, and she had only gone halfway. There was a strong smell coming from one of the men, and she wondered if she smelled, too. At home, she took a shower every day, made sure she always looked nice, spent a lot of time on her hair and makeup, but she had been traveling for days now and had been so consumed with worry about Felipe

175

that she had barely thought about herself at all. She should go to the hotel first, take a shower before she went to the detention center, but that would mean waiting longer to see him, maybe even waiting another day. On the other hand, the prison officials would not be too helpful to an unkempt woman wearing dirty clothes and smelling like trash.

She hesitated for a moment, and then the words came rushing out. Other than a short phone call to her kids, she hadn't spoken to anyone except the waitress, the guy in the cowboy hat, and the Greyhound agent for several days. If they came after her she could just run—they didn't look very healthy and she could probably outrun them. "My husband is in the immigration detention center in Eloy. You know the place?"

"The jail in Eloy? That's a mean place, sister. Hope you can get him out of there."

"Immigration is bad down here, miss," the younger one chimed in. "They would love to send us all back to Mexico. Even the ones that are born here sometimes get sent back."

"Really? They can do that?" she said nervously, wondering if the police could just pick her up on the highway and deport her to Mexico.

"You forget your ID, they think you're illegal, they arrest you and drop you on the other side of the border."

The one with the red, watery eyes laughed. "Like the movie, *Born in East L.A.* You seen it?"

She had seen it; actually, it had always been one of her favorite movies. The main character had gone out without his wallet and had been deported to Mexico because he didn't have identification. It was a comedy, but in real life, it was not so funny. Not a bit funny. Julia pulled the half-eaten burrito out of her purse and waved it at them. "Anybody want some?" she asked.

"Thanks, but we get by, and you're gonna need that food, miss," one of the men answered. "Got at least a day's walk ahead of you. If you move fast, you might make it there by this afternoon. The heat'll slow you down, though, so it might take longer." He picked up a grimy bag from the ground. "Donuts. Take one, for your trip." He put his hand in the bag and pulled out a sugar-covered donut.

"That's nice of you, but this burrito has really filled me up. I couldn't eat another thing right now, and I need to get going."

"Miss, you're always welcome to come back if you need a place to sleep. We take care of each other here. I'm Walter and these handsome fellas are Herminio and Cesar."

"Julia," she responded. She felt grateful for the small camaraderie they offered, the only friendly respite she had encountered on a lonely road in Arizona. She waved goodbye and stepped out of the shadows of the overpass onto the road.

The Eloy Corrections Corporation of America Immigration Detention Center was not a place you could just walk into. There were two outer doors—pressing a buzzer got Julia through the first door but landed her smack up against a second locked door. Pressing another buzzer got her through that one, then a few more feet on the sidewalk and through another door that opened into the lobby. Once inside, she was met by armed guards in short-sleeve white shirts with the red, white, and blue emblems of the Corrections Corporation of America, the CCA, their guns dangling at their side. A clerk at the front desk doled out bits of information regarding identification requirements: who can be an authorized visitor, what you can bring in, what you are allowed to do in the visiting room.

Shorts not shorter than mid-thigh, no jogging shorts, cutoffs, or hip huggers. No underwire bras due to metal detector sensitivity. No spandex, military clothing, tank tops, halter tops, shower shoes, slippers, or hats. All visitors will be dressed appropriately for a business setting.

If Julia passed the clothing rules, she then had to pass the identification requirements.

Legal picture ID, she had that. Authorized visitors only. Visitors were allowed only on weekends and had to be approved prior to the day of the visit, which meant waiting at least another day.

Immediate family will be placed on a waiting list unless strong circumstances exist that would preclude their visit. Visitors may take a small coin purse and coins into the visiting room. All items entering the visiting room will be thoroughly searched and visually inspected by the front entrance officer prior to admission. Lockers are provided for storage of a visitor's personal items.

If they let her in, she could put her bra, her purse, and her bag in the locker, change her tank top for the white blouse that was in her bag.

Conduct in the visiting room: A brief kiss and hug are allowed at the beginning and end of the visit. Disruptive or offensive behavior will be cause for termination of the visit. Visitors and inmates/detainees must obey the rules of the facility at all times. Visitors may only visit with the inmate/detainees they are approved to visit. Fraternizing with anyone other than an approved visitor by an inmate/detainee will result in termination of the visit. Visitors are allowed to stay one hour.

Julia felt she could be satisfied with just seeing him, letting him know she was here for him. A brief kiss and a hug would go a long way. Tomorrow was Saturday, an approved visiting day. All that was left was for the immigration authorities to approve the visit. It would all be worth it, worth the five days of travel and sleeping under the highway, if she could see him.

There would be a wait, they said, pointing to an area where there were benches, but she couldn't sit, so she paced up and down the room, taking deep breaths and trying to remain calm. She put her hand in her pocket and felt something sticky, a piece of gum that must have been Camilo's.

The gum was sweet in her mouth and the chewing alleviated some of the tension, so she concentrated on chewing and tried not to think about seeing Felipe. Chew, walk, chew, sit down, chew, get up and pace again. She didn't smoke but understood at this moment why people did. There were times when any relief would be welcome. She had only been on the outside of the jail and the atmosphere was already terrifying. She could only imagine what it must be like on the inside. But that's what she was here for, to get Felipe out of this nightmare and take him home to his family who loved him.

She decided that she would call the Immigrants' Rights Project right after she visited Felipe, found out what he had been told about his situation. There was still some time left on the pre-paid cell phone card. She could use that to make the call.

As grueling as the trip down the highway had been, it was a good thing she hadn't blown thirty-five dollars on the shuttle van—she could use some of the money she had saved to buy another phone card if she needed it. The kids would be so excited to hear Felipe's voice, know that he would be coming home. The remainder of the cash she had brought was running low, and she still had to buy a Greyhound ticket to get home, maybe two if by some miracle he got released, and a little food to eat on the way.

It wouldn't be long now. A stocky woman in dark pants and a white shirt with the red, white, and blue CCA name tag was strolling toward her with a form in her hand, probably coming to let her know that to-morrow's visit had been approved.

"Señora Sanchez?" Nobody had ever called her that in New York. Julia smiled at her, gave the woman a little wave, a friendly gesture, but the woman didn't smile or wave back. Her voice was cold and business-like, and she seemed impatient to move on to her next task.

Probably just overworked, Julia thought. She could understand that.

"I'm sorry, ma'am," the woman said. "Felipe Sanchez isn't here. They put him on the plane to El Salvador this morning."

Seventeen

The handcuffs cut into Felipe's wrists as the cactuses and the palm trees of Arizona became specks on the ground, nothing left to see but fluffy clouds, puffs of smoke drifting through the atmosphere. He could barely feel the plane moving as it did a slow-motion dance over thin ribbons of highway. A green carpet appeared, then square patches of brown with the tiniest of houses lined up for miles. His family was down there, slipping further away each minute, and the dream, the lover's dream he and Julia had created, was choking and sputtering now, threatening to crumble and disappear forever.

Three weeks had passed since immigration agents whisked him out of his cell at the Westchester County jail, taking him by plane to the immigration detention center in Arizona, where he had no right to a phone call or a court appointed attorney because he was being held on an immigration violation, no way to explain his disappearance to his family. He had paced the tiny jail cell frantically, unable to sleep, stumbling back and forth between the walls, back to front and back again, in a circle with no beginning and no end. He stared desperately through the bars, clutching them, shaking the lifeless iron until his hands were red and raw, closing his eyes and opening them slowly, hoping desperately for a sign that help was nearby, that at any moment life would return to normal and he could go home.

The plane was full of blue uniforms, U.S. marshals watching over them. A plane full of handcuffed Salvadorans, returning to the blood-stained soil of their birth. There were a hundred people on this plane who had crawled through the burning heat of deserts, swam across rivers that threatened to suck them downstream to a watery death. It had been about survival, but more than that, it was about the children, sending them away from the violence, finding a new place where they would have a different life, creating a dream for the ones not yet born.

"Fasten your seatbelts. Do not unfasten them until you are told to do so. Don't touch the window shades or any of the buttons over your head. If you need to use the restroom, you must ask for permission."

A pleasant-looking, middle-aged man with a receding hairline and a belly that was straining against the limits of the seat belt, sat next to him, squirming, trying to get comfortable, but the more he squirmed, the less comfortable he appeared. "Can't wait until these cuffs are off," Felipe whispered to him sympathetically. It seemed the closer he got to

183

El Salvador, the more he whispered. It was something he had learned as a boy, although back then it hadn't helped to save anyone's life.

"They're cutting my wrists," the man said. He eyed Felipe, sized him up cautiously.

"Name's Roberto."

"How'd you end up here?"

"I left to earn some money to send home to my parents and wound up staying in the U.S. fifteen years, getting married, having kids. Worked in a meat packing plant in Iowa all that time, never had any trouble. Last month, the ICE raided the plant, sent everyone without papers to the detention center. I have four kids, one in high school. Three little ones. It's gonna be tough on them without me."

Two young men sat across the aisle from them, their arms and chests tattooed with gothic letters and gang symbols. Eighteen or nineteen at most, dispossessed boys who had no one protecting them so they watched over each other, striking out with fury at anyone who threatened them. The face of a small boy crying in the desert flashed through Felipe's mind, and he glanced quickly at the teenagers out of the corner of his eye, wondering what happened to Cheyo, if he ended up joining the gang life for protection. He and Julia had always fiercely protected their own children, tried to teach them right from wrong. As soon as they were old enough, they helped out at El Patio—at five years old Ricky would stand at the door and greet the customers when they came in and show them to a table, so proud to be helping Papi. His adorable little boy was growing up into a world his parents couldn't protect him from. They couldn't even protect themselves these days.

A marshal roamed the aisle, his eyes wandering the rows for any sign that something might be amiss, and Felipe and Roberto fell silent, gazing intently at the back of the seats in front of them, at the clouds drifting by the window.

"I pray for my children every day," Roberto said when the marshal had passed. "They're out there now without me."

The plane slammed into the tarmac with a thud, zooming down the runway toward the El Salvador International Airport. They had been on the plane less than three hours. Three hours and a million miles. Three hours—less than the time they spent on a subway trip from Oakmont to Coney Island and back. There was no way home this time, no subway, no Metro North ride to an anxiously waiting family, to children missing their father.

A click of a key and the handcuffs were removed, his arms yanked behind his back as he was pushed along into the airport immigration processing center by the *Policia Nacional Civil*, the Salvadoran National Civil Police, shoved into a chair in front of a camera. A blinding light flashed in his eyes, a hand reached out and grabbed his arm, jamming his fingers one by one onto an ink pad, leaving black fingerprints on a piece of paper. His picture. His fingerprints. The *guardia* had his picture and his fingerprints now and could track him anywhere—in the woods, in a village, at a job. A different uniform was coming toward him, asking him his name, typing it into a computer. It wasn't the uniform of a *guardia,* but he watched the immigration area carefully for any sign of dark green uniforms, rifles with the bayonets on the end.

"What are you typing?" Felipe asked.

"I'm looking for your name in our database, searching for a criminal record. If you've ever committed a crime here, we'll find it and you'll be back in handcuffs before you can count to three, on your way to a jail cell."

A balding man in a white lab coat emerged from a small office next to the processing center and headed toward him, cradling a hypodermic needle between his fingers. Sullen brown eyes, hidden behind oversized black glasses that camouflaged an exhaustion from too many things witnessed and not spoken about, crooked yellow teeth and an odor of onions, waving a needle.

Felipe watched in horror as the razor point of the needle floated through the air toward his right arm. The man could be anyone, a *guardia* or someone just pretending to be a doctor. Anything could be inside that needle—maybe a drug that would put him to sleep so they could spirit him away to an ancient stone prison in some hidden place where no one would find him.

The Salvadoran military had murdered Papi and Oscar, torn him from his family, forced him to flee to survive. He had no idea what they would find in the computer, and with no money and no papers, they could keep him in locked in a prison forever and no one would ever know.

He scanned the airport, but there was no place to hide, just some plastic benches, fast food restaurants and thousands of people hustling toward their destinations. If he disappeared into the crowd, he might be able to find his way to a bus, any bus to take him away from the immigration officials, their handcuffs, and their shots. Police were everywhere, strutting around in their black uniforms, carrying guns. Guarding the immigration office, the baggage area. The balding man in the white coat glanced at the policeman standing rigidly by the fingerprinting area, as the needle moved closer to Felipe's arm.

"It's just a—"

Felipe's foot flew out and the man in the white coat fell backward, sliding across the white tiles as the needle sailed through the air, smashing onto the floor, a puddle of liquid and broken plastic. He bolted from the chair and dashed through the door, heading for the crowd of people milling around a nearby baggage carousel. Across from the carousel, he could see a small office with large glass windows and an open door, where a man was gesturing furiously with his hands and bickering with the two clerks behind the counter, something about his lost luggage. The man stomped out, his arms folded, as he returned to the baggage carousel and stared mournfully as it lumbered around without his luggage. The two employees sauntered out behind him, chatting as they headed toward a restaurant at the end of the corridor. Felipe watched them disappear into the crowd, slipped quietly into the office, turned off the lights, and crouched behind the counter.

The black uniform of a policeman appeared in the window, then moved toward the door.

The knob turned slowly, the door inching open as he surveyed the office, then turned and strolled over to the baggage carousel, searching the crowd, exchanging words with a woman at a car rental counter, observing the travelers waiting at the bus stops.

Felipe's view through the glass was clear now, a parade of people being greeted by loved ones, grabbing their suitcases off the carousel, scurrying to their next destination. He had no bags, and no one would be there to greet him, to hug him with joy after a long absence and guide him to a waiting car outside. The airport was full of signs, but he could only read a few of the words. To find the right bus, he would have to stand at the bus stop and ask each driver where the bus was headed.

El Salvador was his birthplace, but it was no longer his home. He had been a child when he left, and except for some short trips to San Salvador with Mama and Papa to buy clothes and one day in the refugee camp in Honduras, he'd never been outside of his village. Mama could be anywhere—still in Honduras, or back in El Espino—and he had heard through the grapevine that many people had moved to San Salvador to take jobs in the *maquilas*, the textile factories.

Another face floated past the door, vaguely familiar. Roberto, his fellow detainee from the airplane, checking out the transportation signs in the baggage area. Felipe crept across the floor of the darkened office and paused in front of the door, peering warily through the window.

No sign of the policeman from the immigration office, but the airport was full of policemen in the same black uniform, and he had only glanced at him. He tried to remember his face, but it had faded, could be any of them. Time was running out. The employees would be coming back from their break soon and would discover him, think he was robbing the place and call airport security. He cracked the door open a sliver, scanning the baggage area for signs of the police. The area seemed clear, so he slid out the door and stepped quietly across the corridor.

"Roberto," he whispered.

"Where did you go, *hermano*?"

"Don't know what the hell was in that needle, and didn't want to find out."

"It was a tetanus shot, in case you step on a nail," Roberto said.

"You sure of that? You trust them? I wouldn't trust these people to give me change of a dollar."

"Actually, you missed six dollars and the pupusas. They give you six dollars to get home, and some pupusas to eat. Don't even need to exchange the money because there's no national currency anymore. They're only using U.S. dollars." Felipe stared in amazement as Roberto unfolded six crumpled dollar bills and slipped three into Felipe's shirt pocket. "I understand, *hermano*. Two of my brothers were killed by the *guardias*. I found one of them myself in the bushes, with five bullet holes." He tugged on a pupusa stuffed in a pocket of his baggy olive green work pants. "Take this, you're going to need it. I took a couple extra, stuffed them everywhere."

The pupusa was wrapped in a napkin, a little stale, but no food had ever tasted so good.

Felipe savored the flavor of the cheese on his tongue and the pasty softness of the flour between his teeth. Twenty years of making pupusas had taught him how to make the best, but there was nothing like hunger to bring out the flavor in food. The pupusa disappeared all too quickly, and he licked the remains of the cheese and the flour off his fingers, one finger at a time, to try to get a little more of it.

"Want another one?" Roberto asked, pulling a pupusa out of a different pocket.

"I hope you left some for the other people," Felipe chuckled. "They're pretty good, but you can keep the ones you stuffed in your underwear."

"Don't laugh, *hermano*. You'll wish you had more in a few hours."

Felipe's eyes caught a sign with pictures of buses and taxis, and a large advertisement with a picture of a coffee plantation. "Looks like a *finca*. What does it say?" Felipe asked.

Roberto contemplated the sign, stroking his throat, tossing a sympathetic glance at Felipe as he read the sign aloud.

Coffee Tours!

Learn about the history of coffee culture in El Salvador from 4th generation plantation owners!

Pick coffee beans in the fields! Learn about drying, roasting, and packaging facilities! Visit unique towns and colorful houses!

We recommend cameras, light clothes, and comfortable shoes! Entrance fees, lunch, transportation, and guide included.

Departs from San Salvador at 8:30 a.m. every day. $87.00.

Felipe felt a wave of sadness and a white-hot burning in his chest. The *finca* was his childhood, his past—it was his Papa and his Mama, it was Oscar and so many others who had endured so much, fighting for a better life. He was stunned that their daily reality had been turned into a tourist attraction, a show for people to enjoy on their vacations. And Mama—he had to find her, but now he was more fearful than ever about what might he find. He numbly followed Roberto as they shoved open the glass doors to the transportation area and hovered near the bus stop apprehensively, watching the tourists struggle with their cameras and their bags, as he waited for a bus to take him to the place he once called home.

Eighteen

Marisol leaned over the white paper tablecloth at St. Michael's and pulled Camilo's plate closer to her, cut the ham into little pieces, placed the fork in his hand. "Eat something, *chiquito*. It's ham, your favorite. M-m-m, delicious meat." Camilo asked for Papi every day, his beaming smile now a fading memory, his dark eyes clouding with tears at the slightest offense. The first time they had come to St. Michael's, he had pushed the meat off the plate onto the table and sat there with his arms folded, refusing to eat.

She checked for her purse on the floor, the cloth one with the floral design Mama bought for her birthday, and shifted uncomfortably in the chair. She tried to eat but didn't have much appetite, so she rearranged the food on the dish with her fork, the ham on the left and the coleslaw on the right, the coleslaw on the right and the ham on the left. Just the idea of having to eat in a soup kitchen made her queasy. The dining room was pleasant enough, full of weathered men in work pants and well-worn boots, their heads bent over the table as they slurped their soup, frowning mothers feeding small children and sneaking pieces of meat into plastic bags they kept in their purses, elderly women carrying tattered brown shopping bags, sitting alone, invisible in a world of busy people zooming through their daily lives. The room was clean and attractive and she liked the flowers and the picture on the wall, made it a little homier, but it was humiliating to take that step through the door asking for help, broadcasting your troubles to a roomful of strangers.

It had been her idea to eat at the soup kitchen to save money. Camilo ate lunch at school, but ever since Mama left for Arizona, Marisol had been bringing him to St. Michael's for dinner, and for both lunch and dinner on the weekend. Mama had left some *carne guisada* for them in the refrigerator, which Marisol had been taking to school for her lunch, leaving the rest for Ricky to eat for dinner. Before she left, Mama had a serious talk with her about money—told her that she and Papi had some savings they had put aside to use as start-up money for their dream restaurant, but without Papi to bring in money, it was going quickly. No new clothes, nothing but necessities until Mama came back and got some more work. Marisol offered to look for an after-school job, but Mama said no to that. Her schoolwork was more important, and she needed her to watch Camilo after school on the days she had work. They would get by somehow.

Mama didn't know that she and Camilo were eating here every day, and never would have agreed to it, but Marisol was afraid that they could end up homeless the way things were going, and that was super scary. At least if she helped Mama save some money on food, they might be able to keep the rent paid, so they didn't have to sleep at a shelter or in the street.

The volunteers dishing out the food were closing up, putting lids on the aluminum pans, moving them from the alcove back to the kitchen. Nice of them to help people out. One of the volunteers, the vegetable soup guy, was staring at her, probably hoping she would speed up so he could finish cleaning and go home.

Camilo had eaten his ham; maybe she should grab a cookie for him, and one for herself. Just one each, not to look greedy. She tossed their paper plates into a large metal trash can, moseyed over to the alcove slowly so she didn't come off too enthusiastic about that cookie, just cool and collected, throwing away her trash and picking up something a little extra for her brother. This morning she had put on her gold hoop earrings, although she hadn't had time to put on any makeup. Jewelry always added some pizzazz to her appearance, even when she didn't feel much pizzazz about anything, and the gold hoop earrings perked up whatever she was wearing.

The vegetable soup guy was young, about her age. She had seen him there a few times and he had tried to talk to her, but she hadn't paid much attention. White boy, kinda cute, with blue eyes and dark blond hair falling over his forehead. His clothes were definitely choice enough—baggy pants, some rock group on the T-shirt. East Oakmont kid trying to be cool. Maybe he was writing a report for a class about life in a soup kitchen. Her life, his adventure. He tossed her a quick, sunny grin, and she smoothed her hair to make sure it wasn't sticking up in some weird way that she hadn't noticed. For a moment she felt a spark of excitement, flattered that he was paying attention to her. She held herself back, though, kept her cool face on. Flirting with some white boy from the east side was certainly not what she needed to be doing right now, as cute as he was. It was the beginning of May; exams were coming up, and she needed to get Camilo home.

If she could keep her life together for one more year, she would have those college scholarships in the bag. Her dream was to go to medical school, help find a cure for cancer or AIDS, although since Papi was arrested, she had been entertaining thoughts of going to law school instead. There was still time to figure that one out, as long as she kept her grades up, but now that she had to be in charge of everything, she was barely making it to class. Mama and Papi had always been there to listen to her problems, to turn her around if she veered off course, but she was on her own right now.

The cute white boy was checking her out as she moved toward the cookie tray. "What's your name?" he asked. "I saw you here the other day, but I didn't get a chance to ask."

Don't answer his questions. Leave now. She felt needy, though, and his welcoming smile was grabbing her, drawing her in. It wouldn't hurt to be a little friendly, especially since she needed to come back again and would have to see him when she did. "Marisol," she answered indifferently as she picked up two cookies from the tray, took a small bite of one and broke the other one in half for Camilo.

"Beautiful name. Mine's Colin."

Chocolate chip, her favorite. She wouldn't mind taking a few home, but that would be pretty rude, considering she hadn't paid for any of it.

"Been volunteering here for a while?" she asked, making more of an attempt to be pleasant. She chewed the cookie slowly, rolled the chocolate chip around on her tongue, relishing the sweetness.

"Just started last week. Doing some community service hours."

Probably some kind of school project. "What school?" she tossed out lackadaisically, giving Camilo the other half of the cookie. He was tired, starting to complain, wanting to leave.

"Oakmont High. You?"

An east side boy. She had been right about that.

"Grover Hill. You like Oakmont High?"

"It's okay. I play football; keeps me from being bored."

That was interesting. She didn't know any football players, especially white ones from East Oakmont. He was finishing up his junior year, he said, like her.

"How did you end up here?" she asked. "Some kind of school requirement?"

"Got in a little trouble, doing some community service."

Not a goody-goody after all, although he probably just did something silly like sneaking into the movies.

"Well, I'm doing a term paper for a sociology class on soup kitchens in churches," she responded quickly, before he had a chance to quiz her about why she was there. "I interviewed a few people who come here all the time, but I thought it would come out better if I experienced the place for myself, actually tasted the food. My little brother likes the meat, so I bring him with me."

It was getting a little too personal now, way more than she had intended, and she needed to take Camilo home. She felt surprisingly attracted to him, though, and there was a part of her that wanted to know more about him. The blue eyes and the smile were getting to her. She had dated quite a few guys, had a boyfriend for a while, but she had never dated anyone with blue eyes. Doing community service, maybe not so spoiled. There were lots of white guys like him in college, and she was bound to meet one sometime. She just hadn't thought it would be this soon. Besides, it didn't matter; they were just talking. Nobody ever died from having a conversation. He would go back to the east side; she would go home to Grover Hill. Never the twain shall meet. She had read that somewhere.

He was ogling her again, probably looking for sex, thinking she was easy and loose because she was a Latina from Grover Hill. A good-looking football player, had to have lots of girls chasing him. A big red flag, waving in her face.

"Maybe we could hang out sometime, have a little fun," he said, hanging his thumbs over his belt, tilting his head to the right a little as he flashed that totally charming grin.

Say no and put an end to this. On the other hand, a little fun wouldn't hurt.

"What did you have in mind?" she asked casually. That would tell her what he was after. He had probably heard about the sleazy run-down motels where the whores took their customers. No-tell mo-tels, everyone called them. She knew exactly what street they were on and stayed away from there.

"Maybe take a walk after my shift sometime, stop someplace and grab a snack. When my dad was driving me here, we passed a Donut House. I think it was on Tenth Street. You know that place?"

He didn't mention anything that sounded like he just wanted a hook-up, even if that was what he was thinking. She felt weak and desirous, attracted to him despite the danger signals. "I do, but I'm pretty busy right now," she mumbled, trying to make her face a mask of calm despite the butterflies in her stomach. "Next week or the week after might be better," she heard herself saying, wondering if she had just made the biggest mistake of her life.

Two weeks later, Marisol sat on the steps of St Michael's, enjoying the last bit of evening sun as she waited for Colin to finish his dinner shift. She had made sure to have her makeup on today and picked out her nicest earrings, the silver hanging ones, and a blouse that her friends always said was pretty. She reached back and pulled off her hair band, letting her hair fall to her shoulders.

The heavy oak door of the church moved a little, then slowly swung open and there he was, right there on the steps next to her, wearing a blue T-shirt with a different rock group on it this time and a pair of green and white basketball shorts that hugged his knees. The blue shirt brought out the blue in his eyes, which was just totally adorable.

It had been an unusually hot day for late spring, and the streets of Grover Hill were teeming with people outside for the evening. Children played on the sidewalk as their parents watched from the steps of their houses, folks drifted down the street, conversing with their neighbors or making a quick trip to the corner store.

Marisol prayed that no one she knew would see her walking with him. She knew exactly what they would think, especially with El Patio closed and her family having money problems, even though she had lived here all her life and had never been that kind of girl.

"You're crazy, girl," she could hear her friends saying. "A football player from East Oakmont? Don't mess with someone like that. Plenty of cute guys around here. Carlos was looking at you the other day—I think he likes you." Despite all of the danger signals, she felt excited about this little adventure, a much needed distraction from all her troubles.

They ambled along toward The Donut House on Tenth Street, where they ordered lattes and shared a Boston Kreme donut and a double chocolate one and chatted about their classes at school and their after-school activities. Colin told her a little about football, and she mentioned her artwork, an okay subject to share with someone you were just getting to know. You couldn't get into too much trouble talking about art.

"You draw?" Colin asked.

"My mother and I both draw," Marisol said nonchalantly. "I've had drawings displayed in the restaurant my dad worked at and some other places in the neighborhood. I used to make extra money selling them to the customers. I haven't been doing much art lately, though. I've been busy with other things, I guess. School, taking care of my brother so my mom can work, all those things."

"Sounds like you're talented. I've always liked art, but I'm not too good at drawing. You'd probably laugh if you saw some of my drawings," he said wryly. "They look like a little kid did them. I'm better at building things than drawing. I still have ashtrays and other things I made in elementary school. My mom has them displayed on a shelf in the living room."

"I remember those ashtrays. I made one in third grade," she said, and they both laughed.

"Yeah, my mom arranged for me to take pottery classes after school for a few years, but then my dad signed me up for Pop Warner football, and that kind of took over my life. Art doesn't get you a college scholarship. I loved it, though. My mom used to take me to the Wakomah Art Museum. We saw some really cool sculpture exhibits and they had some hands-on classes for kids. One time I made a puppet out of paper maché, and another time I learned how to make soap. I even went to summer camp there once for a week and did pottery every day."

"I went to the Wakomah Art Museum on a class field trip! I haven't been there since then, though. Be really fun to go again," Marisol said, flashing a smile at him. "I think it was about a half-hour ride on the bus."

"Hey, I'm game," he said. "You thinking of, like, studying art in college?"

"Well, the art is just a hobby, something I do for fun. I'd really like to go to medical school someday, maybe do research, work on a cure for cancer or AIDS."

"You must get good grades if you're thinking about that," Colin said. "I have okay grades, not the best, so I'm counting on a football scholarship to get me in somewhere. My dad has really been on me about that. You know how parents can be."

"Yeah, I guess," she said, not wanting to get into that one. She glanced at her watch, which read nine-thirty. She had been so engrossed in the conversation that she hadn't even noticed that the sun had completely disappeared and the street outside the window was enveloped in darkness. Tia Rosa was watching Camilo, and she needed to get home to put him to bed and get them both ready for school in the morning. She tapped on her watch and pushed her chair back. "School tomorrow and everything," she said, tossing him a smile, not wanting him to feel like she was trying to ditch him. "This was fun. Maybe we could do this again sometime."

"I have a better idea," he said. "Ever been to the Central Park Lake in the city? They have these little boats you can rent. We can float around the lake and enjoy the scenery, maybe grab a hot dog and a soda."

Central Park Lake was in Manhattan, a long ride from Oakmont, way out of her comfort zone. She couldn't go on a date like that anyway. Mama was still away, and between school and taking care of Camilo, she had no free time at all for an all-day outing.

"Might be okay, but that's a long trip," she said quietly. "How about if I drop by St. Michael's on Tuesday and we can talk some more, maybe plan something for after finals when school is out. And don't forget the Wakomah Art Museum!"

"Definitely on my list!" he said, grinning again.

His hand grazed her fingers as they walked to the door and she inched a little closer to him, feeling more upbeat than she had been for a while.

Nineteen

They fought valiantly for land reform, but there was so much bloodshed and death that in 1990 the UN stepped in to negotiate a truce between the government and the FMLN in order to stop the death squads, the endless killing. A compromise was signed in 1992 and a ceasefire took effect, but not much changed for the impoverished people in the villages. Seventy-five thousand people died during the war, and one million fled the country.

Mango trees, laurel, madre cacao. Through the bus window, banana and avocado, orange and lemon trees floated by, dreamlike and unreal. An illusion, a spell created by a *bruja*, a witch. Someone he had angered in the past had put a spell on him that brought him back here. A volcano rose up in the distance, a sign that they were in coffee-growing country. Julia would have wanted to be here with him, but the seat next to him was taken by someone else, a stranger.

She would have been excited to see the place he lived in as a child, and would already have been sketching in her notebook. Pictures of the people's faces, the children, the fruit trees with the volcano in the background. Marisol, so much like her mother, would have been drawing, too. This was his country, spectacularly beautiful but full of sadness for him—sadness and beauty, a strange combination. The bus slid to a stop; the doors swung open. He knew where he was; he had not forgotten after all these years. He had walked this road time and time again, from the *choza* to the *finca*, to the marketplace, to the church of Father Rodriguez. He wondered if Father Rodriguez was still there, and Esperanza, the *curandera* who had opened her door to him in the middle of the night, given him medicine for Papi. They had asked for nothing in return, but he might try to find them, offer to help them out in return for all they had done for his family.

The dirt road was soft and dusty under his shoes. He had good shoes now, New York shoes from a New York store, but he could still feel the dirt under his feet. He kicked up a little dust, which left a brown blanket on his New York shoes. Loud squawking from a nearby tree caused him to look up, and he spotted a green parrot sitting on a branch, staring down at him curiously. Verdito, welcoming him back! Verdito had been here all the time, watching over Mama, Ana, and Juanito, waiting for him to return.

"*Hola*, Verdito, I'm back! Do you remember me? Have you been waiting for me all this time?"

The parrot cocked its head and looked sideways at Felipe, blinking a beady black eye, hopping from branch to branch as though something exciting, something special was happening today.

Felipe peered through the trees, looking for the *zacate*, the dried grass on the roofs of the huts in the village, and the wood and bamboo walls of the *chozas*, but there was no sign of them.

No sign of people, either. It was midday; they must be out in the *finca* picking coffee, as they always had.

The river would not have changed, would still be there to greet him after all this time. He approached the place he remembered the river to be, and there it was—his river, the Escondido, quietly rolling along as it always had, oblivious to all the violence and the changes that had happened around it. He stood there mesmerized, watching it silently, listening to the birds, feeling the warmth of the sun, and for a moment a feeling of peace came over him, a serenity he had not felt since he was a child floating on this river. He looked around for the *choza* he had lived in as a child, but there was no sign of wooden huts anywhere; in fact, all the *chozas* seemed to be gone. A flash of metal glinted in the sun as he peered through the trees, and he approached it gingerly, stepping slowly through the grass, stopping behind a tree to look around cautiously for any sign of danger. It was too high up to be a gun—it looked more like the roof of a building or some kind of man-made structure. As Felipe moved closer, he realized that it was a tin shack, and he stared at it curiously, wondering what it was used for. The aroma of food cooking wafted through the air, and it then dawned on him—the wood and bamboo *chozas* of his childhood were gone—replaced by corrugated tin huts, *laminas*, lined up side by side. No sign of *hornillas*, either, the holes in the ground fortified with bamboo that were used for cooking when he was a boy.

Several chickens scratched at the ground in front of the shack, cackling loudly as he approached, then scattering in all directions. The door was open, and he peered in to see if anyone was there. A woman with long gray hair flowing down her back was leaning over a stove, her matchstick arm turning a large spoon in a metal pot. It wasn't Mama, he was sure of that.

"*Hola, Señora!* I'm looking for Señora Sanchez, Maria Elena Sanchez. Do you know which house is hers?"

"And who are you?"

"Felipe, her son."

"*Dios mio!*" The woman turned toward him, the spoon suspended in mid-air, the food left in the pot to cook on its own. She bent down to wipe up a drop of sauce that landed on the floor, then stood up quickly, gaping at him.

"*Dios mio!* Felipe Sanchez?"

"*Si, Señora.*"

"Do you remember me? I'm Lydia, Oscar's wife."

Felipe stood there stunned, as a hazy memory tucked away in a corner of his heart, a dream of some distant past that no longer existed, suddenly came to life in front of him. People long dead, reincarnated and speaking to him.

He stepped through the doorway and moved toward her, toward Oscar's wife, searching, trying to find words. "Lydia."

"Felipito." She put her arms around him, hugged him for a long moment. Strong, safe arms, holding him close, the bones under her threadbare cotton dress as sharp as the rocks in the Escondido, her strength unbowed by the storms that cleaved the earth around her.

"I've been away a long time, Lydia, but I've never forgotten Oscar. He's always been in my heart, a hero to me." He could feel her heart beating against his chest, her courage and Oscar's, coursing through him, filling places where emptiness hid, where the sadness of years lay unmoved by time.

"He's a hero to all of us. I still miss him after all these years."

Felipe stepped back, observing her, searching her face. "Lydia, where can I find my mother?"

Lydia pointed to one of the other tin huts. "She lives over there. She's one of the cooks at the *finca* now."

"When did she come back here, Lydia?" Felipe asked.

"When word came that the UN had started negotiations, many people in the camps started heading back here. She came a little bit later, after the truce was negotiated. We lost so much here, so many people were killed, but El Espino is our home. There was really no place else for her to go."

Felipe watched Lydia stirring the *pollo encebollado*, the chicken stew, the scent of chicken and onions and something else he couldn't quite identify, lemon maybe, suffusing into the room. "And you, Lydia?"

"I never left, Felipito. I stayed to fight with the FMLN—that was what I felt I had to do. If Oscar was here, he would have—" Her voice trailed off, and they were both silent for a moment.

The spoon clinked against the side of the plate as she ladled some chicken stew and a mound of rice onto it, handed it to him. "Taste it, Felipe. Real Salvadoran food, like we had in the old days, before the war."

It was lemon he had smelled, he could taste it now, in the sauce that bathed the chicken and the onions. "Delicious," he said, grinning at her. "It's been a while since I've had anything as good as this. I always knew you had many talents, but I didn't know you were a great cook, too!"

"Thank you for those nice words. I don't have that much to do these days, and it's something I enjoy doing. I raise my own chickens. Did you see them out there? I grow some vegetables, too, around the back."

"I saw the chickens. They gave me dirty looks and yelled at me when I came near them. I think they thought I was going to grab them to make some more chicken stew!"

"They're smart, those chickens, and very opinionated!"

A box of oranges, still green from the tree, a bag of rice, a brown burlap sack of *masa*, cornmeal, lay in the corner, stacked against the drab metal wall of the shack.

"Lydia, do my sister and brother, Ana and Juanito, still live here?"

"Ana is married with her own family. The little Ana you remember has four children, Felipe. Juanito is a handsome young man, always flirting with the girls, but he works hard, too."

Little Ana and Baby Juanito, his brother and sister, were grown now. He wondered what they looked like, and whether so many years apart would make them strangers, as unfamiliar to him as people he might meet on a bus or in a grocery store. Juanito was just an infant when he left and would have no memory of him at all.

"And you, Felipe? Why did you come back here? We thought you'd be a rich American by now."

"Did you know Miguel, Lydia? My mother's brother?"

"Ah, yes—he was quite a bit older than I was, and then he disappeared when he was still a teenager. He went to the United States, I heard. I was just a child, but that's what people said."

"He owns, well, owned a café in New York, and I've been working there with him all these years. A small place, not fancy, but we had plans—"

"Do you have a family? Children of your own?" Lydia asked.

"I do—I have a beautiful wife and three children—two boys and a girl. I'm missing them very much, and they are always on my mind."

"So, why—"

"I didn't have citizenship papers, Lydia, and they made it so hard to get them. Julia and I were trying, but because I first came into the country, well, you know, across the desert, getting papers was pretty close to impossible. They arrested me on some fake charges and then deported me, so here I am."

"Does your Mama know you're here, Felipe?"

"No. I thought so many times over the years about how I could visit, but this was not how I planned it." He drifted toward the door, gazing out at the small tin huts that had become the village of El Espino. "Why is it so quiet here? Where is everyone? Picking coffee on the *finca*?"

"No, they've cut down coffee production because prices are low and they're selling the land to build developments. Do you remember how many people used to work on the *finca*? Thousands. Now they only have enough work for about three hundred. Most people work in San Salvador now, in the textile factories or the restaurants. Your mama works in Don Cristobal's kitchen, so they have kept her."

"And the *guardia*? Do they still patrol—"

"You don't need to worry about that, Felipito. When they negotiated the truce, the government dismantled the death squads and replaced them with the National Police. You won't find the *guardias* patrolling the villages or the *fincas* with guns the way they used to."

Lydia pointed to one of the *laminas* a few feet away. "That's your

Mama's house, over there. Go there, rest, wait for her there. She'll be back about seven o'clock. Don't go to the *finca*. She will be so excited to see you, she won't be able to work, and if she angers Don Cristobal, she may not be shot the way they did during the war, but she could be fired on the spot."

The heat in Mama's tin shack was stifling, one large room with clothes hung on a piece of rope strung from wall to wall, a small table holding a *tecomate* to carry water, the bags of rice and beans and the sack of *masa* underneath. The straw mats were gone, and in their place was a bed with a metal frame and pillows, and two chairs.

The bright afternoon sun stopped at the door, leaving the room with only a tiny amount of light coming from a small window. Felipe lay down on the bed to wait for Mama, but the darkness and the heat made his eyes close, and he drifted off into a dream. Loud voices yelling, strange men threatening him and waving machetes. He could hear the voices; they were in the room with him, coming toward him, grabbing him, throwing something wet on him.

A woman's voice now, as he opened his eyes and discovered a short, rotund woman, her black hair streaked with gray and pulled back in a bun, standing over him. Something wet was on his face; it was Mama, shaking him, calling out his name, her tears wetting his face.

She had survived it all—the death of Papa, the refugee camp, sending her child away to a strange land. It showed in her face, a roadmap of all she had endured, but she was still Mama. Next to her was a grinning young man and a beautiful woman with a baby in a *covita* around her shoulders. Juanito and Ana, his brother and sister, his family, grabbing him, shaking his hand, laughing, crying.

Voices floated into the room, the sing-song of children's voices, playing *escondolero*, hide-and-seek, as he had so many lifetimes ago, accompanied by the rhythmic hooting of a bird that sounded like a *torogoz*.

"You must be hungry after your long trip, *mijo*," Mama said, stroking his hair with her hand the way she did when he was a little boy. "There's food outside. Let me get you something. Lydia made it—I think it's *pollo encebollado.* She brought it over for us."

Felipe didn't move, just stood there watching Mama in amazement. "Mama, you look great—beautiful as ever," he responded. "I saw Lydia when I first came here, and she told me you're working at the *finca* in the kitchen. Are they treating you okay over there?"

"Well, there are no *guardias* with guns anymore, but they're still mean. You better not be late or talk back to them, because, you know, they'll fire you just like that. I'm glad to have the job, though. I'm too old to go to San Salvador to work in a clothing factory."

"Did you come on an airplane?" Juanito asked, still smiling. "I've never been on a plane. Maybe when you go back you can take me with you. Mama said you were working in a restaurant. Do you think they would have some work for me there?"

Lydia stuck her head in the door. "Felipe, the whole village is here to see you. Are you going to stay in here the whole day? We have some good food and some old friends who want to see you, too."

"Sure, sure—look, we'll talk later, Juanito—I'll tell you all the whole story—"

Juanito and Ana and Mama laughed then.

"Juanito?" Ana said, looking amused. She gave her brother a small push. "Baby Juanito, Baby Juanito—I'm going to call you Baby Juanito now," she said, chuckling.

"He's Juan now—call him Juan, *mijo*," Mama said seriously.

Word of his arrival had spread through the village, and several people pushed into the tiny room, wanting to see him, to hear his voice, peppering him with questions, but Mama shooed them outside, where Lydia had placed her pot of food on a wooden table. Felipe wanted to be alone with Mama, to ask her about that day in Honduras, but that would have to wait.

It seemed as though the entire village had gathered, waiting patiently for him outside, so he put aside his wish to be alone with Mama and stepped through the doorway to greet them.

Mama had a few chickens, too, now, and a little place to grow some food. Tomatoes and green shoots of onions reached for the sun beside the ridges and furrows of the corrugated tin wall of the *lamina*, and the chickens bobbed their heads up and down as if to nod their approval and offer a hello.

He had been right about the bird, it was a *torogoz* he had heard, the national bird of his country, clutching a branch on a lemon tree, a spot of green and orange among the leaves, a bright blue stripe above his eye and a long blue tail peeking out behind the branch.

The crowd was silent as they listened, enraptured, to the story of his life in New York, his deportation, and then when he had finished, they shared their own stories with him.

"So many people died during the war, Felipe, or disappeared never to be seen again. Your mama did the right thing, sending you to the United States. The *guardia* would have shot you for sure," said an older man with a bald head and a face creased with wrinkles. There was something familiar about him, and Felipe stared at him, trying to place him. The nose—the slightly crooked nose—Rolando—it was Rolando—one of the men who worked with him at the *finca*, ate lunch on the grass with Papa and Oscar. "I lost both my sons," Rolando said quietly. "Now I beat myself because I didn't send them away from here, too."

"Ernesto and Rafael. Where are they now?" Felipe asked. He could picture the three of them playing *escondolero* and *mica* together, a game of tag, hiding behind the trees, shouting with children's glee when they found someone, laughing and running away when they tagged them. Ernesto was Felipe's best friend, Lydia and Oscar's oldest son.

A hush fell over the crowd, now silent except for the sound of people breathing and shuffling their feet in the dirt.

"Ernesto was very brave, Felipe," Lydia answered softly after a long pause. "He died in a battle in Chalatenango fighting the 4th Army brigade at the garrison at El Paraiso. Rafael—the *guardia* came one night and took him away and no one ever heard from him again."

Felipe felt as though his heart would shatter into little pieces, and he struggled to maintain his composure as the realization of what his mother had done crystallized in his mind in a way it never had before. During the twenty years he had been away, he had often see-sawed between sadness and anger, never quite understanding why she hadn't given him the chance to be the man of the family, to prove that he could survive, or even be a hero, save his family, save other people. He understood it completely now—the torment of a mother having to make such a choice. She could keep her child with her, knowing that he would be in constant danger, living every moment under the threat of death, or send him away, facing the possibility of never seeing him again. A mother's hope—that maybe he would be one of the survivors. He wondered what he would do in that situation, what Julia would do, if they had to make a choice like that.

"Your son is very handsome, Maria Elena," one of the women said brightly, breaking the tension.

Mama was appraising him, examining his face, his clothes, the child she had last seen at thirteen. "Very handsome, like his papa."

"There are some pretty women around here, Felipe," one of the men added, giving him an impish grin.

Lydia glared at him. "He has a wife and three children in the United States. He needs to go back and take care of them."

"They're very far away, and he may never see them again. People have needs, Lydia. Guillermo's daughter is looking for a husband. She's a beautiful girl."

Felipe thought about Julia, what it must be like for her raising the children alone, supporting them by herself. He couldn't imagine being with another woman, but returning to the United States was so impossible that it was just a hopeless fantasy. The best he could do would be to get a job here and find a way to send money every month.

Lydia understood, and put her hand on his shoulder. "Something sweet for you, Felipito," she said, handing him a piece of mango. The honeyed taste of a mango, a tortilla filled with beans and rice. Pupusas, tamales, chicharrones. The mango juice was dripping from his fingers, running down his throat, coating his lips, and the air was fragrant with the perfume of orange and lemon trees. The tastes and smells of El Salvador, his country. Mama just stood there, watching him eat the mango. Savoring him while he savored the mango.

Twenty

Frank had been hoping to have the next SIM meeting in the comfort of his own living room, but Bonnie had made a big scene about it—said she wouldn't have a meeting like that under her roof—so here they were, stuck in the crummy back room of the Steak 'n Brew again, pretending they were having a poker game. Business hadn't been great lately, and management wouldn't spend a bent penny to fix the place up a little, even if it would help bring in more customers. The faded beige paint on the walls made the room look shabby, and there was a dark stain on the ceiling where water had once dripped from a broken pipe.

That new regional manager, Kevin Blasington, would probably have a cow if he knew why they were meeting here tonight. Frank had told him the restaurant pulled in some extra money letting cops use the back room after hours for a card game every Friday night. If he knew the real reason, what they were really planning, he would probably fire

Frank on the spot. There had to be something wrong with that. That asshole could fire him anytime, but Frank couldn't say a word back to him, couldn't disagree or make a complaint about anything. He could get a few other people canned, though, like the guys in that little hole in the wall restaurant on Fourth Street. Bradley and Dawson had done a hell of a job getting the health department to close the whole damn place down. Frank had even heard that one of them was kicked out of the country, sent back to Mexico, or wherever the hell he came from.

At the moment, the place was silent except for the nasal drone of a sportscaster on the big flat-screen TV on the wall and the thump of beer glasses being plunked down on the table. It was the bottom of the eighth inning, and the Yankees were leading the Red Sox, 8-5. The group sat mesmerized as the second baseman sauntered up to the plate, displaying the blue and white pinstripes of the New York Yankees for the whole world to see. Frank's thoughts drifted to Colin flying across the goal line, winning the game for Oakmont High. Someday Colin would wear an NFL jersey with the name Sullivan in big letters on the back, flashing across the TV screen for millions to admire. Sullivan—the greatest wide receiver ever, they would say. Maybe not the Giants right away, maybe he would start on another team first, but he'd make a top team eventually. Frank picked up the remote and muted the sound.

"Hey, whatcha doin'?" Mike Torelli said. "We're watching the game!"

"You can still see it—I'm just turning off the sound. We gotta get down to business, bud. Anyway, you were chewing too loud, so no more TV for you until you learn to eat politely."

Roberta, Mike's new wife, put her hand over her mouth to stifle a giggle. "Maybe he'll listen to you. He don't listen when I tell him."

Roberta was Mike's third wife, but they had only been married six months and were still laughing and teasing each other. It had been a long time since he and Bonnie had laughed and joked like that, and Frank winced, feeling a little down for a moment. He shook himself, remembering his marine training—chin up, chest out, shoulders back. When things get tough, just keep going. He rapped loudly on the table several times, and the chit-chat stopped, a roomful of eyes on him now.

"We have a lot of new folks here tonight—welcome, welcome— you came to the right place because this is the group that's gonna make things happen!" There were even a few women now, wives or girlfriends of the cops, or mothers who didn't like all the riffraff in the schools these days. "You just wanna sit around bitching, this ain't the right group for you. You really wanna clean up Oakmont, stick with us, because we're doin' it," he said, picking up some papers from the table and waving them in the air.

Greg Bradley leaned back in his chair, his hands clasped behind his head. "Yeah, well how about you stop blabbering and let's get down to it," Bradley said, only half-joking. You could never really tell with Bradley. He could be a jerk sometimes, always throwing his weight around, taking over the spotlight, but when you needed someone to take care of business, he was the man, so Frank had to give him some slack, let him show what a big guy he was for a few minutes. The world was full of jerks and you had to put up with them. Not much you could do when the jerk was on your side.

"Got a few new ideas to share with you tonight, things I think you'll be excited about," Frank declared, trying to sound authoritative. "You guys have been doing a great job with the picketing at the mall, but Bradley here came up with a suggestion to make us even more effective, and I want to run it by you," he continued. It may have been Bradley's idea, but this was his show. "See, our buddies here can arrest the guys by the fence from here to kingdom come, but new ones keep showing up. So how about we keep up the protests at the mall, but start squeezing the contractors, too, hitting 'em where it really hurts—"

Bradley jumped in, his voice booming across the room. "Yeah, we've had a couple of our teenagers up at the mall, paid 'em a few bucks to jot down the license plate numbers of the contractors who are picking up illegals."

"We stop the trucks from coming in, there won't be any reason for day laborers to show up. No work, no illegals, right?" Mike Torelli threw in.

"You got it, buddy. We're goin' after 'em," Bradley said. "I ran a motor vehicle check on the license numbers and got addresses. We're gonna mess them up good!" he said, smacking his fist against his palm.

A roar of approval swept across the room, along with scattered clapping that slowly picked up steam until it exploded into earsplitting applause. Beer glasses clanged on the table, bottles waved in the air, hands exchanged high fives and fist bumps.

The plan was to target the contractors at their own homes each Saturday, when more of their neighbors would be around to watch the action, to witness their humiliation. One of the cops knew a reporter, so there might even be a story in the local paper or on the six o'clock news. The suckers would never live that down.

The following Monday was one of Frank's days off, but he hadn't slept well and had awakened around four o'clock in the morning, tossed and turned for a while, unable to get back to sleep. He got up and puttered around the kitchen a little, made a cup of coffee and chewed on a donut, then decided that he might as well do something useful, like checking out one of the addresses on Bradley's list to make sure they had the right guy, play a little cat and mouse with him before they pulled out the big guns on Saturday. He could nap later this afternoon, after he had taken care of some business for SIM.

Frank sat behind the wheel of the white Ford van, let it idle for a while, then turned off the engine. Sitting in his van in the dark at six o'clock in the morning was not how he usually preferred to spend his days off, but if he wanted to catch the guy red-handed as he picked up illegals, he needed to start early. He turned on the radio to catch the sports news. The Yankees had won yesterday's game, too—nothing surprising there.

The sportscaster gave a quick traffic and weather update and the seven o'clock news report; a whole hour had passed without any sign of the contractor. The pre-dawn sky was beginning to lighten, and he could now make out the house and the area around it more clearly.

His Marine Corps training was coming in handy these days. Always scope out the place, know the terrain and the layout of the environment before approaching the enemy.

The house was a ranch style house like his, a little smaller, maybe a two-bedroom, with a scrappy little lawn in the front with some empty boxes sitting on it. A plant on the front steps looked like it needed to be watered, and there were several old newspapers pushed to the side, obviously never been picked up. A sign on the lawn said *For Rent,* and more empty boxes were piled up by the curb, like they were put there for the sanitation truck to pick up. The fellow must have just moved in. It didn't look like he was doing well at all, and Frank guessed he wasn't making a ton of money if he was hiring illegals. Too bad, so sad. The guy should get himself a real job.

An old black pickup truck with a large dent on the passenger side door and two ladders sticking out of the back sat idly in the driveway. Frank checked the license plate against the number the kid had written down. They matched, and Bradley's motor vehicle search had come up with 1246

Neville, this address. He was definitely in the right place. Bradley's search had turned up addresses, but he hadn't bothered to list any of their names, so Frank had no idea who the guy was or who lived in the house.

The waiting made Frank a little drowsy, so he leaned back in the seat and closed his eyes for a minute, but sat up quickly when he heard a door slam, startled for a moment. This was it! The show was about to begin! The front door closed and opened again, as a man wearing paint-spattered overalls and a Mets baseball cap struggled with a tool box that didn't want to go through the doorway. Frank's heart was racing, and he felt fired up now, like one of those guys who wait hours to catch a fish, and finally get a tug on the line! He had really only gone fishing once, with a couple of waiters from the restaurant, and he hadn't liked it much, sitting there for hours just to catch a stupid fish. He could've gone to the grocery store and bought one, for god's sake. This was different—this was about catching people—people who deserved to be caught and have their butts handed to them. He wasn't able to make out the man's face from where he sat, but something seemed familiar, although he couldn't quite place it. Maybe the guy had been a customer at Steak 'n Brew, or he'd seen him around town somewhere.

A stream of exhaust drifted out of the tailpipe as the truck backed slowly out of the driveway and puttered down the street. Frank waited until the truck arrived at the first intersection before he pulled away from the curb, trailing about a half a block behind him. The driver continued on Neville for a few blocks, then made a right turn and headed toward Barrington, where he rolled into a gas station. Frank sat idling at the curb, impatient for him to get moving, for the real stuff to happen. He hoped the jerk wasn't planning to spend the morning doing errands. That would be a royal pain, following him all over Oakmont as he picked up groceries and stopped at the cleaners.

The guy was filling up his car with gas now, and Frank felt antsy as he waited for him to stick the hose back on the gas pump and get into the damn truck. Instead, the man locked the car door and trotted toward the convenience store. Five minutes, then ten passed, and he reappeared with a coffee container in one hand, keys swinging loosely from the other.

After what seemed to Frank like hours, the truck began moving again, turning left at the next corner, definitely going in the right direction to get to the mall. He was exhilarated, laughing to himself as he trailed along behind him, keeping his eye on the license plate. There were lots of black pickup trucks out there, and he wouldn't want to end up behind the wrong one.

Frank hit the button on the radio and music filled the van—some seventies or eighties rock. He moved his shoulders to the beat, belting out the song at the top of his lungs, even though he didn't know a lot of the words. He may as well enjoy this party all the way. The dude had no clue he was being followed, and what was coming later would really blow his mind.

Greg Bradley might be a pain sometimes, but he definitely knew his stuff. Everything he had suggested so far had worked. The black truck was taking the road that led right to the mall, approaching the parking lot now, cruising up the fire lane toward the fence. The driver honked, and two young guys hopped in the back of the truck, waving to the others still leaning on the fence. Grinning, like good things were happening for them. Not for long, boys.

The rest of the week dragged by slowly at Steak 'n Brew. Frank tried to keep his mind on the job but was often distracted, preoccupied with thoughts of the big event coming up this weekend. Saturday finally arrived—their first protest at a contractor's house—his chance to take charge, show what a good leader he was. The Neville Street guy, the one that Frank followed, was going to get it today, and Frank couldn't wait. Excitement was building as cars began cruising up and down the street, making sure they had the right block before they pulled into a parking space. Frank had the important stuff in his van—extra signs, buckets of paint, a bullhorn—so he had arrived early and taken the parking space right in front of the house.

Familiar faces were trotting up the street, forming a circle on the sidewalk in front of the house. Ed Wilhelm, a tall, skinny fellow who had shown up for the first time last week, stopped by Frank's van to chat for a minute.

"Great idea you got here," Ed said. "'Course I never understood why the hell those people wanna come here in the first place, crawlin'

225

through the desert and everything. Let 'em go back to where they came from, get jobs there, that's what I always say. And hell yeah—hittin' the guys who are giving them the work—hey, that's the way to go. Anything you need, bro, just ask. I'm here to help," he said, giving Frank a wink.

Frank leaned into the van and pulled out the bullhorn. "Here, this is your chance to tell the asshole exactly what you think. Just press this button and shoot. When you get tired or your voice starts to give out, let me know and I'll get somebody else."

"Hey, I'm up for it. All I need now is a band to back me up!"

Ed picked up the bullhorn, pressed the button. "Stop hiring illegals!" Ed's voice boomed through the bullhorn.

"Stop hiring illegals!" the crowd roared back.

"How's that? Is that cool?" Ed whispered to Frank out of the side of his mouth.

"Perfect," Frank responded. "I've got a few musicians in mind already for the band," he laughed, giving Ed a tap on the arm.

The black pickup truck was parked in the driveway, the two scuffed wooden ladders lying in the back, along with several cans of paint, a tarp, and pieces of sheetrock. Everyone in the SIM crowd knew the guy was guilty as hell—he wasn't even trying to hide it, keeping his stuff out there in full view for anybody to see. The protesters surged toward the truck, kicking the tires, then the doors. A bucket of paint flew through the air, leaving red streaks dripping down the windshield, then more paint—green this time—plastered the back window. No truck, no work. Three pairs of hands pulled the ladders off the truck, threw them on the lawn and poured motor oil all over them. He won't use those again either. He would slip and break his neck if he tried.

Two faces appeared in the doorway and stared at the commotion in front of their house.

Don't even try to call the cops, Frank thought, chuckling to himself. They're already here. The man, definitely the one he had followed, gaped stupidly at the crowd, clearly confused about what was happening, while a woman stood beside him clutching his arm, her eyes wide, her mouth dropping open with shock and horror.

The group was chanting in perfect harmony along with Ed, parading in formation as they waved their signs in the air, and several onlookers from the neighborhood had already gathered to watch the show. *Don't hire illegals! Lawbreakers get out of Oakmont! We understand English! Do you?* the signs read. That should embarrass the hell out of them, Frank thought gleefully. The woman, who was probably the guy's wife, was scanning the faces in the crowd now, most likely looking to see if she could identify anyone for the police when they came.

Chances were good she would turn to her husband, blame it all on him. That was one way to stop the contractors—sic their wives on them. No woman wanted people parading around in front of her house because of some dumb thing her husband did.

The woman in the doorway continued to survey the protestors, then stopped short, almost did a double-take when she caught sight of Frank standing next to his van, handing out signs.

Their eyes met, and Frank felt the blood drain from his face. The guy hadn't been around much, maybe he had met him once, but he definitely recognized the wife now. He glanced at the *For Rent* sign on the lawn, wondering what the hell was going on. Damn it—no one had mentioned a word to him about this.

Twenty-one

A day didn't pass without Marisol worrying about Papi. Mama had returned from Arizona, but her attempt to visit him had been futile, and she had returned sick and with bad news. Deported to El Salvador, they had told Mama at the jail, but nobody knew exactly where he was or what had happened to him, or even whether he was still alive.

The only good news in Marisol's life was that the new guy she had met at St. Michael's was really sweet, and she was totally buzzed about seeing him again. They had gotten together several times after his Tuesday shift, sitting in Washington Park talking, watching the pick-up basketball games, the kids playing in the last hours of daylight. Last week they walked in a different direction and found a new café, one that had a live jazz band in the evenings.

"So after school is out, let's go somewhere special," he had said. "Which is it? Central Park or an art museum?"

She was delighted with his interest in art, something that connected them, but also wanted to show him she was cooperative and easygoing, so she agreed to go to Central Park with him the first weekend after finals. They decided that since the weather was so nice this time of year, this was a good time to do outdoor stuff, maybe save the art museums for cooler weather.

In the meantime, Mama had gotten some more housecleaning work, but then came down with a virus that went to her chest, and Marisol awoke one night to explosive coughing emanating from the foldout couch in the living room. She scrambled out of bed, tiptoeing so as not to wake Camilo and Ricky sleeping on cots across the room.

Mama lay shivering under the white cotton blanket, her face ashen, a whistling sound coming from her chest as she struggled to draw each breath. Marisol bent over to touch her forehead and noted the hollows underneath her eyes and the grayness of her skin as her palm brushed Mama's brow, burning with fever.

"Mama," Marisol whispered. "Mama, you need a doctor." She scooted into the bathroom, pulled a bottle of red cough medicine from the cabinet. The bottle was sticky and about half-full; must have been Camilo's when he was sick. She tipped the bottle and a stream of cherry-flavored liquid dripped onto the spoon. "Take this, Mama," she insisted, and held the spoon to her lips, dribbled it into her mouth. "It'll help the cough, but you need more than cough medicine. When the market opens in the morning, I'll run down and call. Do we have insurance, Mama? Do you have an insurance card?"

Mama bolted upright, doubled over as her narrow frame convulsed from the force of the cough. "Get Papi. Maybe he's downstairs," she mumbled feverishly when the coughing had subsided. "He would—," and she closed her eyes, unable to finish, as tears coursed down her cheeks, ran over her lips, and left wet marks on the pillow. "Get Tia Rosa," she said weakly. "She'll help us."

"Tia Rosa and Tio Miguel are away, Mama. They went to New Jersey to visit her family, but I'm here. I'm right here next to you and I'm not leaving. I'm going to get you to a doctor, Mama."

The wood floor creaked behind her, and she turned to see Camilo's small frame huddled in the doorway, his Batman pajamas rumpled, his doleful eyes riveted on Mama.

"Mama is sick, but she's going to get better, Camilo. I'm going to take good care of her.

"Go back to bed. You have school tomorrow," Marisol said gently.

Camilo ignored her request and plodded into the room, hovering over the couch.

"The emergency room at Westchester General, you know, where we always go," Mama whispered, closing her eyes as though just having to move her lips exhausted her. "Six, number six bus."

The bus didn't run at this hour of the night, and they no longer had a phone to call a taxi or an ambulance, so Marisol pulled a chair over to the couch for herself and piled some blankets on the floor for Camilo, who remained there guarding Mama until his eyes began to close and he dozed off. Marisol hunkered down in the chair with a blanket and sat there all night, watching over Mama, listening for any change in her labored breathing. When she found herself getting sleepy, she stared out the window, focusing on the neon sign across the street as it blinked on and off, on and off, painting eerie shadows on the floor and the wall, on the foldout couch where Mama slept. In the morning she slipped out of the apartment and rushed down the street, searching for an open store, someplace to call for help. The grocery store, El Latino Mercado, opened at seven; Alfredo would let her use his phone.

The ambulance shrieked as it raced through the early morning traffic, rushing Mama to the emergency room, a sorrowful wail ushering in the new day.

A week later, Julia lay on the couch, resting her head on a pillow, staring aimlessly out the window. "Pneumonia," the doctor in the emergency room had said and sent her home with medicine.

Marisol leaned over the stove in the alcove that served as a kitchen, stirring chicken soup in a small aluminum saucepan, then measuring out a cup of rice and dumping it into a pot of boiling water. "Where do you think Papi is, Mama?"

"We know where he is—he's in El Salvador. That's what they told me in Arizona. Why are you asking me this?" She leaned back against the pillow, her eyes closed, and sighed wearily. "I've told you everything I know. There's no point in going over it again and again."

"How do we know they told you the truth? He could still be in Arizona, lying in a prison cell."

Marisol ladled some hot soup into a cup, carried it gingerly to the small table next to the couch, set it down next to Mama. "I just don't understand why they arrested him. They couldn't have thought he was dealing drugs. Why not the other day laborers?"

"They did arrest the others. They were turned over to the ICE, too, but Papi was the one that was picked out of the lineup. And Tio Miguel is a citizen—"

"A citizen? How did he—"

"A long time ago, about forty—no, more like forty-five years ago, when he was a very young man, not much older than you, Miguel left El Salvador and went to Mexico with another brother, Leonardo," she said, taking a small sip of soup. "They worked on a *finca* there for a few years and were recruited by an American company looking for workers to pick cotton in Texas. The bracero program, it was called then. It was seasonal work, so they went back to Mexico at the end of each season but were given passes to commute back and forth across the border to work when the next growing season began."

Marisol was pleased to see that Mama was hardly coughing at all anymore, and the warm soup seemed to be picking up her mood.

"He was a good worker," Mama continued, "so his employer arranged for him to get a residence permit, which allowed him to get a green card and apply for citizenship. He returned to El Salvador a few times, long before the war began, told the family about the program and tried to convince them to join him, but they thought things might get better, so they stayed. When the bracero program ended in 1964, Miguel and Leonardo followed the migrant circuit, working on farms across the United States. They ended up on a dairy farm in New York, then worked at a café here in Oakmont. All this time they were saving money, so they were able to buy the café when the owner retired. Leonardo married and returned to Texas, but Miguel stayed to run the business. He's a naturalized citizen, has the same legal rights as any other citizen, rights Papi doesn't have. Things are much more difficult now; it's so much harder to become a citizen than it used to be."

"So if Papi had come here earlier, things would have been really different for him," Marisol said sadly.

Mama sat up straight, her eyes focused intently on Marisol. "I guess you're old enough to know the truth now. Then maybe you'll stop asking me the same questions over and over again. Listen—your Papi came here by crossing the desert on foot—he didn't go through customs or anything like that—so he has no rights under U.S. law. You know, illegal, they call it. Undocumented, which means he has no papers to prove he belongs here."

"Being here twenty years and having a family and a business doesn't count for anything?" Marisol asked.

"No, it doesn't," Mama said bitterly. "But it's much more complicated than that. If he hadn't been arrested and charged with a crime, he could have gone back to El Salvador and spent ten or fifteen years trying to get some kind of a visa to enter the U.S. I don't really know how that works—I only know that it's a long shot, and the chances are it would have never happened, but it's possible. But since he was deported for criminal reasons, he can never, never return to the U.S. unless the charges are dropped."

"But why, Mama? Why did they pick Papi out of the lineup? He would never deal drugs." Marisol paced the tiny room, beating an invisible path from the foldout couch to the window to the table and back to the couch. "We need to find out what happened, Mama. We have to try to clear his name, so that, like you said, there's some tiny possibility he could try to come home. There must be something we can do, someone we can contact."

"I know, *mija*. Of course I want to help him, but you have to know that we tried so hard to get him citizenship—really, we tried for years, but it was just impossible. Now that he's not even in the country anymore, I don't know who could help us."

"But I've heard that if you are married to a citizen, they can sponsor you."

Julia turned her head on the pillow, her eyes wide open now. "No, it's the undocumented thing, Marisol. If you came into this country without legal papers, your spouse can't sponsor you, even if they are an American citizen, born and raised in the United States, like me. I called Immigration, I even went down there and spoke to someone in person. I got a lot of information I really didn't want to hear. You were little then, too young to understand any of this, but I guess, well, you're old enough now and this is as good a time as any. You just wouldn't believe what they told me. It made me so upset that I didn't even want to tell your father what they said."

Marisol stopped pacing and sank down on the couch next to Mama, staring at her. "I do want to hear it, Mama, but you're still sick. I'm sorry I brought it up now when you need to be resting. I can hear it another time—"

"It's okay. All I do is lie here all day. I may as well do something useful with my time. They told me that there is something called the Green Card Lottery, also called the Diversity Immigrant Visa, which makes permanent resident visas available to immigrants, but—get this— it's only available to people from countries with low immigration rates to the United States. People born in any country that sent more than fifty thousand immigrants to the U.S. in the past five years are not eligible to receive a diversity visa. And guess what countries those are?"

"Oh my god! He's not eligible for it because he came from El Salvador?"

Mama closed her eyes and leaned back. "El Salvador, Mexico, Guatemala—sixteen other countries, which I bet you could figure out yourself."

"There were no other options, Mama?"

"His only other option would be to return to El Salvador and go through the immigration process there, which, like I've already told you, could have taken ten, twenty years, and even then he might not be approved. If he was sponsored by an employer, there would still be a ten-year bar to his entering the country due to his previously undocumented status. During that time, the employer would have to keep the job open for him. That's really a joke, isn't it—can you imagine anything like that ever happening?" she said sarcastically.

Marisol rose from the couch and began pacing the room again, lost in thought. "What are we going to do, Mama? Nothing? We can't just do nothing. We have to try to help him."

"Marisol, do you really think I'm not concerned, that I don't worry about Papi every day? I went all the way to Arizona on the damn bus to help him and got nowhere. I am just as upset about it as you are, but the whole immigration thing is, well, the whole thing is very complicated, way over our heads. No one seems to be able to do anything about it, not even Congress."

"I'm not trying to solve the whole immigration thing. I just want to help Papi!" Marisol pleaded. "Please, Mama—can't we at least—"

"I think I've already explained it to you, so now you can stop bugging me with this," Mama said, her face contorted in an angry frown. "If something can be done, Papi will have to figure it out. I told you that I've tried everything, and nothing worked. I'm out of ideas, and I have a family to support, so I need to spend my time getting a regular job right now."

"Well, here's an idea that maybe you haven't tried. I spoke to my guidance counselor at school, Ms. Torres, and she told me about Legal Aid, that they give free legal advice. We looked up the address on her computer, so why don't we at least go there and try to see if they can help us?"

"What are you talking about?" Mama snapped irritably. "Legal Aid helps people with small things that happen in their life, like if their employer didn't pay them, or something like that. This is way out of their league, too."

The grating bark of Mama's cough had eased some, but her voice was still hoarse, her usually bright eyes hooded and dull, as she raised herself up on one elbow. "You have a future, you're going places in this world. I don't want you to ruin your life worrying about this. I know you love Papi, and you're just trying to help, but this is way, way over your head. Believe me, if I get some useful information, you'll be the first to know. Do you understand me, Marisol?" she said sternly, giving Marisol her sizzling *don't you dare* look. "You have been so wonderful during all this, I can't thank you enough, but now that I'm back, you need to go back to being a teenager and finish school. That's your job right now. I'll take care of the family."

Julia picked up the pill bottle from the small nightstand next to the couch, slid back down and pulled the blanket up to her neck. The remains of the cup of soup, a box of tissues, and a glass of water cluttered the nightstand and the room had a rancid smell, needed the windows opened to let out the odor of uneaten food and feverish breath. A red and white pill fell into her hand and she raised the water glass to her mouth with unsteady hands.

"What kind of places am I going, Mama? The kind of places where they can do this and get away with it? I don't want to go to those places and I couldn't live with myself if I didn't try to help Papi." She picked up the cup of soup, handed it to Julia. "Aren't you going to finish the soup?"

Julia rose to a vertical position, wrapped her fingers around the cup and held them there for a moment, its warmth soothing her as she lifted it to her lips, sniffed it, took a small taste.

"You know, this doesn't taste like the soup we usually get. What brand is this?"

Marisol hesitated, but had no quick answer ready. Better to tell the truth and take the consequences. "I got it at St. Michael's. They serve lunch and dinner there. The food is pretty good."

"St. Michael's? The free food kitchen? Where homeless people eat? We're not homeless, and we don't need handouts." She set the cup down on the nightstand with a thud and pointed to her purse. "Take a few dollars, go to the store and ask Alfredo for two cans of chicken noodle soup. We don't beg, Marisol."

"Mama, I was just trying to save money so we don't get evicted. Then we really won't have a choice." She knew she shouldn't be fighting with Mama, when Mama was so sick. She tried to apologize but the words were silenced by an ocean of tears that welled up inside her.

"You have choices and opportunities that your father and I didn't have. Keep your eye on that medical school, so you can really help people. You have the touch, I can see it, even the way you are taking care of me right now. Don't take a chance on losing it all. We'll manage somehow."

Julia turned away and buried her face in the pillow, her shoulders shaking. Marisol sat down on the couch next to her and pulled her close. Her blouse, the pretty one she had worn to meet Colin, was rumpled and creased now, as she held Mama tight, the blue pillowcase damp with their shared sorrow.

Twenty-two

Felipe's childhood village hadn't changed much in twenty years, but San Salvador was a whole new world. The city now sported cafés, restaurants, and art galleries designed for tourists, and on the outskirts, the edges of town, textile factories loomed menacingly—huge compounds with prison-like walls, surrounded by barbed wire. Rolando's wife worked in one and had tried to help Felipe get a job, but most of the jobs were for women, sewing clothes destined for the U.S. and Europe, and the pay was low. Five dollars a day, eleven or twelve tedious hours standing in front of a machine, without breaks or time to eat. He wondered if Julia was wearing clothes made in one of those places, if his children were. He was able to land some hours bussing tables in a restaurant, a fancy place frequented by tourists, and when a customer found out he spoke some English, she suggested he might also find some work with one of the tour companies.

The pay was still low and the hours long, but at least he was earning a little money. The tour bus meandered around the city, allowing the tourists to observe daily life as it went on in San Salvador, then took them out to the countryside to take in the lush forests and the volcanoes, or to a *finca* to learn about coffee growing, just as the sign in the airport had said.

"Just describe how the coffee is picked and processed," the supervisor had said sternly. "They don't need to hear your opinion about it—that's not your job. You start telling stories and you won't have a job here or anywhere else."

The months went by quickly; six, seven, then eight months passed as he worked both jobs; tour guide during the day, bussing tables at night, which allowed him to give some money to Mama and put some away for himself. The work kept him busy, but watching families enjoying their vacations tormented him, filling him with sadness when he was supposed to be smiling and happy for the customers. Julia couldn't be by his side, but she never left his mind, and he brooded constantly about her—how she was feeling, how she was managing to support the family, whether she had moved on, found a boyfriend who could help her out, give her the love he couldn't. And his kids—they were growing up without him, without a Papi to have fun with, to help them through difficult times in life, to celebrate the good things. Marisol would be graduating from high school soon, and he wouldn't be there to let her know how proud he was of her. Ricky's graduation would be coming up in a few years, too, and he wondered how he was doing in school. He wasn't as motivated to succeed as Marisol was, and had always been more interested in sports, parties, and his friends. And Camilo had been so young when he left—it must not have been easy to explain to him why his Papi had just vanished and never came to see him, never called. Julia had a tough job, raising three kids alone, trying to keep them on track. The frustration of not being able to reach out to them, to touch them, to provide the help they needed, kept him awake for hours at night, leaving him exhausted in the morning, plagued by stomachaches and headaches during the day. He stumbled through the days, praying that he would make it through his shift without any big mistakes. A few times he stopped off at one of the bars after work to have a drink, maybe just one or two, maybe three, hoping the alcohol would relax him some, allow him to sleep, but he found himself dozing off on the bus ride home, then lying awake on the mat on Mama's floor for the rest of the night.

He bought a pre-paid cell phone card and tried to call their old phone number, but all he got was a recording saying the number was out of service, and he didn't have Tio Miguel's number written down. When he called what he thought was Tio Miguel's number, he got a wrong number on that one, too.

In the end, it was Mama who decided. "We've been so happy to see you, *mijo*," Mama said, her voice barely above a whisper. "These have been the happiest months of my life, that I got to be with you again, but things are still so hard here, and you have children. You need to go back to your life in the United States." That was Mama, always trying to do the right thing, even if it wasn't really what was in her heart.

Felipe shook his head. "I can't go back, Mama," he said dejectedly. "They arrested me and sent me to jail. I don't have any way to get there, and if I did, they would just find me and deport me again. Maybe I'll be able to return someday, but right now I think I'm going to be here for a while. Think about the good part. I'll be able to spend time with you and Ana and Juanito—I mean, Juan."

"It happens all the time, to so many people. They get deported and they stay here for a while, trying to earn some money, but many of them decide to take the chance, try to go back," she declared soberly, but he could see that her lower lip was trembling, and she looked away, avoiding his eyes, as though she was talking to someone off in the distance.

"But Mama, I have no idea how to find a coyote and don't have money to pay one, anyway." He hesitated, then cleared his throat and blurted out the question he had been waiting all these years to ask. His tongue felt thick and fuzzy, as though his mouth was full of cotton, and the words came out in a jumble.

"How did you find—I mean, who—um, you must have paid him— um, how were you able to get a coyote to take me the last time?"

Mama's hands were moving nervously, the same way they did that day in Honduras. Tapping her foot, brushing her hair back. "It's not important. I did the right thing, and I'm doing the right thing now. I never had to pray that you were not being tortured or cry over your grave. I could rest at night knowing you were alive, and I knew my brother Miguel would help you. I am the happiest woman alive, that I got to see you again, but you deserve better, *mijo*."

"You deserve better, too, Mama. I have thought so often about finding a way to get you to the United States. You would really like Julia, and I have always promised my children that they would meet their *abuela* someday. If I ever do get back there, you could live with us. My wife and my children are all citizens and we could move to another part of the country where no one recognizes me—"

"I'm not young anymore. I couldn't make a trip like that and Ana has four children who need their *abuela,* too."

"Maybe I can find a way, Mama. What will happen when you can't work on the *finca* anymore?"

This time, she did not walk away, but met his eyes, let him see her tears. "God has kept you alive all these years, and brought you back to me. God will take care of both of us."

"We will see each other again, Mama."

"You have always been with me, Felipito."

"And you with me, Mama."

It was Lydia who explained to Felipe what to do. The coyote had asked for seven thousand dollars to lead him from El Salvador through

Guatemala, then to Mexico and over the U.S. border, but there was another way, Lydia had explained. From San Salvador, he could take a bus to Guatemala City, then another bus to one of the Mexican border towns, where it would be easier to find a coyote who would just get him from one side of the border to the other, and probably wouldn't cost more than five hundred dollars. Everyone in the village knew someone who had made the trip, and information and advice about how to find a coyote once he reached the Mexican border flowed freely. "Go to Enrique's bar and grill in Matamoros and ask for Humberto, or La Plaza in Ciudad Juarez or the Estrella de Oro bar in Nuevo Laredo. El Semental, he's the best. No, if you can find Pedrito, he's the best."

Mama made him some tamales and gave him a plastic bottle of water that could be refilled, which he placed in his backpack along with an extra set of clothes he had purchased for the trip. The sun had not yet come up but there were already people on the road, beginning the hour walk to the *finca*, or heading for the bus that would take them to the *maquila*s in San Salvador, a sea of straw hats kicking up the dust as they trudged along the road. Ana and Juan accompanied him to the bus stop, clinging to their last moments with him, postponing their final goodbyes as long as they could.

The scent of oranges was in the air, and they followed it to a grove of trees, ripe oranges hanging from the branches. Several had fallen onto the ground and Felipe scooped them up and put them in his backpack with the tamales, tossed a few to Ana and Juan to take home. He could hear the engine of the rickety old bus now, grinding, coughing its way up the dirt road one more time, surviving yet another twenty-mile trip from El Espino to San Salvador.

By the time they got back to the road with the oranges, the bus had come to a stop and the driver gestured impatiently at him to hurry up and board. Ana's tears were damp against his face as they embraced, her body pressed tightly against him. He wanted to promise that they would see each other again, but when he tried to speak, no words came out, so he just hugged Juan quickly and gave Ana a last peck on the cheek, then stumbled up the stairs onto the bus.

The seat he slid into was torn and hanging off the frame, so that every time the bus lurched, it slid forward, pitching him against the seat in front of him. He would have moved but the other window seats were filled and he wanted to look out at the world that was once his, to say his last goodbyes. He pressed his face against the window, waving goodbye to Ana and Juan as they watched the bus pull away, their hands waving frantically in the air.

The bus drifted past mango trees with their white blossoms, the lush green of the laurel trees, tin shacks with chickens scratching in the dirt. It had been Papa's dream that they would have a little piece of land, with chickens laying eggs, and vegetables growing next to the house.

Oscar fought for that dream and paid the highest price, and Lydia swallowed her grief and carried on. Mama had a dream, too, that her son would survive.

In the distance, the rocky slopes of a majestic volcano rose up, silhouetted against the deep blue of the morning sky. The sea of straw hats vanished, the tin shacks became gray specks, Ana and Juan faint shadows in the early morning haze.

He scanned the faces on the bus, the faces of his childhood, his village. They would always accept him, no matter how long he was away. This was only partially his world, though, and he was on his way back to the other one, the world of Julia and his children, the only life they had ever known. He had one foot in each world, but would never completely belong in either, as though he was caught in purgatory, trapped forever in a state of uncertainty.

The bus in Guatemala City stank from exhaust fumes and the remains of old food left behind, but the cracked window didn't budge when Felipe tried to open it. He pushed on it, but the crack only got bigger, and it appeared that any attempt to push it harder would make the entire pane of glass fall out. There was no air conditioning, and the heat and the monotony of the ride made him doze off periodically, awakening only when the bus made a stop for people to eat or use a bathroom. He was not quite asleep when the bus lurched to a stop and the doors screeched open.

"Tecun Uman, Tecun Uman," the driver shouted loudly.

"Where are we?" Felipe mumbled drowsily to the man sitting next to him.

"Tecun Uman, border of Guatemala and Mexico."

"Five-minute bathroom stop," the bus driver shouted. "Use the restaurant across the street and be back in five minutes, or we will leave without you."

Through the cracked window Felipe could see police cars, men in blue uniforms with the words *Policia Federal* on the back of their shirts heading toward the bus, pounding up the steps in their black boots, demanding identification and pressing the passengers for information regarding their travels in Mexico. Felipe shrunk down in his seat, his skin clammy and cold, his arms covered with goose bumps.

"Destination?" a policeman growled at a man sitting up front near the driver.

"Going to see family in Chiapas," the man responded quickly.

"Identification."

The man pulled a tattered wallet from his pocket and extracted a wrinkled piece of paper.

"This says you're from El Salvador."

"Yes."

"What is the address of your family in Chiapas?"

"Don't know the address. I just know how to get there."

"You headed for the border, like all the other Salvadorans? We can arrest anyone we think is going toward the U.S. border. Makes it easier for the border patrol if we just prevent you from getting there." The policeman waved a set of handcuffs at him. "Get up, now! You're coming with me."

Felipe slid out of his seat and crept toward the door, trying to not draw attention to himself, just another bus passenger headed for a five-minute bathroom break, but the policeman grabbed his arm as he tried to pass.

"Produce your identification!" he yelled.

"Bathroom stop! Emergency, and I only have five minutes!" Felipe yelled back as he yanked his arm away and sprinted toward the front of the bus, catapulting down the stairs, swerving wildly to keep his balance as he pitched forward onto the gravelly road. His hands and knees hit the ground with a crash, and he frantically staggered to his feet, numb to any feeling except desperation.

"*Detenganlo!* Stop him!" a hoarse voice bellowed. Felipe sprinted past a run-down storefront with a rusty Coca-Cola sign and a faded picture of an ice cream cone, where a young girl, not more than fourteen, was posing seductively in front of the door in tiny red shorts and high-heeled shoes. She wore bright red lipstick that made her lips appear adult-sized on her child's face, calling out to him as he ran by, offering quick sex in exchange for whatever cash he could manage to produce.

He dodged a pig that plodded across the road, stumbled over an obstacle course of rocks and potholes, and sprinted toward a long metal fence. The fence had barbed wire at the top, but he could see a place where the barbed wire was rusty and had broken off, so he stuck his foot in a gap in the fence and shimmied his way up, trying to grab the part of the fence that was broken.

The jagged metal cut into his hands and every muscle he had was on fire as he threw his backpack over the fence and scrambled toward the top. The penetrating crack of a bullet whipped by his ear, followed by the sharp snap of ripping cloth as he rolled over the top and crashed onto the ground. He grabbed his backpack and crawled through the grass as a gun fired again and a bloodstain spread across his left sleeve, dots of blood dripping onto his shirt.

The bus driver honked the horn three times to let the passengers know that this was last call, but the policeman was still hovering by the fence, scanning the area, searching for him. The driver gunned the engine and the bus rolled down the road, leaving him to survive alone in this desolate place.

The skin on Felipe's hands was lacerated from grabbing the rusty wire on the fence, and his arm was bleeding heavily where the bullet had clipped him. The sun was fading and darkness was descending over Tecun Uman, making it difficult to see more than a few feet. Beyond a grove of lemon trees, the howling of dogs on the prowl drifted through the twilight. The police were returning with dogs, and with no shelter and nowhere to hide, the dogs would smell his food, pick up the scent of his body, hunt him down.

The aroma of oranges permeated his backpack, tantalizing him with their fragrance, but he didn't dare stop to peel one. He reached into the bag and tore off a piece of Mama's tamale and stuffed it in his mouth, chewing as he crawled through the grass. His hunger got the better of him and he pulled out another piece and gulped it down. The tamale eased his hunger some, but his mouth was dry and his mind kept drifting to the oranges in his bag. No time for oranges, no time to open up the bottle of water that was a few inches from his hand.

The dogs were barking louder, or maybe they were closer. The rocks and twigs were slicing into the cuts on his hands but he crawled faster, propelling himself through the grass like a snake being chased by a hawk. His arm touched a small log, and he lay across it for a moment to catch his breath. There was a musty odor in the air, as though he was near water or mud, and a faint murmuring of voices from just beyond the grove of lemon trees.

The scent of lemons reminded him of Lydia, the lemon flavor in her *pollo encebollado*, the warmth of her arms when she greeted him. If he returned to El Espino, they would welcome him, care for him, help him start a new life there. Mama would always love him and had been thrilled to see him again, but she had still insisted that he return to his family, to the children that needed him, no matter how difficult the journey. Mama was very wise about most things, but the one thing she never understood was just how difficult it was to cross the border into the United States. She had sent him into the desert of death when he was thirteen, a crossing that he barely survived, and had no idea that this one might even be more difficult, maybe impossible to survive this time. There were people in the village who had tried to cross the border recently, been caught and sent back to Mexico. Things were even more dangerous now than they were twenty years ago, they had said. There were more patrols at the border, more helicopters and even electronic things, sensors that could find people anywhere.

Mama was right, though—his children needed a father. Marisol would always be able to manage, but Ricky was a teenage boy who needed a dad to explain man things to him. Julia was probably working long hours to support the family by herself, so the kids must be on their own a lot of the time. Marisol would look after Camilo, but there was no one to keep an eye on Ricky when Julia wasn't around, no man with a firm hand to keep him in line.

He fought to stay conscious, but the loss of blood was making him weak and his legs didn't want to move. A rustling from one of the branches of the lemon tree sent a few leaves floating to the ground, settling softly on the grass, as Felipe peered up into the branches to see what had disturbed the tree. A small green parrot sat high up on a branch, a black-eyed sentinel, watching over him.

Twenty-three

Ricky should have been home by now. The crimson streaks blanketing the Oakmont sky were dwindling, fading to the smoky ash of dusk. Julia picked up a green pepper, smooth against her hand as she turned it over several times, looking for any bad spots that needed to be cut off. She raised the knife and brought it down on the pepper, slicing it in half, then in quarters, chopping it into smaller and smaller pieces. The knife slipped, slicing into her finger, a river of red dripping down the side of her hand onto the kitchen counter. She ran her hand under cold water, grabbed a paper towel and wrapped it around her finger, rummaged around in a drawer and found a box of brightly colored neon Band-Aids she had bought for the kids.

It was not easy raising a teenage boy with two parents, and she was a single mother now. She worried more about Ricky than her other two children, who were more upfront about their feelings and communicated them easily, allowing her to help them when they needed it. She understood Ricky's pain and desperately wanted to soothe him the way she could when he was younger, when a hug and a few encouraging words could make things all better.

Julia tossed the pieces of green pepper into the *sofrito,* the sauce that flavored the chicken, along with the onions, cilantro, and garlic. Olives, chopped tomatoes, a cup of peas. *Arroz con pollo,* rice with chicken, made the way her mother and her grandmother made it, and generations before that in Puerto Rico. Enough to last a week, so the kids could grab some when she wasn't home.

She stirred the pot of rice, then sat down to work on a drawing in her sketchbook while the food was cooking, but her mind kept drifting back to Ricky. The page remained blank and untouched as she stared out the window watching the evening light slowly fade. She thought maybe she should be more understanding of what he was up against at this age, having grown up in the South Bronx herself, but that only made her more terrified that she was going to lose him to the dangers she knew were out there.

Camilo padded into the room waving his homework, and Julia put her arms around him, holding him close for a moment. Camilo was still young enough to hug, to need her arms protecting him. "Good job," she said, trying to sound more cheerful than she felt. At eight years old, he reminded her so much of Ricky at that age. "Are you hungry?" she asked him. "We're going to eat soon, but I have to run to the store for something, so I want you to stay with Marisol until I get back. You can watch TV until dinner."

Julia wandered around the neighborhood, scanning faces on the street, hoping to catch Ricky coming home, and then turned onto Miller Avenue, where an empty lot at the end of the block served as a hangout for teenagers in the evening. The thumping of drums was coming from someone's open window, reminding her of the vacant lot next to her apartment building in the Bronx, where the neighborhood men played congas into the night when she was a child, the same lot where she first kissed a boy on a hot city night. Her father, Isidro, had washed dishes in a Manhattan restaurant all day, sat in that vacant lot till late at night playing Latin rhythms for the neighborhood. He had been only forty-five when a heart attack took his life, and her mother passed away from cancer a few years later, maybe a combination of cancer and grief. Mama never seemed to recover after Papi died, didn't even bother going to the doctor until it was much too late to save her.

She stepped over a piece of cracked cement that had become dislodged, past a flattened red and white plastic cup from one of the fast food restaurants and a tattered envelope that had escaped from someone's trash, and glanced into the window of the discount clothing store that was just pulling its racks in for the evening. A slinky black and white dress with lace around the neckline hung seductively in the window. If

Felipe ever came home, it would be nice to wear when they went dancing, or on a special occasion, maybe Marisol's graduation. He had always liked it when she wore sexy stuff like that.

Across the street stood the West Oakmont police station, an ancient, crumbling brick building without windows. It sometimes appeared to Julia to resemble an eyeless face, watching over the neighborhood of Grover Hill, judging all that happened there. Felipe had been taken there when he was first arrested, and she usually went out of her way to avoid going anywhere near the place, but tonight she walked by slowly, searching for signs of excessive police activity going on in the community, squad cars or police vans bringing an unusual number of people in, especially teenagers.

She strolled nonchalantly toward the vacant lot, but was greeted only by dead air, some empty soda cans, and a pizza box. She was secretly hoping she wouldn't find Ricky because he had already gone home, and breathed a sigh of relief when he wasn't hanging out in the lot with a bunch of kids she didn't know. Maybe he had just gone to a friend's house, or to play basketball in the park, but he had homework to finish, and school tomorrow.

The sound of voices drifted through the dusk, but it was just a couple arguing loudly in front of the market. Julia quickly scurried around them, waving to Alfredo, who smiled and waved back at her from his usual spot behind the counter. The store was empty, not much business tonight, and Alfredo watched her idly as she rushed over to the dairy case and picked up a container of milk, then grabbed a large sack of rice and two cans of beans. The shelves near the cash register displayed an array of tasty-looking candy bars, so tempting in their colorful wrappers, and she stared at them hungrily for a moment, then snatched a few and tossed them in the cart. Money was tight, but the kids deserved a treat now and then, and it would be nice to have something special for Ricky when he came home.

The evening twilight had turned to pitch black by the time she left the market, clutching the grocery bag. She turned the corner and slipped into the shadows, rushing past the darkened hulks of buildings and rows of empty cars parked along the curb. There was no welcoming yellow glow of fluorescent lights as she approached the darkened storefront that was once El Patio, no Felipe to comfort her with loving arms when she returned home without Ricky, to help search for the son they had brought into the world together. Her heart was pounding and a feeling of desperation was driving her now, as she became more frantic to find Ricky and bring him home. She knew the truth—that even in the suburbs, miles from the mean streets of New York, the sharks would be circling around him, hungry for a young man's blood.

Julia bolted up the first flight of stairs to the apartment, tripping on a step, her arms flailing in the air as she tried to hold onto the groceries and grab the banister to keep her balance. A sharp pain shot through her leg, and she limped painfully up the second flight and onto the landing, where she fumbled anxiously through her purse to find the front door key.

Marisol was sitting at the table in the living room, frowning into her laptop computer, the red and white checked tablecloth strewn with papers. Julia tossed her grocery bag carelessly on the table and slumped into a chair. Seventeen years of motherhood meant she knew Marisol as well as she would ever know anybody, and Julia couldn't help noticing her hand tapping the pencil nervously on the tablecloth.

"Computer not working?"

"No, it's okay," Marisol responded distractedly, as though she was preoccupied with something more important.

Julia bent down to pick up a napkin that had fallen on the floor at breakfast, crumpled it into a ball and threw it at the small wicker wastebasket across the room.

"Good shot, Mom," Marisol said, as the napkin landed neatly in the middle of the basket.

"I played a little basketball in high school," Julia responded. "I never told you about that? It was fun, but I wasn't good enough to make the junior varsity team, so I only played for about a year. I was too short, I guess! You and I should go to the park sometime and toss a few. It might relax us, lower the stress level a little bit."

"Mom—"

"I know, girls your age don't want to be seen playing in the park with their mama. I'm sorry, guess I missed the boat on that one. We should have done it when you were young enough to enjoy it and not care what anyone thought."

"No, please don't say that—it would just be a little weird, that's all, and I have a lot of other things going on right now."

"I know, I know, and you are a wonderful daughter and I'm very proud of you, even if you don't want to play with me!" Julia said, teasing her a little. "By the way, did Ricky come back at all?" she asked, trying to sound casual.

"Mama—" Marisol began, and then stopped. Julia watched her breathe in, exhale slowly, try again. "Mama, the police were here."

Julia leaned forward, her dark eyes riveted on Marisol's face, impatient for her to continue. "Why? What happened? Something happened to Ricky?"

"He's—he's down at the police station. When I answered the door, they flashed their badges and asked for you. I told them you weren't here, and they said to tell you to come down to the station because he was picked up in the park with some other kids. They wouldn't really tell me anything—they said they needed to talk to his parents. Do you want me to come with you?"

Julia closed her eyes for a moment and tried to take a deep breath, but the wind had been completely knocked out of her, as though she had been sucker-punched in the stomach.

"Do you want me to come with you to the police station?" Marisol repeated softly.

"No, you have other things you need to do, and I don't want you involved in this. I can manage it. But what I do need," Julia said wearily, "is for you to tell me everything you know. You're not helping Ricky by keeping things from me. Who's he hanging out with these days?"

"He's not in a gang, Mama. But you know, he's very popular, and some of his friends, kids he's known since kindergarten, some of them might be—"

"He hangs out with the gangbangers?"

"Well, he wouldn't stop being friends with someone he's known all his life because they're doing some things—"

"What things?" Julia interrupted testily.

"I don't know—whatever they do—I don't think he's doing any of those, like, gang things, but he's very loyal to his friends, and he wouldn't just cut them off or stop being friends with them. They play basketball, soccer, maybe hang out sometimes, but that's all, as far as I know. He has other friends, too."

"And drugs? Is he doing drugs, Marisol?"

Marisol sighed and rolled her eyes. "There's a lot of drugs around, Mama. Around the neighborhood and around the school. Most of the kids have tried something, marijuana or something at a party. Not me," she said quickly, "but a lot of the kids do. Ricky's not heavy into anything, but, yeah, he might have tried something."

Julia frowned, her lips drawn in a tight line. As if life was not stressful enough, now she had to venture alone into a police station to retrieve her son. She pulled one of the candy bars from the grocery bag, a chocolate one with almonds and coconut, taking small, slow bites as she savored the sweetness on her tongue, making it last until she had devoured the last drop and there was nothing left but the empty wrapper staring at her from the table.

Twenty-four

The subway platform was airless and hot, and Marisol prayed that she wouldn't start sweating because sweat would make her makeup run and leave a mark under her armpits, which she definitely didn't want. When the train finally came, there was one space available, so she and Colin squeezed in together, their bodies touching, and she felt giggly and silly, something she hadn't felt in a while. The subway rumbled through the blackness of the tunnel, rocking and swaying with a rhythm all its own as it flew around curves, careening along the track at lightning speed, lurching back and forth, causing her to slide into him, feel the warmth of his body against hers.

"Check out that ad over there," Colin whispered, interrupting her thoughts. "I think the people on this train could use some of that soft, gentle toilet paper. They look like their behinds need some kindness."

"Be careful," Marisol whispered back, not wanting to show that she thought his gross joke was funny, preferring to appear cool, classy. "If anybody thinks you're laughing at them, we'll be in a lot of trouble."

"We'll just hand them some comforting toilet paper—that'll calm them down!"

"You carry it with you?" she tossed back, dropping her guard some, and they doubled over with laughter this time.

Marisol was more impressed than ever with his charm. He was not only cute but witty, too. No rock band shirt today—instead he looked amazingly buff in a tight white T-shirt and a pair of cut-off denim shorts with a tear in them right at the top of his thigh. He was more than cute—he was totally hot, so hot it made her tingle just to look at him.

A vendor selling small trinkets dragged a cart through the double doors, presenting his wares to an already annoyed crowd, bored with what he had to offer. He paused in front of Colin and waved a rabbit's foot on a keychain. "Toys, get yer toys, two dollars. How about one for the young lady?"

Colin fished in his pocket and pulled out two dollar bills. "I think I will."

"For you," he said, handing her the rabbit's foot. "For good luck."

They trudged up the staircase that led out of the dank, musty subway station and emerged into dappled sunshine. 72nd street and Central Park West, the sign said. The New York skyline peered over Central Park's sweeping emerald canopy, and across the street, a police barricade indicated that the park was closed to cars, reserved for walkers, joggers, and bicycle riders.

Colin took her hand and they walked side by side, enveloped by the leafy green foliage, the scent of flowers, and the warm afternoon air. They drifted past a meadow where two lovers embraced on a blanket, and she imagined laying on a blanket in the sun with him, finding solace in each other and in the beauty of nature. Mama had told her the story of her first date with Papi at Orchard Beach, where they sat on the sand and watched white seagulls swooping down to snatch fish from the bay. They fell in love there, Mama said, and promised her that she would fall in love with someone like that someday. Marisol had always been fascinated by the idea, but a little doubtful that anything like that could ever happen to her.

She felt a sudden twinge of apprehension, wondering if Colin took all his dates here, whether she might just be one in a long line of girls fawning over him, perky blonde cheerleaders who gave him whatever he wanted. She kicked up a pile of leaves, scattering them across the path. She had promised Mama she would babysit Camilo today, but instead she had dropped him off with Tia Rosa so she could go on this date. If that wasn't bad enough, Camilo had been having some trouble in math, but she hadn't found the time to work with him on it, even though he had asked her at least two weeks ago. Mama had said it was important they stick together as a family, support each other through all this, and here she was hanging out in Central Park with a white boy from East Oakmont while the family needed her at home.

"Do you come here often?" she asked nonchalantly, trying not to let her worries leak out and spoil their day.

"My friends and I come down and walk around, see the sights. We can't get into the big clubs yet, but we've found a few that don't card you. Came down a few weeks ago to hear a band and walk around Greenwich Village."

It certainly sounded like fun, walking around the city, listening to music. New sights, new things to learn and see. She thought about sharing her trip to the Statue of Liberty and Ellis Island, asking him if he had ever been there, but that wasn't as cool as going to clubs in the city with your friends, and it would bring up the immigration issue, which could get awkward. Even Mama and Papi didn't always see eye to eye about the race thing.

"We're all human," Papi would say. "The *guardia* who killed my father was the same color as me, and a white person helped save my life in the desert."

Mama, born and raised in the United States, was more skeptical. "Well, in this country, you need to be careful whom you trust, especially if you have brown skin, or black," she would retort. "White people will sell you down the river before you can blink an eye, and even faster if there's a buck to be made."

The lake was in front of them now, shimmering in the sun, surrounded by outcroppings of rock and yellow flowers, brightly colored butterflies fluttering about the blossoms. A restaurant with tables covered with white tablecloths and wicker chairs overlooked the lake, filled with well-dressed people clattering glasses and silverware, savoring their appetizers and sipping wine coolers in the sun.

"That's a little beyond my wallet," Colin said, laughing.

"Definitely beyond mine," Marisol said, rolling her eyes and nodding in agreement.

"I'm more of a Hamburger Heaven kind of guy. We go to the one in the East Oakmont mall after football practice. Best fries in town. Ever been there?" Colin asked. "Be fun to—" he began, but stopped suddenly in mid-sentence. "It's not that great really. We can find a better place than the mall to eat."

"We don't shop at that mall much, but my father was working over there for a while."

Colin didn't respond and seemed to be lost in thought for a minute. "The mall could be a cool place to work," he finally muttered, speaking slowly as though he was choosing his words carefully. "What did he do there?"

The sharp edge of a rock pressed against her shoe like the blade of a sword that had met its mark, a trespasser encroaching upon the sweetness of the afternoon. She thought about telling him the whole story, but decided not to because it would make Papi sound like a criminal and she didn't want Colin to think she came from that kind of a family. "White people think we're all gangbangers and criminals," Mama always said.

"Construction, painting, odd jobs," she answered, wondering if he had noticed the day laborers waiting for work by the fence, what he thought about them. Maybe he was one of those guys who was too preoccupied with his own life to really pay much attention to a bunch of men in work clothes.

A grimace flickered across Colin's usually cheerful face, as though something was troubling him. An uncomfortable silence fell between them, and she hastily tried to fill the space with small talk, ask about him.

"What about your family?"

"My dad manages a restaurant, the Steak 'n Brew, out by the highway."

"Never been there, either. What about your mom?"

"Nurse in the emergency room at Westchester General."

Marisol flashed on Mama lying on a gurney at Westchester General. It could have been Colin's mother taking her temperature, putting on the blood pressure cuff. A weird coincidence, but possible. She hesitated, then decided she could share that. Nothing too personal about it, everyone got sick sometimes, and it was kind of funny and sweet that his mom worked there, something that connected them.

"Hey, I was just there last month. My mother was coughing and couldn't breathe, so I called 911 and an ambulance took her there. Maybe your mom treated her. That would be cool, wouldn't it, if your mom took care of mine in the emergency room?" she mused, watching his reaction.

That worried look crossed his face again, just for a second, but long enough for her to notice. "She works the night shift, so you wouldn't see her unless you were there all night," he responded quickly. "Your mom okay?"

"They were really helpful, gave her medicine, so she's feeling better, not coughing much at all anymore." It comforted her some knowing his mother was a kind person, someone who helped people, and that he obviously came from a nice family.

A large swan and some ducks were circling the lake in front of the restaurant, hoping for some handouts. "I have an idea," Colin said. "If we swim around in the water and pretend we're ducks, maybe they'll throw us a few appetizers!"

Marisol was relieved they were off the subject of families and Oakmont, back to having fun again. "How about breadcrumbs and a few pieces of leftover fish?"

He began quacking like a duck and flapping his arms, so she pretended to throw food at him and he pretended to catch it in his mouth, smacking his lips as she ran after him, and they chased each other laughing until they fell down on the grass out of breath.

"Ready for a boat ride?" he said, as they lay in the grass laughing. She could see a fleet of rowboats moored to the dock and a building with a sign for boat rentals. *$10.00 per first hour,* the sign said. *$2.50 per each additional ¼ hour or portion thereof. $30 deposit per boat.* They headed over to the boathouse, and Colin pulled a credit card out of his pocket. "My dad's credit card. As long as I stay on the football team and get decent grades, he lets me use it sometimes."

"That's pretty cool of him," Marisol remarked. If his dad worked in a restaurant, they probably didn't have a lot of money, so it was super nice of him to trust his son with a credit card, another good sign.

"Yeah, I guess," Colin mumbled, slapping the card down in front of the clerk at the booth.

"Sounds like a nice guy," Marisol said brightly, but Colin was busy checking out the boats.

"Wouldn't want to get one with a hole in it," he whispered in her ear playfully.

At first, he did the rowing and she lay back, luxuriating in the warmth of the sun, admiring his athletic body and the strength of his muscles as he pulled the oars through the water. This was exactly what she needed, something wonderful to happen in the midst of all her troubles. Colin stopped rowing, let the boat drift for a few minutes, and they floated aimlessly, feeling the water lapping against the side.

"Ever rowed a boat?" he asked after they had floated for a while. "Wanna try?"

She never had, so he sat behind her at first and rowed with her, showing her how to move the oars in a circular motion and how to use one oar to turn the boat. His body pressed up against hers as their arms moved in sync, and Marisol could feel his chest moving, the rhythm of his breathing. She thought he might be breathing a little faster than usual, and she might have been, too. A little embarrassed, she focused on the oars, but the newness of it and the closeness of his body made it difficult for her to concentrate and control the boat.

They found themselves heading for a clump of trees by the shore, but he didn't seem to be able to help her turn the boat in a different direction, or maybe he wasn't really trying. The boat drifted under the trees into a little forest hideaway, surrounded by overhanging branches, and the mud next to the shore had a clean, earthy smell, untouched by the civilization a few hundred yards from it. Small water creatures darted around in the water, flitting in and out of the algae, and something leaped from a rock, maybe a frog.

Colin turned around and reached for her hand again, and for a few minutes, they were quiet, listening to the slapping of the water against the shore and the warbling of a bird somewhere above them. He leaned toward her and she thought maybe he was going to kiss her, but he didn't, instead he just sat there looking at her.

"You're very pretty," he said finally.

"And you're very nice," she said and laughed a little nervously. "I think we'd better be getting back. Our hour is almost up, and they might make you pay another ten dollars if we're late."

She rowed back this time, feeling more confident, and he stretched his body out over the back of the boat, letting her take the lead. The boat thudded against the side of the dock, rocking gently as they climbed onto solid ground and strolled along the path, their pinkie fingers entwined. The blue and yellow umbrella of a food cart appeared ahead, diffusing the aroma of sizzling meat over the wildflowers and the plush velvet earth.

"How about them hot dogs?" Colin said.

Marisol ordered one with just mustard because she didn't want to chance having food dripping down her blouse, but Colin ordered the works—sauerkraut, relish, and onions.

"That's all you want on it? Only mustard?" he asked, raising his eyebrows as though he was seriously alarmed.

"Those other things are a little messy, that's all," Marisol answered with a small giggle.

"Try the sauerkraut. What's a hot dog without sauerkraut?"

Marisol had never had sauerkraut, and it looked a little strange, but she agreed to have the man put a little chili on the hot dog, just a little, and took a lot of napkins just in case. They found a bench and sat silently for a few minutes, munching on their hot dogs.

"Good, huh? You like it?" Colin asked.

Marisol swallowed the piece she was chewing quickly, wiped her mouth before she spoke, the way Mama had taught her. It wasn't polite to talk with food in your mouth, Mama used to say when she was little.

"Delicious! Better than anything we could get in that snooty restaurant."

"Yeah, I'd love to get one of these carts to come to my school at lunchtime. Be a lot better than those crappy school lunches, too," Colin said, and they both laughed.

"Fat chance of that!"

"Well, this cart is always right here, but they have them all over the park, so the next time we come here you can have another one, and then you can try the sauerkraut!"

Despite her efforts to be cool and cautious, the fact that he was mentioning another date sent a thrill of excitement through her, and at that moment she would have agreed to just about anything he asked— well, not quite anything, but almost. She flashed a smile at him, the most flirtatious smile she could muster. "Yeah, it would be fun to come here again. Next time I can bring a blanket, and we can relax in the sun. The art museum can wait!"

"Sounds good!" he said, grinning. He jumped up to toss their trash into the nearby can, then quickly sat down again, this time close enough so that their bodies were touching. Waves of desire flooded through her and she wanted to kiss him right then, but that would definitely be too aggressive and would send the wrong message, so she sat quietly, just feeling the warmth of his body. A lot of guys would have already made a move on her, but he didn't even try, which surprised her. Maybe he was actually being respectful—she hoped that's what it was, and that he hadn't decided that he really wasn't that into her and just wanted to be friends, not go any farther than that. Anyway, she needed to get home because she had to pick up Camilo from Tia Rosa before Mama got home.

"We should probably be heading back to the subway," she said finally. "We have a long way to go."

"I can take you home and then take the bus across town. It would give me a little more time to spend with you," he said wistfully.

She wanted that, too, but she definitely didn't want him to take her home, to see where she lived, and this would be an especially bad time for him to run into Mama. "You don't need to take me home. I'll be fine."

They still had a long subway ride ahead of them, and then a transfer to the Metro North train to Westchester. "I can get home from the train," she said. "You probably have things to do, and I have to pick up my brother."

"That cute little guy you brought to St. Michael's?"

"My aunt is watching him today and I have to pick him up by five-thirty. My aunt and uncle have some church thing they're going to. Same time, same place at St. Michael's next week?" she said, trying to sound casual.

"I still have quite a bit of community service to do, so I'll be around your neighborhood for a while. I'll be there Tuesday after school, as usual."

"I'll come by then, but I may be watching my little brother this week, so I'll have to bring him with me."

"Great!" he said, grinning again. "I'll make sure I save him some ham!"

Twenty-five

The room was hazy and had a sour smell. A bulb outside the door illuminated what appeared to be a hallway, and as Felipe's eyes became accustomed to the dim light, he could see that the space was filled with people lying on cots, lined up from one end of the room to the other.

A young man in faded blue medical scrubs had spotted him lying semi-conscious in the grass last night, his arm covered in blood from the bullet wound, and had half-carried, half-dragged him into the building. He guided him to an empty cot and dressed his left arm with some kind of medicinal-smelling ointment, then began bandaging it, wrapping it with white tape that didn't look very clean. Bone-weary and drained, Felipe's eyes began closing the minute he lay down, and he fell sound asleep before the guy had even finished bandaging him. In the morning, he found clean clothes at the end of the cot—a threadbare white T-shirt, and a pair of black pants that were made for a thinner, taller man. The waistband was so tight it pressed into his stomach, and he had to roll up the cuffs so they didn't drag on the floor.

The walls were a dingy gray, pockmarked with holes and places where the paint had peeled off, leaving bare, crumbling plaster. A shadow of a woman in a white dress was silhouetted against the wall, an apparition floating among the bodies on the cots. The apparition moved toward Felipe, smiling at him, extending her hand.

"Welcome to *Casa de Bienvenida*. I'm Sister Clara."

"Is this a hospital?"

"There are no hospitals in Tecun Uman. The nearest one is twenty-eight miles away in Tapachula. You're in a Catholic mission."

"Who was the person who found me last night? He looked like a doctor."

"Not exactly. He's just a person we trained to do first aid, help with bandaging, things like that. We couldn't afford to pay a doctor to stay here, or provide the equipment they would need."

"He saved my life," Felipe said quietly. "I'm very grateful to all of you." He peered around the room again, gaping at the sleeping bodies on the cots, then back at the nun standing patiently in front of him, remembering a white church in the desert, kind people nursing him back to health.

"That's why we're here," the nun said. "We believe that this is what

God has called upon us to do. Are you hungry? Would you like a banana, maybe some rice and beans?"

He felt a little sick, but the smell of the food reminded him of how long it had been since he had eaten. "Thank you. I would love some, if you can spare it. If not, I had a backpack with some food in it. Have you seen it? A black backpack?"

The nun smiled at that. "The one with the oranges? It's right here by the cot. You should eat them before they go bad or someone steals them. And if you want to give me your dirty clothes, we'll wash them and give them back to you. They probably fit you better than the ones you have on."

The bodies on the cots were beginning to move in the early morning light, some struggling to hoist themselves up from the cots into wheelchairs. Two legs were leaning up against the side of the cot next to his. Plastic legs. Sister Clara pushed the wheelchair close to the cot, placed a hand on the man's back and the other around his waist to steady him, and boosted him into the chair. He glanced at Felipe, who had stopped eating and was gawking at the scene around him. "*Hola, amigo.* You must have just gotten off the bus."

Felipe wondered how the man would know that. Only the police had seen him get off the bus, and he wondered what kind of deals might be made in a place like this.

"How did you know I just got off the bus?"

"You have legs."

A strange answer, although when he looked more closely he could see that the man only had stumps that were bandaged at the top of his thigh.

The man stuck out his hand. "Hector. Welcome to *Casa de Bienvenida.*"

"Felipe."

"Headed for the United States?"

Felipe didn't answer.

"I'm not going to turn you in, if that's what you're worried about. We're all here because we tried to make it to the border and failed."

"What happened to you?"

"There's a train that runs between Tapachula and the Mexico-Texas border—"

"A train that goes to the border?" Felipe interjected, feeling a surge of excitement.

"Where can I get the train? How much does it cost?"

Hector made an attempt to laugh but it came out more like a cough. He pointed to his legs. "That's how much it costs, *amigo*. It's a very expensive train. You'd be better off going back to your country. Look around the room at all the people who tried to make it. We can't work anymore and our lives are ruined. I was trying to join my family in Texas, but instead I've been here for six months. This your first time trying to get across?"

"I left El Salvador when I was thirteen, crossed the Arizona desert with a coyote. Almost didn't make it out alive, but I was rescued by some very kind people. I lived in the U.S. for twenty years, got arrested for something I didn't do, and they deported me. I'm going to try to get across some other way this time. I was lucky to survive the first trip, but I don't think I could make it across the desert a second time."

"I understand. I lived in Texas for ten years, worked my butt off in a slaughterhouse all that time. One day, immigration raided the slaughterhouse and I was deported and sent to Hutto Prison and then back to Honduras. I have a wife and five children in Texas. I was trying to get back to my family, to help support my children, but I fell off the train. At first, I didn't think I was hurt, but then I looked down and my legs were gone."

Sister Clara was handing out tortillas and bananas, and the mournful twang of a guitar drifted over from another room. Felipe took some bananas and gulped them down, but even with the rice and beans, his stomach wasn't full.

"This seems like a pretty good place. Is it safe from police and border guards?"

"This is a Catholic mission that helps the poor in Tecun Uman. It's also a migrant shelter, a stopping point on the Guatemalan-Mexican border for Central Americans. Many of us are here because we tried to jump the train and fell off, others are on their way to the border, like you. Some don't make it over the border and stop here on their way back to their country. The mission took me in, bandaged me up, fed me, gave me a wheelchair, got me some artificial legs. They are very good people, but they don't have much money. *Casa de Bienvenida* scrapes by with donations, and some of the women staying here go out and get money other ways."

"Yeah, I saw them out there when I was running from the police."

Another amputee sitting nearby had been listening to the conversation and extended her hand. "Zoraida, from Guatemala. You be careful if you go out there. You don't make any moves in this town without paying off the police, and they are not kind to anyone who causes them a problem. It's a good thing they didn't catch you."

Zoraida pulled her wheelchair up close to Felipe, looking him over. "Where are you trying to get to?"

"New York, where my family is."

"Everyone who comes through here is trying to get to their family or else needs to get a job in the U.S. to feed their family back home, but it's too dangerous to go this way. You have to get a coyote. They'll pay off the police to let you go through."

"I have enough to pay a coyote to get me across the border, but I don't have enough to pay one to take me all the way from here. I'll have to find some other way to get to the border."

"How did you pay your way the first time you crossed?" Hector asked.

"My mother gave some money to the driver. It wasn't as difficult or expensive then."

"It was still expensive back then. Your mother must have been young and pretty."

"She was. She is still very beautiful."

"Did you think the coyote took you for ten pesos? Your mother made a deal to provide services for someone."

Felipe glared at the ragged man with stumps for legs and matted black hair, wearing a frayed green shirt, the material worn so thin his brown skin was visible through the holes, and a pair of plaid pants cut off above his stumps. Torn between pity and the desire to rip off whatever limbs he had left, he grabbed Hector by the shirt and pushed him. The wheelchair spun around and began rolling backward.

"What did you say about my mother?"

Hector rolled until his hands grabbed the wheels and paused them, deftly turning the chair around until he was facing Felipe. "That she loved you that much, *amigo*. Your mother loved you so much that she was willing to sacrifice herself for you. Save yourself—go back to her."

Felipe sat silently on the cot, rocking back and forth, sadness flowing through every vein in his body. He had no tears, only an agonizing grief tearing at his heart. He could go back to El Salvador, work in the tourist industry and help Mama as she got old, but his children would grow up without him, and Julia would find somebody else and move on with her life.

"I can't go back to El Salvador. I have a family in New York."

Zoraida took his hands in hers, held them tightly for a moment. "Listen, Felipe. A drought dried up everything on our farm in Guatemala, and my children had no food to eat. I thought if I could make it to California, I would be able to earn some money to send home, so I jumped a train, but it was going too fast and I slipped off, and now I'm no good to anyone. I had wanted so much to do something better for them, but I ended up like this." She whirled the wheelchair around until it was facing directly in front of him, so he had to notice.

"Look at what happened to me, Felipe, to the people in this room."

"I have to try. I have no other way to get home."

Hector shook his head. "It's not worth it. Go back to El Salvador and save yourself."

Zoraida backed the chair off. "I know how you feel. I felt that way, too, that I was desperate and had to take the chance. Everyone hopes they will be the one that makes it, and sometimes you can't live with yourself if you don't try."

"And I have to be one of those who tries, Zoraida. I have two boys, one nine and one fifteen, and a daughter about to graduate from high school. I'm willing to take the chance or die trying."

"Alright then, about a half-mile from here, Guatemala and Mexico are connected by a river, the Suchiate. If you cross it, you will have passed over the Guatemalan border into Mexico."

"How wide?"

"It's very shallow, not deeper than waist high and about two hundred meters wide. A riverman will take you across on a raft for twelve pesos, seventy-five cents. On the other side of the river is Ciudad Hidalgo, where there is a trainyard. You can follow the group from the raft. They'll all be going there. The freight train to Tapachula comes through there, and if you can grab onto a ladder, you can hoist yourself up and try to climb to the roof. The train is going very fast, and it's very dangerous. Even if you can get onto the roof, you still have a long ride ahead of you, one thousand miles to the U.S. border. They call it the train of death."

Twenty-six

Frank parked his van in the driveway of the house he and Bonnie had bought together so many years ago and sat frozen behind the wheel, breathing hard. None of the New York dailies had covered the protest on Neville Street, but an article had shown up in the *Oakmont Gazette*, the local paper that was tossed in the driveway once a week. Bonnie would hit the roof if she saw the article in the paper, found out whose house had been targeted. If he came in quietly, maybe he could grab the paper and dump it before anyone had a chance to read it. Bradley had good ideas, but he really hadn't thought this one all the way through. No one had considered what would happen if one of the contractors they were picketing was someone they knew, someone they had to work with or deal with in some way.

He nudged open the car door and stepped out into the balmy spring air, closing the door slowly behind him so it didn't slam. The paper was gone from the driveway where the delivery person usually threw it. Someone had definitely picked it up and brought it in. Frank pondered for a moment how he would explain this to Colin, how to clean up this mess.

The paper was there, sitting on the table. Frank grabbed it quickly and stuffed it into the trashcan, then took off his sandals and stuck them on the rack by the door. They were well-worn and comfortable, but the floor squeaked in places and the sandals were a little loose and slapped when he walked, so going barefoot would be quieter. The toes on his right foot touched the floor lightly, then his left, as he tiptoed toward the stairs that went down to the family room. Maybe he could sleep there tonight—there was a refrigerator, a couch, and a TV down there.

"Frank!" Bonnie called from the living room as he opened the door to the basement. She was sitting on the couch, her hands curled around a cup of coffee.

"I'm really tired," he called back. "Long day—I'm going downstairs to take a nap."

Bonnie was off the couch now, her hands still wrapped tightly around the coffee cup as she stepped into the hallway, glaring at him. "What the hell are you doing, Frank?"

"I said I'm going to take a nap!" he responded irritably. "I had a long day at work. The new regional manager was hassling me, said the customer numbers are down and the kitchen is too slow getting the food out. Like those things are all my problem. Maybe he should—"

"I'm not talking about that, Frank. You know what I'm talking about—Luke's father."

Frank frowned, pretending to look concerned. "Something happened to Luke's father?"

There were more footsteps in the hallway, and Colin plodded in slowly, dragging his feet, looking as though he was about to cry. As if things weren't tense enough, now his sixteen-year-old son was going to act like a big baby. Some football player. He'd have to have a word with him about that.

Bonnie and Colin stood there silently for a minute, glowering at him. "Carol Harper called me," Bonnie finally sputtered. Her face was drawn and pinched, and she stood ramrod stiff in front of him, gripping the coffee cup so tightly between her fingers that her knuckles were white, as though that was the only thing keeping her from slapping him silly. "An anti-immigrant group was picketing in front of their house last week, and she saw you there, acting like you were in charge of the whole thing. Are you out of your goddamn mind? Or maybe you never had one in the first place. You certainly don't have much of a heart."

"Why did you have to picket Luke's house, Dad?" Colin mumbled, his voice so low Frank could hardly hear him.

"I don't have much of a heart?" Frank retorted. "What about him—whatever his name is—"

"Ray—his name is Ray," Bonnie shot back. "Ray Harper, like Luke Harper, his son."

"Yeah, Ray. Does Mr. Ray care what he is doing to the children in this community? Ruining their lives?" Frank said, tossing the sarcasm right back at her.

"Dad, Luke saw the article in the paper. Everyone in Oakmont knows about it by now, and Luke is embarrassed to come to school, even said he might quit the football team. He said he's never coming over here again, wouldn't step foot in your crappy van if he was bleeding to death."

"I don't understand," Bonnie said. "How deeply are you involved in this, anyway? You really haven't mentioned much about it, except for wanting to have meetings in our living room. You having meetings somewhere else, Frank? Secret meetings we don't know about?"

"Mr. Harper lost his job a few months ago," Colin added, choking up now. "Luke told me they couldn't make the mortgage payments on their house, and the bank took it away. They just rented that new place, moved in there about a week ago. They don't even have any friends in the neighborhood yet, and now they never will. Why did you have to do this? You're ruining his life and Luke's, and mine, too."

"No one's ruining your life, son, and Ray Harper is ruining his own life, and his family's. He made the decision to pick up illegals at the mall—"

"That's what this is about Frank? The damn mall again? Well, you have really blown it this time! Call him, Frank. Apologize!" Bonnie demanded.

"How about Ray stops picking up illegals at the mall, and apologizes to us? We'll be glad to call off the picketing then," Frank grumbled testily, but he wasn't so sure about this one.

It was Ray's wife, Carol, who always came to pick up Luke. Ray hardly ever showed his face, and Frank had always assumed he was a traveling salesman or something, out of town a lot.

He rarely even came to the football games, which was why Frank hadn't recognized him right away. Well, Colin would just have to deal with it; there was no use crying about it. He would just have to accept that there were hard knocks in life sometimes, although Frank had to admit to himself that he had really stepped in it this time, couldn't argue about that.

Maybe SIM could stop protesting the contractors at their homes and just continue to focus on the mall, arresting the guys who showed up there to get work. It wouldn't be as personal, wouldn't rip the contractors to shreds, which had been the plan, but at least this would still get the message out. Ken Dawson had also talked about closing down another restaurant, El Pollo Sabroso, some little chicken place in a strip mall over near the highway. Definitely had to be illegals there. Dawson was hot to trot on that one, and it was a safe bet that none of them would be friends of anyone's family.

"We just want to send the contractors a message," Frank said wearily. "We're done with Harper. We don't hit the same guy every week, anyway. We've got a few others we need to go after, and maybe some businesses. Ray Harper will put the word out, advertise somewhere and find some other work and everything will calm down. Give it a few weeks and no one will even remember it happened."

Colin rolled his eyes, then jammed his hands into his pockets and leaned against the wall, as though he needed to prop himself up. "How's he gonna get work when you ruined his truck and his ladders, Dad?" he retorted indignantly.

"Don't you roll your eyes at me, young man, and you better watch your tone, or you'll have some consequences of your own to deal with," Frank snapped.

"No, he will not have any consequences! Did you even consider that you might be embarrassing us, too?" Bonnie shouted furiously. "How do you think Colin feels when he has to face his friends at school, explain why his father acts like an asshole?"

Frank hated it when he and Bonnie fought, especially when she started yelling. There was nothing worse than having a woman screeching at you. It made him feel like a little kid, being yelled at for something he didn't understand. Things hadn't changed much in that area. He really didn't get why Bonnie was so concerned about the stupid illegals. It must be her damn liberal friends who were influencing her—probably that Melissa woman—the one that was always volunteering places, trying to help people. Bonnie used to be a pretty cool person, did just what a woman should—raised her kid, cooked dinner for the family, went to work to bring in some extra money. Now she was defending every low-life who crossed her path, wanting to help everyone. It was probably that change of life thing women get, making her moody and strange.

"He'll just have to understand that this cause is bigger than him and his little friends. Sometimes you just have to man up, son, take the hit and move on." He turned toward Colin, looked him squarely in the face. "You worried about the team losing their quarterback? The team would have lost their wide receiver, too, if I hadn't stepped in and rescued you," he said acidly.

"Dad, the guys on the team—"

"You don't know what they think, son. Maybe they agree with me, or their parents do. You think I'm the only one who wants to run those guys out of town? And hey, Luke is a good quarterback, but everyone is replaceable. If he wants to quit the team, that's his choice. There are plenty of kids waiting in the wings, hoping to grab a spot."

Bonnie grimaced, her face contorted with rage. "I don't believe this—I just really don't! Damn it!" She swung the coffee cup in the air, flinging coffee all over him. The cup slipped out of her hand and smashed against the wall, sending broken shards flying everywhere. Jagged slivers of glass glittered on the floor around Frank's bare feet, but Bonnie made no move to clean them up. "Colin and I are going out for dinner," she snapped. "You can fix your own and eat by yourself!" She turned and stomped out the door, with Colin following close behind. The door slammed abruptly with a loud crack that echoed hollowly through the empty hallway.

Warm coffee ran down the side of Frank's face, dripping brown stains onto the front of his shirt. He wondered how long it would take for things to cool down. He could disappear for a while, stay in a hotel somewhere, but he'd still have to come back to get his clothes and some other things, and he couldn't afford more than a few nights in a hotel. Staying with his mother in her little apartment in the Bronx would just about kill him, and probably her, too. He didn't really have any other place to go.

Frank stumbled down the stairs to the basement, washed the coffee off his face, threw the stained shirt in the laundry basket next to the washing machine. The smell of coffee still permeated the room, and he reached up to feel his hair, what there was of it, to see if it was wet.

He had been losing a lot of hair lately, maybe it was time to shave it all off. A lot of guys his age did that so they didn't look bald, just looked like a tough guy with a shaved head. Right now, a hot shower might help, wash off the coffee smell, relax him some before he crashed out on the couch. He definitely wasn't sleeping upstairs tonight.

He and Bonnie had done a lot of work fixing up the family room together and it was looking pretty nice, not a bad place to stay at all. It used to just be a funky old basement, but they had painted the floor and covered it with some kind of linoleum, good-looking stuff, which really brightened things up a lot. The best part was the home theater they had installed, a seventy-inch TV with a high-tech entertainment center. He could watch TV, movies, sleep on the couch just like he did upstairs.

Big glass windows looked out onto the backyard, and he gazed outside for a moment, watching the leaves on the trees tossing in the breeze. There was a forecast of rain tonight, probably drizzle all day tomorrow, which meant fewer customers at Steak 'n Brew. People hunkered down at home when it rained, ate whatever leftovers they could scrounge up.

Management would probably keep blaming him for the lack of business—not much he could do about that except tune it out, pretend he was listening when he really wasn't. When the SIM organization got really big, had all kinds of success, maybe he could pull in a paid position there as a professional big shot. They'd had a few setbacks, but the article in the paper might actually be a good thing. They were getting publicity, getting known around the area, even if some people didn't like it. He would just have to get used to the fact that the better SIM did, the more crap would be thrown at them.

There was a patter of paws on the linoleum floor, and Turkey lumbered into the room and nuzzled against him. That dog loved him no matter what he did, so Frank stretched out on the couch and ran his hand over Turkey's soft fur. Petting Turkey was better than a hot shower sometimes. Turkey probably needed a walk soon; better do that first. Too bad women weren't as easy to deal with.

It was nothing unusual for him and Bonnie to fight; they had battled it out before, but everyone usually calmed down in a day or two. This one had really turned into a hot mess, though. He wondered how Colin's friends would react. He had always enjoyed it when they came over to toss the football around, and he wondered if any of them would ever talk to him again. Teenagers could be funny sometimes, and his hope was that they would be too wrapped up in their own lives to even pay much attention to any of it. Colin would still need him for things—money, especially—so he'd just have to get over this. He didn't have much choice about that.

There was no reason why he couldn't survive down here for a few days, although he couldn't cook anything. There wasn't even a microwave to warm things up, and Bonnie sure wasn't going to be cooking for him. He guessed he'd be eating fast food for a while. There was a half-bath but no shower, so he would have to go upstairs for that, and it would be weird running into Bonnie in the bathroom when they weren't talking to each other.

It was funny how things turned out sometimes. You had the best plans, thought they were all worked out, and then some stupid glitch blows the whole thing, kinda like those cop shows where someone plans the perfect murder, only they forget one small detail and the whole thing unravels.

Twenty-seven

Julia recognized him immediately, the cop with the big belly and the slicked back hair who used to come into El Patio and harass Felipe and Tio Miguel. Officer Bradley, he had said his name was.

Julia's mouth was dry and felt like it was full of sawdust, the words stuck somewhere at the back of her throat. She approached the counter, asked to see Ricky, explained that she was his mother and had come to take him home. Officer Bradley scrutinized her, the muscles in his jaw flexing as he chewed on a piece of gum, grinding it between his teeth, turning it around on his tongue. Bradley shot a look at the other cops, as though they had a secret understanding that they were not about to share.

"He's upstairs being questioned. Have a seat."

The voice came from a young cop with a military buzz cut, so blond it was almost white. Julia thought he couldn't have been more than twenty-five years old, one of those young guys with a permanent smirk. She knew that kind of guy, the dangerous kind, who had no experience but always needed to prove himself. A chill went through her as she thought of accidental shootings, mistakes made by scared policemen who shot first and asked questions later. A few years ago, a twenty-three-year-old immigrant from Guinea had been standing in front of his apartment building on Soundview Avenue in the South Bronx and was shot forty-one times by police who mistook him for someone else. The policemen involved in the shooting were all acquitted, never served a day in jail for the life they took.

Blond buzz cut was running his eyes over her body, staring at her breasts, exchanging glances with the other cops.

Julia folded her arms over her chest and stared into his face, meeting his eyes. "Can I see him now? Ricky, Ricky Sanchez. He's—"

"You sit down right there, ma'am," Bradley interjected, pointing to the plastic chairs. "He's being questioned. Wait until you're called, like everyone else." He moved toward her, his hand on his nightstick. "Sit down, or you'll be facing some charges of your own."

She sat for an hour, then two hours passed, but she seemed to be invisible, submerged in a sea of faces waiting to be heard. A middle-aged woman with ebony hair pulled tightly behind her head in a bun, a teenager with tattooed arms leaning back in a chair with his eyes closed, a gray-haired couple sitting side by side, waiting patiently until they were acknowledged.

Finally, she rose from the chair and straightened her blouse, making sure it wasn't wrinkled. "I want to see my son, Ricky Sanchez."

Officer Bradley's face went from light pink to red and he began moving toward her, until he was close enough that she could smell the garlic on his breath, see the red lines on his bulbous nose, his belly straining at the buttons on his shirt. "*Sit down!*" he bellowed.

"I've been sitting for two hours already." Her mind felt clear, strong, for Ricky, who would always be her baby boy. For Felipe, in a hell of his own. "I want to see my son, right now!"

"You're not in much of a position to give me a hard time, lady." A pair of handcuffs swung back and forth, the key clicked in the lock. The handcuffs fell open, grazing her arm. "One more time, ma'am, and you will join your juvenile delinquent son in a holding cell."

A slender woman who had been looking over some forms stepped toward Julia. "Sergeant Tanisha Jackson," she said, extending her hand. "I believe we're ready for you now."

She touched Julia lightly on the arm and quickly led her out of the office. "Follow me," she said, as they began the trek up the stairs to the holding area.

As they emerged from the staircase, Julia glanced through the open door of a room just ahead and could make out the contour of a body, a head laying on a table with tousled black hair and a white T-shirt. Julia let out a small gasp.

"That's him," she said, rushing toward the room, almost banging into a policeman that was standing near the door.

Ricky's right eye was swollen shut and the whole right side of his face was purple. There was blood on his lip, which looked lacerated and torn.

"Oh my god, Ricky. What happened to you?"

The interrogation room in the West Oakmont police station had no windows, the only furniture a pitted wooden table and four folding chairs. An officer she hadn't seen before pointed to a chair, motioning for her to sit down as Bradley slipped in the door behind them.

Julia stood behind the chair, her hands gripping the metal frame. "I don't need to sit down. I want to know who did this to my son."

The sight of Mama caused Ricky to sit up, scowling glumly. He glanced at her, then slumped in the chair with his head back, his eyes closed.

"Ricky was picked up with several other young men in Washington Park for being a co-conspirator in a felony drug sale. He was not cooperative, and when we tried to bring him in he tripped on the curb and scraped his face."

"He was arrested in the park?"

Ricky was mumbling now, trying to form words without moving his torn lip too much. "We were just playing basketball, Mama. They busted us for playing basketball."

Officer Bradley shifted in his chair, pursed his lips and breathed out loudly, shaking his head. "Undercover police observed a drug sale behind a building on Grant Street and arrested several members of the Miller Avenue Kings. We have photographs of Ricky associating with various members of that gang and have no doubt that he is involved. Drug running, theft, and other criminal activity. We've been watching them for a while. Not much wiggle room here."

"Mama, I know some of those guys from school, but I don't deal and I wasn't there when they busted them. I just hang out with them sometimes, listen to music, play basketball or soccer."

Julia crossed her arms and glared at Officer Bradley. "Not everyone who grows up in Grover Hill is a criminal or in a gang. Do you see any signs of gang membership on him? Tattoos? Jacket? Gang colors? Did you see him selling drugs to anyone?" She brushed her hand over Ricky's hair. "He needs medical attention. I'm taking him home so I can get him to a doctor."

"Sure, ma'am, and you think we don't know about the family history of criminal activity, that he grew up learning how to be a criminal in that crummy little storefront of yours?" Bradley circled around the table until he was standing next to Ricky. He leaned over until his face was an inch away, his mouth adjacent to Ricky's ear. "Do you think that we don't know that you learned how to run a criminal enterprise at your daddy's knee?" he yelled into Ricky's face, banging his fist on the table, his face contorted with fury. "If you think we are just going to let you carry on his business for him, you'd better think again."

"Oh, no," Ricky snapped angrily, his voice rising. "You don't talk about my dad—"

"Shut up!" Bradley yelled, "or you'll find yourself locked up. Now get the hell out of here. We're lettin' you go this time, but you get picked up again and you'll go straight to central booking. We have a spot in juvie just waiting for you." He glared at Julia. "We're watching all of you. That means you and the rest of your little criminals, too!"

Twenty-eight

The lawyer at Legal Aid was a middle-aged woman with short, curly blonde hair that circled her round face like a halo and wire frame glasses that were slightly crooked. A Christmas angel with crooked glasses, Marisol thought. She couldn't wait to describe this one to Colin so they could laugh together, share another one of the funny things they had seen. He didn't know about Papi or that she was going to Legal Aid, but she could describe the face, tell him she noticed her on the subway. Not the whole truth, but not a big lie that really mattered. She had debated asking Colin to accompany her to this appointment, but she wanted to have fun with him, not creep him out with her problems, so she decided against it.

The lawyer, Linda Malone, her desk plate announced, leaned her head back, rubbed her eyes and readjusted her glasses, examining Marisol carefully. Marisol wondered if she looked too young to be taken seriously, or if the woman had just seen too many hopeless cases to have the energy for another one.

"Let me see if I have this right. Your father was arrested for drugs and then deported because he was in the United States illegally. That's quite a tall order. What is it you are asking me to do?"

The Legal Aid office was sparsely furnished: a honey-colored wooden desk, orderly and immaculate, occupied only by a computer, an in-out box with neatly stacked papers, a telephone, and a pencil holder with four black pens. Bookcases lined every wall, packed with law books. Marisol slid forward to the edge of the chair, clasped her hands together and folded them in her lap, her body stiff and tense. "He's innocent, and I want to help him."

Linda Malone took off her glasses, stuck the end of the frame in her mouth as though she was pondering deeply. Pondering how to end this conversation so she can get back to her real job, Marisol thought.

"You want to help him? How old are you, honey?"

"Seventeen. I turned seventeen last week, but Ms. Torres, the guidance counselor at—"

"And how do you propose to do that? He's probably not even in the country anymore."

"That's why I'm here, because Ms. Torres thought you could—"

"Okay. I really don't have a lot of time, but tell me briefly what you think happened. And I mean briefly!" she said, checking her watch.

Her fingers curled around her glasses again, scooping them up and casually sliding them on so they sat at the end of her nose, enabling her to peer over them authoritatively. She picked up the pencil holder, cradling it between her hands as though it was a glass of fine wine, then slapped it down on the desk. "This is a very complicated situation, and it's quite possible that you don't have all the facts, but now you've got me curious. Go on, tell me what you've heard."

Marisol touched her earrings, made sure she hadn't lost one, which sometimes happened and could make her look silly. "He was picking up day labor work at the East Oakmont Mall when the police came and arrested all of the guys waiting there. They put him in a lineup and some-body picked him out, said he was a drug dealer, supplying drugs to kids at Oakmont High. He was in jail for a while, the county jail, so we could visit him every week, but he isn't a citizen, so one day we went to visit and he was gone. My mom checked it out, even went down to Arizona to visit him, but he'd already been deported to El Salvador."

Mama had done everything she possibly could, but had hit a brick wall and had warned her to stay out of it, to keep her life on track. She wanted to listen to Mama, but Papi's arrest had been so awful and scary that she often woke up in the middle of the night, in a panic that she couldn't stop people from hurting Papi. Most mornings her stomach was so upset that she could barely eat anything for breakfast. One night she dreamed a pack of lions was in the house tearing everyone apart with long, sharp, fangs, leaving body parts and trails of blood along the floor, and woke in a cold sweat, lying sleepless for hours. That morning she had fallen asleep in her first period class, of all places, and didn't wake up until the teacher threw a piece of chalk that bounced off her desk with a sharp crack and landed on the floor. When she lifted her head groggily from the desk, she was greeted by the sound of the class breaking into uproarious laughter.

The lawyer dangled the glasses from her lips, not even a drop of lipstick to add a little color, then pulled them out of her mouth and waved them in the air officiously. No makeup, either. A little pink blush on her cheeks would definitely brighten her up a little.

"I don't know if you realize what you're getting into," the lawyer said, "but you may be biting off a heck of a lot more than you can chew, and you might not like what you find out."

Marisol stared at the wall of law books, full of words that didn't mean anything. She wouldn't want to be a lawyer if she had to carry out those laws. It wasn't about doing the right thing, it was about the words in those books, making them work so you could win. She watched those legal shows on television, saw the way the words were twisted to win a case. Papi had been sent away because of those words, laws that made him invisible, a problem to be cleaned up, dismissed.

"What have you heard from him?"

"Nothing—"

"That's not surprising. They're not usually allowed phone calls at immigration detention centers."

Marisol straightened her blouse and uncrossed her legs, which were becoming numb from not moving. Keeping herself super busy with school took her mind off her troubles sometimes, but it was her decision to actually do something constructive to help Papi that was helping her bounce back, keep going through it all. Maybe it was an impossible task, the way all the adults said, but she knew she would never be able to live with herself or accept any success in this crappy world unless she tried.

"My whole life, he worked in a restaurant below our apartment and came home every night. He spent his free time at home with our family, and he and my mom are totally into each other. I would have noticed something. He would never sell drugs, and I want to know why this was done to him."

"The best I can do is to suggest that you and your mother go to the County Clerk's office in White Plains and ask for a disposition. It'll cost you five dollars, but it'll give you some information about what happened."

"They'll just give it to me?"

"Pay the five dollars, and they'll give you what they have. There's no risk in doing it. It's the public record of the case, the part that is available to you. They probably assigned him a public defender, and you can find out from the disposition who it was. Contact that lawyer and he or she can look into it for you." A honey-colored drawer squeaked open and

Linda Malone shoved a business card across the desk and shrugged her shoulders. "Good luck, honey. Call me if I can help with anything."

It was drizzling outside, a fine mist that turned the usually busy streets into a ghost town, as people sequestered themselves indoors to stay out of the rain. Marisol raced from the office building to the awning of a restaurant, trying to stay dry, propelled by a surge of anger, a furious energy galvanizing her into action. It would cost a few dollars to take the bus to White Plains and five dollars to pay the clerk for the disposition. She didn't have the money, but she would get it, and she knew exactly who she was going to ask.

Twenty-nine

The Suchiate River was just as they said, chocolate brown and reeking of sewage. The river was dotted with small *camaras*, rafts being pushed by men waist-deep in the water who were moving the rafts with long poles or by hand, back and forth across the river between Guatemala and Mexico.

People waiting for the next raft were huddled under the shade of trees to escape the searing heat, some eating tortillas and drinking water, others licking flavored ice sold by vendors working the crowd. Scattered throughout the water were people who had tired of waiting for their turn on a raft and were attempting to cross the river on foot.

Felipe felt a twinge of excitement as a raft approached the shore, and he waved both hands in the air to catch the attention of the riverman. "How much to get across?" he yelled.

"Twelve pesos, seventy–five cents," the riverman yelled back.

The raft was packed with goods from Mexico, which would be unloaded to sell in Guatemala.

"How much if I help you carry the boxes?" Felipe yelled again.

"Four pesos, twenty-five cents American money, if you don't have pesos."

The bullet wound was healing well, and he was pleased to find that he had no pain as he lifted the first box from the raft. Sister Clara had re-bandaged his arm before he left the shelter, a clean white bandage, tightly wrapped, to make sure the wound stayed clean and continued to heal. He hoisted a box onto a waiting truck, followed by several other boxes of television sets, disposable diapers, and potato chips, judging by the pictures on the cartons. A man in a thin white undershirt and white pants spattered with brown dust leaned casually against the truck, observing him as he loaded the boxes. A huge straw hat was pulled down over his forehead, and droplets of sweat glistened in the creases that lined his leathery face.

"Looking for work?" the man asked.

"I wasn't, but what do you have?"

"*Finca* not too far from here. Picking papayas and mangoes."

"How much?"

"Good pay. One dollar per day. Work seven days a week, you can make seven dollars. That'll go far around here."

"How many hours a day?"

"Ten to twelve hours, depending on how much needs to be picked."

Felipe wrapped his arms around the last box, tossed it onto the truck, and waved the man off. "Thanks, but I'm not staying here," he answered.

"You could make some good money," the man continued. "Maybe even enough to pay for a coyote," he said, grinning at Felipe, as though they shared a very important secret. "It's a very dangerous trip, and a coyote could really help you."

"One dollar a day will pay for a coyote? I don't think so, although at that pay, I might be able to afford to take a taxi home. It would probably be cheaper than a coyote, anyway!" Felipe responded facetiously, grinning back at him. "Actually, I'm trying to get home to my family, and I want to get there before I'm old and gray. Thank you for the offer, though. I'll keep it in mind if I come through here again."

He wandered over to the fruit ice vendor and handed him five cents for some pineapple-flavored ice. The ice was cool in his throat and the sugary sweetness of the pineapple syrup was a treat he hadn't had in a while. He sprawled out under the shelter of a tree, gazing languorously at the empty raft bobbing in the water, the breeze from the river washing over his face like a soft morning kiss. He wondered if Julia missed him, if she was thinking about him today. Someday they would take a real vacation together, stay in a nice hotel, sit out at night sipping margaritas, watching the sunset. In the meantime, she had needs, and he wondered if she would be swayed by them, by some good-looking guy who paid attention to her, flattered her, helped her with money, took their children places on the weekend. She was a beautiful woman and other men would certainly be interested.

The riverman had returned and was collecting money, seventy-five cents from each person, twenty-five cents from Felipe because he had loaded boxes. Felipe climbed onto the raft, two huge tractor inner tubes covered with wooden planks, large enough to hold five or six people. He watched in amazement as the riverman navigated the little rig swiftly across the narrow stretch of water with his pole, the Guatemalan shore still in sight behind him, the Mexican soil visible ahead. Zoraida had been right. A few short minutes would put him in Mexico, that much nearer to his family. The raft smacked against the riverbank with a thud, bobbing and swaying in the shallow water.

Mexico! He had made it to Mexico! He was elated that he had gotten this far without being turned back, but he had no idea where to go now or what to do next. One of the other guys who had been on the raft with him was strolling confidently toward a dirt path, as though he had done this before and knew exactly where he was going, and the others were trotting along quietly behind him. Zoraida had told him to just follow the group from the raft, so Felipe slipped into the line behind the last person as they tramped briskly along, the Suchiate River fading until it was just a dot in the distance. The trail wound through a grove of mango trees, and he grabbed two mangoes that had fallen on the ground and slipped them into his backpack with the oranges.

They had been trudging along the dirt path for a while, fifteen or twenty minutes, Felipe thought, when the line ahead of him stopped so abruptly that he almost smacked into the man in front of him. He craned his neck to see what was happening up in front. It appeared that the path had suddenly ended, with nothing ahead but a thicket of trees and dense underbrush. One by one, they each squeezed through a narrow space between the overhanging branches and hanging vines and found themselves in a small meadow dotted with gravestones.

Felipe tapped the man in front of him on the shoulder. "What the hell is this?" he asked nervously. "Why are we in a cemetery?"

He wondered if he had made a terrible mistake following these people blindly, and was about to be robbed, or worse, killed on the spot. Maybe this was a set-up, a way for the police to dispose easily of un-suspecting Central American migrants, lost on their way to the border, desperate to get there any way they could. His body was on full alert now, adrenaline rushing through him as he debated whether to turn and hightail it back to the river as fast as he could, when the man pointed to some bushes with a small pathway cut through them.

"The train to the border stops on the other side of those bushes," the man whispered. "We hide in the cemetery, listen for the whistle of the train, and then run out and try to jump on. We have to be very quiet, because the police are out there, waiting to arrest us. When the train comes, you have to run very fast and jump on before they can grab you."

"How often do trains come by here?" Felipe asked.

"Hard to say—they come when they come, and we just wait. But I heard down at the river that they're expecting a train at midnight tonight."

Twilight was setting in, blanketing the cemetery in a bluish-gray haze, as the other people from the raft vanished behind the tombstones to wait out the time until the train came. Felipe removed an orange and a tortilla from his backpack. Sister Clara had washed his clothes and given him a bag of tortillas, which he had placed carefully into his backpack. He leaned against a tombstone and peeled the orange, biting into it slowly, savoring the juice as long as he could before it went down his throat. He could have eaten a bushel of oranges and a pound of tortillas, but he had a long journey and needed to save the ones he had left.

Hours passed; the twilight long descended into blackness before the wail of a train whistle and the rumble of an engine pierced the eerie stillness of the cemetery. There was a rustling noise from behind one of the tombstones, and then the sound of footsteps crunching on grass. "It's time," he heard someone say.

Felipe could barely see them all in the dark, faceless shadows, darting toward the bushes. Five people had been with him on the raft, but since the rivermen continued to ferry people from the Guatemalan shore all afternoon, a steady stream of new arrivals had shown up until there were no more tombstones to hide behind. They sprawled out in the grass, stretching out flat, praying that they would be invisible in the darkness. An army of ghosts waiting in a graveyard, gambling everything on a chance for a new life.

They crept silently through the bushes as the train whistled again, louder this time, and the *bestia*, the huge metal beast, came into view—a freight train carrying goods from Central America to Mexico and the United States. Felipe was too excited to be frightened. His heart was racing and energy surged through him, making him feel strong, invincible. The train to the border!

A flurry of blue descended on the train yard, uniformed men with rifles pointed at the first group to emerge from the bushes surrounding the cemetery. The majority of the crowd slipped back, disappearing into the darkness as the police grabbed two men and pulled them away in handcuffs. The police disappeared with their detainees, and Felipe followed the group as they snaked through the bushes again, swarming into the train yard.

The train was moving toward them at a much faster rate than Felipe had expected, roaring and bellowing as it belched thick black smoke, its huge metal wheels sending yellow sparks into the darkness. He could see a ladder on the side of a freight car and he leaped, grabbing the ladder with both hands, squeezing with all the force he had. The train swerved back and forth along the tracks, his hands sliding on the rungs, his legs swinging in the air as the train picked up speed, his shirt flapping in the wind like a flag as he dangled precariously over the railroad ties below.

Visions of legless torsos danced on the walls of the freight car, disembodied legs floated across the wispy clouds wandering the night sky, rootless and disconnected. Felipe managed to propel his left leg onto one of the rungs and curl it around the metal. He was perspiring heavily and his hands were soaked in sweat, making the ladder slippery and difficult to hang onto, causing his right hand to slip, leaving him hanging on with one leg and one hand. He wrapped his left arm around the rung of the ladder, clinging to the writhing beast like a *toreador* wrestling the bull from hell, frozen in place until the train rounded a bend and slowed down a bit.

Summoning every last ounce of energy and commanding every muscle in his body, he snatched the ladder with his right hand and swung his left leg up, wiping one sweaty palm on his pants and quickly thrusting it back on the ladder. The train slowed again as it rounded a curve, and he stretched one hand up at a time to grab the highest rungs, his legs following behind. A small piece of metal was sticking up from the roof of the freight car, and he wrapped his hands around it and hoisted himself up on the roof. Felipe lay there, shaking uncontrollably, clutching the metal rod so tightly that his hands were hot from the friction. He moved one leg, and then the other. Legs. He still had his legs.

The train chugged down the tracks for quite a while before he finally lifted his head, scanning the area for his companions from the raft. He spotted two of them sitting on top of the next car, and several shadowy figures on top of other cars further down. A few had made it, most of them hadn't. He wondered if anyone had jumped and been pulled under the wheels, or whether they were still in the cemetery, waiting for another train, and how many had been arrested and sent back to Guatemala or their home country. The train slowed again as it pulled into the Tapachula train yard, twenty-eight miles from Ciudad Hidalgo and Tecun Uman. He had completed twenty-eight miles of a thousand-mile trip.

Summer, 2006

Thirty

The world outside the bus window flew by quickly while Marisol entertained herself with thoughts of Colin. She needed things with him to stay exactly the way they were right now, a fun escape from her troubles, even though this trip would certainly be easier if he was sitting beside her, his shoulder resting against hers, the warmth of his hand soothing her. She thought about them chasing each other in Central Park, pretending they were ducks, and almost laughed out loud. Colin was so much fun, but more than that, he was special, kinder and less pushy than other boys. She had desperately wanted him to kiss her in Central Park, but in a way she was relieved that he hadn't demanded that they hook up right away, grateful that she would have time to get to know him better before anything like that happened.

The frosty stone and glass façade of the county courthouse appeared sooner than she had expected and a chill ran through her body, as though July had morphed into January, the warm summer air driven out by a blast of icy winter wind. Papi's fate was inscribed in ink on a disposition in that forbidding fortress, twenty floors of secretaries watching over closely guarded offices, guards observing silently from hallway corners. Walking through those doors and facing those condescending eyes would be the scariest thing she had ever done, but she had to try to help Papi. Right now, all she needed to do was get that piece of paper, a document anyone could get for five dollars, the Legal Aid lawyer had said. It was a written record of his felony conviction, and would have the name of his public defender on it, a name she needed. There was no reason why she couldn't just walk in there, hand over five dollars, get that piece of paper and leave. She wouldn't even have to tell Mama, who had been pissed off as hell at her for even considering doing this.

"You have no idea what you would be getting into," Mama had said. "I tried everything I could and I got nowhere, so what are you going to do? Take on the Oakmont police department by yourself? There are some mean cops out there, and you don't want to mess with them. I know you want to help Papi, but think about what he would want. He would want you to go to college and have a good life. That's what your Papi would want you to do."

She had managed to pass her final exams with her usual high grades, and burying herself in her books for a few weeks had been a good distraction. Now that she didn't have school to consume her time, though,

317

she suddenly had an ocean of time to think about Papi. Ms. Torres had given her some leads on summer jobs she should follow up on, too, but that would have to wait.

Anyway, she wasn't taking on the Oakmont Police; she was just getting a form so she could have a conversation with Papi's lawyer. Marisol couldn't see any reason why that would make the situation worse or endanger her in any way. Mama was just burned out from everything that had happened and would probably change her mind when she saw that Marisol was actually doing a good thing, something that would benefit the whole family.

She stepped into the spacious lobby of the courthouse, surrounded by a continual stream of people entering and leaving the elevators, parading in and out of the surrounding offices, completely engrossed in whatever business they had there. She stood there for a moment, unsure of what to do next, and then walked tentatively up to the security guard at the front door. Linda Malone had said something about the County Clerk's office—that was what she needed to find.

"I'm looking for the office where I can get a disposition of a court case. I think it's the County Clerk's Office," she said to the guard.

"Third floor," he said stiffly, as though he was tired of being asked questions people should have figured out some other way. "Directory is on the wall over there," he said pointing across the hall to a glass display case with hundreds of names on it. That was a new one for her; she hadn't known that big office buildings listed the office numbers that way, and tucked the information away in her mind to use in the future. "You have to go through security," he said, pointing to a line of people taking things out of their pockets and throwing them on a conveyor belt. "Then go to the third floor and follow the signs."

A form had to be filled out, five dollars handed over. She handed the clerk the five dollar bill she had borrowed from Colin, promising to pay him back as soon as she got a summer job.

Another wonderful thing about him, she thought. He hadn't asked any invasive questions or been patronizing about it—he had just placed the bill in her hand and smiled. "Pay me back when you can," he said, flashing that sexy grin of his. She was getting to be mad crazy about him—

"Miss!" the clerk was staring at her, annoyed. "Are you done with the form?"

The clerk returned a few minutes later with a document which she tossed in Marisol's direction, already motioning to the next person in line. The man behind her grumbled audibly about how long she was taking, but Marisol's hands were so shaky she couldn't grasp the form, which seemed stuck to the counter. The clerk finally grabbed the page and shoved it into her hand as she called the next person forward. There was his name, Felipe Sanchez, the words "aggravated felony"—and the name of an attorney.

July passed by slowly, turning into August before Marisol landed an appointment with the public defender, the man who had been Papi's lawyer. He was younger than she expected, maybe in his late twenties or early thirties, with long, brown hair pulled back into a ponytail, a slightly wrinkled white shirt and a blue tie with splotches of orange and yellow. Steven Rosenbaum sat behind a spacious, mahogany desk, tapping on a computer. He eyed Marisol curiously, continued typing for a few more minutes, then pointed to an oversized dark brown leather chair and motioned for her to sit down.

"What can I do for you? School project?"

The walls were lined with the same law books she had seen at Legal Aid, but the desk was a little messier, overflowing with file folders, an in-out box stuffed with papers, a coffee can crammed with pencils and pens of various sizes. Potted plants occupied the empty space between the bookcases, giving the cramped room a slightly earthy odor.

"You had a case, a man who was arrested for drugs and then deported because he wasn't a citizen."

"I've had quite a few of those."

She sank into the soft leather chair, clearly designed for larger, more important people to conduct serious business. "His name is Felipe Sanchez and he was a day laborer in Oakmont. He was waiting for a job in the parking lot at the East Oakmont mall when he was arrested, taken to a police station, and put in a lineup. Someone picked him out of the lineup, and he was convicted and sent to the county jail. Then one day we went to visit him and he wasn't there—he had been sent to an immigration detention center in Arizona. My mom tried to find him but was told he'd been deported."

The lawyer stared at the computer, absorbed by something on the screen, his fingers clicking intermittently on the keyboard. Maybe he was playing a game of some kind. He could be a gamer, bored with his job, whiling away the time playing video games while his clients rotted in jail or were deported without so much as a word from him. "And what is it you are asking me to do?" he said finally.

"He's my father, and he's innocent. He would never sell drugs."

"Your father? He must be a really nice guy, to have raised such a concerned daughter," he said quietly, his brown eyes focused on her now, studying her face. "How old are you? College student?"

"Seventeen. I'm in high school. I'll be a senior when school starts up again."

The cloth purse with the floral design sat on her lap, and she twisted the strap on her purse around and around, something she often did when she was nervous.

"I went to the County Courthouse and I got this," she said, opening her purse, taking out the disposition and pushing it across the desk toward him.

He picked up the disposition and glanced at it. "An aggravated felony. That's not great."

"What is that, an aggravated felony?"

"Some things that are misdemeanors under criminal law are felonies under immigration law. If you're not a citizen, you have very few options."

"But how could they find him guilty? I just don't understand it. He wouldn't have had drugs on him—there's just no possibility of that. He was at the mall trying to get some work, that's all."

"Any other adults at home?"

"Just my mother now."

Marisol had tied her hair back to make her look older; the hot weather always brought out the frizz in her hair, and she thought it would be better not to have her hair flying out everywhere. She had spent at least a half-hour getting her eye shadow and mascara just right and borrowed Mama's lipstick to make her lips look pinker. Mama probably wouldn't have minded, but Marisol didn't want her asking what the occasion was, so she snuck into her dresser when she was at work, swiped on the lipstick and slipped it back in the drawer. Her black shoes, white blouse, and black skirt matched perfectly. She and Mama had picked them out together, for special occasions like communions and weddings.

"She know you're here? Why didn't she come with you? I don't usually meet with—"

"She's working today. The guidance counselor at school told me to go to Legal Aid, and the Legal Aid lawyer sent me here. I have to do this—my Papi has no one else who can help him. In my government class, the teacher said—"

"I understand how hard this must be on your family and how much you care about him," Rosenbaum interjected, drumming on the desk with his fingers as he gazed at her solemnly. "The problem is—well, this is a very difficult situation, and um, I would love to try to help you, but hey, there are some limits as to what I can do. From what you're saying, he was here illegally and he was convicted on a criminal charge. A conviction for a criminal offense is an automatic deportation for an undocumented person. He's already been deported—he's not even in the country to return to court, if we did reopen it. He may never be able to come back here," he said gently, as though he was trying to soften the blow.

"But that's wrong—he's not, he's really not a criminal—he's innocent. I don't see why you can't reopen the case and help me prove him innocent."

The lawyer leaned forward, regarding her sympathetically. "Prove him innocent?" he said, in the same gentle voice. "The case already went to court, and they found him guilty and closed the case. I really don't know what—"

"We have to start somewhere, and I'm starting here. The Legal Aid lawyer told me that once you've been someone's lawyer, you remain their lawyer, even if the case is closed and they're not here. If there's new information, you have to open up the case," Marisol said, pleading now, fighting back tears. She took a deep breath, pushing the tears back down. Crying would make her look childish, when she needed to be taken seriously.

Steven Rosenbaum sat up straight, raising his eyebrows in astonishment. "New information? You have new information?"

"Well, when our restaurant was still open, my brother and I worked there on the weekends, and the police would come into the restaurant and harass my father, insulting him about him being illegal and threatening him. I pretended I wasn't listening, but I heard them say stuff about how the restaurant was a front for drug dealers in the area, and that they were going to call the health department, get them closed down. I think my father was set up because I know he never did any of the things they accused him of. Don't you think I would know if he was getting drunk or stoned? And nobody came in and out buying or selling anything except pupusas and burritos. That's just crazy."

The lawyer was quiet for a moment, his eyes searching her face. "You're a smart girl, very mature for your age. Your father is a lucky man to have you for a daughter." He stared out of the immense glass window as though he was searching for something.

Marisol couldn't see anything out there except the blue sky and more buildings, but maybe he was just thinking, stalling for time until he could figure out how to dismiss her. If she craned her neck, she could see people twenty stories below going about their business, tiny little people and tiny little cars moving about like ants. She felt small like that, like a little ant in a giant world, trying to avoid being squashed flat.

"Okay. You have me a little intrigued here. For some reason, I believe you, but I'm not going to promise you anything, because what you've presented me with is—well, very, very tough is an understatement. I still want you to promise me something, though. From now on, no more detective work. I don't know what kind of people you are up against, so let me do the investigating. I have a daughter, and if she was in your situation, that's what I would want her to do."

He picked up the disposition again, scanning it for a moment, then pressed a button on his telephone.

"Yes, Mr. Rosenbaum?" a woman's voice answered.

"Roberta, pull up the file on Felipe Sanchez. #367008.

"I need some time to look this case over. Make an appointment with my secretary and come back in about a month. We'll talk then."

Thirty-one

Tortillas and oranges churned in Felipe's stomach as he lay on the roof of the freight car, clinging to the metal bar, the wheels vibrating hypnotically as they rolled past shuttered warehouses, darkened fields, sleeping villages. He had almost drifted off when his eye caught a shadow moving beside the train, then several. The shadow moved faster, and a figure leaped, arms outstretched, grabbing for the ladder. A scream rang out as the body flew off the ladder and slid under the train; the sound of a woman wailing faded into the darkness as the train hurtled down the track, oblivious to the tragedy it left behind.

A hand tapped his leg. "Don't fall asleep, *amigo*. You have to stay awake, or you'll end up under those wheels, too. There's a tunnel up ahead, so stay down! When the train stops, we can try to get inside the car."

"Thanks," Felipe mumbled, glancing up to see who the voice belonged to. A boy, not much older than Ricky, wearing jeans and a black shirt with a picture of a race car on the front, was stretched out next to him on the roof. "Thanks," Felipe said again, louder this time to make sure the boy had heard him. "Sounds like you've been this way before. What's your name, *hermano?*"

"Emilio," the boy answered. "Done this twice already and haven't made it all the way yet. My mama is in Los Angeles and I'm trying to join her there. I'm not giving up—hey, look out! The tunnel's coming! Get down, get down!"

Felipe flattened himself against the roof as the train entered the tunnel, filling the narrow space with exhaust. Fumes choked his lungs, seared his eyes and his throat as he lay with his face pressed into the metal, gasping for air, not daring to move for fear of being crushed between the train and the ceiling of the tunnel. The train lurched and swerved in the smoky blackness, and several minutes dragged by before the brown palm leaves that crowned the rooftops of a village emerged on the horizon. Felipe sat up slowly, his hands still wrapped tightly around the metal post. He sucked in the clear mountain air, felt it rush into his lungs, drinking it in as though it was a cool glass of water on a hot day. The roof of the freight car was already warm under his body, and there would be no protection from the burning Mexican sun as the day heated up.

The outline of a train yard appeared ahead, and Felipe could make out container trucks and forklifts lined up in front of the corrugated steel doors of a warehouse. Men in wide-brimmed hats and shirts with cutoff sleeves stood on the platform, waiting for the train to arrive, their muscular arms shining with sweaty blue tattoos. With so many people around, someone was sure to spot them on the roof and give a shout to the inspectors and the police who were wandering the train yard, making safety checks, cruising for stowaways. No way they could manage to climb inside the train without being seen.

The train screeched to a stop, and the men began pulling open the heavy doors of the boxcars, tossing cardboard cartons onto the concrete and piling them on the forklifts with such amazing speed that the whole operation was done in a matter of minutes. Felipe flattened himself on the roof and peered across the parking lot, where he could see the inspectors in their blue uniforms examining freight being loaded into the container trucks, laughing and conversing with the forklift drivers.

Emilio moved toward the ladder, motioning to Felipe to follow him. "We can get inside now," he whispered. "They went so fast, they left some of the doors a little open, so we can get in there now. It's better to ride inside."

Felipe hesitated, sure they would be spotted, thinking it might be better just to stay flattened on the roof and hope that the train would quickly resume its journey, but he noticed that some of the migrants were already slipping down the ladders and disappearing from view.

He grabbed the top rung of the ladder and stepped down tenuously, one rung at a time, until the comforting crunch of gravel told him he was on solid ground. A hand was sticking out of the door of the boxcar, motioning. Arms pulled at him, hoisting him up into darkness. The train was beginning to move again, and the arms that had pulled him in grabbed at the door, closing it behind them as the train accelerated, leaving the train yard and the inspectors behind.

Felipe was grateful to be inside the boxcar, away from the heat of the sun and the constant danger of falling under the metal wheels or being crushed as the train went through a tunnel. As his eyes adjusted to the dim light, he could see several people sprawled out on the floor, and the air was rank with the odor of urine and vomit, the remains of those who had huddled in this boxcar before him.

He dozed on and off for a while as the train rattled and banged over the tracks, then just sat there awake, feeling the train rumbling beneath him. He tried to comfort himself by imagining the moment he and Julia reunited, what their first kiss would be like, the joy on her face when they were able to touch each other again. The kids would be older and taller— Marisol would be getting ready to graduate from high school, and Ricky might look more like a man than a boy now. Even Camilo, his baby, would have grown some. If Officer Bradley was still on the Oakmont police force, the family might have to move out of Oakmont, go someplace where he wouldn't be recognized by the police. New Jersey, maybe, or even the Bronx or Brooklyn, where he could disappear into a crowded neighborhood, stay out of sight. He wondered how the kids would take that.

Hours went by as he lay on the floor, a whole day possibly, until he finally pulled himself back up to a sitting position. He had eaten all of the mangoes and most of the oranges, and shared what was left of Sister Clara's tortillas with some other people in the boxcar. His head throbbed; he had long since finished up his water, leaving him unbearably thirsty, and he was down to his last orange.

The odor in the car seemed to have intensified far beyond the stench of food and human waste, and felt like a rope around his throat, choking him. He did a quick scan of the boxcar to see if anyone had some water they might share with him, even a small sip would help alleviate the dryness in his mouth and throat. Emilio was leaning against the wall across from him and gave him a small wave, but no one appeared to be drinking anything at all. A few empty plastic bottles lay scattered around the car, their last few drops long since drained.

"Hey! Emilio! Any idea where we are?" Felipe called weakly.

"Still in Mexico, I guess," Emilio responded, shrugging his shoulders.

"Can't wait to get the hell out of here," Felipe tossed back.

He sat there absorbed in his thoughts, lulled by the rhythmic clacking of the wheels, until he felt the rumbling begin to slacken, the high-speed clatter ease into a softer chugging, indicating that the train was slowing. He glanced over at Emilio, who was crawling over the bodies sprawled across the floor and pointing vigorously at the door. A shirtless man lay motionless as Felipe climbed over him, his shoes scraping against his legs, but the man didn't give the slightest flinch or moan of complaint, and his chest was still, with no sign of a breath being taken. Felipe clawed at the heavy metal door, starving for some fresh air.

"What the hell are you doing?" a voice called out in the dark.

"Trying to open the door a little to get some air, to see where we are."

The hands that had pulled him into the car to safety were grabbing at his legs, tugging on his shirt. "Hey! Don't open that door!"

Felipe gripped the door handle, pulling on it with all the strength he could muster. "We're still moving. The police are not going to come in while we're moving." He jerked the door open a crack and peered at the track moving beneath the train.

"Close the door. You're crazy, man. Close it!" a man pleaded. Two others tore at his arms, another wrapped his hands around one ankle.

"There's no air in here. Need some air—"

An ominous clicking, the glint of a steel blade as a knife swung open, pointed at him, moving toward his throat. "We'll all end up getting air in a Mexican jail if you don't close it, now!"

Felipe kicked at them, twisting and thrashing to free himself from their grip, desperate to escape the boxcar. Without food or water in this suffocating, airless hot box, he knew he would just continue to get weaker until death came knocking. He could now see several other bodies lying motionless near the door, as though they had crawled toward the door in desperation to escape, but had been so weakened by dehydration and hunger that their hearts just gave out. He had no idea how much farther they had to go or where they were, but he couldn't spend another second in here, surrounded by dead bodies, he was sure of that. If he couldn't get onto the roof, he could take a break, sleep outside in the grass for a while and try again later. There would be another train—if not today, there would be one tomorrow.

"Get out of my way," he snarled, propelling himself through the crack in the door, hurtling through the air like a piece of tumbleweed blown by the wind in a desert storm. He sailed from the train onto the gravel below and lay crumpled on the ground as the metal door of the boxcar clattered shut behind him and the train slowed to a halt. Stunned and dizzy, he struggled to his feet and limped furiously toward the nearest ladder.

There was nothing to do on the roof but watch the endless miles of track and sagebrush roll by, but at least he could breathe. He looked around for Emilio and caught sight of him on top of the next car.

"How'd you get out of there?" Felipe yelled to him, glad for the companionship.

"I saw the guy with the knife and decided to go a different way. I jumped from the space between the cars," Emilio yelled back. Emilio turned away briefly as a man's head appeared at the top of the ladder of his car, then two more. Felipe watched, waited for them to find a place near Emilio. He considered attempting to climb across the roof to join them, but still wasn't confident about shifting his position while the train was in motion. Maybe when the train stopped, though, he might try to get over there, or maybe Emilio would join him over here.

He gazed back amiably at Emilio, but something was very wrong. The men who had joined him were fishing through his pockets, taking his money, his shoes, and his clothes. Emilio was crying now, pleading for mercy as the men kicked and punched him, cracking a stick over his head powerfully enough to be heard down the track. Legs without pants and feet without shoes flew into the air as they threw him over the side of the train. They slithered across the roof, coiled snakes ready to strike, scanning the other freight cars, scoping out the area for their next victim, leaping silently across the space between the cars, springing toward Felipe. Instinctively, without a second of hesitation, he hurled his backpack over the side, slid halfway down the ladder and catapulted through the air, landing inches from the wheels, his body rolling over and over across the gravel, down the side of an embankment. The train whistle moaned, the wheels chanting a song of lament as the last rusty brown boxcar disappeared down the track and another body sailed over the top of the train and crashed to the ground, a lifeless, broken heap.

Dirt filled Felipe's mouth and his eyes burned from dusty grit as he plunged to the bottom of the hill. Pain shot through his leg when he tried to move it, his arms and legs were bruised and covered with cuts and scrapes, and his back felt like a ten-ton truck had rolled over it.

The early morning sunrise turned to midday heat, then cooled as evening set in and darkness fell. He had no idea how many hours he was sprawled there, in and out of consciousness, dozing and waking, then dozing again, until hunger roused him and he sat up, staring woozily at the hill, scanning the area for his backpack. A patch of black next to the tracks caught his eye, and he crawled gingerly up the hill, his hands clutching at the grayish-brown sandy clay soil, hard and unyielding under his fingers.

A few feet away, Emilio's lifeless body lay slumped in the gravel. A feeling of sadness swept over him as he stared at Emilio's body, sadness for another young life lost, but also sadness for the loss of a friend, a stranger who had offered him camaraderie on a lonely journey.

Felipe wondered if he should try to give him a burial of some kind, but quickly abandoned that idea. He had nothing to dig with but his bare hands, and if the police spotted him they might think he had killed him and arrest him, throw him in jail. The best he could hope for was that the police would eventually find the body, maybe have some way to determine who he was and contact his family. His mama was in Los Angeles, he had said, and would be waiting for him. The police wouldn't even know her name, and he doubted the police would really try to find a family member in another country, but maybe he had relatives in Mexico who would help them out. The cops would probably just dump him in an unknown grave somewhere, but there was always a chance.

Hobbling along next to the tracks, he reached a bend where the train would have to reduce its speed, maybe even brake for a moment. One lone orange was left in his backpack, and he peeled it furiously, tearing off pieces and stuffing them in his mouth. There was no source of drinking water and no river to cool him, nothing for miles but tracks and sagebrush, surrounded by an endless expanse of parched brown earth. He had no idea where he was, or whether all the trains that came through here went to the U.S. border. Maybe some of them just circled around Mexico and went back to Tapachula, and he would have to start the journey all over again. The orange was about half eaten when his ears caught the sound of a train whistle. He quickly stuffed the orange into his backpack and slung the straps over his shoulders, ready to leap when the train curved around the bend.

Thirty-two

At noon on Saturday, Colin ladled soup from the ancient aluminum pot, its underside blackened from years of service at St. Michael's. The soup was thick and chunky, a bean soup, onions and tiny cubes of carrot swimming in a brown sea. Volunteers were scarce at lunchtime on Saturday, so Wesley worked beside him, serving ground beef from one pan, cooked carrots from the other.

He glanced briefly at Marisol as she nibbled on a piece of bread at the dining room table across from the alcove, the ground beef and cooked carrots barely touched on her plate. Colin checked his watch and gave her a thumbs up, and she caught his eye and held it for a minute, her lips creasing in a slight smile, that sexy smile that made heat spread through his body. Marisol scooped some ground beef onto her fork and lifted it to her mouth. He watched her chewing the meat, as slow and sensual as everything else she did. Colin had never thought he would find chewing meat captivating, but every movement she made mesmerized him.

He was becoming quite comfortable being at St. Michael's, even though many of the people there didn't speak English and it wasn't his usual scene, for sure. Dad had offered to pick him up today, but he declined, insisting that it wasn't worth the trouble—the bus ride across town was an easy twenty-minute ride.

He dished out his last bowl of soup and danced out of the alcove, a hip-hop move he had seen on TV that made Marisol throw her head back and laugh right out loud.

"Pretty good. You like to dance?"

"I'm ready anytime," he grinned.

"I'll have to teach you to cumbia," she responded, the sexy smile broader as he squeezed in next to her at the table, so close that he could almost nuzzle her neck, although he didn't think she was quite ready for that, to be seen snuggling with him in public.

"Ready for some sand and surf?" he said in a low voice, trying to make it sound deeper and sexier, more charming. On their train ride home from Central Park, they had decided it would be her turn to show him someplace new, and she had chosen Orchard Beach in the Bronx. It was a place her family often went on weekend outings in the warm weather, she had said, and seemed to have some special meaning for her, so he easily agreed.

"You'll have to show me around this time. Never been to Orchard

Beach." The Bronx wasn't a place his family chose for recreation, except for visiting Nana. Weekends were generally saved for football, puttering around the yard, kicking back in front of the television.

Marisol held up a large woven tote bag. "Start with towels, a bathing suit—"

Colin peered into the bag. "Ah, a black bikini. Looks nice resting in there, but I bet it looks nicer when it's on you." He held up a tiny olive green army bag. "Swimming trunks!"

"How about if your swimming trunks and my bathing suit head toward the Metro-North?"

Wesley, who had been in the kitchen cleaning up, shuffled into the dining room as Marisol held up the woven bag. "Where are you off to, young people?" he asked. "Looks like you're going somewhere." He extended his hand to Marisol. "Seen you here a few times, but don't believe we've been introduced."

"Wesley, this is my friend Marisol. Marisol, this is Wesley, one of the coolest guys you ever want to meet. Smart dude, already taught me a bunch of stuff."

"How to ladle soup and empty the trash," Wesley grinned. "You young folks have a pleasant afternoon. Looks like it's turning out to be a beautiful day."

"My swimming trunks are going to follow her bathing suit to Orchard Beach."

"Ah, Orchard Beach, best kept secret in the Bronx," Wesley replied. "I lived in the Bronx myself for a while, but I like it better here. Sleeping on a heating grate in the city gets old, so I decided to raise my standard of living, move to the suburbs." They all laughed. "Great neighborhood, Grover Hill. Love it here," he added, grinning again. "Wouldn't live anywhere else."

He gave Marisol a quick appraisal. "You live in Grover Hill?"

"All my life, on Fourth Street," she said, glancing over at Colin.

A wave of anxiety flooded over Colin, who wanted more than anything to distance himself from his father's condescending attitudes. "Definitely a cool place," he responded eagerly, hoping to reassure her that he wasn't going to put down Grover Hill.

Marisol looked at him curiously. "Why do you say that?"

"Because you live there," he said, trying to sound playful, but he could feel heat rising in his face as it flushed, turned beet red right in front of her. He hated when that happened, and he hoped Marisol didn't notice, or didn't know the reason if she did notice. It was a little hot in the church; if she said anything about it, he would just say something about how warm it was in there.

"I know Fourth Street," Wesley interjected. "Used to be a terrific little restaurant, Salvadoran, I think—"

"Nice to meet you," Marisol said to Wesley, extending her hand, "but we better get going if we want to get to the beach before the sun goes down. Got an hour ride ahead of us—the Metro North and a bus in the Bronx."

"More time to spend together!" Wesley said, clapping Colin on the shoulder.

Colin pushed open the front door of the church, brushing Marisol's fingers with his as they stepped into the bright light of early afternoon. It was a little dance they had been doing lately, brushing fingers, then curling them together, sometimes just their little fingers, sometimes their whole hand.

The blast of a car horn jolted them out of their reverie, diverting their attention to a van parked at the curb, its driver playing little games with the horn. *Dun, duh, dun-dun,* the horn sounded, and then some long and short honks, like some kind of Morse code. A white Ford van with a dent in the passenger side door. Dad had come to pick him up, even though he had asked him not to. It was too late to slip back into the church. Dad had seen him, knew he was here.

"Gotta talk to someone. I'll be right back," Colin murmured to Marisol, in a voice barely louder than a whisper. He raced down the gray stone steps of the church, slid around to the driver's side window.

Dad was sitting behind the wheel with his elbow resting on the open window frame, but he wasn't alone. Sam was next to him in the passenger seat, and Cory, the new quarterback, was spread out in the back, sitting where Luke would have been. Luke and his family had high-tailed it out of town shortly after the SIM rally in front of their house, so quickly that Colin barely had time to say goodbye. He and Luke were keeping in touch, though, texting each other regularly. His family was in Florida, Luke had texted him, staying with his grandparents until they could find a place of their own. Colin had tried to apologize for what happened, but Luke wouldn't hear it, said he knew it wasn't his fault and he didn't need to apologize for Frank. He would never come back to Oakmont, ever, but maybe Colin could come visit him in Florida sometime.

Colin gripped the window frame of the van as he peered into the back, trying to control the panic surging through him. These guys knew him, would spot the edge in his voice, his hurry to leave. "What are you doing here, Dad? I told you I would take the bus home."

"What does it look like we're doing here?" Frank said sarcastically.

"Just gonna toss the ball around a little, practice a few plays," Sam threw in.

"Yeah, play around for a while, go out for burgers afterward, like we always do," Frank responded impatiently. "C'mon, get in the car. You waiting for some kind of private invitation? It's hot in here."

"Well," Colin responded, trying to choose his words carefully. Sam and Cory knew about his arrest, that he had to do this community service thing. Shane, the other guy with him at the mall that day, had gone into Hamburger Heaven to buy a soda, leaving Colin alone outside when the police came. Shane had watched the whole arrest thing from behind the door, then had blabbed about it to their friends at school. Sam and Cory would be sympathetic, understand that he had to get the community service finished so he could put it behind him, forget it ever happened.

"I, uh, I'm sorry, I'd love to go with you guys, and, uh, how about we get together this weekend—that would be a better time for me—"

"What the hell are you talking about?" Frank said testily.

"I wasn't planning on leaving right now. I need to work another shift, get this damn community service over. Why stretch it out, have to come back here extra days? I just came outside for a break, goin' right back in," he said, trying to sound casual.

Sam was sprawled leisurely in the front seat, his long legs stretched out in front of him as he stared out the window. "Dude, who's the girl on the steps?" he asked, taking a big bite of a candy bar, chewing slowly as he spoke. "She's watching your moves, bro, checking you out."

"One of the people that ate lunch here today, probably waiting to be picked up by someone," Colin answered, continuing to try to sound indifferent. "I just serve the food, dude. Don't keep track of where they go after lunch."

"Homeless people have cars?" Cory piped up from the back, bringing guffaws from all three.

"Probably gets picked up by a limo. You can save a lot of money eating for free at the taxpayers' expense," Frank added, glaring indignantly at the girl on the steps.

"She's watching you, dude. Can't fool me," Sam continued.

"I wouldn't go near that one if my life depended on it. Probably has a two hundred and fifty–pound brother somewhere who'll beat your ass for looking at her, kill you before you can turn around," Cory tossed in.

"Slimy bastards, always tryin' to get somethin' for nothing," Frank proclaimed. "Not a bad idea, trying to finish this up as soon as possible. The less time you spend walking around Grover Hill, the better. Not today, though. Go tell 'em you can't stay today, that something's come up and you'll make it up tomorrow or some other day. They won't care—"

"It's summer, Dad. The football season doesn't start 'til fall. Anyway, I signed myself up for a double shift today, so they're expecting me to stay. Don't worry about it. I can take the bus."

"Maybe that chick can give you a ride in her limo," Sam offered.

"I don't care if it's the middle of January and it's snowing. Great players practice all year. No practice, no scholarship." Frank pulled out a cigarette from the pack in his shirt pocket with his left hand, stuck it between his teeth, his right hand on the steering wheel. Hadn't even turned off the motor. Colin could feel the van rumbling as Frank gave a tap on the accelerator and the engine roared loudly. Good thing the emergency brake was on, or the van would have flown down the street with him hanging onto the window.

"Dad—"

"Now! Go back in there and tell them you're not doin' an extra shift to-day, and tell them when you'll be back. Then come back and get in the damn car! You're doing them a favor, helping them feed these scumbags for free."

"They kept me out of—"

"They didn't keep you out of anything, son. I did, and the cops and the judge agreed to it. These people had nothing to do with the charges being lowered. They just mark off the sheet showing you put in your hours here. Do you need me to talk to them? I can go in there and take care of it, if you don't have the balls. G'wan, move." He placed his hand on the door, pushed it open with a shove. Colin stumbled, scrambling to keep from falling backward. At the top of the steps, Marisol leaned against the handrail, the beach bag sitting idly at her feet. The door to the van was open now, and Frank slid out of the driver's seat, threatening to blow into the church, act like an asshole.

"I'll handle it, Dad," Colin said desperately. "I'll be right back, okay?"

Colin sprung toward the stairs but slowed down when he hit the first step, his feet dragging as he tried to buy a little time to think, figure out what to do. He stopped halfway up the stairs, wiped off the sweat that was collecting on his forehead before resuming his trek to the oak door, the longest journey he had ever taken. Step up, pause, step up, pause. He had climbed the highest peak in the lower forty-eight states with the Boy Scouts, a fourteen thousand–foot hike with a pack on his back, a piece of cake compared to this.

Marisol, watching, waiting, within earshot now. "What was that about?" she called.

"Come inside, we have to talk," he said quietly, as he pulled open the door and rushed into the front lobby, hoping she would follow slowly so it didn't look like they were going back in together.

"I have a problem, a big problem," he said, as she stepped into the lobby behind him. "That's my dad in the van down there—we, um, have an emergency at home and he came to pick me up. My mom woke up sick this morning and he needs me to help him out with some things."

She would understand that, said her mom had been sick, taken to Westchester General in an ambulance. Couldn't fault a guy for helping out his family.

"I, uh, well, could we go to the beach another day? I'm really sorry, but I'm, just like, jammed up here."

Marisol was silent for a moment, then gave him a fake little smile, as though she was hurt and was trying to cover it up. "Well, yeah, I guess so, I mean I'm disappointed, but things happen, I guess."

Colin had thought a lot about when to kiss her and had hoped maybe something would happen at the beach today, but that would have to wait. This was terrible, disappointing her like this, and he was desperate now to show her he cared, that he wasn't just a total jerk blowing her off, so he moved in closer to give her a peck on the mouth before he rushed out. His lips met hers, but what started out as a goodbye peck quickly intensified into a feverish heat as she moved in closer to return the kiss, pressing her body against his.

The long blast of a car horn reverberated faintly through the double doors, and Colin pulled away quickly. "Gotta run—Tuesday—be here Tuesday—we can talk then," he said breathlessly. Marisol nodded, nervously patting down her hair and straightening her blouse, looking flustered as she watched him scurry toward the door. He turned and gave her a quick little wave before he swung the door open and stepped onto the landing, nearly smacking into his father, who had marched up the steps and was moving toward the entrance, a few seconds away from entering the building.

"I told you I'd take care of it," Colin said curtly. "No need to go in there. C'mon, let's go throw some passes."

Thirty-three

Felipe could now make out the silhouette of a train, miniature at first, like a child's toy, then larger, its headlights beaming like warm, welcoming eyes, beckoning him to climb aboard.

It stopped momentarily to allow a train to pass in the other direction, and he limped toward the coupling between the cars as quickly as his bruised body allowed. He spotted a ladder, dark and rusted, flat against the wall of the freight car, and grabbed the third rung.

Faces were peering down at him from the roof, strange faces. There was no way to be sure they weren't bandits, lying in wait for him. He stopped, motionless, not sure whether to continue. He could climb down and wait for the next train, but he had no idea how long that would be, and he had no water and nothing left to eat except for that last piece of orange in his backpack. Climbing to the roof was his best shot at surviving, even though those guys up there could easily rob him and throw him from the train, kill him the way Emilio was killed.

Two arms reached out to grab him as he clung tenaciously to the ladder, frozen in place with the massive wheels churning beneath him, the faces staring down from above. He wouldn't survive another jump, but he was groggy and weak, might not make it up the ladder, either.

"You don't want to stay there," one of the men called down to him. "Better to come up here," he said, holding out his arm. Another face peered over the side, another voice. "*Carajo!* He's in bad shape, all bloody." A second pair of hands tugged at him. "Grab onto us, *hermano*. You can do it. Hold on, just a little bit more."

"I'm Fredy, and this is my brother, Alfonso," one of the men said. Felipe flopped down next to them, his breath coming in short gasps. "Where are you from?" Fredy asked.

"Felipe, from El Salvador," Felipe answered, his voice faint.

"Hey, we are, too!" Fredy responded, grinning enthusiastically. "What part?"

"El Espino. My father and I worked on the *finca*—"

"We're from San Salvador. We worked in a clothing factory there.

Felipe managed a small smile. "I was working in San Salvador before I decided to try to get back to the U.S."

"In one of the clothing factories? Which one? Maybe you know my sister—"

"No, in a restaurant for a little while, then as a tour guide," Felipe answered.

"Tour guide? That's a pretty good job. You gave it up to do this?" Fredy said, eyeing him curiously. "What did you do? Get drunk and get fired? That happened to me—"

"I have a wife and three children in New York. I'm trying to get home to them."

"Ah, you got caught by *la migra*, right, *amigo*?" Alfonso said. "Me, too—that's what happened to me. Got family in Texas—Dallas—that's where I'm headed." He gave Fredy a punch on the arm. "He's going to Texas, too."

Fredy surveyed Felipe's bruises, the purple welt on the side of his face, his torn and dirty clothes. "You don't look too good. What the hell happened to you?"

"Maybe you need to shut up for a minute and help him," Alfonso said to Fredy playfully.

Fredy pulled the red bandana from around his head, tying it around the wound on Felipe's arm. "*Bandidos* on the other train," Felipe mumbled. "They killed two people, and I had to jump—"

"What's in the backpack?" Alfonso broke in, staring at Felipe's backpack hopefully. "You got some water? We could really use some water."

"Just half an orange, that's all I have left. I finished the water a few days ago, haven't had a drop since then," Felipe murmured.

"There's a church in the next town that will take us in and give us some food and water. It's a very small town, so the police and *la migra* are not all over the tracks," Fredy said.

Felipe looked at him skeptically. "How do you know that?"

"I've taken this trip four times, never made it over the border. When the train crosses the border at Nuevo Laredo into Texas, *la migra* is standing on the bridge, checking out the trains as they come through. They scan the cars with infrared telescopes, and they have dogs that circle the train yard sniffing at the cars looking for people inside," Fredy said.

"If they see you, it's *adios,* bye-bye to the United States, and *buenos dias* to Mexico. No money, no job, say hello to a Mexican jail," Alfonso added.

"You've done this before, too?" Felipe asked incredulously.

"Third time."

"But you think you can get past *la migra* this time, when you couldn't before?" Felipe asked, puzzled.

"Oh, no, we won't try that again, but there are other ways. Stick with us—you'll see!" Fredy said.

"You ever really been in a Mexican jail?"

"Once for three months, and another time for a month. You wouldn't like it. Sleeping on a concrete bench in a little room packed with people and crawling with *cucarachas*. They want money, and if you don't have it, they don't like you. But I know the game now, and I'm going to make it over this time."

The brakes hissed as the train pulled into a tiny village, a patchwork of ramshackle wooden huts draped with strands of dried palm leaves. A line of people gathered beside the tracks, waving bottles of water, and a woman was selling tortillas and beans from a cart!

"They expect us," Fredy said, responding to the look of amazement on Felipe's face. "People come through here on the trains every day, seven days a week. They have family and friends who have ridden these trains, children who have crossed the border. The water is free, to help us, and you can buy food from them for a few pesos. They make a little money and the migrants coming through can get something to eat."

The church courtyard was cluttered with people, some without shoes, some with dirty clothes they had clearly been wearing for days, maybe weeks, their hair matted from not having bathed. Felipe wondered if he looked like that, if he smelled like that. They walked through the open door of the church into the hallway, where people were sleeping on pieces of cardboard on the floor, in the hallway, on the patio. Hapless as they were, they were the survivors, the ones who still had arms and legs and had made it this far. There was water, rice and beans provided by the church, and a place to rest, away from the vigilant eyes of the police.

Fredy lit a cigarette he begged from a man in the courtyard, blew a stream of white smoke into the air. "They let you stay here three days, then you have to leave to make room for other people."

"The police come here?"

"They harass the church workers and arrest them sometimes. Father Gregorio was arrested for harboring fugitives, but he paid the police enough money and they let him go."

"How far do you think we are from the border?" Felipe asked.

"Six hundred more miles of Mexican police, and then the big one."

"Big one?"

"Getting across the U.S. border."

They had been at the little Mexican church for three days, when Father Gregorio approached Felipe, just as Fredy said he would. "Son, we're glad to have you, but we need to make room for the others coming off the train. I wish you good luck on your journey. Know that we'll be praying for you."

There was a small, filmy mirror in the bathroom at the church, so Felipe was able to give himself a quick once over before leaving. Although he looked like he had been in a boxing match, with cuts on his face and bluish-purple bruises on his arms and legs, miraculously, nothing had been broken or seriously damaged in any way. The respite at the church had revived him some, and the bruises from his leap off the train were beginning to heal, but he still felt run-down and sluggish, as though he could sleep for a week if he had the chance. Just a few more days to rest, to be in the safety of Father Gregorio's church would have been helpful, and he did not feel at all ready to get back on the roof of a train. Julia and his children had waited so many months to see him, a few more days to rest would not make such a big difference. He looked in the mirror again, and this time it was Mama's face staring back at him, and then Lydia's, encouraging him to continue, strengthening his resolve to keep going for as long as he could.

As the train clattered along the tracks, the clear mountain air gave way to factories belching black smoke. Rows and rows of run-down wooden shacks danced by the train and disappeared into the yellowish-brown horizon, and the air smelled like rotten eggs.

"We should jump off when the train goes through Mexico City," Fredy said. "There's a metal recycling plant that operates twenty-four hours a day, doesn't ask you any questions. We can pick up some work there, save a little money and catch a bus to Nuevo Laredo, the last border town in Mexico, just across the river from Laredo, Texas."

"And you know some way to get across?"

Fredy laughed. "Find a coyote, or swim across the Rio Grande."

"Wouldn't mind earning a little money, getting some good food."

"Yeah, some enchiladas, or a burrito."

"No, I think a pupusa filled with cheese."

"A Coke, with ice."

"Ten Cokes with ice."

"Something with chocolate."

"Chocolate ice cream."

"No, chocolate cake."

"A beer!"

"Tequila!"

Alfonso gave Felipe a playful punch. "How about a bar where they have lots of girls dancing with, you know, not much!"

"Yeah, a different kind of food. Food for the spirit," Fredy laughed.

Mendoza Metal Recycling was dirty and hot, the immense warehouse floor littered with giant bins of aluminum cans, piles of car radiators, and mounds of twisted metal. Felipe spent his days tossing scraps of metal into a machine that tore them apart as though they were pieces of meat fed to a ravenous dinosaur, while another machine with giant claws swept across the floor picking up the crushed metal, dumping it on top of a thirty-foot pile waiting to be baled into bundles, on its way to be melted down to be reused. Pick, toss, pick, toss, pick, toss. The racket was deafening, making friendly chit-chat to help pass the time impossible. Felipe tore a rag into small pieces and stuffed a piece in each ear to drown out the roaring, but it didn't help much.

They found shelter in a transient hotel, where they occupied a room with three sagging cots, a light bulb dangling precariously from a wire on the ceiling, and a bathroom in the hall shared by all of the patrons. Nothing much to do in the evenings except occupy a barstool at El Paraiso, tossing down beers, savoring the aroma of tequila. Days grew into weeks, but at least he was away from the constant danger of riding the trains. The money he was earning meant that he had food to eat every day and a place to sleep, and he was intensely grateful for the company of his new friends, Fredy and Alfonso.

On Saturday night, El Paraiso featured a girl wearing nothing but a G-string dancing on a table, twisting and shimmying to the music, gyrating her body a few feet from the customers.

Felipe sipped his tequila, absorbed by her swaying body.

"Nice-looking," Fredy said, smiling at Felipe. "You like her?"

"Pretty good dancer," Felipe responded.

"Wouldn't mind a few minutes with her," Alfonso chimed in. He leaned over and whispered in Felipe's ear. "I think someone is looking at you. At the end of the bar, in the red dress."

A woman with wide, dark eyes was checking him out, sliding out of her seat, strutting toward him in a skin-tight red dress that clung to the curves on her body. Fredy and Alfonso were smirking now, egging him on.

"She's definitely coming toward you. Maybe you can share her with Fredy. He don't have nobody looking at him."

Felipe shrugged. "Don't need a bar girl. I have a beautiful wife waiting for me at home."

"Your wife is far away, probably having some fun behind your back."

"No, she wouldn't," Felipe said vehemently, but in his heart he wasn't sure.

"How do you know? Women need love, and you're sitting here in a bar in Mexico City, working ten hours a day at a metal recycling plant. How long have you been away?" Alfonso continued.

"A while." It seemed like forever—at least eight months, maybe more. The woman was beside him now, running her hand over his arm. He hadn't had any food yet, and the alcohol was making him woozy.

"What's your name, handsome?" the woman cooed in a low-pitched voice, her mouth so close to his face he could smell the alcohol on her breath.

When he didn't answer right away, Fredy jumped in. "He's a little shy. His name is Felipe."

Felipe's thoughts drifted to Orchard Beach, sitting in the sand with Julia, watching the seagulls. He wondered if Fredy was right. He had been gone for so long, and she would be lonely. Julia, holding him close, dancing to love songs at the club.

The woman's leg was touching his, and her breath was warm on his cheek now. "I'm Marta. Haven't seen you here before. You new in town?"

"Arrived last week. Only here for a short visit."

"Where are you from, Felipe?"

"El Salvador, New York, a lot of places. I'm just traveling around."

Felipe touched the ring on his finger. It was still there, along with the picture he always carried in his wallet. Julia, the artist who could turn anything into beauty. Forever, they had promised each other.

"Buy the lady a drink, Felipe."

The bartender had been waiting for this. "What are you having?"

"Two beers. One for the lady."

Such a long time since he had seen Julia, felt her touch. Fredy and Alfonso moved away, left him alone with her. She had appeared beautiful from across the room, but up close she looked worn and tired. Her eyes had a yellowish, unhealthy tinge, with dark circles underneath them, and her skin was mottled and blotchy. He wondered what the life of a Mexican bar girl was like.

"You have any children?" he asked her.

She moved away a bit. "I do. I have four."

"Where are they?"

"At home."

"I have three children in New York," Felipe said.

"That's a long way, and I find you very cute." Her fingers caressed his wrist. "Might as well enjoy yourself while you're here. Come with me. I want to show you something." A curtain, a back room with a couch.

Felipe and Julia, in the back room of El Patio. Marta was pulling him down onto the couch, her face moving toward his. Julia's face, then Marta's. Not Julia's face. A stranger's face in a bar in Mexico City.

"I'm not feeling too well—think I might be sick." He rolled off the couch and stumbled through the curtain, back into the bar, where Fredy and Alfonso were nursing beers at a table near the window.

357

Fredy winked at him. "Was she good?"

Felipe pushed open the rickety screen door of the bar and breathed in the night air, which was cooler, almost a little chilly. Two-thirty a.m., the clock inside had read. He found an empty bench and pulled out his wallet, opening it slowly, removing the picture of Julia. He cradled it in his hand, gently, tenderly, as though he was embracing her, the closest he could come to touching her. He remained there for a long while, holding Julia close.

—

Thirty-four

The Garden Café in Hamilton Falls didn't smell at all like El Patio. No familiar smell of sizzling chicken, cilantro, and onions, no sweet smell of Felipe, always within kissing distance.

A little peck here and there in the stockroom, a touch on the hand, a way of keeping them connected, no matter what else was going on.

Julia's new employer had stationed her behind the counter, making sandwiches for the downtown lunch crowd. She presided over a long row of food trays while customers paced anxiously, trying to decide between roast beef, turkey, chicken salad or tuna fish, strips of lettuce, cut tomatoes, chopped onions or sprouts, mayonnaise or yellow mustard.

Julia had never eaten a sprout before she entered the doors of the Garden Café, but customers all seemed to want them. Green hair, it looked like. Green hair with seeds. She could do an interesting painting of sprouts, something abstract. Shoppers trying to catch sprouts as they floated through the air, sprouts being chased by an army of sandwiches. She could probably sell something like that; maybe they would put it on the wall of the café.

She glanced out the spacious glass window that overlooked the street, a quick mental break from making sandwiches. Hamilton Falls was the upscale suburb that bordered Oakmont, and her post behind the counter afforded her a full view of its well-dressed inhabitants meandering in and out of restaurants, perusing the boutiques that dotted the street, relaxing on benches in front of the old-fashioned ice cream shoppe, shielded from the sun by an array of striped awnings and the luxurious cascading branches of leafy green trees.

A couple passed by holding hands, and a teenage boy wearing baggy shorts that hung down to his calves leaned against a tree and stared into his cell phone, entranced by what was happening on the screen. The cops had let Ricky go with a warning, taunting him about Papi, threatening him with juvenile hall if they picked him up again. "You need to find some new friends," she had said. "I don't want to ever see you in that lot, or even in the park. There's no reason why you can't play basketball in the gym after school. Don't give the cops any reason to focus on you." Not that they needed a reason. She wondered if leaning against a tree in Hamilton Falls would be considered just cause for them to detain him.

Fatigue had plagued her since her fruitless trip to Arizona, her body finding solace only in the oblivion of sleep, and even that escape often eluded her. Marisol had been a godsend, taking on responsibilities way beyond her years, but lately she had also been out a lot, coming home late, leaving early, spending an excessive amount of time putting on makeup and fussing with her clothes. Julia suspected she had a boyfriend, but Marisol's lips were sealed. She wondered why Marisol had never brought the boy home, introduced him to the family. Marisol deserved to have some fun, but Julia couldn't help worrying a little. Marisol usually told her everything, and Julia was concerned, maybe even a little hurt, that her daughter wasn't sharing this one.

The tomato tray needed to be refilled, so she lifted it from its place in the row, leaving the sprouts and the lettuce to cope with an empty space where the tomatoes had been. She quickly carried the tray to the back room, where another line of people was cutting up lettuce into strips and slicing tomatoes, filling up trays to replace the ones that became empty. One of the tomato slicers smiled at her, a nice-looking guy with a wise-guy grin and black hair cut close to the scalp, stocky and athletic looking. He wore a white apron spotted with food stains, the sleeves and the collar of a black T-shirt peeking out from underneath it, and she found herself imagining his body without the apron, dressed up to go partying, and then naked, without any clothes at all.

The full tray of tomato slices was heavy and cumbersome, her steps clumsy as the tomatoes sloshed back and forth in the tray, threatening to spill over the side as she returned to the counter and slid it carefully into the empty space, noting that the tray of sprouts was about half full and the onions were getting low and would also need to be filled soon.

"I've been waiting ten minutes for my sandwich," an annoyed voice grumbled. An angry face in a three-piece black suit and a dark blue silk tie glared at her from the other side of the counter, irritated and impatient. His white shirt was buttoned at the collar, squeezing his neck so tightly she could see the veins standing out.

"Sorry for the delay, sir. I went to fill up the tomato tray."

"I gave you my order and you walked away. You could've made my sandwich first. I've a mind to file a complaint against you."

"What would you like, sir?"

"I already told you what I wanted. Just make it, damn it."

"It's right here, sir. Let me make sure I got it right. Turkey sandwich on wheat bread with mayo, lettuce, and tomato."

"Is something wrong with your hearing? I asked for roast beef!" he asserted vehemently, in a deep voice that resonated across the room.

At least she had gotten the mayo, lettuce, and tomato right. He looked like a mayo, lettuce, and tomato man. Make enough of these sandwiches and you begin to know what they want before they ask for it. Definitely not a sprouts kind of guy.

"You're right, sir. Roast beef coming right up."

Julia slapped the sandwich together so fast it almost fell off the counter onto the floor, but she managed to wrap it and hand it to the man just as the manager came over to investigate the commotion. "Problem here?" he asked, eyeing her dubiously.

She couldn't afford to lose this job. There were times you had to save yourself even if you told a little white lie, and luckily for her, the man had already moved on. "He was complaining about traffic, said it took him half an hour to find a parking space."

"He must really like—"

"Yes, he does, I've seen him here before, a regular customer. He said the sandwiches here are so good that it was worth driving around for thirty minutes, and that the service is always excellent."

"Good, that's good," the manager said indifferently, strolling away to find some other problem to solve.

The lunch crowd had thinned, and Julia had a ten-minute break coming. The break room was a tiny space in the basement with only a table and a few chairs, some vending machines, and a coffee pot, but it was a relief just to sit down for a few minutes.

"*Hola*," a voice said from the doorway. "May I join you?"

It was the cute tomato slicer, sliding into a chair opposite her. "I'm Antonio," he offered. "I know you're new here, and just wanted to say hi, you know, give you a little welcome. What's your name?"

"Julia," she responded politely. She wasn't feeling up to having personal conversations with strangers about her life, but he was a fellow employee trying to be nice. It wouldn't be a good idea to have her new co-workers thinking she was an unfriendly bitch.

"I heard that guy giving you a hard time. Don't let it get to you. Been here three years, and it happens to me all the time."

"I've got three kids to support. I can't afford to get fired."

"Raising them alone?" he asked.

"At the moment," she said wearily, hoping that would end the conversation.

"My mother raised four of us alone," he continued. "I know how it is. Not an easy life." He rose slowly from the chair, ambled over to the vending machines. "Want a soda?" he asked, dropping coins into the machine. "I'll buy you one. What do you like? Coke? Sprite?"

Accepting favors from men you hardly knew was not a good idea. "Thanks, that's nice of you, but I brought some food with me," she said, opening her purse and pulling out a bottle of water and a small plastic bag with a sandwich in it.

"You got kids?" she asked as a way of keeping the conversation pleasant, making small talk with him. Everyone liked to talk about their kids.

He pulled the tab on the can, snapping it open with a sharp crack, the liquid fizzing as it bubbled up to the top. He had long, thin fingers, which he wrapped tightly around the can as he raised it to his lips. A little unusual for a man to have fingers like that, Julia thought, as she stared at his hands. No wedding ring there.

"Got two, a boy and a girl. I'm divorced," he said, parking himself in the chair across from her again. "I got married right out of high school, but it didn't work out. My ex has the kids, and I see them on weekends."

"That's pretty tough, too," Julia said. She watched him enjoying the soda, which looked really appealing now, better than the water sitting on the table next to her, but she had already turned down his offer. If she bought her own soda now, he might feel insulted.

"Yeah. Maybe I'll do better the next time around," he said quietly.

He was a father, so he must like kids, or at least be comfortable around them, which made her feel a little safer. It would be nice to have a friend at work, and they did have the parent thing in common.

He lowered his voice, smiling, talking gently to her. A flirty kind of gentleness. "Sounds like we both could use some fun. You like to dance?"

It had been a while since she had done anything she could call fun. Felipe would always be the love of her life, her one and only, and they had shared so many special moments together.

Sitting on the beach watching the sunset, dancing till two in the morning. The moment their first baby was born, his proud face, the tears in his eyes. Felipe had been gone nine months now, and she wondered how long you should wait for someone to come home.

"Yeah, I love to dance, makes me forget my troubles. We used to—"

"You're too pretty to be working so hard."

He was talking in that gentle voice again, that enticing "I know you need some loving and I can give it to you" voice. "Where do you live?"

"Oakmont."

"What street?"

"Fourth and Miller. You?" She half-hoped that he lived somewhere far away, like Brooklyn or Queens, too far away to make getting together a reality. Far enough away to mean she didn't have to make a decision about this. She had kids who came first, and had no time to be running around the subways at all hours to see him. That just wouldn't work at all.

"Hey, that's great. I live on Cedar. There's a new club that just opened up right near me—La Cabana. The music is terrific."

About eight blocks away, walking distance. She would never forgive herself if she ran into someone she and Felipe knew. If Marisol or Ricky saw her with another man, they would never forgive her for betraying Felipe. The shame would consume her, eat her alive for the rest of her life. She wasn't sleeping with the guy or marrying him, though, just going out dancing with a co-worker. She could always just meet him there, which would make it more casual, less like a date. There would be other single guys there, and she could dance with them, too, making it clear that she just wanted to be friends, nothing further.

Tia Rosa had heartily agreed to watch Camilo, with no questions asked about why Julia was going out alone on a Saturday night. Maybe Tia Rosa had figured it out and was too polite to say anything, or just understood that she needed a break. Julia folded her dress, placing it neatly in her black and red cloth bag next to her black heels and her pantyhose, and headed toward the nearest fast food restaurant. She slipped furtively into the restroom, where she put on her makeup in the bathroom mirror, then stepped into a bathroom stall to change her clothes, stuffing her slacks, her shirt, and her everyday flats into the bag.

As the minutes ticked by on her watch, she dilly-dallied in front of the mirror, fixing her hair, reapplying her lipstick. It was too late to turn back. Antonio was waiting for her at the club, and she would have to face him at work tomorrow if she didn't show tonight. Standing him up would not be a good idea. No reason why she couldn't dance with him for a little while, then excuse herself because she had to check on the kids. There shouldn't be any problem with that. The three-inch heels she had chosen to wear clicked loudly on the tile floor as she scurried past the counter, past the customers quietly eating hamburgers and French fries at the tables next to the front window, and stepped tenuously out the door in her best black dress.

La Cabana was dark and glitzy, with strobe lights flashing back and forth across the ceiling, the walls, the floor. A place of illusion and sur-real dreams, where you could dance to the heartbeat of your secret lover and no one would know. The energy flowed between them, sweaty and breathless, the thump, thump of the beat consuming her, transporting her to a place where nothing existed but the present. Antonio, the cute tomato slicer, became Antonio, *el bailador,* the dancer, the choreographer, as they matched each other's steps in perfect time. For the moment, the world they had entered at La Cabana was all there was. The DJ switched to a different beat, a slow, romantic one this time, and she felt Antonio pull her close, her chin resting on his shoulder.

She was doing something terribly wrong, leading Antonio on, being unfaithful to Felipe. She should excuse herself, go to the ladies' room, throw cold water on her face, and leave. Tell Antonio she was married, that she would wait as long as she had to, for the rest of her life, for Felipe to come home. She could feel Antonio's breath in her ear, his hand on her back, holding her. Holding her up. It had been a long time since anyone had been there to hold her up. She had been the one holding everybody up for so long now that she couldn't remember what it was like for someone to be her strength, to catch her when she tripped. Still, she needed to stop all this right now, go home to her children.

How long should she wait? A year, two years? Ten? When someone vanishes from your life, possibly never to return, at what point do you move on, start anew? The song ended, and she glanced anxiously at her watch.

"I've really enjoyed this, but I left my nine-year-old with a friend, and I need to pick him up. I'll see you Monday, at work," she said, giving Antonio a quick peck on the cheek. She grabbed her bag from the floor next to the little table they had occupied, took a last sip of her margarita, and hurried across the dance floor toward the front exit.

New York
Fall, 2006

Thirty-five

The trip to Orchard Beach had been postponed for several weeks, while Marisol waited for Colin to finally have a free Saturday with no football practice and the good news that his mother was feeling better. In the meantime, they had continued taking walks on Tuesday evenings after his dinner shift at St. Michael's, and last week they had gone to a movie, a chick-flick romance about some college students who meet on a year abroad in Paris. The movie wasn't great, but they had sat holding hands, their knees touching, while they whispered silly comments about the movie. Colin bought some popcorn and fed pieces to her, brushing her lips with his fingers, holding them there a moment as she ran her tongue over them sensuously, licking them slowly. "The popcorn here is amazing," she whispered.

The day Colin's mother had gotten sick, Marisol stood on the steps of St. Michael's watching him open the passenger side door, climb into the van and drive away, disappearing into the afternoon sun until nothing remained but a wisp of smoke from the tailpipe. She had reluctantly picked up her beach bag and descended the stairs slowly, one step at a time, praying that Colin's mother was suddenly feeling better and his dad would turn the van around, bring Colin back. Despite her disappointment, she was deeply moved by the fact that he would give up his plans to help out his family during a crisis, something she could certainly relate to.

The best part of summer had now passed, but the fall weather was still warm, and the sea air at Orchard Beach smelled clean and fresh. A small breeze blew, carrying with it the scent of smoke from the barbecue grills in the grassy area. Marisol slipped off her shoes, the sand under her toes soft and velvety, her feet sinking into its cozy warmth. They walked along the sand holding hands until they found the perfect place to spread out the oversized towel she brought from home, a more secluded spot toward the end of the beach, away from the families and the rest of the beach crowd, a few feet from the water's edge.

In the bright sun, the towel appeared worn and frayed, a casualty of years of Sanchez family baths and trips to the beach, and hundreds of washings in the laundromat on Fourth Street.

Although the red and yellow designs she loved as a child had faded into pale versions of their original selves, it would always be special to her, a reminder of the good times her family had together. She peeked at Colin out of the corner of her eye to see if he had noticed how old and worn the towel was, but he was sitting at the edge of it with his feet in the sand, gazing out at the blue-green water, absorbed by its sun-streaked radiance.

"It'd be cool to be on a beach for a week," he said finally. "My family went to Cape May in New Jersey for a few days once when my dad had some vacation time. Best vacation I ever had—riding the waves, laying in the sun."

She wasn't sure she wanted to open that door yet, to get into family stuff, but she was also aching to get closer, to find out more about him. She hesitated for a moment, then plunged ahead. "So, what's your dad like?" she asked.

"Tough guy, yeah, real tough guy sometimes. You don't say no to him. Works hard, though, and wants the best for me. Can't fault him for that. How about yours?"

"Nicest guy in the world. If you need help, he's there, even if he just worked twelve hours."

They were side by side now, watching the breakers rippling in the wake of distant boats, shadowy silhouettes gliding across the horizon. Colin turned his face toward her, hesitating for a moment before he spoke, as though he was debating whether to ask the question she knew was overdue, hovering silently between them since the day they met.

"Where's he from?" he asked quietly.

"My dad's from El Salvador, but my mom was born here. Her family's been in New York for a long time—my grandparents moved here from Puerto Rico in the 1950s."

He turned away, staring off into the horizon, retreating into silence. Sweat was collecting on her neck and dripping down her chest, so she suggested they play around in the surf for a while. They waded in up to their knees and stood there shivering until Colin splashed her and she splashed him back and they were back to being totally silly, giggling and thoroughly wet. He dove down and grabbed her legs, lifting her up and tossing her in, then came up for air and floated on his back. Marisol floated alongside him, drinking in the deep blue of the sky, luxuriating in the afternoon warmth, the water lapping gently against her skin. They paddled back to the beach, beads of water trickling down his chest and his back like tiny sparkling jewels, his dark blond hair plastered against his head, intensifying the blue of his eyes.

The sand at the edge of the water was cool and wet as they strolled along the shore, their pinkies intertwined. Marisol stepped gingerly around shells and piles of seaweed that had washed up on the beach, catching sight of a small, perfectly formed pink and white shell, which she picked up and gave to him. The tide sloshed in and out, tickling her feet, and the cold water made her jump as it ran over her toes, but Colin was there holding onto her, keeping her steady.

The aroma of grilling meat drew them toward the boardwalk, their bare feet padding softly on the creaky wooden planks as they meandered past vendors hawking hats and T-shirts, the odor of hamburgers and hot dogs wafting from a kiosk, reminding Marisol how hungry she was.

Colin had some cash on him and offered to pay for both of them, so they bought hot dogs, sodas, and an order of fries to share, and carried them to the Sanchez family towel, her contribution to the picnic. She even agreed to try some sauerkraut on her hot dog this time, just a little, to show him that she was willing to check out new things. The sauerkraut wasn't bad, kind of cold and vinegary. It did add a little zing to the hot dog, and if it dripped on her, it would be easy to wipe off.

"Hey, you're trying the sauerkraut!" Colin teased. "How is it? Pretty good?"

She swallowed the bite that she was chewing, wiped her mouth with the napkin. "Yeah, I like it. It definitely adds something! What about you? No credit card this time?" she said, teasing him back.

"Nah, that's really just for special occasions, like if I'm going to some event or someplace special, and—if my dad's not mad at me. I think it helps him keep track of where I've been, too. We're not getting along that well right now, so this is not a good time for me to ask him for it."

"I'm looking for a part-time job, something I can do after school or on the weekends," she asserted, letting him know that she was no mooch. "Um, so... what are you and your dad arguing about?" she asked, curiously.

"Well, it really wasn't about me. He had a... well, a problem with my best friend's dad, and now my friend doesn't come over anymore. It's kind of a mess. Anyway, you don't need to worry about paying. I can pay when we go out."

"It's not just that. My family is having a hard time since my dad lost his job. I should be helping out," she said, offering as much explanation as she was willing to give him right now.

Colin was digging a hole in the sand with his fingers, scooping it up, piling it into a little hill. "What happened? Why'd your dad lose his job?"

"He worked in a café that his uncle owned, but it closed, so he got some temporary jobs doing painting, putting up drywall, that kind of stuff. Not real steady work, though."

Colin stared down at the sand, silent again. "Yeah, that's a bitch, having to go through all that," he said finally. "My dad works in a restaurant, too. He didn't lose his job, but he didn't get the promotion he wanted, so he's been in a really pissy mood lately, more than usual. I don't know what we'd do if he totally lost his job. My mom would still be bringing in some money, but we'd have to cut back on lots of things. Your mom works, right? I guess that helps a little."

"She worked in the café with him, so when it closed she was out of a job, too. She just got a new job in another café in Hamilton Falls, but I'm still trying to help out as much as I can."

"I'm sure your dad will find another job, in some other restaurant or something. I wish there was something I could do to help you guys.

I'll ask around school and see if anyone has heard about any places hiring right now, for you or your dad."

"I, uh, well, that's nice of you," Marisol stammered, not sure what to say, wondering if he could pick up the quaver in her voice. She couldn't imagine telling him that her father wasn't even in the country anymore, deported because of criminal charges. Maybe someday, but not now, when the relationship was so new and wonderful. If a time came when she was really, really sure he loved her enough to stick around no matter what happened, then she might be able to share that part, but definitely not yet.

"My football coach taught us some meditation, ways to breathe and calm yourself down before a big game," Colin said. "Football can be really stressful. Having to play in front of a crowd can be scary sometimes, people screaming and yelling, demanding that you perform. It's like your whole life depends upon winning the game, and if you lose you're a piece of crap. I could show you some breathing and stuff. It's pretty helpful, really."

There were so many things about Colin that impressed her, touched her in some deep way. He actually listened, wanted to help, cared about what happened to her, to her family.

"That'd be really cool. I've heard a lot about meditation, but I've never actually done any. Maybe next time I see you at St. Michael's, we could find an empty room after your shift."

"Okay, sounds good!" he said enthusiastically. "Wesley could probably help us find a place. He might even join us."

She picked up a handful of sand, molded it into a little ball and placed it gently on top of the sand castle he had begun building. "Digging in the sand is relaxing, too," she said, smiling at him. "I used to do it for hours when I was a kid."

"I'm still a kid, I guess," he said, but he wasn't smiling and she thought he seemed nervous.

"That community service must take up a lot of your time. Too bad they don't pay you for that."

"Just somethin' I have to do. Guess there's a silver lining to everything. If I didn't have to do community service, we wouldn't have met. I'm almost done with it, though, and then I'll be a free man."

"Free from what? I thought you liked helping out at St. Michael's," she said. She still hadn't found out why he had to do the community service, what he had done wrong. It couldn't be anything that serious, though. It was obviously nothing that would have put him in juvie or gotten him kicked out of school. Maybe he was just embarrassed that he had done something foolish and didn't want to look dumb in front of her.

"Come on, help me out with this," Colin said. He scooped up some more sand with both hands and placed it around the sand castle, patted it down.

"I saw a really cool sand sculpture on the beach once—a huge castle with sculptures of people around it and everything," Marisol responded.

"Hey, let's build one. How about a castle with moats and turrets—the whole thing? It's been a really long time since I've done anything like this. I used to really love it. Guess I still do," he laughed, but not a hearty laugh, more like an uncomfortable little snicker.

"Yeah, I remember you told me about that. I mean about the ashtrays and the classes at the art museum! It's never too late to pick it up again!" She began piling some sand on the top, molding and shaping it with her fingers, until it began to look like a tower.

"Beautiful," Colin said. "I'm going to make one on this side." He held up a popsicle stick that had been laying in the sand. "Here, take this. You can use it to carve out windows. In those art classes at the museum, they let us use a tool called a clay shaper. Guess this is as close as we'll get to a real one, but it's a lot cheaper, and will work just as well," he laughed, a real laugh this time. He stood up, looking around. "I'll be back in a minute. Gonna find another stick—clay shaper, I mean!"

Colin returned a few minutes later with several popsicle sticks and some empty cups. "Found a few more things we can use." The castle was looking more like a real sand sculpture now, and Colin began carving out windows with the stick.

Marisol sat back for a moment, grabbing her purse to pull out her sunglasses. A friend had told her that sunglasses made her look sexier, more appealing, so she tilted her head a little to the side and flicked her hair back to increase the effect, something she had seen models in television ads do.

She tried to be casual, not to stare at him as he worked painstakingly on the sand castle, but each moment seemed to bring a new discovery. The excitement on his face as he carefully carved out the windows, the broadness of his shoulders, the strength of his arms, drew her like a magnet, enticing her to move closer, until her leg was touching his.

"I'd like to watch you play football sometime, maybe come to one of your games."

"Yeah, that'd be good," he responded, but he didn't sound very excited.

She thought that she would love to sit in the stands at his school, cheering on his team, watching him run down the field in his uniform, but maybe it was too soon for that. They had been dating for several months and he acted like he was really into her, but for some reason, he wasn't ready for her to meet his family and all his buddies. Well, she wasn't ready for him to meet hers, either, so she could understand that, but there were some other things she didn't get, like why he hadn't answered her when she asked about his community service.

"You work after school?" she asked, wondering where his cash came from.

"Not really, with football practice and all, don't have much time left."

He put down the stick and moved toward her, stroking her arm with his finger. "I have time for you, though," he said, his voice low and husky, his eyes fixed on her. Marisol felt a thrill travel through her body, as though a flame had been lit, starting an unquenchable fire that grew hotter by the minute. She inched closer, and then his lips were touching hers, his chest and legs bare against hers. Her hands caressed his back, feeling the softness of his skin, as their bodies moved together, in perfect rhythm. She stroked his face and his hair, and he nibbled on her neck, licked her ear. "I can't get enough of you," he whispered, and she felt dreamy, as though nothing mattered but this moment and being here with Colin, far, far away from the turbulent waters that continuously swirled around her.

Thirty-six

The Bronx hadn't changed much since Frank had been there last year for his mother's birthday. The same grimy, pitted sidewalks with an occasional blade of grass struggling to grow between the cracks, the mom-and-pop stores hidden behind metal gates and barred windows.

Tony's Pizzeria and the deli-grocery on the corner with the graffiti-covered Coca-Cola sign had survived all the neighborhood changes over the years, but some of the other shopkeepers the family had frequented during his childhood had moved on, replaced by Caribbean storefront restaurants and groceries with signs in Spanish.

The neighborhood was full of memories for him—playing ball in the street, getting a slice of pizza at Tony's, picking up a loaf of bread for his mother at the Irish bakery. He and his siblings were the first generation in the family to live in the Bronx. His parents had grown up in the slums of Manhattan's lower east side, moved to the Bronx to provide their children with a better life.

Frank and Bonnie had tried forever to get Nana to move to Oakmont, but even when offered a room in their house, she preferred to stay in the Bronx. "I have everything I need right here," she said. "Stores I can walk to, the subway down the street, the church two blocks away. I don't know anyone in Oakmont and you would have to drive me everywhere."

The turn of the century red brick building Nana had called home for fifty years was sandwiched between a bakery, La Panadería, and a small storefront church, La Iglesia Pentecostal, its façade still handsome despite having endured generations of rain, snow, and burning summer sun. Colin peered in the window of La Panadería, attracted by a whiff of fresh baked goods that wafted out onto the street.

"Used to be McGinty's Irish bakery," Frank said. "Best soda bread you ever tasted. The chain stores have never been able to match it."

"Next time we come, we should buy Nana's birthday cake here instead of lugging it all the way from Oakmont," Colin offered. "The cookies look good. Let's get some cookies!"

Frank rolled his eyes and shook his head. "I wouldn't buy anything here. Might not be clean, and we don't want to encourage these people—"

"Don't be ridiculous," Bonnie shot back at him irritably. "They couldn't stay in business if they weren't inspected by the health department." Things between him and Bonnie had improved some since the argument about the SIM protest at Ray Harper's. At least they were talking now, but they seemed to disagree on everything these days and tempers flared up easily, sometimes over the smallest things. He had moved back into their bedroom for a few days, but she wouldn't touch him and they snapped at each other a lot, so he retreated to the basement again, hoping it was just temporary. Nothing changed, though, and he was still camping out there, sleeping on the couch, getting his meals from fast food restaurants.

"I doubt if the health department comes around here anymore," Frank retorted.

Bonnie pursed her lips and squinted at Frank. "Colin knows better than to believe that." She glanced hastily at Colin, as though she was suddenly unsure. "I hope you do."

Colin shrugged. "I don't really care about the health department one way or the other," he said. "I'll eat anything. I even eat at Lou's Burgers, across from school. Their burgers are so greasy, the grease runs down your arm and leaves little puddles on your plate, and they have a big dog that walks around the kitchen. Don't think they ever change the oil they cook the fries in, just toss new fries in the same old sludge. Burgers still taste good, though." He pressed his face against the bakery window to better appraise the goods on display. "Wouldn't mind one of those cookies with the chocolate on them. Bet Nana would like one." He turned expectantly to his parents to see if anyone was buying, but they had already walked away and were pushing open the front door of Nana's building.

The door to the aging, six-story building opened onto a narrow, dimly lit hallway with four apartments on the first floor: 1A, 1B, 1C, and 1D. The corridor reeked of fried fish, and the drone of a TV and the faint murmuring of voices hummed from behind the dark wooden doors.

Nana's doorbell had long been disabled; it was nothing but a piece of wire hanging from a hole in the wall, so Frank banged loudly on the door that said 1C until he heard a shuffling and then a clang and the squeak of a police lock opening. Folks in the Bronx had secured their doors with police locks for as long as Frank could remember, a metal bar that reached from the floor to the middle of the door to deter anyone who would even think of breaking in.

"She doesn't need that police lock, never did," he chuckled. "Anyone who would consider breaking into Nana's apartment is gonna get a shock, might find a lamp flyin' across the room!"

A wrinkled face with a mop of curly white hair and bright blue eyes peered at them from the doorway, her cheeks as pink as the roses Frank had brought for her. No one knew the secret to Nana's bright cheeks, whether it was makeup, her naturally ruddy complexion, or just her rosy spirit showing through.

"Come in, come in. How's my Colin? Look at you, you've grown so much, but you're still my good boy," she said, holding out her arms to give him a hug. "You'll have to tell me all about what you've been doing."

"Of course he's good—he's my son!" Frank said, answering for him. "He's a better football player than I was, though. Are you ready to be the grandmother of the next superstar with an Ivy League degree?"

"I'll love him no matter what he decides to do," Nana declared. "I'm sure he'll make the right decision when the time comes," she said, winking at Colin.

Nana took Bonnie's hands and grasped them tightly. "You look lovely, as always. And Frankie, how's the restaurant going?" she said, patting his stomach. "Looks like those steaks have been good to you."

Nana's living room held a seven-foot couch with ornately carved wooden arms, its cushions sporting a vivid red and yellow floral design, softened only by the plastic cover that lay on top of it. Her furniture had always been covered in plastic, and Frank imagined that was how she managed to keep it looking clean and new for fifty years. He always made sure not to wear shorts when he visited, even in the summer heat, so he wouldn't stick to the plastic, which made a loud sucking noise under your bare legs when you shifted positions. The couch was too heavy for anyone to move, so when Frank sat there, he was destined to gaze eternally at the array of family pictures on the opposite wall. They spanned several generations and included a photograph of the green rolling hills of Ireland along with several pieces of embroidery with Nana's favorite sayings. *"Be true to who you are and the family name you bear,"* one said, and *"The smallest good deed is better than the greatest intention,"* on another. *"Love, faith, charity,"* read a third.

Frank purposely avoided the couch today, kicking back in the faded old armchair on the other side of the room instead. His eyes closed and a wave of fatigue washed over him. A nap wouldn't be a bad idea at all right now. Managing the restaurant, chauffeuring Colin's football buddies, and organizing for Stop Immigration was a demanding schedule, and a little time to just relax would be nice.

He had traded his warm-up suit for a pair of khakis and a white golf shirt with an alligator over the pocket, not something he would do for just anybody, but his mother's birthday was a special occasion, a long-standing family tradition, even though nowadays the family was scattered all over the country. He never knew what to expect with her, though, and she always had some surprise for everyone or something new to share. Last year she had been determined to have her birthday party at the church so the priest could attend, and the year before she had insisted they move it to the park, where she gave out pieces of her birthday cake to the children playing there.

She hadn't mentioned any cockamamie ideas this year, and he had his fingers crossed that she wouldn't come up with one.

"Michael and Noreen are on their way, Mother," he murmured sluggishly. His brother Michael, a high-end lawyer, worked at a fancy law firm on Wall Street and was busy, busy, busy, rushing from one swanky event to another. Never missed a chance to show everyone how important he was. He always made it to Nana's birthday party, though, even if he arrived when the party was half over because he had something else to attend to.

"They said they'd be a little late, some program they were involved in," Frank said. At least they showed up. The other siblings rarely ventured back to the Bronx. They just sent one of those Hallmark cards every year and thought that was enough.

"Then we're going to have a full house today," Nana responded. "I want you to meet some new people. You're never too old to make friends, you know."

A knock at the door brought Nana to her feet, shuffling across the room to unbolt the police lock and usher in several people Frank had never seen before.

"This is my new friend, Nita Moreno, her husband, Tomás, and this little sweetie is Maya. They live in 1B and do some shopping for me when I can't go out, and help me get to Mass on Sunday. I watch Maya for them sometimes. Maya likes to come over and watch TV with me.

"Would you like to watch TV, Maya? We're going to have a birthday party with some cake and ice cream. Would you like a piece of cake?"

Maya nodded, and Nana turned on a small television set perched on a stool near the kitchen and flipped the channels. A children's show appeared with puppets dancing on the screen. "I've learned all about Froggy and Peaches and Mr. Bob. Maya has taught me some Spanish and I make sure her English is correct. "*Tengo ochenta años, hoy.* That means I'm eighty years old today. Maya has only been in the U.S. two years, but she speaks English very well," Nana continued. "How old are you, Maya?" Maya smiled broadly, showing a missing tooth. "I'm seven years old," she answered.

"Please sit down, make yourself comfortable," she said to Nita and Tomás, who were standing awkwardly near the door. "I'm so busy blabbering I didn't even introduce my family. My son Frank, his wife, Bonnie, and my handsome grandson, Colin. They have a nice house in Westchester County. A little too quiet up there for me. Makes me nervous. I like people on the street and police sirens wailing all night."

The arrival of Michael and Noreen prompted Bonnie to remove the cake from the box, light a row of eight candles and lead the group in singing a chorus of the birthday song.

"Teach us the words in Spanish," Nana said, and the Moreno family promptly began singing a round of *Feliz Cumpleaños* to Nana. Nana sang along loudly, waving her arms like a conductor, pleased that she knew all the words to the song in Spanish, exhorting everyone to join in.

Frank glanced over at Bonnie, who was grinning joyfully and singing at the top of her lungs. Just watching her act so happy about this crap pissed Frank off, and he felt an irritation in his belly, like when he had eaten too much spicy food. She was probably overdoing it on purpose, he thought, just to annoy him. Colin was slapping the table in time with the music, as though he was some kind of a drummer or something, and Frank reached over and poked him with his finger, pointing at the table and shaking his head. Bonnie turned to Colin and mouthed "It's okay," nodding a yes to him as she glowered at Frank.

Frank slumped in the armchair, his lips pressed tightly together, determined that not one word of Spanish would ever slip from his mouth. He stared gloomily out the window, his hands clenching the arms of the chair, while the whole group filled Nana's living room with an exuberant rendition of *Feliz Cumpleaños*. Nana had gone too far this year, inviting the Hispanics right into her apartment. A police lock wouldn't do a bit of good if she was unlocking it for them, and that was not a safe thing to do for an older woman living alone. The next thing you know, she would be getting a tattoo and hanging out on the corner with the teenagers. He thought it might be time for him to have a talk with her, bring up the subject of moving again. He couldn't leave her in this place forever. If she didn't agree to move, they would have to find some way to get her out of here, into a retirement home in Oakmont, near them.

The vase of flowers he brought adorned the center of the coffee table in front of the couch, and presents wrapped in multi-colored paper sealed with various lengths of Scotch tape lay beside them, waiting for her attention. "Smell the flowers, Maya. So beautiful," Nana said, bending over to breathe in their fragrance, trying different arrangements until she was satisfied with the result.

"Thank you all for coming to celebrate my birthday, and for the wonderful presents and the chocolate cake. Chocolate has always been my favorite, and I can't wait to taste it and see what is underneath all that beautiful paper."

"Next time we can get a cake from that nice bakery next door," Bonnie said, turning to the Morenos. "*¿Te gusta esa panaderia?*" she asked.

"You speak Spanish, Mom?" Colin said, his eyes widening in surprise.

"I took Spanish in school and practice it at the hospital," she said. "A lot of the patients speak Spanish."

"Yes, I do—it's a very good bakery," Nita Moreno answered.

"I like the *tres leches* cupcakes," Maya said. "They have frosting on them."

Nana grabbed her cane and tapped it on the floor a few times, then pulled herself up from the couch, smiling enthusiastically. "I have a present to give, too, a present for all of you Sullivans, something I came across when I was going through some things last week. I won't be around forever, and this is something very special that I want you to have."

Thirty-seven

Marisol sat patiently in the front lobby of the public defender's office, waiting for her appointment. There were no other clients in the waiting area at the moment, and the room was excruciatingly quiet; no people to stare at, conversations to eavesdrop on, or comings and goings of clients to watch. Her two o'clock appointment became two-fifteen, then two-thirty. Mama had wanted her to eat something this morning, but Marisol had been in such a rush that she had skipped breakfast, grabbing a candy bar at the corner market before she got on the bus. The package of peanut butter crackers she had bought from the vending machine for lunch hadn't tided her over for long, either, and now she could feel the beginning of a headache coming on.

Three or four magazines lay on a small table—*Golf-Pro*, *Sports World*, *Home Decor*—nothing that really interested her, but she picked up the *Home Decor* and stared distractedly at an article about the latest trends in kitchen remodeling. She had skipped out on her afternoon classes to make this appointment, and she was beginning to wonder if Steven Rosenbaum really didn't want this case and was giving her the brush-off.

An hour passed before the secretary finally called her name. "You can go in now," she said, looking puzzled when Marisol stared at her from the couch, frozen in place. "Are you Marisol Sanchez?" she asked impatiently, glancing at her desk.

Marisol nodded and tossed the home decorating magazine back on the table. She thought about reminding the woman that she had been waiting an hour, but she held her tongue. Probably not a good idea to get into an argument with her.

"You can go in now—he's ready for you," the secretary repeated, louder this time, scrutinizing Marisol more carefully now.

Marisol slowly pushed open the door to the lawyer's office, taking a quick peek into the room before she stepped inside, edging warily toward the big leather chair in front of his desk. Steven Rosenbaum was sitting at the desk, tapping on the computer as usual. "You can come in," he said amiably, motioning to her to sit down.

"Beautiful day today," she said, trying to sound cheerful, make friendly small talk.

"Yes, it is," he mumbled. "Sorry for the delay. I was in court, and it ran longer than I expected." He looked up at her and smiled. "So, how've you been? You doing okay?"

"Yeah, managing, I guess, Mr. Rosenbaum," she responded. "School keeps me busy."

"You can call me Steve," he said. "Everyone else does."

The office door scraped over the carpet as a young woman scurried in and handed off a folder, pivoted on her heels, and slipped back out the door, leaving the office silent, the only sound being the rustling of pages being flipped back and forth. Steven stroked his cheek, then curled his hand around his chin.

"So, since you were here last month, I've had some time to review your dad's case, see what we had in the records about him," he said. "I remember this case now. I met with your mom several times and called the detention center in Eloy for her, but I wasn't allowed to speak to him. What happened with that? Did your mom ever go to Arizona?"

"She did—she went all the way there on the bus, but by the time she got there, he had already been deported. We haven't heard anything from him, and we have no idea where he actually is or if he's even still alive."

"I understand how difficult this must be for you, and of course, for everyone in your family," Steve said sympathetically. "Your mom is a lovely person, and I'd love to be able to help you, but like I told you last time, I really can't promise you anything. It's funny, though— looking back at the records, I'm reminded that he was not in possession of drugs when he was arrested, so there was no actual evidence of sale or personal possession."

Marisol was speechless for a moment, at a loss for words. The words that finally came out were hoarse and whispery, not the way she wanted to sound at all. "You're saying there was no evidence and they convicted him anyway?" she said, fighting back tears. "I don't understand. Weren't you supposed to be defending him?"

"He was convicted based on—"

The barking of a dog, followed by a mournful howl, interrupted him in mid-sentence as he picked up his cell phone from the desk, slapped it against his ear. The ring tone coming from his cell phone was actually a dog barking—she would have to tell Colin about that one. Steve leaned back in the chair, listening to someone on the other end of the cell phone, periodically muttering "uh-huh," and "yeah," until he finally slapped the phone down on the desk and turned his attention back to her.

"So, where were we?" he asked absentmindedly, as though he was still preoccupied with the phone call. "Uh, your father was convicted based on eyewitness testimony about something that happened on another day. Someone picked him out of a lineup."

"Yeah, the lineup. When we visited my father in jail, he told us about that. You know, he never found out who was behind that glass pointing at him, or why they picked him and not any of the others."

"Well, they wouldn't have told him that, but I can tell you that he was picked out of a lineup by someone who claimed to be a customer of his. This person testified that your father personally sold him drugs. Actually, it happened to be a minor, someone about your age, a student at Oakmont High. My guess is that the kid got arrested and made a deal with the police to finger his supplier," he said pensively, his brows knitted in a frown.

"But my father couldn't have been one of his suppliers. He doesn't know anything about Oakmont High. He probably doesn't even know it exists and wouldn't know how to find it if he did. So why would this kid pick out my father?"

"Most likely he wasn't targeting your father specifically. He just picked someone out randomly, to save his own skin. An arrest record doesn't look good on a college application."

Oakmont High. Marisol wondered if Colin would know the kid. Drugs weren't her scene, but she still knew who the stoners at her school were, who was dealing.

He opened the drawer and took out a tin of round, white peppermints, popped one in his mouth. He pushed the tin across the desk at her and motioned for her to take one, so she carefully plucked a mint from the box with the tips of her fingers and slipped it onto her tongue. She liked the taste of the mint, tangy and sharp. The tin lay open on the desk and the aroma of peppermint lingered in the air, a sweet, pungent odor.

"Isn't there anything you can do?" Marisol asked.

"Well, legally I can file a motion to reopen the case based on new evidence—the problem is we really don't have any new evidence at the moment. What you told me about the police harassing your father is interesting and does give me something to look into, but it's not something that could be used in court. Why don't we start by reviewing some background information? Was anyone else giving your father a hard time besides the police? I mean, did he have any enemies, or someone who was angry at him?" He flipped through the file, absorbed in his thoughts.

"I can't imagine that. He went to work, came home, took us places on the weekend. Everyone in the neighborhood liked him. Our restaurant was a very popular place."

"Then why did he give up working at the restaurant and become a day laborer? I find that curious. What was he running from? Any problems with gangs in the neighborhood?"

"No, just the cops who stopped in to harass him. One night they came in, found two empty beer bottles in the trash, which they called 'selling alcohol without a license,' and music playing on the radio, which they called 'operating without a cabaret license.' The next day, someone from the health department showed up and claimed the stove had a gas leak and would have to be replaced, and some other things, like rodent droppings on the floor. I never smelled gas or got headaches or anything, and I never saw any mice or rats, but the health department fined them big-time for all those violations. My family didn't have the money to pay all of them and buy a new stove, so the restaurant was closed. A friend told him about getting day labor work in East Oak-mont, so my father went there with his uncle and the friend because we needed the money."

"Maybe we've been focusing on the wrong person. The kid who picked him out was a teenager. Anyone angry at you, or maybe someone else in your family? Where do you go to school?"

Marisol eyed the tin of peppermints, which was sitting on the desk in front of her next to the pencil holder. The flavor of the first one lingered in her mouth, which was watering for another. Having something to chew on calmed her nerves, but it wouldn't be polite to ask, and he wasn't offering, so she stared at the pencil holder instead. It was getting toward four o'clock; she had been here for hours and she needed to pick up a few groceries for Mama and head home to help with dinner.

"Grover Hill, in West Oakmont."

"Grover Hill. Definitely gang activity there. Look, I want to help you, but in order to do that, you need to be totally up front with me, tell me everything you know."

"I am telling you everything. My brother was picked up once by the police with some other kids in the neighborhood, but they let him go, and anyway, that was several months after my father was deported. He was never in trouble before my dad was taken away, and he definitely isn't a gang member. We go to the same school, and I would know that."

"What about you? Anything happen at school you might want to tell me about?"

"Why would someone from school target my father?"

"They wouldn't. The police would target your father and make a deal with someone. If they want to stay out of trouble, they do what the police tells them to do."

"Can you tell me the name?" she said, staring at the file sitting on his desk. "Maybe it'll trigger something."

"Well, I really shouldn't, but if there's even a slim chance it might help your father's case, I'm willing to show it to you, on one condition. You have to promise me that you will let me handle this from now on. If it does trigger any thoughts, feel free to share them with me, but no more detective work—none! No confrontations—do you understand?"

Marisol nodded, and Steven Rosenbaum picked up his file, turned it around towards her, and pointed to a name. "Ring any bells?"

Thirty-eight

Nana shuffled out of the room to get the surprise or present or whatever it was she wanted to give them. She always had cool things to share, and Colin couldn't wait to see what this one was. He cut himself another piece of birthday cake, making sure he got all the frosting that went with it. Chocolate layer cake was his favorite, and he shoved a big bite into his mouth, practically inhaling it, it was so good. He licked the remains of the frosting off his fork, then sliced off another chunk.

Nana was using a cane when she walked now, and Colin wondered if she was okay, if she had fallen or hurt herself lately. It couldn't be too bad because mostly she just swung it back and forth two inches off the ground, didn't really seem to need it that much. She reappeared, striding purposefully into the middle of the room swinging the cane in one hand, carrying what appeared to be a notebook with a set of yellowed pages inside of it in the other.

"I'm so happy to welcome Nita and Tomás and Maya to the neighborhood, and of course, to our country," she said loudly, making sure everyone heard her over the buzz of chit-chat drifting across the room. She waved the notebook in the air excitedly, waiting a moment for the chatting to stop before she continued. "Sometimes we forget that we came from another country, too. I wanted my children to be Americans, so I didn't teach 'em too much about the past. I used to think, the past is gone, it's the future that is important. I'm old now, and I think a lot about the past and how we were new once, too, forced to leave our country, tryin' hard to make another life here."

She handed the notebook to Colin. "This is a story told by my great-great-grandfather, Johnny Murphy. I'm not sure how many greats, really—I get confused by all the greats, but anyway, the story was written down by Johnny's daughter, Mary Murphy Callahan, who was my grandmother. 1872—that was the year she was born, down in the Five Points neighborhood at the bottom of Manhattan. Grandma Mary worked in the needle trades—that's what girls did back then—and gave birth to nine children, but only four survived."

"What are needle trades, Nana?" Colin asked as he cut himself another piece of cake.

"Factories where people cut and sewed material to make clothes. Hellholes, they were," she said, shaking her head indignantly.

Nana squeezed in next to Colin on the couch, flipped a few pages of the diary. "You can read it for yourself, but I love to tell stories and I'm going to tell you a little bit, to whet your appetite. Would anyone like a cookie?" she said, smiling to herself as though she was laughing at a joke only she understood.

"Mother—" Frank began.

"I know, Frankie, you have other things to do today, and you've heard this story before, but I hope you'll be patient with me while I bring the young ones and our new friends up-to-date. I've kept it in a special place in my dresser drawer for forty years, and it's time for me to pass it on. It's yours now, Colin, and someday it will belong to your children."

"It's easy to lose your way in this world if you don't know who you are and where you came from," Bonnie tossed in, glaring at Frank.

"Thanks, but I already know where I came from. If you don't, maybe we need to have a little talk," Frank shot back, chuckling to himself. "Anyway, I don't know how much of this story is—"

"Well, I think Colin might like to hear where he came from," Bonnie retorted. "Why don't you go ahead, Nana? Frank can take a walk around the neighborhood if he doesn't feel like listening."

"The TV in the bedroom working, Ma?" Frank asked.

"Of course it works," Nana answered. "I've had that TV for thirty years."

Frank stood up and stretched. "Wouldn't mind watching some football. Big game today between Penn State and Miami," he said, winking at Colin. "More important to know where you're going than where you came from." He sauntered out of the room, disappearing into a small room off the kitchen.

Nana sat up straight and clasped her hands together, peering slowly around the room, appraising each person. "Don't mind Frankie—he's just a grump sometimes. Do you still wanna hear the story?"

"Please go ahead, Nana. I really do," Colin said.

"I like to hear stories, too," Maya said. "In school, the teacher reads us stories every day."

"Yeah, yeah, we're good," Tomás added. "We would love to hear it."

"Sounds great, Ma," Michael said, "but Noreen and I have to get going. I have a big case coming up and I have some work I have to get done."

They hugged Nana, waved goodbye to everyone, and scurried out the door.

"Well, then I'll tell the story to the rest of you," she said, but Colin thought there was a little sadness in her voice, and not quite as much enthusiasm. "Okay, so here it is. My great-great grandfather, Johnny Murphy—your great-great-great-great-grandfather, Colin—came to the United States from County Kerry, Ireland, in 1847, at the age of fifteen, to escape the potato famine. There we go again with all those darn greats. Maybe you can figure them out, Colin, and let me know if I have it right. Anyway, it was his wish that this story would keep bein' told, but he didn't read or write much, so it was handed down by word of mouth until my grandmother decided to write it down. Johnny Murphy wasn't his real name, you know. His name was Eamonn, Eamonn O'Murchada. *O'Murrakoo* was how they pronounced it in Gaelic, but when he came through the immigration place—it was in Staten Island in those days—they changed his name, told him if he wanted to be allowed into America, he would be John Murphy, so John Murphy he was.

"They were very poor in Ireland, worked as tenant farmers on the estates of wealthy Englishmen, who rented 'em tiny plots of land to live on, about half an acre, too small to grow anything but potatoes. The English, they grew all kinds of crops on those estates, but shipped them off to England in big boats to make money, paid the Irish next to nothin'. They had nothin' but potatoes to eat and a one-room hut to live in if they were lucky. The rest of 'em lived in holes in the ground called scalps or in the county workhouse. Clothes were so ragged you would'a thought they was naked."

She glanced over at the Morenos, who were listening raptly. "Sorry for my language, but that's the way it was. Nothin' but a few strips a' cloth on their backs.

"Potatoes morning, noon and night, and they were glad to have 'em. Do you like potatoes, Maya? I like 'em mashed, myself. Nothin' like some good mashed potatoes with butter and salt. Kept me healthy all these years. What is your favorite kind of potatoes?"

"French fries," Maya answered. "I like McDonald's fries."

"They didn't have French fries or McDonald's restaurant back in 1847," Bonnie said to Maya. "How did they cook their potatoes back then, Nana?"

"Well, they boiled them, made potato cakes, potato soup. Praties, they called 'em."

Colin leaned forward, his hands on his knees, entranced by his grandmother's story. "What kind of house did the Mura—what was their name again?" he asked. "Johnny Murphy's family, where did they live?"

"A one-room mud hut, until the famine, when the potato crop got a disease and all the potatoes turned black and spoiled. They couldn't pay the rent and Lord Byrne's agents threw 'em out. Broke down the door with a battering ram, chopped down the walls right in front of 'em."

Frank appeared in the doorway, leaning against the frame. "Ma, you have to let me get you another TV. That one is a piece of junk. I can't even get channel 45. You need to call the cable company—"

"Oh, I don't care about that," Nana said. "I don't watch TV much. I prefer to read a book or take a walk. I can still get a few channels, so I can watch my soaps, and that's enough for me."

Frank trudged back into the room and slid back down into the armchair, glaring silently out the window.

Colin turned to Nana. "So what happened next?" Colin asked. "You interrupted the best part of the story, Dad!"

"When we get home, we can go to the library and take out some storybooks," Frank said peevishly. "Maybe Mom can read them to you at bedtime."

"That's enough, Frankie," Nana said. "You're welcome to listen, but you can always go take a walk if we're botherin' you too much. Anyway, where was I?"

"The soldiers were throwing them out because they couldn't pay the rent," Bonnie said.

"Right. Johnny's mother was a proud woman and refused to take her family to the workhouse. She was a healer, collected herbs and things and tended to her neighbors when they got sick. Wild garlic and honey for the cough, comfrey for the fever, my grandmother told me. I still use those, been handed down all these generations, although the garlic isn't wild, comes from the supermarket," and she lowered her voice to a whisper when she said "supermarket," as though not to offend the ancestors.

"Brigid, her name was, she took care of them all, even if they were strangers, just wandered into the neighborhood." She paused, glancing at Frank, who was sitting with his arms folded, his heel bouncing against the floor. "If they were sick she healed 'em. Delivered babies in the middle of the night, prayed for their souls. Never denied anyone, even when she—"

"That was a long time ago, Mother," Frank snapped. "Lotta things have changed since then."

"Frank Sullivan, don't you interrupt me!" Nana shot back, shifting her weight on the couch. "And don't you start changin' the story! Frankie likes to make up stories, too," she said to her audience, "but I'm tellin' this one."

"I wrote a story in school," Maya added.

"And maybe later you can read it to us, honey. What is it about?" Nana asked.

"About a little girl, she come from Honduras," Maya responded.

Nana nodded. "Sounds like a good story. I better finish up, then, so you can read it to us. I know we'd all like that."

Maya's mother pressed her lips together and stared at the floor, twisting her wedding ring around and around her finger.

"Don't mean to be taking so long," Nana apologized. "You all have other things to do besides listen to an old lady ramble on about the past."

"No, please, tell your story, Nana. We want to hear it," Nita responded softly.

"So as I was sayin'," Nana continued, "Johnny Murphy's parents were too proud to take their family to the workhouse, that was the poorhouse where you worked all day in exchange for a little food and a place to sleep, so they slept out in a field with their four children. The baby was very sick, and as bad luck would have it, that was the night the Lord decided to take her, so they had to bury her little body in the field across from the workhouse. The whole family slept there that night, next to the little grave."

Nana took a deep breath, as though she needed to pause to collect herself, then picked up the plate of cookies. "Have one and pass it around," she said, handing the plate to Nita. "Stories go better with cookies."

Maya took one, Colin took three and put them on a small paper plate. The chocolate cake had filled him up, but no reason why he couldn't manage a few cookies.

"Want one, Frank?" Bonnie asked, passing the plate to Frank. "Got chocolate in 'em, your favorite."

Frank took a bite, chewed it slowly. "Good cookies, Mother. Bet you made 'em yourself. An old Irish recipe?"

A mischievous grin creased Nana's face. "Can't tell a lie, Frankie. Don't cook so much anymore. No one here to eat it. But I do love the sweet stuff, so I buy them at the Spanish bakery next door. Best cookies in the world. Like 'em?"

Colin almost choked on his cookie, the crumbs sticking in his throat as he tried not to laugh and ended up in a coughing spasm.

"Delicious cookies," Bonnie chimed in, grinning back at Nana.

Nana kicked off her sneakers, white with pink and black designs, and wiggled her feet. "My feet bother me these days. Hope you don't mind if I tell the story barefoot. The Irish were often barefoot in those days, so it'll add a little flavor to the story," and she smiled to herself in that funny way again.

"So anyway, in those days, people were fleein' Ireland by the thousands, gettin' on ships coming to America or to Canada. Padraig, that was Johnny's father, didn't have the money to pay for passage for the whole family, so they dreamed up a wild plan to get Johnny on a boat so he could go to America, get a job and send money to the family, maybe send for them later.

They went down to the docks, and Padraig engaged the ticket agent in a conversation. Brigid pretended she was sick, threw a regular fit, layin' on the ground, screamin' and carryin' on. Everyone ran to help her, and Johnny slipped behind a family and followed them onto the boat. Broke the law, I guess, sneakin' on for free, but when your family is starvin' and people are livin' in caves and dyin' in the fields, you do what you need to save yourself and your family. He didn't hurt nobody, just snuck onto the boat so he could come to America and have a better—"

"Can't prove that one," Frank said, leaning back, his arms folded tighter.

"This is my story, Frankie. Now you just hush up, let the children learn something."

"Sound like pretty brave people," Colin added. "Stay and starve or have some guts, make a break for a new life. Makes me feel proud to come from people like that."

"So, the ship was packed with people—two to a bunk, sleeping on the floor, whatever space they could find. They were supposed to get one pound of bread or potatoes a day, but that ran out quickly and they were as hungry as they were in Ireland. Water leaked in, rats ran over them as they slept, and the typhus, that came next. Half the people on the ship dyin' from the fever, the ones still alive sleepin' on the floor next to the dead bodies."

"I saw a rat once," Maya said. "In our—"

"Maya!" her mother scolded. "Let Nana finish."

"They arrived at the quarantine station on Staten Island, where they checked 'em out for diseases, then they had to be approved by the agents, who laughed at them, they were so skinny and their clothes were all dirty and raggedy. They checked 'em over to see if they could work, and that's when they changed his name, told him he couldn't come in if he didn't. The Lord was lookin' out for Johnny; he didn't have typhus, and he had met a girl on the boat, Dairinn O'Braiain, became your great-great-great-grandmother. They changed her name, too. Daisy O'Brian is your name now, they told her. America was a strange country to them, all kinds of foreign ways they didn't understand. Didn't even speak the language, had to learn to speak English."

Frank slid to the edge of the armchair, wide awake now. "Come on, Mother. They spoke English. Go to Ireland, you'll hear them speaking—"

"They did not! The Irish had another language of their own, Gaelic, that's why you can't pronounce their true names. You don't hear it much anymore, but there are people in Ireland who still speak it."

"Be way cool to go there," Colin said.

"The Americans made fun of 'em, spit at them when they walked down the street, threw rotten oranges. Daisy still had a few coins her parents had given her, so they paid sixpence to a man for a room in a boarding house, but the man ran away with the money, and they had to sleep in an alley. Back then a whole lot of people couldn't pay the rent in the boarding houses, so there was a whole community living in the alleys behind the tenements. The Irish in one alley, the Germans in another, the Italians a few blocks down. Johnny tried to get a job, found signs everywhere that read NINA, No Irish Need Apply."

Nana picked up the plate of cookies and waved it around. "Anybody want another cookie? I know I'm goin' on here, so maybe it's time for a cookie break. I know you want one," she said to Colin. "I used to give you cookies when you were a baby. You loved 'em, could suck on one for hours. 'Course your mom and dad didn't know, probably would've been really mad at me if they had found out!"

"Anyways, the Americans didn't want us here—the Irish, I mean—told us to go back where we came from, but we hung in there, stuck with our own for protection, helped each other and shared what we had, held that St. Patrick's Day parade every year, despite it all. Daisy got some work sewing, and since the ships were coming into the harbor every day, Johnny got a job loading ships, sent money back to Ireland. His parents never did make the trip, but his younger sister came a few years later. Pretty soon, Daisy had a baby and Johnny wanted to name her Clodagh, after his sister that died in the field, but Daisy said no one in America is called Clodagh, so they named her Catherine, Katie for short. She was the first of seven, the beginning of the Murphy clan in America."

Nana's hand went up to her mouth to cover a coughing spell, while she waved the other one in the air to signal her audience to be patient. "All this talkin' is dryin' up my throat."

"Can I get you something to drink, Nana?" Bonnie said, looking concerned. "Colin, honey, would you go into the kitchen and get some soda from the refrigerator? And I think there are some paper cups on the kitchen counter; maybe you could bring those, too."

Nana slapped her hand to her forehead and rolled her eyes. "I didn't put out anything to drink—guess I'm gettin' a little forgetful nowadays. Probably shouldn't tell you that," she said, taking a quick peek at Frank. "Some people want to put me away in some home somewhere, you know, where they send old people to die."

"Thank you, dear," Nana said to Colin when he brought in the soda and the glasses.

"Who'd like some soda? Colin, pour some for me, if you wouldn't mind."

She took a sip of soda, placing the cup on the table in front of her. "You know, we're a strong lot, we Irish, and we know the meanin' of hard times, but we always found time to sing and dance and tell stories. I always tried to teach my children that hard times don't have to make you mean, like it does some people. Mike always said that—my late husband,

411

may he rest in peace. Frankie's father and Colin's grandfather," she explained to the Morenos. "Mike Sullivan was his name. He worked on the docks loading ships like Johnny Murphy, but he died young, never had a chance to see his children grow up. He did a little too much drinkin' and his heart gave out. Mike always said he never wanted to see a Sullivan being mean or cruel, 'cause we have felt that meanness and cruelty, we know what it's like and would never wish that on anyone. We had six children, but I ended up raisin' the younger ones all by myself. Some of them got it, some didn't," she said, wrinkling her nose at Frank. "That's why I want this story told. You take this diary, Colin, hand it down to your children, tell them this story. That's what Johnny would have wanted."

Colin wrapped his arms around Nana, gave her a big hug. "Very cool story," he said, taking a bite of one of the cookies from the Spanish bakery next store. "I'm gonna read the diary as soon as I get home."

"I'd like to read it, too," Bonnie added. "Let me know when you're done with it."

"Don't leave yet," Nana said. "We still have another story to hear. Maya, go get your story. We can't wait to hear it."

Thirty-nine

Marisol hunkered down on the steps of St. Michael's, her arms wrapped tightly around her knees like a rubber band stretched beyond its capacity, ready to snap at any moment. Marking time until Colin arrived.

Loud music blared from an open window in the apartment building across the street, some kind of Caribbean reggae. The music was loud enough to hear down the block, a welcome distraction from her thoughts about Colin. She didn't know the song, but it gave her a reason to tap her foot on the step, a release from the jitters in her stomach. Helped her cover it all up so nobody would guess her insides were on fire with grief.

She had ignored the red flags, the voices whispering in her ear to walk away from this one, but she couldn't deny that she had enjoyed the time she spent with him. It had been more than enjoyable, it had been wonderful, thrilling. She had thought maybe she loved him and that he returned it, but the truth was on that paper in black and white. The sweet boy who had taken her boating in Central Park on a warm spring day had done this to Papi. Being an honor student didn't teach you everything, and she had certainly stepped in it big time on this one. Reached for something way over her head, maybe over both their heads, a fantasy world that didn't exist, beautiful until it floated away, a beloved brightly colored balloon vanishing into the upper reaches of the atmosphere, leaving her wondering if it had ever really happened at all.

The sketches she did of him, of the things they did together, lay in the bathroom sink, staring up at her, awaiting their grisly fate as she held a matchbook over them, ready to turn them into a pile of charred ashes and wash them down the drain. The lake in Central Park, the beach at sunset, a funny cartoon of the subway ride and some of the people they had seen, a sketch of him stretched out on the Sanchez family towel at Orchard Beach, serving food at St. Michael's. His dark blond hair and his charming face would burn quickly, disappear in a puff of smoke, never to be seen again. She had hovered over the sink holding the matchbook, then picked up the sketches with shaking hands and tossed them in the back of the closet under a pile of clothes.

Colin wouldn't think she was pretty today. She hadn't slept well in days, tossing and turning, holding back tears in public, crying at night when no could see. Her eyes were puffy and she had no earrings and no makeup, just an old blouse and a pair of jeans she had thrown on, along with a pair of sneakers to make it easier to run if she needed to.

She could have easily never spoken to him again, simply disappeared and gone back to her life, but she harbored the tiniest bit of hope that a mistake had been made, that it was some other Colin Sullivan who picked Papi out of the lineup, or a typo by some overworked clerk at the County Clerk's office. Maybe his father or some other relative had the same name. Colin, Sr., and Colin, Jr. That would make sense based on what he said about his father, a tough guy, not a very nice person.

The reggae music coming from the building across the street had changed, although not by much, the same beat with different lyrics. As she sat on the steps absorbed in the rhythmic pattern of the guitar and the reverberations of the drums, her ears picked up a second set of drumbeats, thumping through another open window in a different apartment building. Latin music, a song that she knew. The rhythms of the two songs blended and clashed at the same time, alternately dissonant and harmonious, a unique mixing of two worlds, a blending of cultures that seeped into the pores of everyone who heard it.

Marisol spotted a woman pushing a stroller, moving her head to the music as she wended her way down the street, and wondered which song she was dancing to, or whether it was the intertwining of both that was energizing her.

A familiar navy blue T-shirt emerged from around the corner, along with a pair of long gray basketball shorts and leather sandals, his hair rumpled in a sexy kind of way, falling loosely over his forehead, one wavy lock over his right eye. There was still time to crawl away, save herself, but she felt rooted to the steps, frozen in place. She focused intently on a piece of gum stuck to the cement, a flattened, used up piece of gum some previous occupant had discarded, on their way to St. Michael's, maybe seeking guidance or else just coming home late at night tired and drunk. Chewed up, spit out, tossed aside without a second thought. Stepped on again and again, by everyone who passed this way.

Colin's chest rose and fell as he raced up the steps, close enough for her to feel the heat of his body and breathe in the sweet smell of the soap he had used this morning, but she felt distant, far away, as though she was in an underground tunnel listening to footsteps echoing on the path above. She sat with her head bent over, her eyes fixed on the piece of gum, the drums pounding in her ears. She tuned out the Caribbean music and heard only the Latin, a lamenting song of love that had been lost. Her music, her world, a world he would never be able to touch.

"Marisol." That voice had excited her, made her want more, but now she couldn't look up, couldn't bear to hear it or see his face. He sat down on the steps next to her, his shoulder touching hers, expecting a response, but she had none.

"Marisol. What's wrong?"

She searched desperately for a reserve of strength; it appeared faintly at first, a vaporous, misty image in the back of her mind, then surfaced, deep and rich. Mama's steady endurance, Papi's indomitable spirit. They had provided a legacy of courage for her, more than enough to do what she had to do. She rose to a standing position, towering above him, her arms folded as she stared down at his face, his blue eyes, his quirky grin. She wanted to just slap him and leave, but this was bigger than that.

He had the right to defend himself, to say his piece. In America you were innocent until proven guilty, unless you were an immigrant with no education and no citizenship papers, then you were presumed guilty, never innocent. She would give him a chance to tell his story, a chance Papi never got.

The street was empty and quiet, the only sound the cooing of pigeons on the roof of the building across the street and the muffled growl of an occasional car as it passed by. She searched his face for a clue that would tell her where to begin, but picked up only surprise and confusion.

He glanced at his watch and attempted a smile. "They're expecting me at twelve. This is my last day here. I've finished my community service—back to my boring old life, I guess."

"They can wait. The people in there are used to waiting."

Colin was silent for a moment, obviously taken aback by the edginess in her tone. "What gives?" he finally muttered stiffly, clearly uncomfortable now.

She imagined him with a hand mark across his cheek, blood dripping from the side of his mouth, and stuck her hand in her pocket, holding onto a special smooth green stone she had found once on Orchard Beach.

The piece of paper was in her purse, folded up into squares, the damning words right there in black and white. Black marks that changed Papi's life, her life. Silently, because there were no words, no way to explain it all, she unfolded it, extended her arm, placed it in his hand.

Blood drained from his cheeks, his eyes glued to the page. "Where did you, how—"

"From a lawyer."

"A lawyer? Why?"

"Is that you?" she snapped angrily, hoping he wouldn't notice that her hands were shaking.

He leaned back against the step, his long legs sprawled out in front of him, and closed his eyes. "This is uh, kind of a personal thing. I thought about telling you, just didn't, I guess. I didn't want you to think I was—"

Marisol pointed to Papi's name on the form. "Open your damn eyes and look at what you've done."

"Are you worried that I'm some kind of messed up guy, some kind of criminal?" he said softly, as though he was trying to soothe her, ease the tension. "Well, I did make a mistake, a stupid mistake, I'll admit to that, but I've never been in trouble before and don't plan to be again.

There's nothing to worry about. It's over. I paid my dues, did my community service, and I'm done with it. I'm looking at a football scholarship, not jail time," he added, reaching for her hand.

Marisol, the ambitious one that had toed the line all these years and followed all the rules, quietly determined to get ahead, struggled to contain herself but could not control the sound that came from somewhere so deep even she didn't know what it was. She yanked her hand away from him, and a furious, guttural sound flew at Colin with the force of a tornado and the high pitch sound of a gale force wind, threatening to ravage both of them.

"*Cabron!* You bastard!"

Colin ran his hand through his hair, gaping at her with his mouth open. "What?"

"I know what this is about, so you can stop pretending you're clueless. You picked an innocent man out of a lineup to save your sorry ass—a man you'd never laid eyes on before."

Colin squinted at her quizzically. "Do you know him? Is that why you—"

"The man you accused is my father, you asshole! My father! A human being, in case you hadn't noticed, even if he didn't have papers. Did you think for one minute that this person you were telling lies about might have had a family who loved him, children who needed him? Or was he just some brown-skinned person who wasn't worth more than a piece of trash?"

A red flush crept over Colin's face, and his voice was flat and quiet. "Your father? He was your father?" He clapped his hand to his forehead and ran it slowly through his hair again. "Oh god, this is so messed up. I'm like, incredibly sorry about the whole thing."

Marisol's voice echoed across the steps and the street rocked with the force of her rage—for Papi, for Tio Miguel, for all of the other voiceless people whose lives were destroyed by forces beyond their control. "Laws are made by human beings who sure as hell are not perfect themselves. They're not always fair and you're just damn lucky if you're born on the right side of them. Slavery was legal, too, passed fair and square by an elected government, enforced by law. 'Oh, the slaves have broken the law by running away, I'll help catch them and send them back to be whipped and enslaved, collect a reward, too.' Is that what you would have done?"

"No, of course, I—"

Two guys wandered up the street dribbling a basketball, glancing over to see what the commotion was about, but Marisol saw nothing, felt nothing except for the heat in her face, the trembling in her hands. "Do you have any idea, the slightest notion of what you did?"

"I'm so sorry, Marisol. I—I don't know what to say. The police offered me a deal and my dad forced me to take it," Colin stammered.

"No one can force you to do something like that. I would have expected more of you, but now I know you're just a coward. Worse than a coward."

"You don't know my dad. I was scared, and I didn't know what else to do."

"Have some courage? Take the consequences for what you did? Did that ever occur to you?" Marisol sputtered angrily.

"I guess I really didn't think about anything except getting out of the situation I was in. My dad said I could never get a football scholarship or financial aid if I was found guilty and my chance of going to a good college would be ruined, so I just did what he told me to do."

"Well, isn't that just too bad. Better to ruin someone else's life, someone with no resources to defend themselves."

Colin gazed blankly at the building across the street. The two basketball players were watching them, looking to see if there was any kind of trouble going on, if she needed help. She waved them away and they resumed their dribbling practice.

"Do you care at all about what happened to him? Do you even want to know?"

"I do want to know, because of you. You've made me care enough to want to know," he mumbled dejectedly.

"You're sorry because of me? What if it wasn't me? What if it was just some poor guy that you sent away and never had to face? You bet you're sorry! A sorry excuse for a human being!" Marisol snapped. "But if you really want to know, I'm going to tell you the truth, and I swear to god, I hope it eats you up for the rest of your life! My father went to jail and then got deported. That's right. Deported."

Colin stared at her, a look of astonishment on his face. "Shit! He was deported? I didn't know anything about that. I thought they'd just give him a ticket for loitering or something and let him go. What can I say besides telling you I'm sorry? I really messed up, but if there's some way I can help, I want to make it up to you."

"Well, now he's somewhere in El Salvador with criminal charges on his record. He can never return home, and we don't know if we'll ever see him again. We don't even know if he's alive or dead, or locked up in a prison somewhere. I'll introduce to you to my mother and she can tell you what it's been like for her raising her children alone, or you can meet my nine-year-old brother, who asks for his Papi every single day. You want to help? Well, here's what you can do."

She grabbed the paper and crumpled it into a ball and threw it at him. It flew through the air and smacked him in the face, just below his right eye. "Go to the lawyer whose name is on that paper, and tell him what a lying little shit you are, and that you want to tell him what really happened."

Marisol turned her back to him and bolted down the stairs. She raced across the street, dodging a car that swerved wildly to avoid her, its brakes squealing as it smashed into a car parked at the curb. The driver yelled something out the window, but the words were garbled, a distant humming in her ears. Her body was on automatic pilot, fleeing to a safe place, away from danger. She sprinted down the cement sidewalks of Grover Hill, running for several blocks, not slowing down until she reached the corner of Fourth and Miller. Winded, she paused for a second to catch her breath and took a quick glance behind her. In the distance she could still see the wooden door, the stone walls of St. Michael's, could see him. He was still sitting there, holding his head in his hands, a tiny figure in blue slumped on the steps.

She darted quickly around the corner, the shuttered doors of El Patio looming up in front of her. The doorway was filled with a pile of ad sheets someone had dropped there, the windows boarded up. Her hand closed around the doorknob that opened the way to the little apartment upstairs, to Mama.

Forty

Colin stood in the hallway outside the kitchen, clutching Johnny Murphy's diary. He had pored over it till late into the night, reading it and re-reading it, painting pictures in his mind of his ancestors, his blood. His father was hunched over the breakfast table, drinking his coffee and scanning the morning paper, his white undershirt stretched across the muscles in his back. The table, scuffed and stained from its years of service to the Sullivan family, had a dark spot where his father put his hot coffee cup every morning. The same black coffee cup with the red and white Harley insignia, in the same spot for years of mornings. It left a permanent mark, as though he had stamped it with an inscription with his name on it, his personal place card. Frank Sullivan sits here, his coffee cup goes there.

"Mornin', son." Frank tore open three packets of sugar, dumped them in the coffee, swirled it around with his spoon. A wisp of steam rose from the cup as the sugar dissolved into the inky black liquid. Liked his coffee black, no milk, no creamer. Strong and black with lots of sugar. Frank lifted the coffee cup to his lips, took a small sip, and set it back on the dark spot.

"Stick a couple of these in the microwave for me, will you?" he said, pushing the box of frozen waffles across the table. "And while you're standing there, grab the jam from the refrigerator."

The aroma of coffee filled the kitchen, an earthy, morning smell that usually made Colin feel cheerful and homey, signaled the beginning of a new day, an anticipation of good things to come. Didn't mean much today, though. Even the sweetness of morning coffee couldn't erase the bitter taste in his mouth, relieve the sick feeling in his stomach.

"This coffee is the best there is, comes from somewhere in South America, I think. I poured some for you," Frank said, pointing to an identical red and white cup across the table from him. "I didn't take the milk out—you can get that yourself. I don't know how you can stand milk in your coffee. It's not coffee anymore, once you start puttin' milk in it. Turns into a woman's drink. You'll get over it, though, son. A few more years of football will cure you of that. Believe me, the pros don't drink that weak beige stuff you like," he chuckled.

Colin flipped through the pages of the diary one more time and flung it on the kitchen table. Frank eyed him curiously. "You okay?"

"Have you read this?" Colin said curtly.

"Don't need to. I've heard Nana's story many times, heard it long before you were born. She loves to tell it, over and over, whether anyone wants to hear it or not. I don't think half of it is true. Nana's always been a character, and now I think she's gettin' a little wiggy in her old age, like havin' those Hispanics to her birthday party. I'm worried about her, alone there, surrounded by those people. Bunch a' criminals, all of 'em, wouldn't hesitate to rob an old lady. That guy, that Tomás guy—wouldn't let him in my house. You can tell by the eyes; those shifty eyes give it all away."

Colin shoved two frozen waffles into the microwave, jerked open the refrigerator, and grabbed the strawberry jam from its usual nesting place on the side of the door. The jar was sticky on his fingers, the remains of a past breakfast left on the label. He raised it high in the air as though he was going to throw a pass, plunked it down in front of Frank with a thump.

"What's with you? Not eatin' today? Must be girl problems. Can't think of anything else could make a teenage boy not want to eat," Frank said, grinning widely this time. "I got lots of advice about that, if you need any. Women are funny ducks, have you flyin' high one minute, crawlin' in the dirt the next. You just gotta learn how to play 'em so they'll keep givin' it out," he said, giving Colin a knowing wink. "Takes a while to get it right, but you'll learn."

Colin picked up the waffle box, tapped it distractedly on the table a few times. "Stayed up last night reading that diary, Dad. Johnny Murphy was a pretty cool guy. Made me feel proud to be descended from someone like him."

"Now you're talkin'. Proud Irish stock, that's us. Always loved St. Paddy's Day. How about you and me make a deal to go to the parade on Fifth Avenue in March? I used to take you there when you were little, but we haven't been there in years. It's quite a sight, all those Irishmen in one place. I like watching the high school marching bands, you know, the girls in those little skirts twirling the batons. Great food, too. Corned beef and cabbage, soda bread and green beer. Hell, I'll even buy you a green beer, son." He slathered some butter and jam on his waffle and winked at Colin again.

"Wasn't nothin' in the diary about corned beef and cabbage and green beer. Well, you know the story—they didn't have much food at all, just a few potatoes if they could get them. The part that really got me was where the whole family lived in a one-room hut, and if they couldn't pay the rent, the rich landowners threw them out, didn't care if they died from livin' outside in a field somewhere. Bunch'a mean s.o.b.'s, those landlords," Colin said, shaking his head.

"Whoa, you are in some mood today. Whatever, that's history. Some bad things may have happened back then, but things change, and now you're here in Oakmont, New York, getting ready to go to a fancy college. History is interesting, but it's the past. I wouldn't put too much stock in it. The Irish worked hard and overcame all that. The green beer thing—well, that's just for fun. Gotta have a little fun in life sometimes."

"They fled to America, but the Americans didn't want 'em, treated 'em like dirt, said they were all criminals. What do you think 'No Irish Need Apply' meant?"

"A few jerks. We kicked their asses, though. We became cops and arrested 'em all," Frank laughed. "That taught 'em not to mess with us."

Colin hooked his fingers over the back of a chair to steady himself, slid onto the edge of the seat. "Some things haven't changed, Dad. Those day laborers at the mall are not any different than Johnny Murphy trying to get work and being told they didn't hire the Irish. Probably broke a few laws in their time trying to survive, too. Tammany Hall and all that. I read all about it on the internet."

Frank took a bite of waffle, chewed it slowly, gaping at Colin. He couldn't have looked more shocked if a grizzly bear had walked into the room and taken a seat at the table. "Don't think I heard you right. Must have been something on the radio, some commercial or something. *WHAT* did you say?"

Standing up to Dad had to be the scariest thing he had ever done, but if he didn't go forward, he couldn't live with himself. Besides, he was already a pathetic piece of crap in Marisol's eyes for what he did, so he may as well go down telling the truth. "The new immigrants are not any different than the old ones. They're just trying to survive and make a new life for themselves."

Colin could see the veins moving in Frank's neck, his jaw tightening as he chewed the piece of waffle, took a swig of coffee and washed it down with a gulp, then slammed the cup down on the table. Colin thought it would break into little pieces, that was how hard he slammed it. Coffee sloshed over the top, leaving a trail of brown liquid dripping down the side, forming a puddle beside the cup. Had to hand it to Harley Davidson, their mugs were tough—strong enough to withstand the wrath of Frank Sullivan.

"You're comparing your proud Irish ancestry to a bunch of illegal Hispanics? People that are breaking the law, sneaking over the border, coming here and taking our jobs? We weren't illegal. We got here fair and square, paid our dues, became good citizens. Damn, maybe you really are doin' drugs. Either that or you've lost your mind completely, havin' some kind of breakdown or somethin'. Looks like I made one hell of a mistake, makin' that deal so you could get off with community service. I should'a let you go to a youth facility for a few months. You would'a come back with a hell of a different attitude, wouldn't be all high and mighty, spoutin' this shit."

Colin's face was flushed, the white T-shirt and blue basketball shorts he had been wearing since yesterday sweaty, sticking to him, his brain foggy from lack of sleep. He had been in and out of dreams all night, barely slept a wink. In one dream he was chasing Marisol down a busy highway, gasping in horror as she was catapulted into the air by a speeding car, her lifeless body stretched across the black asphalt. In another, he was tramping through a jungle while a group of people followed him, wailing and crying. The jungle was sweltering and steamy, a smoky mist rising from the ground obscuring his view, causing him to stumble and pitch into muddy quicksand that sucked at his legs, dragging him down. A swarm of insects swirled around his head, biting his face, his arms, his hands, as the mud choked him, suffocated him.

"They didn't use the word 'illegal' back then—they used different words, but they meant the same thing. Go back where you came from; you're not welcome here," Colin declared wearily.

"Where the hell you gettin' all this from? School? Because if that's what they're teachin' you in school, I'm gonna have to go up there and make some noise. Damn multicultural crap is drivin' the schools into the gutter. Which teacher told you all this?"

"I read the diary and looked up some stuff on the internet, talked to people. That's all."

"What people?"

"People."

"I've about had it with your attitude today, boy. You got some kind of stick up your ass, have some waffles and get over it." He curled his hand around the jar of jam, heaved it across the table, sent the butter sliding right behind it. Shoved them so hard they almost flew off the edge, forcing Colin to scramble to catch them before they crashed onto the floor.

Colin sat up straight in the chair and breathed in, then out, his eyes riveted on his father's face. Underneath the table, his hands were balled up into fists and his right foot was tapping nervously against the linoleum floor. Better to get it over with quick, like pulling off a Band-Aid.

"Somethin' I need to tell you," he muttered.

"Better be something good, 'cause I've about had enough, Mr. Know-It-All. Spill it quick, 'cause I been about to walk outta here for the past twenty minutes."

A hush blanketed the room, a perilous, stormy silence, broken only by the high-pitched cry of a bird cruising the neighborhood for scraps of food. The outstretched wings of a crow flickered outside the window, a shadowy omen hovering briefly before vanishing, a black speck soaring into the brilliant blue sky.

"About the case, my drug case."

"Your drug case? You don't have a drug case. I went to a lot of trouble to take care of that so you wouldn't have it standing in the way of your future. You did your community service, and it's over, finished."

Frank rose from the chair, his bulky frame looming over the table, the chair teetering, falling backward, hitting the floor with a crash. "Somethin' wrong with you, son? You sick? Havin' mental problems or somethin'?"

"No, no—nothing like that. It's just that—I do appreciate all the help you gave me, it's just that I made a big mistake that I have to fix."

"There's nothing to fix. I told you it's already been fixed."

"Well, it's time to like, unfix it. I lied about that guy in the lineup, okay? I never saw him before—never, ever."

"You didn't lie, son. You got yourself into a little trouble that's not worth ruining your life over and made a deal to get off. It's done all the time. We were all young once, partyin' and raisin' hell, made a few deals to survive. The cops know you come from a good family, expect you'll grow out of it, like we did. Nothin' to feel bad about, should be proud of yourself. You made the world safer for the kids in Oakmont."

Colin gazed dejectedly at the remains of Dad's waffle, forgotten on the plate, the splotches of coffee lying motionless next to his cup, and prayed for a major emergency to happen suddenly, something huge like an earthquake or a gigantic power outage that could force a swift end to this conversation, put it on the back burner for a while. Not much chance of that. Oakmont never had earthquakes and the weather was supposed to be beautiful for the rest of the week, no storms forecast at all.

"What I did ruined someone else's life."

Frank's face turned beet red and his voice boomed across the room, bouncing off the walls, coming back and wrapping itself around Colin's throat. "What the hell is eatin' you? You're telling me you're worried about some guy who skulks around schoolyards selling drugs to kids? His life isn't worth a bent penny compared to yours. Never heard such a bunch a' damn bullshit in my life."

432

"He was not selling drugs to kids, and he has a family who cares about him."

Colin was really in deep shit now, sinking deeper every minute. He should never have started this. It might have been better to do the time, not be indebted to his father for bailing him out in the first place.

"How the hell do you know that? What'd he do? Send someone to threaten you? Is that why you're actin' this way? 'Cause you're scared they're gonna hurt you?" Frank asked, softening his tone, the angry edge in his voice subsiding. "If they come near you, son, you call the police immediately. Some of these people are connected with drug cartels and are very dangerous. We'll have Johnny Loman put some security around the house, and I'll let your school know that they've been hassling you. In the meantime, don't go anywhere by yourself. Have Sam or one of your other friends with you at all times."

"No one is hassling me. I've just been thinking about this and need to set things right." The floorboards creaked in the hallway, a whispering of rubber soles brushing the wood floor, the emergence of blue hospital scrubs in the doorway.

"You have something to do with this craziness?" Frank grumbled irritably at Bonnie as she sauntered into the room to see what all the yelling was about.

"No, but from what I've heard, I'm very proud of my son."

A wave of relief swept over Colin, gratitude that his mother had gotten him out of the line of fire for a moment, but even that might not be enough to help him face Dad's rage. Mom gave in to Dad all the time to avoid facing it herself. Colin wasn't fooled by her brave little talk one bit. They'd have a big fight and then things would go back to the way they were: Dad in charge, Mom toeing the line. Even when they fought about race stuff, she often backed down to restore peace in the house. Might have to fight this battle alone, not much anyone could do to get him out of this one. He stuck his finger in his coffee cup and swirled the coffee around in circles. A muddy puddle, ice cold and stagnant, a lost cause on its way to the netherworld at the bottom of the drain. "Need to tell the truth about what happened," he mumbled into the cup as though there was no one in the room.

"I'll give him some paper and he can write a story and get it off his chest. A set of crayons, too, and he can draw a goddamn picture. Then he can throw it away and forget about it," Frank snapped at Bonnie. "Is that what you want? You want me to treat him like a big baby the way you do?"

"I treat him like a human being who makes mistakes and can learn from them. You're not exactly Mr. Perfect, who never makes any mistakes. That's actually kinda funny," she snickered, trying to suppress a giggle. "Yeah, you really have a lot of nerve expecting a teenager to be perfect when you—"

"Do you know what this means?" Frank thundered. "You're going to make me look like a damn fool. I pulled strings to get you off and convinced the police in this town to back you, and you're telling me you're going to change your story? I pulled strings with the goddamn police department. Don't you get that?"

"Frank, he's just trying to do the right thing," Bonnie shot back. She touched Colin's arm gently, her lips pinched in a forced smile. "What do you need to say, honey?" she asked softly.

"I'm turning myself in."

The sun was getting higher in the sky, sending streaks of light through the window that were making odd designs on the table. Frank glared at him, a chilly glare, cold enough to shrivel the leaves on the trees. The furious, withering look Colin had spent most of his life trying to avoid. Frank Sullivan, ex-Marine. Not someone you wanted to make angry. The little boy in him that always wanted to please Dad was struggling to not cave in, to be able to go through with this. "We already did the right thing. Are you out of your fucking mind?"

"I'm going to see a lawyer about changing my statement."

"You're going to change your story to free one of those scumbag illegals? They're better off locked up."

Colin sucked in his breath and let it out slowly, his eyes riveted on Dad's scowling face.

"Exactly what I'm going to do."

Frank's fist flew out and caught Colin on the jaw, sending him flying into the window. A searing pain shot through Colin's head as he struck the glass, but before he could steady himself, another blow hit him in the stomach.

"Like hell you will."

Spring, 2007

Forty-one

The coyote called himself *El Lobo*, the wolf. Five hundred dollars each to guide them across the Rio Grande, cover the cost of the driver on the American side. Felipe, Fredy, and Alfonso crouched in the tall brush, hidden by the thick stalks of Carrizo cane and mesquite bushes that sheltered them from the helicopters whirring overhead and the ICE vans lying in wait.

A rustling in the bushes, muffled footsteps padding across the hard clay soil. Fredy tugged on Felipe's shirt and pointed silently to a shadow moving through the brush. El Lobo, camouflaged in a black shirt, black pants, and black sneakers, barely visible in the darkness as he crept stealthily toward them. A sliver of a quarter moon provided no light and he carried none, not so much as a flashlight to illuminate the winding, circuitous path. The ground was rugged and uneven, strewn with hidden obstacles, but El Lobo knew the route as well as a flock of birds wending their way south in the winter, gliding along with the agility of a panther, as the migrants slipped out from the cover of the cane and tailed him up the path that led back toward Nuevo Laredo.

A long white van sat motionless in the far corner of a parking lot behind a church, no engine running, no driver visible in the front window.

"What is this?" Felipe whispered to Fredy. "Doesn't *la migra* drive vans like that? Maybe it's a trick."

"Only a trick on *la migra*, Felipe. El Lobo wears black in the dark and drives a white van to fool them. He'll take us far down the river to a hidden place they don't patrol as much. He's very smart—he'll get us across."

"Not smart enough to get you across last time."

"That could happen to anyone. We just have to be careful," Alfonso whispered.

"Looks like at least ten people here, maybe more. How are we all going to fit in there?" Felipe whispered back.

"It's a very friendly ride. He's taken the seats out, so everyone sits on the floor. It's pretty tight, though. You might have to sit on someone's lap. Or maybe one of the women will sit on yours," Fredy chuckled.

El Lobo sprinted across the lot, pulled the door open quickly and motioned to the group. "Go, go—climb in fast!" he whispered.

Felipe crawled into the van and found a space where he could lean against the wall, stretching his legs across the bodies of several people lying on the floor. "Sorry," he said to a woman as his legs pressed into hers.

"That's okay," she said, giving him a small smile. "Not much else you can do."

He took his shirt off and used it to wipe the sweat from his face, then folded it the long way and tried to use it as a fan, without much luck. The woman lying under his legs was watching him, so he fanned her with the shirt, and they both laughed. "Doesn't do much, I guess," he said. "Name's Felipe. What's yours?"

"Lupe," she answered, her eyes wandering over his shirtless chest.

"Where you headed?" Felipe asked.

"Los Angeles—got kids there," she responded. "You?"

"New York. Got kids there, and a wife," he said, and she nodded understandingly.

The vehicle swerved wildly and then lurched to a stop. "I guess we're stopping here," Felipe said. "Well, thanks for riding under me. It definitely made the trip better," he said, and they both laughed again.

The doors swung open and they found themselves in a murky, wooded area, a blind alley, silent save for the occasional crackling of twigs as an animal scuttled through the bushes. Ten people followed El Lobo down a dirt trail in single file, their belongings in plastic bags. The dank, musty odor of wet mud and the faint lapping of water against a shore let Felipe know the Rio Grande was somewhere nearby, taunting yet another group of migrants to dare to risk everything to cross, not knowing whether the river would save them or betray them this time.

The *put-put* of a helicopter broke the silence, but when Felipe peered upward he could see nothing but the midnight sky and a sprinkling of clouds. The aircraft was somewhere up there in the atmosphere, its location hidden from the vigilant eyes of the migrants, like a hungry bird lying in wait for its next meal. A small animal scurried across the path into the bushes, escaping from the claws of an owl that could be heard *whoo, whooing* nearby. The hooting of the owl blended with the whining of the helicopter, predators searching for their prey.

He could see it now, the Rio Grande at one of its lower points, rolling along quietly in the darkness. A searchlight panned the river and disappeared for a few moments, then returned to pan again. The migrants, carrying the plastic bags with their belongings on their heads, slipped noiselessly into the water, their eyes peeled for the amber lights of the helicopters, on alert for the drone of an engine. The muddy river bottom sucked at his feet, making each step an entanglement from which he had to disengage, only to find that the next move forward sucked him down again.

An engine roared overhead, an electrifying jolt that sent ten heads diving under the water, their plastic bags following close behind. Felipe held his breath until his lungs were on fire and he had no choice but to surface. The helicopter had vanished again, but now he was chilly and shivering, his teeth chattering as he slogged through the water, listening intently for any sign that the helicopter had returned. The water was shoulder-high, then waist-high, until he finally reached a shallower area covered with reeds, tall grass, and thick, sticky mud that licked at his ankles, squished between his toes. He collapsed on the riverbank, exhausted and soaked.

Fredy gave him a nudge with his foot. "Have to keep moving. Just because you can't see *la migra* doesn't mean they're not here. They're all over this place."

They crawled on their bellies through the mesquite brush, thorns scratching their skin, leaving raw red lines on their arms and legs as they inched toward an enormous tractor-trailer parked on the shoulder of a paved road, a company name imprinted in fancy black letters on the door.

"What does it say?" Felipe whispered.

"Delgado Trucking," Alfonso replied. "Moving and hauling."

"Good news—we just arrived and they already have a job for us," Felipe chuckled.

"What do they haul? Smells like animals."

"Cows, or maybe pigs. Whichever one you prefer," Fredy said.

"We sit with the cows?"

"Under them, unless you want to go back to Mexico, take another train ride. If we don't get stopped by the border patrol, the ICE, or the police, the truck should take us to a safe house here in Laredo. You're on your own from there. We're going on to Dallas. Why don't you come with us? You can meet our family."

"Wouldn't mind visiting sometime, but I need to get home to my family in New York."

Parting from Fredy and Alfonso would be bittersweet. They had saved his life, provided friendship that survived a trip through hell, a journey that had no end. A wrong move anywhere, anyplace, could find them snatched up and returned to the Mexican side of the border.

The other migrants were squeezing into a crawl space beneath the truck bed about a foot and a half high, a false bottom that would separate them from the cargo. Felipe slithered into the space on his back, wedged into an opening next to Fredy and Alfonso, just big enough for him to lie flat, his faced pressed against the metal underside of the truck bed. The overloaded vehicle moved slowly at first but picked up speed on smoothly paved roads, bumping and jerking over rougher, unpaved ones. Pain was shooting through his right leg, and the left one felt completely numb, but there was no room to move around, to get comfortable. It was only a short ride from the Rio Grande to wherever they were going in Laredo, Texas, but to Felipe, the ride seemed endless, another harrowing journey on a road that went on forever.

The truck finally lurched to a halt, the back gate banging and clattering as it slowly slid open. A rush of cooler night air seeped into the trailer, a welcome breeze circulating through the stifling heat. The chatter of men's voices drifted into the van, and Felipe felt panic rising in his chest, a sinking feeling that the police or immigration had finally caught up with them and would drag them all out of the truck any minute now, to be arrested, locked up in an American jail, then dumped back in Mexico.

Forty-two

Gusting winds and a driving rain whipped against Colin's face as he and Bonnie raced up the wide, flat steps of the courthouse and bolted for the doors at the top. The sudden downpour had intruded without warning, turning a cool, hazy spring morning into a damp and soggy one. Colin's navy blue sport jacket was spattered with unsightly wet blotches, his carefully pressed pants wrinkled and clinging to his legs, his hair dripping and disheveled. Not the best way to appear before a judge when you're recanting your previous testimony, admitting that you lied.

Colin and Bonnie wandered through the cavernous lobby of the courthouse, their footsteps hushed as they slipped silently across the shining marble floors. Armed guards appeared at every turn, standing watch in front of important offices, reigning over the metal detector, demanding impatiently that he empty his pockets, throw all his possessions on the belt. The place looked like an enormous palace, making Colin feel small and insignificant, a hobbit in an imperial court getting ready for an audience before the king.

Despite his relief at having the chance to set things right, Colin felt jittery, a queasiness that rippled through his body, leaving him shaky and unsteady. He hadn't seen his father since the fight in the kitchen, and it would be a miracle if he showed up in the courtroom today. When Dad punched him, his mother had immediately hustled him out of the room, her arms wrapped tightly around his waist as he leaned against her, groggy and dazed. They had gone to stay with her brother, Uncle Jim, where Colin slept in the basement on an old cot, nursing his swollen jaw and worrying about how he was going to carry on with his school-work and football practice when his life was falling apart. Mom stayed there with him for a few days, sleeping on Uncle Jim's living room couch, but had difficulty managing her night shift sleep schedule and reluctantly returned home. They agreed that it was better for Colin to continue to stay at Uncle Jim's right now. A cooling off period would be best for everyone, even though it felt strange to be hiding out, like he was some kind of fugitive or escaped criminal.

His mother wasn't cooking much—she wasn't about to cook for Frank and she didn't want to impose on Uncle Jim, so she often came by in the evening and took Colin out to a fast food place, or ordered some takeout from a nearby restaurant that they ate in front of the TV in Uncle Jim's basement.

A week passed, and Colin and Bonnie were sitting on the couch eating meatball subs from the local pizza place, one of Colin's all-time favorites. There wasn't much on TV, just the usual goofy sitcoms and the evening news, so Colin hit the remote and switched it off. They were comfortable enough with each other to not have to say much, just a few pleasantries about how his day had been, how the emergency room had been unusually calm yesterday—some broken bones, cuts that needed stitches, but nothing major. Colin stuck his hand in his pocket, felt for the paper, the one Marisol had thrown at him that day at St. Michael's, and tossed it on the couch next to her. It had been as good a time as any to have that talk.

"What is that?" she asked curiously.

"Uh, the name of a lawyer, Mom. I'm going through with it. I'm turning myself in, and that's the lawyer I need to see."

She was silent for a moment, staring down at the paper, then back at Colin. "Well, that's a big step. I understand how you feel, but why not just learn from it and get on with your life? Opening it all up again— that's huge," she said, with a worried frown.

"I messed up someone's life, really messed it up," he said dejectedly. "And mine, too."

"How do you know that?"

It was Colin's turn to be silent, then the words tumbled out. "I met a girl at the soup kitchen at St. Michael's, and we dated for a while. Her father was one of those guys who waits by the fence at the mall to pick up work and turns out he was arrested when the cops swept the place. The guy went to jail, and then was deported, and somehow she found out that I was the one who picked him out of the lineup. I don't know how she found out, but she did, and she let me know what I did to her family. Let me have it, big time."

His mother's jaw dropped, her eyes wide with amazement. "Oh, Lord. I, uh, well, I'm sorry you had to go through all that, honey. Your father and his damn group—they're the ones really responsible, but you're sure as hell not going to get any help from him," she said bitterly. "I'm here for you if you need me—anything I can do, let me know."

They made an appointment with Steven Rosenbaum, the name of the lawyer on the form, and he agreed to meet again with Marisol, this time with her mother present. If they consented to re-opening the case, he would file a 440 motion with the District Attorney's office to vacate Felipe Sanchez's conviction. Because Rosenbaum was representing the Sanchez family, though, Colin would need to get his own lawyer and would have to file an affidavit declaring the facts as they really happened. If the D.A. decided that the evidence warranted a hearing, Colin would be a witness, providing evidence for Felipe Sanchez's case.

Bonnie called the American Bar Association, got the name of a lawyer, said she would put it on a credit card if it was more than she could pay. The lawyer, Sherrelle Davis, accompanied them to the District

Attorney's office, where Colin told his story, offered to recant his original statement and plead guilty to the drug possession charges. He thought that would be the end of it, but for some reason, the District Attorney didn't believe him. Called him a liar, said he could be charged with perjury if he had lied under oath in his drug case about what had really happened.

The lawyers were waiting for them outside the courtroom. Steven Rosenbaum, looking trim and fit in a gray pinstripe suit and a bright red and white striped tie, Sherrelle Davis in charcoal gray with a white blouse underneath. "Call me Sherrelle," she had said when they met at the District Attorney's office, smiling cheerfully at him. She was young and pretty, couldn't be more than thirty, with a short afro, large gold hoop earrings and a curvaceous body that even the conservative gray suit couldn't hide.

Lists of names were on the wall, today's docket. Colin found Felipe Sanchez on the list, up there with a long list of criminals. There was no turning back now. It was kind of like getting a shot—once things were in motion, there was nothing you could do but close your eyes and wait for it to be over.

"Ready?" Sherrelle asked.

Colin shrugged. "I guess."

A hulking man in a dark gray suit lumbered across the floor carrying a leather briefcase with the initials *DT* engraved on the front. A narrow band of white hair circling the back of his head framed an otherwise shiny scalp, and he carried himself with the confidence that went with years of experience. Serious guy, not a stripe or a polka dot anywhere. Must be a class in law school on how to pick out the right gray suit, or navy blue if you wanted to be really wild. Colin wondered what would happen if a lawyer came to court wearing a T-shirt and jeans. Might be a cool thing for a lawyer to try, see what happens.

Gray suit stretched out his hand, gave each lawyer a firm shake. Colin waited expectantly for his turn, but no handshake was offered. Didn't give Colin a second glance, looked right through him like he was invisible, a piece of dust that drifted by, easily blown away by a slight whoosh of breath.

Colin glanced at Sherrelle quizzically, mouthed the word "who?" silently. "Daniel Taylor, the prosecutor," the lawyer whispered in his ear. "One of the assistant district attorneys, from the D.A.'s office. There are several ADAs, and the one who interviewed you in the office is not always the one who ends up prosecuting the case in court."

"But I turned myself in," Colin whispered back, as the man drifted off, slipping through a side door into the courtroom. "Why—"

"The D.A. has already closed the case and isn't interested in starting all over again, admitting they made a mistake. They're going to maintain that the original decision was correct, that there is some other reason why you are recanting."

When Colin had first informed Sherrelle that he had been dating the daughter of the man he had helped to convict, just mentioning

Marisol's name made him so upset that he could barely get the words out. He prayed that the DA wouldn't ask him about it front of the entire courtroom—that could be about the worst thing ever. He had really been into her and had blown it, big time. It wasn't even like they had broken up and were still friends, like with other girls. Marisol totally hated him now, never wanted to see his face again, blamed him for all the bad things that had happened to her family.

A court officer in his blues swung open the courtroom doors, directed people to enter.

"Bailiff," Sherrelle whispered. "Keeps order in the court."

The bailiff stood stiffly next to the empty witness stand, scanning the crowd, searching for anything out of order. In football, if you lost, there would be another game. There would be no second chance if he blew this one. The judge floated through a side door and perched on the dais, the judge's bench, like a bird of prey alighting on a branch, ruffling its outstretched black wings as it contemplated a scattering of field mice.

"Sit here," Sherrelle whispered, pointing to the defendant's table in front of the judge's bench. "I'll be here with you."

Colin turned around and glanced at his mother, who was slumped in the second row of benches behind them, focused intently on peeling the nail polish off her thumb, her face crumpled in a frown. She had picked him up at Uncle Jim's straight from the night shift at Westchester General, still wearing her blue hospital scrubs, her usually neatly combed brown curls bedraggled from the downpour. Dad had been furious when she took Colin's side and spent the night at Uncle Jim's with him, making sure he was okay, getting ice to put on his bruised face. In the morning, she had snuck back into the house to grab some clothes for Colin, pick up his backpack and a few other things he might need, hoping Frank would still be asleep, but he had been sitting at the table in the kitchen, silently drinking his coffee.

"After all the screaming and yelling, now he's not talking to me," Bonnie had told Colin when she called him that afternoon. "He just sat there with his head down, staring into his coffee cup, refusing to say a word. Can you believe that? He has a hell of a nerve being angry at anyone, after what he did."

Daniel Taylor shuffled some papers at the prosecutor's table across the aisle, then began tapping his fingers on the file, as though he was impatient for the proceedings to begin. The courtroom was packed, the right side of the room behind the prosecutor agitated, seething, like a swarm of hungry mosquitoes thirsty for blood. The *Stop Immigration* crowd, here to throw catcalls at Colin, shoot daggers with their eyes, demand that the conviction of Felipe Sanchez be upheld. Colin spotted familiar faces, members of the group his father met with in their living room or at the Steak 'n Brew, but his father wasn't among them. He spotted Mike Torelli, his neighbor, sitting next to cops in civilian clothes, their wives sitting earnestly beside them. Even Sam was there, slouched in the last row on the right side close to the door, in case he decided to slip out of there quickly. Across the aisle, several Hispanic families whispered quietly to each other.

Three lawyers, a judge, and himself. You didn't need a jury trial for something like this, Sherrelle had informed him. A hearing was sufficient; one judge alone would decide Felipe Sanchez's fate. If they won and the judge issued the order to vacate, Mr. Sanchez's records would be sealed and immigration records would no longer indicate that he had been convicted of a crime. The part that Colin had been responsible for would be gone, except for the fact that Mr. Sanchez was deported because of it. Colin would never be able to forgive himself for that. He wondered if there was any way Mr. Sanchez could get back into the country, or if his family had really lost him forever. If he did somehow make it back, he would still be illegal, the way he was before, but at least he wouldn't have a criminal record hanging over him. Marisol and her family would be able to see him again, and maybe she would be grateful for what Colin had done and forgive him. Probably not, though—she would probably still hate him, but maybe he would be able to forgive himself, to sleep at night.

He hoped desperately that the judge was feeling good, had just come back from a nice vacation. A restful week on a beach in the Caribbean, or a villa overlooking a lake in France. He thought about Nana, wished she was here today, egging him on with her feisty attitude. She didn't let anyone intimidate her.

The creaking of the double doors at the back of the courtroom caused him to twist around to catch a glimpse of the latecomer. He imagined for a second that it might be his father, then silently scolded himself for even thinking such a thing. Frank had been a pretty good dad for a while, when it was just about little kid things. Better to brush those thoughts away. No reason to expect that his father would change, that things between them could ever be okay after all this.

A somber figure in black, her hair pulled back tightly into a bun, crept quietly through the double doors into the courtroom and slid onto a bench in the very last row on the left. Marisol, dressed in black, in mourning for all she had lost. Not the Marisol who laughed with him on the subway and held his hand in Central Park, but a grim, unsmiling Marisol, leaning her head on the shoulder of the older woman who accompanied her. That had to be her mother—same jet black hair, almond-shaped eyes. The wife of the man he had picked out of the lineup, the mother of the little boy eating with Marisol at St. Michael's. Marisol's presence in the room unnerved him, left him breathless, yearning for another day, another minute to spend with her. His body slid awkwardly on the bench, almost fell off as he turned away, flustered and ashamed.

Another creak of the swinging door, along with the high tones of a child's voice and the gentle shushing of an adult. The clicking of a cane, tap, tap, tapping on the floor slowly behind them. A shock of white hair and deep blue eyes. It was Nana, shuffling along behind Nita and Tomás

Moreno and little Maya, who clung tightly to her father's hand. Mom must have had a private chat with Nana, invited her to attend the hearing. Bonnie spotted them and waved, pointing emphatically at an empty space on the second-row bench.

"Latecomers, please take a seat without further disruption. Court is in session, hearing the matter of the People vs. Felipe Sanchez. Counsel, do you wish to proceed?"

"We do, your honor."

"Mr. Rosenbaum, call your first witness."

"...swear to tell the truth, the whole truth and nothing but the truth..." the court clerk droned. Told the truth once, got punched out by Dad. The second time had to be an improvement.

"I do," Colin muttered, his voice hoarse, his face tight and stiff, as though he had been stranded for hours in an icy blizzard. His clothes were still chilly and damp from the rain, and he felt like he was coming down with a cold on top of everything. A court reporter tapped on a recording device, getting down every word uttered, every hesitation, every misspoken syllable.

Judge McKenna peered at him from behind Ben Franklin glasses perched on the end of his nose, as though he could suck out the truth through the power of his penetrating stare. A sea of faces gawked silently, restrained by the judge's gavel, waiting to pass judgment on him as he told his story. Colin Sullivan, football hero, liar, criminal.

"Mr. Sullivan, tell us what happened the day you were arrested at the East Oakmont mall."

He felt like a clown, a monstrous, misshapen buffoon on a rickety platform performing a crummy little show, on display for all the world to laugh at, to gossip about.

"Uh, I guess I was with a friend in the back lot behind Hamburger Heaven, waiting to meet up with a kid from school who was going to buy some stuff from us. My friend went into Hamburger Heaven to buy a soda, and I stayed outside to wait for the kid. Saw some cops and tossed the bag behind the dumpster, but they must have been watching. They searched the area, found the bag and—well, they busted me."

"What was in the bag, Mr. Sullivan?"

"Uh, some marijuana, and uh, well, a little cocaine, too, I guess."

"Where did you purchase the drugs, Mr. Sullivan?"

"Uh, a guy on the football team goes to Manhattan, gets it for us. He knows somebody there."

"What happened next?"

"My dad was totally freaked that I got busted. He said the arrest would get me kicked off the football team and totally ruin my chances for getting into a good college. My dad has—well, friends. Friends in the—"

He glanced over at the cops sitting behind Daniel Taylor in the first row on the right. Mike Torelli and his wife, Roberta. Tossed a football around with him lots of times, ate dinner at his house.

"Continue, Mr. Sullivan. Your dad has friends where?"

"I don't know, didn't really mean that, meant my dad is very friendly, everyone likes him. The cops just wanted me to give them a name and pick the guy out of the lineup, that's all. They said if I could name my supplier, they would cut me a deal for helping them out."

He was sinking, the quicksand sucking him further and further down, choking him, like in his dream. Funny thing about dreams, in the dark of night the truth sneaks out, makes you face what you didn't dare think about during the day.

"And you didn't consider giving the police the name of the person on your football team who was actually supplying you?"

"Whoa, that would've—to be honest—not really."

"And why was that?"

Colin raised his eyebrows and shook his head. "Well—I don't think I should—"

The judge leaned over and glowered at Colin. "Answer the question, Mr. Sullivan, or I can charge you with contempt!"

The courtroom was silent, dead silent, as an entire roomful of people listened attentively for his response. Colin drummed his fingers against the side of the witness box, desperate to buy a few seconds.

"Well, okay, here it is," he muttered in a low voice, hoping only the judge could hear him.

"Speak up!" the judge admonished him.

"So this kid on the team has an uncle who lives in the city, gets stuff for us. The dude brags about it, thinks his uncle is really cool. If I ratted on him, got his uncle busted, and they found out I'd snitched, nobody at school would ever talk to me again. I'd have to move away somewhere, go to some other school. I wouldn't have a friend left in the world," he said, staring glumly at the dark brown wood of the witness box.

"Tell us what happened next."

"It was very quick. I went to the police station with my dad and checked out these guys behind the one-way glass. I just wanted to get it over with, get on with my life. My dad said all the guys in the lineup were criminals already, one more charge wouldn't make much difference to them, that I had more to lose than they did."

"What kind of deal were you given by the police for naming this alleged drug supplier?"

"One hundred hours of community service, and I'd be done. No trial, no record."

"And how did you decide which person in the lineup to choose, Mr. Sullivan?"

"I didn't really decide—just picked one out and pointed."

"Has anyone threatened you, forced you to change your testimony, or promised you favors of any kind to come forward?" Rosenbaum continued.

Colin held his breath for a minute, then exhaled slowly. "Well, no, I decided—thought about what I had done, understood that it was wrong. Didn't need anyone to threaten me. I couldn't sleep at night, couldn't look at my own face in the mirror in the morning."

"Thank you. The defense rests, your honor," Steven Rosenbaum said, moving toward the defense table.

There was a murmur of voices from the spectators, and the judge banged his gavel emphatically on the podium. "We'll have quiet!" he bellowed. "Mr. Taylor, you can cross-examine now."

Daniel Taylor, the Assistant District Attorney, sprang from his chair and bounded excitedly toward the witness stand, waving his arms in exasperation. "A man was convicted based on your statement. Are you telling us that you lied?"

The courtroom became a misty haze as Colin flashed on Marisol's fury on the steps of St. Michael's, felt it burning into him now as he glanced at the back row where she sat silently, seething with rage at him.

"Yes, I—"

"Then why should we believe you now? You're a liar and have a history of lying. Did you ever sell drugs prior to the time you were arrested?"

Colin hesitated, his eyes fixed on the space between the witness stand and the judge's bench. Good thing his father wasn't here. Dad would definitely hear about it later, though, from Mike Torelli or one of the other cops, probably all of them. "Well, uh—yes," he stammered.

"So not only did you lie to the police, but you have a history of criminal activity. I'm not impressed by your honesty and your reliability, Mr. Sullivan."

Steven Rosenbaum was on his feet, his voice stern. "Objection. The witness has a clean record with no prior arrests. He has never been arrested or convicted of a crime."

"Just reinforces what a good liar he is."

The judge peered over his glasses again. "Restate the question, Mr. Taylor."

"So, what is your reason for suddenly having this change of heart that could possibly ruin your life?"

Colin fixed his eyes on Nana, in her best navy blue polka dot dress and pink and black sneakers, his mother beside her in blue scrubs, and tried to hold them there, an island of safety in a dangerous and turbulent storm, but he found himself sneaking a peek, another quick glimpse at Marisol in the back row. Her black dress morphed into a black bikini— Marisol holding his hand as the incoming tide tickled their toes, their bare feet sunk into the cool wet sand.

"Who are you looking for, Mr. Sullivan? Is there someone out there who has forced you to do this? Tell the court why you waited so long to come forward and why you are changing your story."

Colin remained silent, pondering the question. He had no answer, barely understood it himself. Just because it was the truth didn't mean it sounded believable. Real life could be incomprehensible, things just developed a certain way and you went along with it, didn't know any other way to do it. His father and his crusade against immigrants, Marisol, Wesley at the soup kitchen. Nana, telling the story of Johnny Murphy. No way the judge would buy that story, but he had no other story to tell. No point in making another one up, getting himself into hotter water.

"Answer the question, Mr. Sullivan," the judge ordered.

Forty-three

Felipe lay motionless in the darkness of the crawl space, listening to the mooing of the cows, breathing in the smell of manure, the sweet odor of hay. Texas! He had made it to Texas! The men bickered and squabbled with each other as they directed the driver to back up this way, then that way. Thundering hooves pounded above him as the cows were herded and prodded along a ramp positioned against the truck.

Two faces peered into the false bottom of the truck. "Quick," one of the men drawled in a low-pitched voice. "Come out of there and follow us."

Felipe trailed Fredy and Alfonso as the men led them down an unlit dirt path to a small, dilapidated shack in a secluded wooded grove. The house was barely visible in the darkness, but Felipe could make out the front steps, broken and cracked in some places, completely rotted out in others.

"Careful where you step," Alfonso warned.

Another man in work clothes and a wide-brimmed straw hat appeared, directing them inside to a large room with mattresses scattered across the floor. The mattresses were crammed with bodies, some snoring loudly, others sitting up, puffing nervously on cigarettes as they stared idly at the wall, their rough, calloused hands stained yellow with nicotine. Food wrappers and empty beer cans were strewn everywhere, and the room stank from the cigarette smoke that hovered in the air and tainted everything it touched—mattresses, clothing, the cracked and peeling paint on the walls. A powerful odor of human waste emanated from the tiny bathroom, mixing with the cigarette smoke. The boxcar had smelled like this, the stench of desperation and fear and death. Felipe's throat tightened and he felt sick to his stomach, frantic to escape this place.

"This here's your safe house," the man was saying. "Bathroom is over there, but there ain't no hot water in the sink, and the place don't have a shower. You can stay here tonight, but then you have to move on or pay us room and board. Twenty-five dollars a day, plus extra for food. If you can't pay that, there's a working ranch down the road and you can work there to pay for your room here. You made it over the border, you're back in the U.S., but you're on your own now. There's a Greyhound station in town that has a pay phone you can use. I know—don't see too many of those anymore, but they can give you change for the phone and info about how to get wherever it is you want to go. Convenience store next to the station has food and other stuff you might need.

"How much do you pay for working on the ranch?" Felipe asked.

The man snickered. "Like I said, the work covers the cost of your rent here, and you can make an extra dollar an hour," the man said. "Hey, you work sixty hours, you make sixty dollars. That'll pay for your food, and a bus ticket out of here."

Felipe's thoughts flashed on another safe house, a little white church in the desert, where he had been nursed back to health by a pretty red-haired woman named Sarah. "This is a safe place, a sanctuary," Sarah had said, "a place where you can rest until you feel strong enough to move on." Kind words, but only a fanciful daydream, a desert mirage, an illusory place that never existed for him. He would return to Oakmont a fugitive, always having to lay low, hide in the shadows. He wondered how he would find work without being discovered. Officer Bradley would still be in Oakmont, would surely spot him. His family would have to move, his kids change schools and leave the only home they had ever known. Maybe they could stay and he could get a little apartment and a job somewhere nearby, close enough for them to visit, but away from the watchful eyes of the Oakmont police. It might be possible to disappear, forge a new identity in Brooklyn or Queens, even parts of New Jersey. He and Julia would have to live apart, but at least they could see each other.

Felipe stood in front of the pay phone, his hands shaking. He remembered that directory assistance was 411, but the operator didn't have a number for a Julia Sanchez in Oakmont, New York, and could only provide landline numbers, not cell phones, which is most likely what Julia had.

Tio Miguel probably hadn't changed his number, so he called the number he remembered, but instead reached a recording for some computer business, definitely not Tio Miguel. Felipe's legs felt weak, but there was no chair to sit on, nothing even to lean on, and now there was a man standing behind him waiting to use the phone, glaring at him for taking too much time, gesturing impatiently. He called 411 again and they had five numbers for people named Miguel Gonzalez in Oakmont, but one of the numbers was almost identical to the one he had called—he had only been one number off! The man behind him shot him an angry look, so he tried to hit the numbers quickly, but his fingers were slow and jerky and he misdialed again, this time reaching a bank recording. The third time, he pushed each number slowly and carefully, and a woman's voice answered.

"Hello? Hello? Is this the home of Miguel Gonzales?" he asked hoarsely.

"He's not here right now. Who is this?" the woman said crossly.

"Well, Felipe Sanchez. I'm looking for Miguel Gonzales. Is this Rosa?"

"Felipe? Oh my god! Where the hell are you?"

"Texas—Laredo, Texas."

"You just hold on—I'm going to get Julia. You just wait right there. Stay right there— don't you go anywhere. I'll be right back!"

Maybe Julia hadn't married someone else and moved away, maybe she still lived next door to Tio Miguel and Tia Rosa, above El Patio, as they had since they were married. He could hear Rosa tearing through the house, pounding on Julia's front door, yelling her name. A door slammed, then footsteps, faint at first, then louder, and the murmuring of voices as someone approached the phone.

"Felipe?" a muffled voice said, then nothing except the sound of weeping, then sniffling. "Oh, god! I'm so happy to hear your voice—"

Felipe's eyes welled up with tears and his body was shaking all over, but he took a deep breath and sucked it in. This would not be a good time to make a scene or call attention to himself. He had just crossed the border illegally and he had a criminal record. The police would not hesitate to grab him and toss him in jail.

"I'm coming home, *mi cariño*. I missed you so much," he whispered, his voice barely audible. "Listen, I can't stay on the phone, but I'm in the U.S., in a bus station in Texas. I'm going to get a bus to New York, and if all goes well, I should be there by Friday. We can talk then."

"Marisol is graduating Friday at 10:00 in the morning, in the school auditorium. If you could make it by then—"

"I'll try, but it's better that you don't tell her I'm coming. I don't know how long it will take, or if I'll even make it there. Let her enjoy her graduation, not spend the whole day worrying about me and whether I'll show up. I'll see her whenever I get there. I'm going to try, though. I'm really going to try to make it, but I can't promise. I'll try to stay away from the—you know who—"

"*Te amo*, Felipe. I'm just so glad you're alive, I—"

"*Te amo tambien*, Julia. I can't stay on the phone. Bye."

Forty-four

"Tell the court why you are changing your story, Mr. Sullivan. A sudden change of heart without an explanation is not very convincing," Daniel Taylor repeated, his voice dripping with contempt. Colin squirmed on the witness stand, tried to move his lips, but no answer emerged. "I—"

Nana leaned forward, her fingers gripping her cane, her blue eyes boring into him.

Johnny Murphy, whispering to him from the grave. *Never want to see a Sullivan being mean or cruel... When you feel pain so bad you think you can't go on another day, play music and dance, help your neighbor with a sick child or welcome a newcomer.*

Judge McKenna's black robes rustled as he shifted in his chair, scowling at Colin from his perch on the bench. "You what, Mr. Sullivan? We don't have all day."

"Found out something," Colin mumbled.

"Found out what?" Daniel Taylor demanded.

"How much I hurt the Sanchez family by what I did. I ruined Mr. Sanchez's life."

"Found out from who, Mr. Sullivan? How would you come by information like that?" the prosecutor intoned peevishly.

"From, uh—"

The prosecutor slapped his hand on the table with a loud smack, indicating his displeasure and warning of the retribution that would follow.

"Who, Mr. Sullivan?"

"His—"

"His what, Mr. Sullivan? Tell the court who provided you with information about Mr. Sanchez's family."

"Daughter," he mumbled.

"You are changing your testimony based on information from the family of a convicted drug dealer? How did they contact you?"

"I met her at the church where I was doing community service," Colin said, choosing his words carefully, the way Sherrelle had advised.

"So, the family found you at St. Michael's and threatened you unless you changed your testimony?" Daniel Taylor turned his palms toward the ceiling, his voice booming across the room, as he shook his head in disbelief. "The state believes that Mr. Sullivan is being unduly influenced by persons connected with Mr. Sanchez, the person who was legally convicted of this crime."

The judge leaned on one elbow, his hand cupped around his chin. "Who would that be, Mr. Taylor? I understand that Mr. Sanchez has been deported to El Salvador."

"Mr. Sanchez is connected to Salvadoran gangs who have been moving large amounts of illegal drugs into the area. He was convicted of being a major drug supplier in the New York area. We contend that Mr. Sanchez's gang affiliates are threatening Mr. Sullivan and that the conviction should stand. And we all know that the drug cartels have lots of available cash. It's entirely possible that they're paying for his testimony today. We rest our case, your honor," he said confidently, as he turned to sit down.

"Call your next witness, Mr. Rosenbaum."

The prosecutor sat down, the public defender stood up. Musical lawyers, one up, one down. He remembered playing musical chairs at birthday parties as a kid. When the music stops, everyone rushes to find a seat—tough luck if you're the one who loses.

"I call Officer Anthony Scoletti to the stand," Steven Rosenbaum said.

Tony Scoletti, one of Dad's buddies, the one who had offered him the deal at the police station. The cops had defended him, taken him under their wing, made him a part of the brotherhood. They would have always been there for him, shielded him, but he had turned against them, a snitch, a turncoat. It didn't get much worse than that. Could have been the most foolish thing he had ever done. It was okay for a woman to be all touchy-feely, sensitive to some poor fool out there, but that didn't sit too well in the guy world. You'll never get ahead that way, his father would have said. Tough guy, Scoletti, staring at him from the witness stand, his blue uniform saying it all, the only evidence the judge would need to decide who was telling the truth.

"…swear to tell the truth, the whole truth and nothing but…" Colin wondered if he would.

"Officer Scoletti, did you or anyone in the Oakmont police department witness Mr. Sanchez selling drugs to anyone?"

"Not—"

"So, you didn't see this crime occur. Tell the court what the basis for arresting Felipe Sanchez was."

"We picked up the day laborers from the East Oakmont mall for making a public nuisance."

"What kind of nuisance was that?"

"Loitering in a public place, littering, harassing local business people."

"Harassing?"

"Overuse of facilities in private businesses without purchasing from the store."

"Facilities?"

"Bathrooms. They don't buy nothin', just come in to use the bathroom. They scare the hell out of the customers, which is not good for business. Customers don't patronize a trashy area, garbage on the ground, shady characters lurking in the parking lot. The mall was startin' to look like the South Bronx, people think they're goin' to get mugged. Terrifies the women, those guys ogling them, gotta worry about being raped every time they go shopping."

A loud whoop reverberated through the courtroom, then applause. The gavel hit the podium with a crash. Judge McKenna's face was flushed as he glared scathingly at the crowd. "Any more outbursts and I will clear this courtroom. Please continue, Mr. Rosenbaum."

"Anyone been robbed or raped at the East Oakmont mall, officer?"

Scoletti played with his tie, straightened it, shifted his weight around on the seat. "No."

"No? You're arresting people because of what you imagine they might do at some unspecified time in the future?"

"Right—we're not gonna wait until a major crime happens. I can't wait to see that headline in the paper. Police turn away while criminals control East Oakmont mall. Immigrant crime rises, police do nothing. The community would be screamin' bloody murder, wanting to know why we allowed these people to hang around. Better to nip it in the bud, get 'em out of there so people can shop in peace. Anyway, disorderly conduct is against the law in this state, along with unlawful assembly and loitering. We can arrest them on a 240.20—causing public inconvenience, annoyance or alarm. It's in the penal code. Look it up."

"After you arrested the day laborers, what happened then?"

"Brought 'em down to the station, put 'em in a lineup."

"On what charges? Littering? Maybe the town of Oakmont should provide some public bathrooms and some trash cans."

"That would encourage them to continue gathering there, and I told you, they were endangering the customers, and we had information they were trafficking in illegal drugs, selling them to high school students."

Muttering drifted across the right side of the room, and the gavel slammed down on the podium again.

"And what reason did they state for gathering at the mall?"

"Waiting for contractors to come by and offer them work."

"So, they're there because they want to work?"

"So they say."

"You arrest people because they want to work?" Rosenbaum said mockingly.

Daniel Taylor approached the bench, pacing in front of the judge. "Objection. Question is leading."

"Overruled," the judge responded. "Answer the question, Officer Scoletti."

"Depends what you mean by work, I guess. S'pose you could call drug trafficking work."

"Answer the question, yes or no!" the judge thundered.

"Uh, yes, if you insist on putting it that way."

"What happened after you put these people into the lineup?" Rosenbaum continued.

"We had Colin Sullivan look at the lineup, identify whoever sold him drugs. He picked out Mr. Sanchez, sir," Scoletti retorted defiantly.

"And Mr. Sullivan got involved in this, how?"

"He was arrested for drug possession, offered a deal if he would identify his supplier. Gave him a chance to be a leader, protect the community he grew up in."

"Colin Sullivan was given a deal by the police for providing this information?" Rosenbaum queried sharply.

Tony Scoletti fiddled with the top of a brown and yellow box of cigarettes that protruded from his shirt pocket. "Yes, he was told he would get off with community service if he cooperated," he said, narrowing his eyes disdainfully in Colin's direction.

"And he picked out Mr. Sanchez."

"Yes."

Now it was Rosenbaum who was raising his voice, pacing up and down. "But you have never seen Mr. Sanchez selling drugs to anyone. When you arrested him for littering, loitering, and urinating, did you find him to be in the possession of drugs?"

"No, not at that time, but we knew there were drugs being sold to high school kids."

Rosenbaum surveyed the faces in the courtroom, then addressed the

473

judge. "The defense contends that Colin Sullivan falsely accused Felipe Sanchez of selling drugs to keep from facing drug charges of his own, to protect his own future. No other evidence has been presented proving that Mr. Sanchez is guilty of these charges. The defense rests, your honor."

The gavel banged again. "The court will take a short break. Please be back in fifteen minutes," Judge McKenna thundered.

The throng drifted toward the door in an unruly mass, the humming of voices turning into a loud clamor. The veneer of politeness forced by the judge's gavel and the stern control of the bailiff vanished as the spectators from the courtroom filtered into the lobby. A protective phalanx of bodies encircled Colin: Bonnie, Nana, the Morenos, Sherrelle Davis. Sherrelle patted Colin on the back.

"You did a good job up there. The D.A. was trying to intimidate you, but you didn't bite, kept it together just fine."

"I'm proud of you," Bonnie murmured softly, squeezing his shoulder.

The crowd in the lobby was edgy, milling about restlessly. "Asshole," a voice muttered, and then a hacking sound, deliberately loud. Spit flew through the air, landing on his navy blue suit jacket, dripping slowly down, followed by snickering and whispering, then a roar of laughter. A figure stepped out of the circle, moving toward him, his fist aiming at Colin's face. Bonnie's hand gripped his arm, pulling him away, out of the man's reach. Another hand on his back, Sherrelle's, pushed him back toward the courtroom, where the bailiff stood with his gun.

"Spoiled piece'a crap," a voice near him croaked.

"Go back to the Bronx and live with 'em, if you love 'em so much," a woman yelled across the lobby.

"Nothin' wrong with the Bronx," Nana hollered back. She darted across the floor, waving her fist in the woman's face. "You should be ashamed of yerself, behavin' like a bunch a' damn fools."

"Get into that courtroom," Bonnie snapped at Colin and rushed to rescue Nana from the fray. "Nana, please," she said, pulling on her arm gently.

"And you're not one to be callin' anyone an asshole. You're the asshole!" Nana shouted at the woman as Bonnie hustled her into the courtroom, her white hair flying in all directions, her navy blue polka dotted dress flapping impudently behind her.

Nita Moreno rummaged around in her purse and passed Colin a rumpled tissue. He quickly wiped off his jacket, stuffed the tissue in his pocket and scrambled into the front row next to his lawyer. He checked his watch, praying that this would end soon. It had to be over soon; it was almost noon and the judge would want a lunch break. Marisol hadn't appeared in the crowd in the lobby, but there she was, laying low in the back row. Sam had returned, too, and was sitting quietly on the last bench on the other side of the aisle.

"We should be finished soon," Sherrelle said. "Your part is done; the rest is lawyer stuff."

Bonnie leaned forward, curled her fingers over the edge of the bench, and murmured into Sherrelle's ear. "What is the possibility that Colin will be charged with perjury and face jail time?"

"The judge will probably rule that if he stays clean for six months, his original drug charges will be dismissed and the records sealed because he is a minor. Not much will happen to him because of all this, but the stakes are much bigger for Mr. Sanchez. If the judge upholds the conviction, he will never be allowed back in the United States under any conditions. If the charges are vacated based on Colin's testimony and the records sealed, Mr. Sanchez will be free of criminal charges and can continue to pursue legal citizenship."

"Well, we all have our fingers crossed that the best happens for Mr. Sanchez," Bonnie said enthusiastically. "We certainly owe his family one hell of an apology. Have you seen them here, Colin? I think it might be a nice thing to do—"

"Haven't seen any sign of them, Mom. Good idea, though. Maybe some other time."

Colin Sullivan, football player, criminal, liar. He had sworn to uphold the truth, but there were some things that were just too awful, and having your mother apologize to your ex-girlfriend and her family was one of them.

The court was reconvening, the crowd shuffling back into the courtroom. Back and forth, the defense and the prosecution traded barbs, quibbled over points, argued that Colin was lying, was not lying, that Mr. Sanchez was guilty, was not guilty.

The judge appeared to have relaxed some, his stern countenance more neutral now. Colin thought he was probably relieved no fights had broken out in the courtroom, no one had to be dragged out screaming like you saw on television sometimes. His stomach was probably rumbling, too, like everyone else's in the room.

The judged banged his gavel again, silencing the courtroom, getting ready to begin. "In most cases, I would take the decision under advisement and rule on it when we reconvene the court in two weeks. But in light of the suffering already caused to the Sanchez family, I am going to rule on this today. I am issuing an order vacating the judgment and conviction of Felipe Sanchez, effective today," he declared emphatically. "Unfortunately, Mr. Sanchez is not present here today to receive this information, and, I have been informed, was deported because of his conviction and is not currently in the country. As a result, I will have to leave it up to his family to find a way to share the results of today's proceedings with him."

An angry chattering of voices, then shouting and another crash of the gavel. "We'll have quiet in here until we are done! As for the charges now pending against Colin Sullivan, he will be sentenced to one hundred hours of community service, time already served."

Both lawyers clapped Colin on the back, and cheers erupted from the row behind him.

"Please exit the courtroom through the double doors in the back," the bailiff called, moving closer to the crowd. Another sound drifted through the chatter and the shuffling of feet—muffled sobbing from the back row.

Forty-five

Marisol peeked out from behind the curtain at the multihued sea of faces drifting into the auditorium, a mélange of colorful clothing, bright reds, yellows, blues, and greens, serious black, sedate brown, tan, and beige. A hum of excitement buzzed in the aisles. Families were decked out in their best dresses and suits, sisters and brothers of the graduates in tow, girls in sparkly outfits and small boys in tiny suits.

The paper that held her speech was crinkled from being read and re-read, the corners bent and frayed, the margins creased, thumbed repeatedly by sweaty fingers. Valedictorian! Despite all her troubles, she had managed to keep studying and come out with the highest grade point average in the senior class. Mama bought her a new dress but refused to get one for herself—said she already had a dress that would be perfect to wear to the graduation, no reason to buy another one. It would cost too much, and she wasn't the one making the speech, she said.

Ricky, in a tan sport jacket, and Camilo, in a navy blue one, sat on Mama's right. Each graduate had been allotted three tickets, so Tio Miguel and Tia Rosa had not been able to attend.

Marisol Sanchez! It was her name they were announcing, her time to come forward. She took a deep breath, smoothed down the blue graduation gown draped over her new black and white backless dress and brushed her fingers over her hair, done up in a twist with flowers woven through it, a special present from Tia Rosa. A pair of two-inch heels made her appear taller, more dignified. She had practiced walking in them several times a day; it wouldn't do to trip and fall in front of the entire graduating class and their families. Her heels clicked on the polished veneer of the stage as she approached the podium to address the Grover Hill High School graduating class.

Ms. Torres had worked on the speech with her, showed her how to walk across the stage with poise and control. "Scan your notes, then look out at the audience. Talk to them, not to the podium," Ms. Torres had said. A blur of colors and rustling bodies waited for her to begin, out of focus like a photograph taken with a camera held by shaky hands.

"Good morning teachers, parents, fellow graduates." If it went smoothly, it would be over in a couple of minutes. "We are gathered here to celebrate the achievements—"

A loud noise startled her, causing her to lose her place. Her valedictory speech, the one she had practiced for weeks, was being up-staged by a commotion at the back of the auditorium.

This couldn't be happening to her, today of all days. Just three more minutes, and she would be done.

"As we prepare to leave Grover Hill High School and take our place in the wide world…"

Keep it going, Ms. Torres would have said, they're counting on you, but heads were turning away from the stage, distracted by what was happening at the back door.

"…we can look back," she continued as she glimpsed at the double doors at the back of the auditorium, "and know that the wonderful years…"

Security guards were rushing toward a man wandering down the aisle, clothes dirty and torn, hair standing out in all directions as though it hadn't been combed in a while, surveying the room anxiously, clearly disoriented. The audience was turning away from her en masse, gawking at the scene, ignoring her, so she paused, waiting for the situation to calm down. A woman rose abruptly from her seat and fought her way down the row, tripping over feet, waving her hand at the security guard. Yelling at the guards who had twisted the man's arms behind his back and were dragging him back toward the door.

"…the wonderful years we have spent here have prepared us well to take our place in the world."

Something was tugging at her about the man in the aisle, something familiar, and then she knew. *Papi!* It was Papi, struggling with the security guards, Mama who was negotiating, pleading with them. Ricky and Camilo sunk low into their seats, embarrassed by the drama taking place around them. Mama, holding Papi by the hand, apologizing to everyone for the interruption as she pulled him down the aisle toward Camilo and Ricky, Camilo sliding over onto her lap so Papi could have his seat.

The ache in Marisol's chest was so intense it threatened to collapse her, and she struggled to catch her breath, to suck in some air, or she was going to pass out right there on the stage in front of the entire auditorium. In that brief speck of time, an image came to her: Papi, optimistic and hopeful, on a ferry that floated over the green waters of New York Bay, the statue of Lady Liberty towering over the harbor, welcoming the ragged and the tormented. Now, amidst the blur of Sunday best, it was Papi's threadbare clothes that stood out conspicuously, and she understood then as she never had before, that for Papi there was no yesterday, no tomorrow, only the never-ending struggle to remain upright in the gale force winds that raged around him, tossed and turned in the eye of a political storm created by forces far beyond his control. At that moment, she knew what she had to do. She turned the pages of her speech over, took a deep breath, and began again.

"Many of you are the first in your families to graduate from high school, and their hopes and dreams are riding on you. I, too, am the child of an immigrant, and I know that our road is hard and full of obstacles, but wherever our future leads us, we must always be proud of where we have come from, of our family and our community. Some members of our family may have been forced to leave the country of their birth, a country that they love, only to find themselves an outcast, an unwelcome trespasser in their new land. We are here today looking forward, ready to begin the next leg of our journey to success, to a better life, but any road we choose must include them, must fight for them, because it is their hard work, their sacrifices and their love for us that have allowed us to be here today, looking out at a brighter future than they had the chance to have. Every road we take must show our pride in them, our pride in ourselves."

The clapping started slowly, as though people were hoping to hear more, but when it was clear she had said her final words, the auditorium echoed with thunderous applause and the entire roomful of Grover Hill families, many of whom were immigrants themselves, rose to their feet, hooting and cheering. Her speech finished, Marisol remained there for a moment until they settled back down in their seats, then turned and clattered toward the black curtain that led to the backstage area. The auditorium was stuffy and hot, the heels were cutting into her feet, and she was roasting under the gown.

A few more speeches, then the dispensing of the diplomas would begin, but the name Sanchez would be toward the end of the list, giving her a few minutes' leeway. She kicked off her shoes, tossing them into the anteroom behind the stage, then scrambled down the stairs, slipping on the last step and flying forward, her blue gown crumpled under her, her cap on the floor. She quickly righted herself, sailing across the auditorium floor in her stocking feet. Heads were turning toward her, but they were still as blurry as they had been when she was on the stage. She fairly flew down the side of the auditorium, toward them. Papi's hair, smooth and combed, Mama quickly shoving the comb in her purse as they moved down the row toward the aisle, toward her. Marisol waved at them, motioned toward the lobby.

The valedictorian of the Grover Hill class of 2007, admitted to Columbia University with a full scholarship, was crying unashamedly in the lobby at her high school graduation, her feet bare beneath her blue graduation gown, strands of black hair dangling from her carefully coiffed twist.

"You made it, Papi. I can't believe you're here. I'm so happy," she said, wiping her tears with a tissue Mama handed her. She took a breath and tried to collect herself, then looked at him quizzically.

"How did you... I mean, how did you know to come here?"

"When we got to Texas, we were brought to a house, what the coyote called a safe house, and there was a pay phone in a bus station nearby. I didn't have Mama's new cell phone number, but I was able to get hold of Tia Rosa—"

"Oh wow, Mama!" Marisol said, regarding Julia curiously. "You must have been so shocked to hear from him. Why didn't you tell us about it?"

Julia was quiet, didn't answer at all, just stood there shaking, tears rolling down her cheeks.

"I know, Mama," Marisol said, putting her arms around her and holding her close for a minute. "That must have been a tough decision. I'm not mad, just a little shocked. Let me see if you have any more tissues in your purse." Marisol fished around in Mama's purse, pulled out a tissue, and handed it to Mama.

Julia wiped her face, sniffling softly as she struggled to get herself under control. "Well, I have to worry about all of you, and I knew how important this day was to you. I wanted you to be able to focus on what you had to do, not be all nervous thinking about Papi. Besides, we didn't know how long it would take him to get here, or if he would even make it back in time for the graduation. And there's always a chance that something could happen along the way, and he wouldn't make it at all."

"I knew I had to get here in time because she told me I better make it here or else!" Papi said. "Sorry I didn't have time to clean up, but the trains were running late!"

Papi still had a sense of humor, despite what he had been through. Marisol told him he looked great, although he didn't. He had deep hollows around his eyes and he was disheveled and dirty, his face thin and gaunt, his arms like sticks, but he was here, alive, touching them, hugging them. She took his hand the way she had when she was a little girl and they crossed the street together, feeling the warmth of his rough fingers around hers, keeping her safe.

"We missed you so much, Papi. Did Mama tell you about the court case? That they dropped the criminal charges against you?"

Papi nodded silently but didn't answer, and she could see that there was something terribly sad behind those hollows around his eyes, stories that he might never tell, even to Mama.

So handsome, Mama always said, teasing him about the beautiful coffee-colored eyes that captivated her at eighteen, made her follow him anywhere. Handsome Papi had sad, yellow eyes now.

"He called me again when he made it to New York, honey," Julia said quietly. "He knows about it. I wouldn't have suggested that he come here if that was still hanging over him."

Back in the auditorium the principal was giving diplomas to students whose last names began with the letter R. Papi accompanied her until she took her place in line behind Cristina Salgado, then strolled down the aisle to sit with his family. Camilo slid onto Papi's lap, his navy blue sport jacket and khaki slacks camouflaging Papi's torn shirt and grimy pants, clothing him in his Sunday best. Loving him, shielding him. Nothing unusual to stare at now, just a small boy sitting on his father's lap. As she was about to ascend the stairs to receive her diploma, she turned and glanced back quickly at her family, at Papi.

It was then that she spotted him in the last row. A navy blue suit, dark blond hair falling over his forehead, those blue, blue eyes, trying to catch her gaze. Colin, arm outstretched, giving her a thumbs-up.

Oakmont, New York
Fall, 2009

Forty-six

Frank Sullivan sat on the front steps of his white ranch style house on Woodbridge Street, watching the high school kids play football on the grassy field across the street, just like the old days, when Colin had practiced there. Fall had come and gone and come again, the months drifting by slowly, like one of those soccer games where nobody ever scored.

The house was quiet now. Bonnie left during that rough patch a few years back, called him all kinds of names. He tried to change her mind, but she wouldn't budge. Sometimes when he was alone in the house, he imagined that she still lived there, that he could hear her walking around at night, or maybe it was Colin he heard, raiding the refrigerator at two a.m.

She had insisted he'd be better off complaining about the way he was treated at his job than hassling immigrants. They were just trying to make a living like he was, she said, but he didn't listen, didn't like being told what to do by a woman. Maybe he should have listened—if Steak 'n Brew had fired him for complaining, he probably would have ended up in another crappy job somewhere, but at least he'd still have his family. He kept a few of the old family pictures on the coffee table—just couldn't bring himself to take them down. His favorite was a picture of him and Bonnie on his motorcycle, her arms around his waist as she leaned against him. When they first met, they had taken some really great trips on that Harley. Zipped around to some of the state parks, hiked through the woods and pitched a tent, made love under the stars.

One of the kids across the street threw a long pass, the way Colin used to. Colin never did get his football scholarship, ended up at one of the city colleges in Manhattan, right in the middle of Harlem. Foolish kid. Tried to steer him straight, but he couldn't stay out of trouble. First drugs, then that crazy thing he did turning himself in to the police so they would let that Hispanic guy go. Couldn't figure that one out—had it all worked out for him and the kid blew it off.

SIM had gotten the illegals out of the parking lot across from the Quik Shop grocery, but they just went somewhere else. Never did get them out of Oakmont. Some do-gooders opened up some kind of resource center for them, so now they go there to look for jobs instead of the mall. Probably get food stamps and free medical care, too, always trying to get something for free. The cops couldn't do a thing about it—can't even bust 'em in a place like that. Two Hispanic families even moved onto Woodbridge Street, bought the houses, sent their kids to the neighborhood school.

Folks stopped showing up for the SIM meetings once they got the illegals out of the mall, until they were down to two or three people and the group finally disbanded. Never did get to become a national organization with him as the leader, as he had hoped. Mike Torelli was the only SIM member he even heard from these days. The others had drifted away, busy doing other things. Mike called him once in a while to see how he was doing, told him he heard from one of his kids that Colin was dating some cute girl. Never met her, though. Probably wouldn't get along, anyway.

He was still stuck in the same damn job at Steak 'n Brew—hadn't had a raise in years, and the regional manager had demoted him to bussing tables and serving customers, gave the restaurant manager position to another young guy just out of high school. Probably paid the kid minimum wage and saved money for the company. Steak 'n Brew had never provided health insurance—Bonnie's job at the hospital had covered that for him, but with her gone he didn't have that either, so he just hoped he didn't get sick. Getting older, things happened sometimes that you didn't expect.

A kid in a white jersey was running with the ball now, dodging and weaving, waving the football in the air. The leaves on the tree in front of the house were bright yellow, but they were dropping quickly. More leaves on the ground than on the tree, a sure sign that winter was coming. It was getting a little chilly, so he limped back into the house and slid into his old easy chair. His knees bothered him these days—couldn't move his left leg at all without pain and he had put on some weight, so he didn't walk much, not that he had any place to walk to. He and Bonnie used to take walks after dinner, holding hands and enjoying the sunset, chatting about their day, before she got all mad at him. Not much fun walking by yourself with no one to talk to.

He picked up the remote and flipped on the TV to see if there was a college game on. Not much else to do on the weekend, and it filled up the silence, the empty places where doors no longer opened and the floor no longer creaked.

About the Author

ADRIANE BROWN, a long-time political activist and teacher, has been writing poems and stories since childhood, when she became enthralled by the immigrant tales that were passed down in her family, both orally and in literature.

As a public school teacher, she personally witnessed the heartbreak that occurs when a parent is deported and the palpable fear with which immigrant families live daily.

She honed her love for the written word by taking dozens of writing classes at the Bethesda Writer's Center. She grew up in Chicago and the Bronx, and currently lives in Maryland with her husband.

To stay in touch with the author regarding contact information, upcoming events, and links to purchase books, please visit Adriane's website at adrianebrown.com.

www.ingramcontent.com/pod-product-compliance
Lightning Source LLC
Chambersburg PA
CBHW020227110726
47898CB00004B/1185